Sayed Haider
RAZA

The hues and colours, struggles and anxieties, aesthetic vision and nobility of spirit of Sayed Haider Raza have been meticulously and rigorously explored by the outstanding art critic Yashodhara Dalmia in this first-ever biography of the great Indian artist. It illuminates, in an engaging and unprecedented manner, the life and times and the art of an iconic figure.

– Ashok Vajpeyi, Poet and Cultural Critic

This is a compelling biography of a master artist who impressively represents the secular enthusiasms of modern India. Dalmia opens a window to reveal a landscape of changing art practices and transforming histories as she carefully traces the arc of Raza's multi-hued life and work.

– Abhay Sardesai, Editor ART India

Sayed Haider Raza traces the journey of a major twentieth-century painter, whose life and work straddled the art worlds of France and India. Dalmia's fine-grained narrative digs deeply, illuminating how post-war decolonization enabled artists from elsewhere to pry open and enrich modernism, transforming it from a parochial Western school into a global movement. A rewardingly rich account for enlarging perspectives on trajectories of art practices in the twentieth century.

– Susan S. Bean, Curator and Scholar

Sayed Haider
RAZA

The Journey of
An Iconic Artist

YASHODHARA DALMIA

HarperCollins *Publishers* India

First published in India in 2021 by
HarperCollins *Publishers*
A-75, Sector 57, Noida, Uttar Pradesh 201301, India
www.harpercollins.co.in

2 4 6 8 10 9 7 5 3 1

P-ISBN: 978-93-9035-164-0
E-ISBN: 978-93-9035-157-2

Typeset in 11/15.1 Adobe Caslon Pro at
Manipal Technologies Limited, Manipal

Printed and bound at
Thomson Press (India) Ltd.

For Maseeh

Contents

Preface

It was when Raza passed away that I thought of and was commissioned to write this book. Not only was it a feeling of a grave absence but in many ways it was the loss of an epic generation of artists which was engrossed with art and art-making rather than its paraphernalia. Their masterly techniques gave us some of the richest practices in art history. The grace and humility with which they met people from all walks of life made them irreplaceable. Sayed Haider Raza seemed one of the last of that generation and his irrevocable loss was to make a big dent in the art world.

To write about Raza was to encounter two different worlds – India of the 1940s, now lost forever, and Paris, France of the next few decades with its post-war rubble and rise, and the last remnants of its modernist practices which continued to inspire artists from South Asia and elsewhere. It was their collision and coexistence which marked the heady period that formed the matrix of Raza's practice. The constant oscillation between these realities created the splendid intermixing of metaphor and métier in his work. It would also be the intertwining of their separate existences that made Raza the polyglot personality that he was and richly infused his art. It mixed seamlessly in his personal life, often juxtaposed dexterously with his daily chores. He would, for instance, begin his day with a remembrance of Islamic, Hindu and Christian teachings or start painting after reading a verse by a poet like Rainer Maria Rilke. His soirées at home would have a mix of French and Indian friends and the music would come from Ravi Shankar's sitar. He was one of the few artists whose work and life were inscribed by actually living in a cosmopolitan Western city like Paris. But when asked if he felt exiled from India, he would say that he had never left home. Perhaps the truth was that he was a global citizen of his time – rooted in the country of his birth and yet living in Paris.

In tracking his long life, we encounter countless people and events which are embedded like nuggets in a piece of ornament. It was his absence which created the need for this book and yet also added to the difficulties. Most of his acquaintances have passed away and could, therefore, leave behind no account of their engagement with his life. Added to this is the fact that many letters and notes exchanged by him are now in Pakistan, since his entire family had been compelled to leave after Partition. There were, however, a few artists who vividly remembered their times with him, the most notable amongst them being Krishen Khanna. The children of a few friends of his have preserved some of his letters for he was a prolific communicator. Most importantly, it was Raza himself who had retained a vast archive of correspondence, notes, photographs and virtually every slip of paper from his adult life, which came to the rescue of this book.

As a biographer I do not presume to have covered every event in Raza's life, for there were numerous and now rest with the artist, but the significant ones have been documented. It is interesting to note that in his early years, his correspondence with F.N. Souza was the most prolific and that there were nascent plans to make the Progressive Artists' Group into an international forum for modernism. Even if this ambitious scheme did not go very far, it is commendable for its vision and foresight. Raza's friends and other artists from India visited him often in Paris and learnt from him and his surroundings; and in turn kept him abreast of the prevailing situation in India and shared with him his great yearning for his homeland. The most frequent of these visitors were Krishen Khanna and Ram Kumar – their letters to him provide a vivid account of his life in Paris and the difficulties he surmounted to make a life for himself there.

When Raza married Janine Mongillat, a fellow student at the École nationale supérieure des Beaux-Arts, it was to be a long, rewarding and stimulating relationship which transformed their lives. Their continuous dialogues and exchanges, while retaining their separate artistic profiles, were to provide the role model of a truly generative and rich partnership. The lesser-known fact was his passionate desire for her that he seldom revealed, perhaps because of a reticence in these matters since his childhood, but which emerge in his letters to her. This book highlights a seminal period of their courtship where his letters provide a glimpse not only into the intensity and passion which he felt for her, but also his erudition as he ruminates on writers and poets from Gide and Rimbaud to Rilke and Rumi. Though younger in years, Janine's death precedes him and leaves him enormously bereft. His attempts to overcome his subsequent loneliness, which he mostly succeeds at by immersing himself in his work, are also recounted in this volume.

Raza's relationship with other French artists, his correspondence with the Berkeley professor Karl Kasten who invited him for a stint there and which transformed Raza's work, his consistent dialogue with prevailing trends in art, are some of the other factors which emerge. He did at all times retain an equidistance from both pure formalism as well as an effete revivalism in his work. As he stated, 'My present work is the result of two parallel enquiries. Firstly, it is aimed at pure plastic order, form-order. Secondly, it concerns the theme of nature. Both have converged into a single point and become inseparable. The point, the bindu, symbolizes the seed-bearing potential of all life, in a sense. It's also a visible form containing all the essential requisites of line, tone, colour, gesture, and space.'

It is with some astonishment that we discover his passionate involvement with Hindi writers, Indian culture and music while living many miles away in a completely different sphere. He visited India every year and travelled to different places in it to stay in touch with and to overcome his longing for the country. But the most touching of those trips was when he visited his birthplace and the teachers of his formative years to whom he felt overwhelmingly grateful. It was characteristic of Raza to not only remember each one of them, but also to believe that it was their contribution to his life that had made him reach the heights he had. His consistent involvement with Hindi poetry made him inscribe those in his paintings. When he did return to India at the end of his life, it was to Delhi – the city which his grandfather had fled from originally during the Uprising of 1857, making the wheel come full circle.

In working on this biography, I am aware that I have touched the tip of the iceberg. Many facts about Raza and the period remain unknown and will emerge in the course of time. If at all I have succeeded in writing about the most critical periods of his life, it is also to touch upon an artist's struggle to overcome the difficulties that lay strewn on his path and his courageous and optimistic ways of dealing with it.

In the Midst of Forests

Little did the infant who opened his eyes in a settlement of barely a few huts in Barbaria, in Narsinghpur district of Madhya Pradesh, know that one day he would be a famous Indian artist living in the metropolis of Paris whose works would be highly sought-after. As a young boy, Sayed Haider Raza had an idyllic childhood amidst lush green trees with birds, bees, flowers and fruits for a roof and the brown, warm earth for his hearth. In this thick forest area, the gushing waters of the Narmada River flow, coursing between the Satpura and Vindhyachal ranges.

This is Kipling country. A lush, overgrown thicket of plants and animals known as the Kanha National Park, which was used as inspiration by Rudyard Kipling for his famed collection of stories for children, *The Jungle Book.* Kipling's 1894 classic is about a boy raised by wild wolves, but the forest is known for its significant big cat population. It has a fair number of Royal Bengal tigers, Indian leopards, sloth bears, wild dogs and barasinghas. The Kanha National Park, which was established in 1955, is one of the oldest wildlife zones and has, in recent times, brought the barasingha back from the brink of extinction. It is believed that Kipling himself never visited Kanha, but the writings of British travellers who visited the region kindled his imagination and he knit the captivating story around Shere Khan the wild tiger and Mowgli the jungle boy, while being surrounded by snow in faraway Vermont.

In this region, the oldest rock formation in India, the rugged Vindhya mountains with their red laterite slopes form an awesome natural barrier and create a sense of the majesty of nature. As a child, Raza would witness the gushing waterfalls that would spring from these formations and hide in holes and crannies here and there. On the banks of the Narmada, right from its source in the Amarkantak, would be lined richly carved temples and mosques as a tribute to its mighty swell.

Sayed Haider Raza was born on 22 February 1922 to the sounds of birds and the mooing of cattle in his surrounding environs and from that moment onwards sprang his engagement and passionate involvement with nature.

When he was five years old his family shifted to Kakaiya in Mandla district, where for the next few years he attended the primary school to imbibe a basic education. Raza's father, Sayed Mohammad Razi – a man of integrity and a very cultured person – was posted there as the forest warden. Raza mentions that despite being profoundly religious and performing namaz five times a day, his father was very open and liberal about other religions. 'We would go to the Hanuman temple or to other Hindu temples [in Damoh]. We would recite chaupais and dohas from the *Ramcharitmanas* and my father would never object to that.'[1] He was well versed in Urdu poetry and would recite Ghalib and Iqbal and many other poets. There would be evenings full of soulful poetry where not just verses by Urdu poets were recited, but men and women from the local tribes, mostly Gonds and Bhils, would sing and dance. '…At the centre was a fire, and on two sides, men and women, mostly from tribes. They would sing, dance and walk rhythmically towards each other. And we were told later that in the dance there was a question of winning a woman. If there was a mistake in the song, they lost.'[2]

His father knew Verrier Elwin well and had learnt about the rich traditions of the tribals from him. According to Raza, he learnt about these choreographic conventions later, on reading Verrier Elwin, but he remembered the evenings vividly. 'Even today I can clearly see those evening parties, with fire and rows of men and women singing and dancing, moving towards each other.'[3]

Sadly, in 1968 a large tribal population from this region was relocated. The area was the ancestral home of many of the Baiga and Gond tribes. When they were rehabilitated on barren lands, many of them suffered from alcoholism and malnourishment, and were in dire need of support. Indeed, according to a report from January 2010, members of the Baiga tribes were illegally evicted from the park without proper compensation from the government.[4]

As the child of a forest warden, Raza recalls a comfortable existence with little that was left wanting. 'Father was planting and growing vegetables. Several acres of land was ours, more or less, in the forest. Sometimes there was also the Deputy Ranger's quarters, some 500 metres from our own… It used to be a big complex, with often hundreds of people working for the Forest Department.'[5] To dress and work in the colonial manner was of course the norm, 'Father used to go everywhere in the forest dressed in shorts and long socks. He always carried a gun. There were shooting parties held where all kinds of officials would come, sometimes British, sometimes Indian. They would go in for a hunt from specially made machans on the trees. But Father would shoot from the ground without climbing up. He was a good shot. He often used to practise shooting. He would ask someone to put a pot, an earthen pot, against a wall and would have his eyes blindfolded. Then somebody would take the pot and put it on a prominent spot. He knew it was in that direction, but not where exactly the pot had been placed. The person who would place the pot was to strike the pot thrice. Then he would go away and Father would shoot; invariably he would hit the pot. Excellent shot.'[6]

His strictness in many other ways led to a certain seclusion in Raza's childhood. He recalls that at the age of six, he was playing with a little girl, Phoola, who was his friend and daughter of the Deputy Forest Ranger. She had bought some sugar-coated peanuts and gave a few to him. But when he came back home munching on these peanuts, his father got very angry and forbade him from eating anything from outside. 'We were very scared of him; he had a very strong personality. We were not allowed to mix with other people. Yet it was marvellous.'[7]

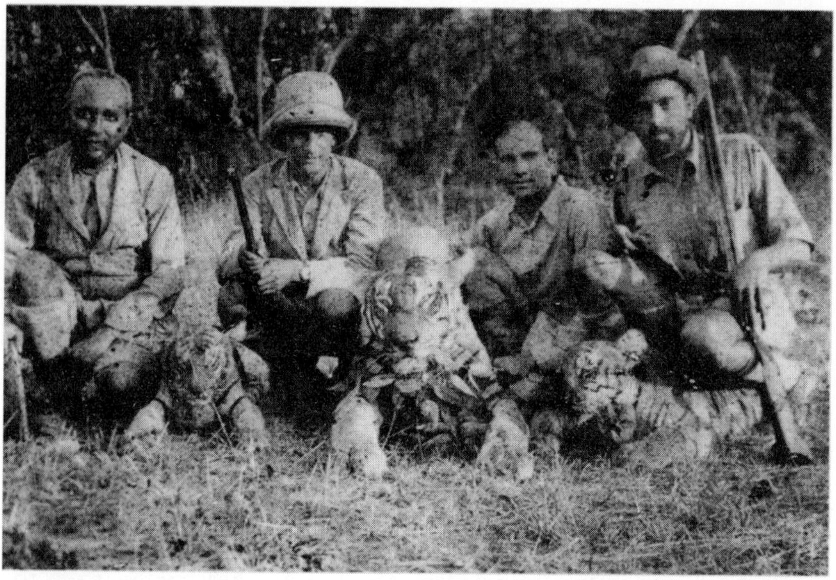

Raza's father, Sayed Mohammad Razi (extreme left) on a hunting expedition with a group in Mandla district.

Perhaps in his aloneness Raza turned towards the natural world and found it a reservoir of wonders. Keenly attuned to its nuances, he was sensitive to the slightest stirring in the forest. The wild animals, the furious rush of wind and the eerie darkness stirred his imagination as much as it frightened him in the dark and exalted him in daytime. As he recalls, 'It is in Kakaiya, where I remember, I became a bit more conscious about the beauty of nature, of life, of pleasures which were intimately mixed up. Nights were terribly anguished hours for me. You could have a snake crawling in. Father would take a gun and shoot it down soon. During the day, you might have a scorpion. Some day or some night in the range, not far from the house, you would have the guards rushing in, one of them having fought a leopard with a stick. He had made so much noise that the leopard ran away. But the guard would be wounded. And the next day, the beautiful sun would come out. The birds flew as usual. There were mango trees, imli trees all around. There were camels in the corner; sometimes even an elephant. And beautiful gardens.'[8] He also speaks of tigers in the forests: 'It was really fantastic that at times you would have all the good things of life, beautiful things linked up with fear because at that time tigers also came to villages and attacked the inhabitants. It was really dreadful and, at the same time, it was beautiful.'[9] This sharp awareness of the duality of life which characterized Raza's work later existed in him from an early age.

The Circle and the Square

If night and day cast a spell over Raza, so did his memories of the forests and his school in the midst of the clearing. His mind would wander off and he was unable to concentrate on his studies. Worried that he would fail in his exams, his parents contacted his teacher Nandlal Jharia and spoke to him about it. According to Raza, 'As a child, I lived in the superb forests of Madhya Pradesh, where I loved to play around the house in the midst of animals. On the other hand, I was rather inattentive in school. One day at the primary school at Kakaiya, my teacher Shri Nandlalji Jharia asked me to stay back at school. On the white wall of the veranda he drew a black dot and asked me to sit before it and look at it. I was then only eight years old and failed to understand his intention, but I obeyed.'[10] Raza was mesmerized by the circle and the experience continued to haunt him even in his later years. It also came back to him in a rush of memories in the '70s and led to the emergence of the Bindu in his work.

While they were in Mandla, Raza entered the middle school. The lush, green surroundings and particularly the Narmada made quite an impression on the young boy. 'From the range quarters where we stayed we could see the Narmada River a few miles from our house. Narmadaji made a round of the city of Mandla almost like a "pushpmala", a garland of flowers.'[11] Even more splendid to him were the ghats. 'The ghats were beautiful. There was a beautiful Gond fort and there were magnificent temples with statues around. Our range quarters were almost on the border of the city where already the forest started. There were no houses in between and we could see the Narmada. All that was very beautiful. But when it rained heavily, there was flood and the flood would lay siege to the whole city. People would be in a state of terror and so would we. Particularly I. I used to find this incredible. Something that I loved, which

I found very beautiful, could be a source of anguish as well, and could even kill. The flood would last for a few days. [Then the] rains would stop and the water would recede. Everything would come back to normal.'[12]

Between the ages of ten and twelve, Raza's range of activities began to widen – he was surrounded by a circle of friends. But the most important thing to him was his involvement with nature. 'Father liked sowing vegetables. We had a gardener who helped us and I liked working with the gardener. Time and again, someone who would make us ride a horse. There were elephants which used to carry timber and one of them would come and stay for the night at the range quarters compound.'[13]

After the 1857 Uprising

Although Raza's father, Sayed Mohammad Razi, was a high-ranking officer in the British government, historically his family had had a relationship of trials and tribulations like many others. His grandfather belonged to an old and well-known family of Delhi and was possibly linked to the Mughal emperor Bahadur Shah Zafar's court; for though the kings were of the Sunni order, the scribes were mostly Shias as they were thought to be very learned. He was in Delhi during the Uprising of 1857, and sensing that he would be persecuted for opposing the British he decided to leave Delhi with his family. We know that the famed poet Mirza Ghalib did not flee from Delhi after the Uprising though he feared retribution for his support to the Mughal king. As the court poet, he had composed many verses during the fight to encourage and champion the side of the Badshah. Now that defeat had followed and many of his fellow men had been killed or persecuted while Bahadur Shah had been exiled for life to Rangoon, Ghalib had no other recourse but to pay obeisance to the British to continue living in Delhi and to obtain his pension. After the British recaptured Delhi, Ghalib wrote the *Dastanbuy*, which is a diary of the Uprising and is intensely pro-British and strongly condemns the 'revolt'. But this was a sign of desperation of someone who was well-located and had chosen to stay behind. The underlying purpose was to help establish his innocence in the eyes of the British. As Pavan Varma pointed out, 'To do so was not a matter of intellectual toadying; it was a matter of survival.

The British were ruthless in victory; the slightest suspicion was sufficient for a man to be hanged.'[14]

Although Ghalib is fulsome in his praise for the British in the *Dastanbuy*, he could not overlook the savagery that ensued after the recapture of the city. As Pavan Varma observed, 'He could not avoid some reference to this aspect; it was essential to give his narrative the garb of authenticity. But his effort is far from convincing. He writes: "I have told you that when the angry lions (the British) entered the town, they killed the helpless and the weak and they burned their houses. It may be that such atrocities always occur after conquest… At noon on Friday, the twenty-sixth of Muharram, which is the eighteenth of September … the victors captured the city and the Fort. The horror of mass arrests, assassinations, and slaughter now reached our lane and the people shook with fear… Beyond the (Chandini) Chowk mass slaughter was rampant and the streets were filled with horror." The truth inadvertently comes out in spite of his best attempts to conceal it.'[15]

Raza's grandfather and others had been fighting the British and fleeing from them. Some of them went to Bundelkhand first and settled there. His grandfather's love for forests took him to Mandla where he became an adviser to the Gond ruler of the kingdom. Raza's father also loved the forests and after he completed his studies at Balaghat, he became a deputy forest ranger (and later the forest warden). He was well-liked because he was a very honest and upright man. In due course, he also gained position and a certain social standing.

Belonging as he did to a privileged place and time, his grandfather appears to be a sensitive man who was well versed in literature and poetry. It is likely that he belonged to the milieu of Ghalib, Zauq, Shefta and other court poets in Delhi. Music and nautch girls had proliferated during this period, adding to the heightened cultural renaissance of the time. To the enhanced courtly culture of Bahadur Shah Zafar's court could be added the new consciousness of individuality and freedom, which was being evoked by the presence of the British – men like the enterprising Company officer William Fraser and his brother, the artist James Baillie Fraser, and their friend, the Anglo-Indian cavalry office Colonel James Skinner. The predominant artist of the period, Ghulam Ali Khan (active 1817–1855), painted lifelike portraits of human figures, often of the ordinary people like peasants and farmers in villages. Women also figured in these albums, not peripherally, but often centre stage and their individual features were etched with great sensitivity. Ghulam Ali worked for Emperor Bahadur Shah, the British and the neighbouring courts – melding together an exciting new amalgam of western and eastern traditions.

Mohammad Razi had also imbibed an awareness of art and culture, and so it was no wonder that he would often host concerts and poetry readings at this house. He was himself well versed in the Urdu poetry of Mir, Ghalib, Iqbal and others. Growing up in this liberal atmosphere, Raza had a great deal of respect for all religions and would bow before temples, mosques and churches all his life.

His mother, Tahira Begum, was equally cultured and seemed to be of Iranian origin. According to Raza, 'But on the side of Mother, it was even more refined. Her father was a man with a big beard. Most probably they were of Iranian origin. They came to Delhi. Then they came over to Madhya Pradesh, particularly the north of Jhansi, Gwalior and Sagar. I have a vivid memory of my mother's mother. She had a very light complexion. So had my mother. Father was brownish. Everyone was interested in poetry, religion and the higher things, apart from everyday living.'[16]

That harmonious and gracious atmosphere was, however, to be disrupted quite soon. Despite the common interests and beliefs, trouble brewed in the household when his father fell in love with another woman. It is not certain who his second wife was, but from all accounts she was a maid working for the family. This led to strain and distance in the relationship not only between the couple, but also between Raza and his father. In his later years, however, he seems to have reconciled with his father and even stated that if he was to be buried in India it should be next to his father's grave in Mandla.

According to his close friend, the poet and writer Ashok Vajpeyi, '…He insisted that he should be buried next to his father. That was the final act of rapprochement. If you look at it that way, a father who had betrayed his mother, from whom he was estranged [yet] he wanted to be buried next to him. In this, he was insistent. Even when [we were] in France, he told me several times – if I die in France I must be buried in Gorbio next to Janine [his wife] and where there is an empty grave. If I die in India, then next to my father in Mandla.'[17] Raza had no clue then that this would actually come to be.

Years of Learning and Forgetting

Hurt and rejected, all the more so since she had shared many happy years with Raza's father, Tahira Begum shifted with her children to her family in Damoh, her hometown.

Damoh is a small town in the Sagar division in north-eastern Madhya Pradesh that has had a long history of successive rulers dating back to the Stone Age; tools found in Singrampur Valley testify to the fact that this area was a cradle of human civilization for thousands of years. Interestingly, its rulers had fought courageously against the British in the Uprising of 1857. But it is also known for its valiant queen, Rani Durgavati.

Born on 5 October 1524 in the family of the Rajput Chandel emperor Keerat Rai, she was married in 1542 to Dalpat Shah, the eldest son of King Sangram Shah of the Gond dynasty. As a result, the Chandel and Gond dynasties got closer and fought successfully against Sher Shah Suri. When her husband died around 1550, Durgavati took the reins of the Gond kingdom in her hands as her son was considered too young. It was during this period that trade flourished and she extended her territory and accomplished the political unification of Gondwana with courage, generosity and tact. Rani Durgavati attained martyrdom fighting the Mughal Empire, represented by its general Asaf Khan and his army.

Not only was she valiant and beautiful, she also respected scholars and generously extended patronage to them. She welcomed Vitthalnath of the Vallabh community and took diksha from him. She was also secular and appointed many eminent Muslims to important posts.

When Raza was in Damoh in the '30s, it is likely to have been a clean, ordered town. There was a large statue of Nandi near the lake called Phutera Talab, which he was very fond of, and would often sit next to it while chatting and spending time with his friends. Many years later when he was visiting from Paris, he came to Damoh and had the statue of

Nandi restored. Their house, on the way to Phutera Talab, was a big, old, beautiful house which would inspire Raza to again live in a similar place in Paris later. His brother and he had space on the first floor as well as in the basement where they would sit, study and receive friends.

A new life began for Raza in Damoh where he joined high school. In school, he began to get seriously involved with his studies. This was so because of his teachers. 'In high school, the teachers were extraordinary. I remember with special gratitude at least two of them. Daryav Singhji Rathore was my teacher in drawing. He encouraged me to draw.'[18] He was not good in mathematics, but he had a fascination for geometry and we see that geometrical forms surfaced in his work later. The other teacher he was particularly close to was Gauri Shankarji Lahri, his Hindi teacher. 'He was young, full of idea and vitality. Not only did he teach Hindi, he recited Hindi poems to us. He encouraged us to read poets like Mahadevi Verma, Pant and others and also recited his own poetry.'[19] Raza, even at this early age, had the ability to internalize his surroundings with sensitivity. Hence, it was not just a respect for all religions but also a keen awareness of the Urdu and Hindi literary and poetic worlds that he was exposed to in his youth and which also emerged in his art later. He could recite verses of Mahadevi Verma or Subhadra Kumari Chauhan without hesitation. It was clear that Raza's formative years were flush with the arts and that this would have an impact on him, sensitive as he was, which would have long-ranging effects. 'Knowing that I was interested in painting he [Gauri Shankarji Lahri] gave me lectures not only in school but even after school. We used to meet in the school compound. He used to pass by our house and would sometimes drop in. He always said that deep relationships existed between poetry, music, dance and painting.'[20]

Over the years, the same teacher continued to have a profound effect on Raza. 'My elder brother Yusuf Raza was an excellent student, one of the best in school. I dragged along but improved. Janaki Prasad and Purushottam Lal were fellow students and there was Raheem also. They were all interested in literature. And encouraged by Shri Lahri we thought – particularly my brother Yusuf – that we should bring out a handwritten magazine. We thought about it and later talked to Gauri Shankarji Lahri. He encouraged us and we got down, three-four of us, to writing poetry and articles in Hindi. We called the magazine *Pushpanjali* and I did a woman's hand with flowers as the cover. Shri Lahri was the first to see it. He said you must show it to Shri H.P. Roy, the headmaster of the school. Shri Roy was from Bengal and was a very cultivated though somewhat reserved person… Next day in the prayer meeting he referred to this magazine done by four-five of us, and added in a very convincing tone: "These students are the jewels of my school." I must have been sixteen years of age. It was a tremendous stimulation to us.'[21]

As his world expanded, Raza would often be naughty and do things which his parents would not have approved of. He recounts, 'I had a wonderful friend in Damoh whose name was Raja Ram Rai. His father was a moneylender. The boy was strong and hefty, not particularly good at studies. He would force me to go to the gymnasium with him. He would also take us to his house and to a place where there were other young people and we would do warm-ups and other different exercises including the surya namaskar [salutation to the sun]. Sometimes I would not tell Father about these things. My mother knew about it. One day Raja Ram said that I should go with him to Phutera Talab, the tank in the town, since I didn't know how to swim. The talab was a beautiful tank, not far away from our house. On the bank were a few temples and a statue of a beautiful Nandi, which later I realized dated back many centuries. He took me over to the talab and said one must know how to swim. He literally pushed me into the water. With all my life I tried to swim and in a few weeks I could. This would mean a lot later since I could swim, not only in India but also in France. In Southern France, we used to go to the sea and I could swim along with Janine [his wife] several yards without any fear and with very great pleasure.'[22] In hindsight, Raza felt that life is laid out by higher powers and you invariably meet the right person and if you are attentive to them, the whole course of your life may change. This could not have been more true for his own life.

He did very well in his studies and after he had passed the High School Certificate Examination brilliantly, his father came to meet him. Drawing and sketching was the one art form that was Raza's own, different from that of his siblings and one which was innate to him. Sensing his talent, Daryav Singhji Rathore, his drawing teacher, told him that he had a talent for drawing and should be trained further in it in Bombay or Santiniketan. The family conferred and it was decided that he would go and study in Nagpur, which was nearer. It goes to his credit that Mohammad Razi wanted to retire from government service but decided instead that he would work for another two years to be able to finance his son's studies. Raza's brother-in-law accompanied him on a bus to Nagpur, for Raza had hardly ever gone outside the town without his parents, and enrolled him in the Nagpur School of Art. A new life was about to begin for the seventeen-year-old Raza.

Shift to the Big City

The move to Nagpur was a big change for the young artist. The hustle and bustle of the city confounded him; he longed for the rarefied world of nature, birds and animals. At the same time, he became exposed to a larger world which expanded his knowledge and awareness.

Raza always remembered his mentors with gratitude. 'In the month of October 1939 a new life began. I am grateful that at the Nagpur School of Art, Shri Bapuraoji Athawale gave me his attention, affection and guidance. He was interested in music. I used to come early in the morning and work through the day and even stay till eight. His wife, Mrs Athawale, would bring samosas or some such thing for me to eat [and ask]: "Why do you work so long and late?" Sometimes, they would have a musical evening where Mrs Athawale sang. It was classical music. As young people we were interested in cheap films, cheap cinema songs: *Sawan ke nazare hain* ... that kind of thing. And here was Indian classical music, both vocal and instrumental. In the beginning, obviously, I could not understand. But just imagine, late in the evening, after a whole day's work, after we had stopped painting, washed the brushes, there was this classical Indian music going on for half an hour. It seemed to go on for hours and then I would go back home. In a few days, I developed a taste for Indian classical music. Then I saw some dances. I was reminded of the Gond dances I had seen in my childhood without knowing a thing about them. This evolution of the mind is important. I can compliment myself for only one thing: that my eyes saw, my ears heard, I recorded, I thought of things that seemed important and formed my own opinions.'[23] In many ways, Raza's bonding with his teachers was reminiscent of his relationship with his father. The two were never very close to begin with and became even more distant after his father married again. For Raza, his father was both present and absent in a duality which confounded him. He had a father and yet did not have him.

As his sensitive mind imbibed the deep, rich tradition of classical music, it seeped seamlessly into his art later. But his training in art left him dissatisfied. While grateful for the kindness and commitment to art by teachers like Bapuraoji Athawale, who was the principal of the school, he found the teaching very academic.

The Victorian concepts of art imposed by the British had led to a distancing from his own reality and indeed a deference to a form of art far removed from his own sensory experiences and had little to do with the Indian traditions of aesthetics. Athawale himself was known for his portrait painting and had a sound knowledge of the Western and Indian techniques of painting. His students alternated between the two styles but were left floundering about the direction their art should take. The training made Raza acquire skills but still left him confused about the path he should take. The academic tradition was unrelated to the Indian reality and, indeed, was considered outdated in the West itself. The Indian method of painting was inadequate for present times. A new aesthetic had to be found which would be rooted and yet modern, but that time was still far away. Nonetheless, he worked in both the Western and Indian traditions and the three years with Bapuraoji Athawale passed swiftly.

The grounding in art he had received, however, along with his innate skill led him to make watercolours like *Machawas Loading Cotton in Broach* (1941), where the painting reflects the scene at the mouth of the Narmada. In this work, a group of people are busy arranging bales of cotton while others are unloading cotton from sailing vessels. The coastline visible on the other side of the river creates an enhanced spatial sense. While the mottled brown of the sand and the boats predominates in the work contrasting with the translucent green, the radiant orange and white brushstrokes light up the painting. His earliest works touch upon the daily life of people and their means of livelihood like growing cotton. The distilled energy of this work would become his hallmark in later years.

He did very well at the Nagpur School of Art and came first in the class with distinction. As his principal wrote, '...His paintings were exhibited in the Annual Art Exhibition of this School, for the last three years... His pictures are purchased by some of the High Officials of this Province. The distinctive features of his work is correctness of outline and excellent treatment of colour, specially in Landscape and Pictorial composition. His manners are very pleasing and I have found him very regular, hard working and honest in his school career. I strongly recommend him to the patrons of Art and the Heads of the Educational Institutions to give him a chance to work as an Art Instructor and allow him to show his artistic ability.'[24] This enabled him to get a job as his father had retired in 1942. To begin with, he became a drawing teacher at the Municipal High School in Gondia but within a month he had obtained a government scholarship of the Central Provinces for studies at the Sir JJ School of Art in Bombay – the premier art institute in the country at the time. Consequently, he resigned in August 1943 and received a letter from the headmaster that praised him effusively: '...He [Raza] has left a deep impression on me and the school. He had to go being spurred by his ambition to be an artist worthy of the name. He has left us but has also left behind the sweet memory of his sincerity and honest work. As a teacher he has taught "Art" to his pupils. As a friend he has taught us the appreciation of "Art". He loved those who came in his contact for learning and always inspired them to learn more...'[25] Raza came to Bombay but found that it was too late to be admitted to the art school; if he had joined he would not have had the percentage of attendance necessary. Hence, the scholarship was withdrawn and he was offered a job in the city of Akola as a drawing teacher but Raza decided to stay on in Bombay.

While he was in Nagpur, his marriage to his first cousin Fatima took place in 1942. This was something Raza wanted very much and his aunt, his mother's sister, had encouraged him. While it decreased his loneliness in the city then, it also led to disastrous results later. 'I got married in 1942 to Fatima, a cousin of mine, in Damoh, of my own choice. Unfortunately, after a few years of life together, differences in views and temperament came to the surface. I was passionately involved in my work as a painter and it was difficult for her to understand my ambitions...'[26] At any rate, he had to soon leave for Bombay to continue with his studies where his life would be irrevocably transformed.

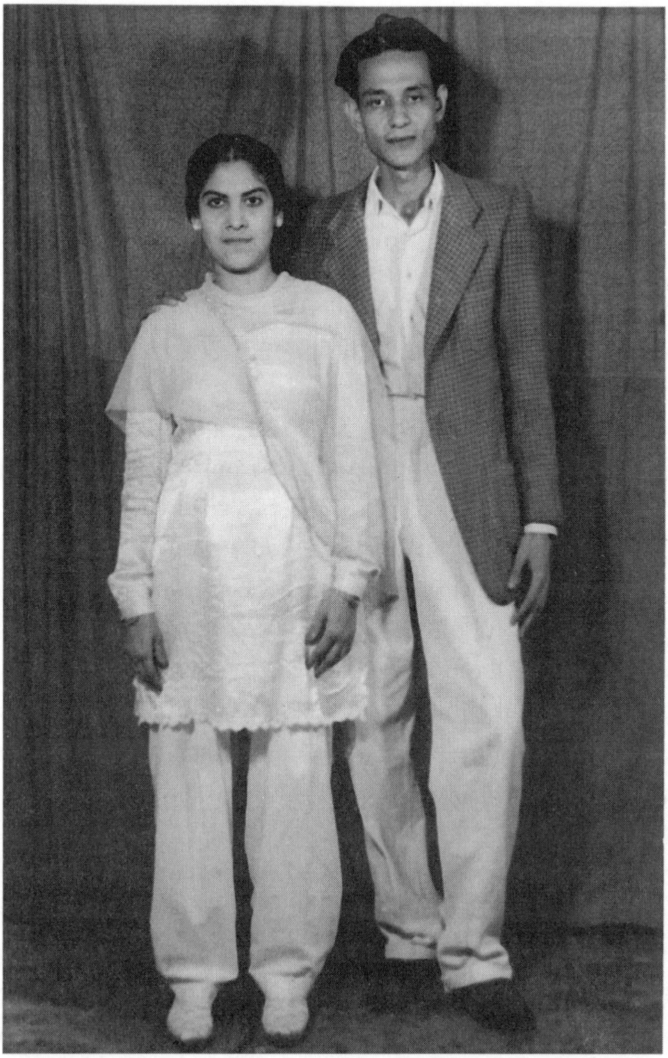

Raza and Fatima after their engagement in Damoh in Madhya Pradesh.

Bombay: City of Hope

When Raza reached Bombay he was only twenty-one years old. Bewildered and dazzled by the big city, what was even more challenging for the young artist was to find a means of earning a living. Almost immediately, however, he found a job as a designer in the Express Block Studio located on Phirozeshah Mehta Road in South Bombay. Hard work paid off and in about a year's time he was made the chief designer by the proprietors Jalil Sahib and Ashfaq Husain. He would work in the office from 10 a.m. to 6 p.m. In the evenings, he attended classes at the Mohan Art Club which was run by M.Y. Kulkarni, an artist himself and a teacher at the Sir JJ School of Art.

Late in the evening Raza would return to his temporary home at Jacob Circle, a suburb of Bombay. A taxi driver, whom his brother knew, gave him a place to sleep in at night since he drove his taxi only during those hours. During the day he would come and use the room, so it suited Raza to return late. But a dramatic event finally turned him out of there for good. 'One day when I came back from my studio at about 9.30 p.m., I found a policeman standing in front of our room. He said I could not get in, since there had been a murder case. We had never been involved in politics or in any other doubtful activity. I was really shocked beyond my wits. I went immediately to the commissioner at the police station and presented myself. I told him that I was a student and was staying at Jacob Circle, a policeman was standing in front of my room not allowing me to get in. He told me that I was out of the picture and even Mr Ralf, the taxi driver friend of mine. There had been a murder in his car. Somebody had stabbed the client, a customer in the car. The next day I narrated the story to the proprietor Jalil Saab and he offered me room in the art department. I used to lie down on the floor. He would find me working till eleven or twelve in the night drawing street scenes or doing some other kind of sketching. Sometimes he would say I was working too late and must go to sleep.'[1] According to Raza, a few months later Mr Jalil proposed that he stay in a posh residential building in the two-bedroom flat where his cousin was staying and so Raza left the sleazy atmosphere of Jacob Circle to stay in more comfortable surroundings. 'I said to myself "In the kingdom of God there might be delay but not injustice."' [*Bhagvan ke raaj mein der hain, andher nahin.*][2] One might add that the unsung hero of these difficult times was the owner of Express Block Studios without whose timely help Raza would not have been able to stay and work in Bombay.

Raza himself felt that there was an advantage in studying in a private institution instead of joining JJ School right away as it provided opportunity for discussions and personal attention to a relative newcomer. The Mohan Art Club had been established in 1942 by M.Y. Kulkarni, a senior artist who had studied at the JJ School. Kulkarni had been there when Charles Gerrard was the principal and he, along with Bendre, Hebbar, P.T. Reddy and others, belonged to the Young Turks Group. Gerrard had come in 1936 and had earlier been with the Royal Academy and also belonged to the contemporary art circle in the UK, where it was believed that in a work of art, the subject was as important as the manner of representation, with emphasis on light, colour and design. Gerrard's support for self-expression had encouraged a few students such as P.T. Reddy, M.T. Bhopale, C.B. Baptista, A.A. Majeed and M.Y. Kulkarni to form the Young Turks Group and forge a front for modern art. The first exhibition of the artists was held in 1941. But for all its brave beginnings, the group was not able to form a cohesive front which would leave a mark. Kulkarni's own work echoed British ethnographic prints with a picturesque description of temples or hills and distant, miniscule figures which were non-differentiated. Yet the move towards modernism was evident in the teaching and the activities of Kulkarni. Under his careful tutelage, Raza prospered and learnt the elementary skills of an art linked with the times. It was through him that Raza came into contact with artists like Shiavax Chavda and K.K. Hebbar when he eventually joined the JJ School.

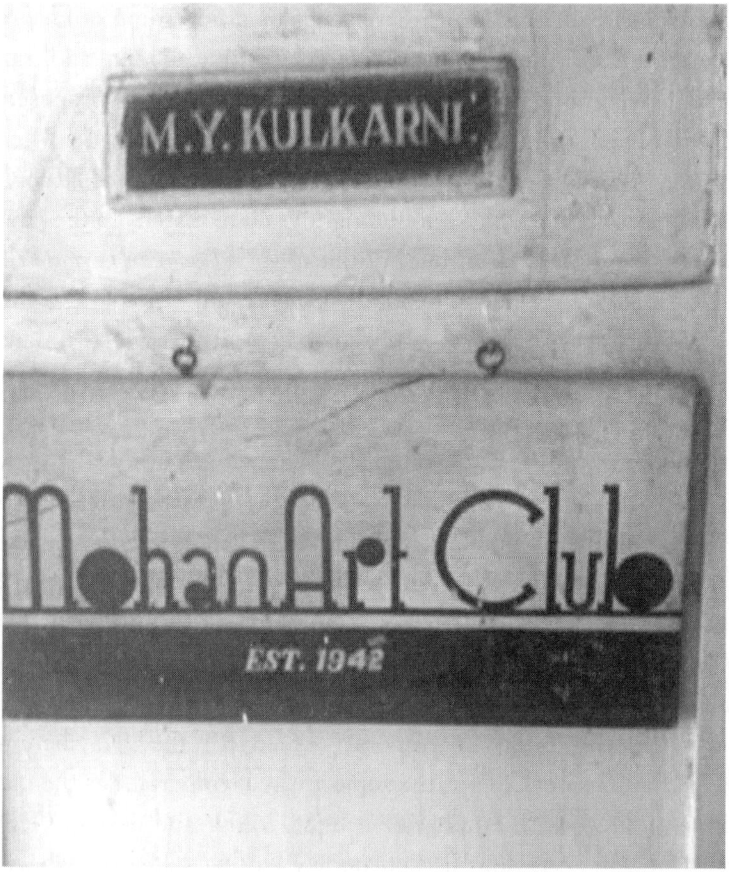

Sign outside M.Y. Kulkarni Art Club, Bombay.

Streaming Traffic, Roaring Ocean

In the mid '40s, Bombay was going through a period of churning and awakening as the Indian freedom struggle reached a crescendo. It would be reflected in the city's cultural and intellectual life as powerful voices expressed a need for autonomy and identity. The city itself was like a huge open studio for Raza. The soaring buildings representing both wealth and power, the constant stream of traffic and the roaring ocean with its lapping waves would hold him spellbound. The cross-currents of people of all classes and colour would jostle his imagination like the eddying waves moving back and forth. In the domain of art and culture, there was a plurality of views and experiments embodying new sensibilities. Invariably, he would come across other artists like N.S. Bendre whose carefully worked out ebullient landscapes and elongated, graceful forms would evoke a startlingly different means of expression in one.

The shifting, translucent light falling on the lanes and by-lanes of Bombay became the subject of many of Raza's works during this period. The view from the window of Express Block Studio situated in the throbbing commercial area of Bombay was like a periscope of light and colour. In works like *Bazaar Gate*, one can traverse the shapes of houses, the light filtering through the parked cars and the patterned shades of teeming life in the street. A painting of the Flora Fountain during the monsoons consists of fluid washes of colours as the pouring rain dissolves all shapes of houses and buses. Most of all *Bombay* (1943) is a panoramic sweep from the Bay Area of Bombay where the entire city with its myriad tonalities, swelling and contracting shapes and shiny surfaces comes bewitchingly alive. Rudolf von Leyden, the art critic of the *Times of India*, would write, 'When he came out of his shell at the age of twenty, he was a painter of light, deft, fluid watercolours of landscapes and town-scenes.'[3]

Raza's expanding vision began to draw upon atmospheric effects on buildings, the changing lights of the day and the glimmering shadows of people and he learnt to transform the same composition in varying lights. The city could be seen during different periods of the day, different seasons and boundaries began to dissolve into mood and movement. Even at this early stage, his work could be distinguished from that of other landscape painters with its abstracted shapes and rhythmic colour tonalities which would lend it an exuberant sensuality.

Raza stated, 'My stay in Bombay was exactly between 1943 and 1950 and these seven years of my life and work were a sort of awakening, a realization of the real values involved in painting. The idea of nature, the impact of nature from childhood, was an important element. But in Bombay I realized that a painter should know his language as a writer should know the vocabulary, the grammar, the meaning of words and has to have a mastery of them in verbal expression. A painter should know what colour is; he should know the organization of colours, their values, and how to render a theme on paper, or on canvas.'[4] Two paintings made by Raza were selected for the group show at the Bombay Art Society in November 1943. One of these was a street scene from the Express Block Studio and the other a depiction of the Parsi fire temple. But he was not considered significant enough to be invited to the show.

The War Emigrés and Their Contribution

The Bombay Art Society was formed in 1888 for encouraging art among the 'natives' and was initially an outlet for many resident Englishwomen to exercise their amateur skills. It was only in 1892 that an Indian student M.V. Dhurandhar carried off a prize, thereby opening the door for his fellow students. By 1937, the Indo-Hungarian artist Amrita Sher-Gil had won a gold medal from the Society for her oil painting *Group of Young Girls* – it launched off not only her own career but also established the early contours of modernism.

When Raza's work was shown, it was noticed by the *Times of India*'s Rudolf von Leyden. He wrote a review of the exhibition where he mentioned Raza's paintings. Both the watercolours were sold for Rs 40 each, which was the monthly salary Raza was getting at the Express Block Studio after working for eight to ten hours a day! The day after the review came out, Emmanuel Schlesinger, the director of the Indo-Pharma Company and a generous patron and collector, visited Raza and invited him to von Leyden's apartment, where he also met Professor Walter Langhammer. In fact Langhammer, the art director of the *Times of India*, called Raza home and also lent him his studio to work in during the day when he was at work. Raza stated, 'I would paint in the day and show my works to him in the evening whereupon he gave very beautiful analytical comments.'[5] These early sessions with him became invaluable, 'Langhammer would show me different examples of prints – Rajput miniatures, Persian miniatures, a painting by Van Gogh, Monet. He would say, "Look at them. Try to find the difference. You must dissect the painting, analyse it. You must see the difference between a Matisse and a Picasso painting or the difference between Monet and Cezanne." It was very hard in the beginning but it was an initiation. By the end of 1949-50, I was analysing not only my own work but also of my colleagues and to them I was saying, "There is a disparity of concept in these paintings." It was great, great I tell you.'[6] As Raza evolved, Langhammer and others began to acquire his works enabling him to leave his job and work full-time on his paintings. He also joined the Sir JJ School of Art in 1947 because he could finally afford its fees and secured a diploma from there in 1948.

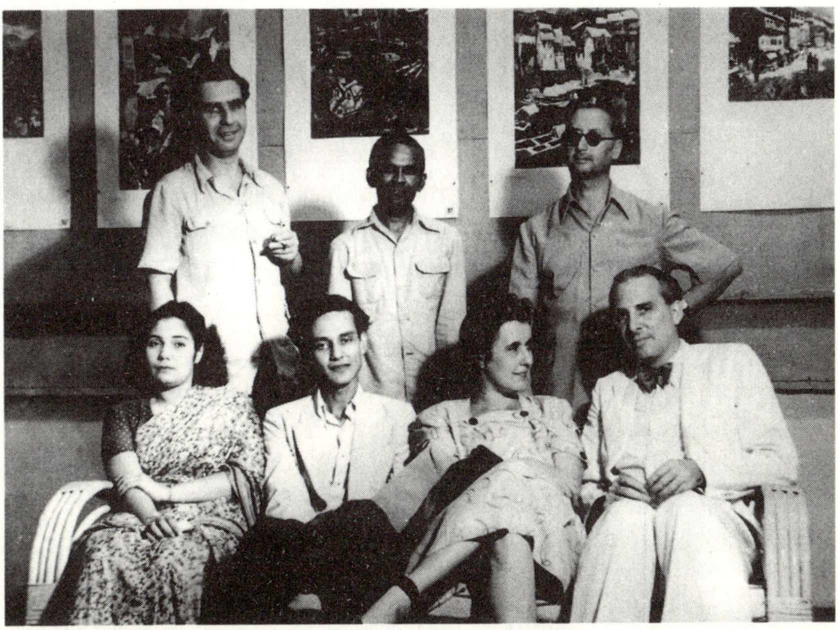

Bombay, 1946
Raza, Kathe Langhammer, Rudolf von Leyden (sitting front row)
Walter Langhammer, Ara (standing behind)

It has to be noted that the presence of certain foreigners in Bombay at this point played a crucial role in the development and promotion of the artists in the city, including Raza. This would create an awareness of the artistic situation outside of the academic art taught in the art colleges and evoke a different modernist idiom. As mentioned earlier, Walter Langhammer, along with his wife Kathe, was a great patron of the artists. A former art teacher himself, he introduced the artists to the new trends prevailing in Europe and held regular discussions with them. He was also an artist who exhibited frequently at the Bombay Art Society and one of his paintings was a portrait of Raza made in the Expressionist mode with leanings towards Kokoschka. Rudolf von Leyden and his comments and in the *Times of India* reviews had a decisive influence on the artists. It was he who had spotted Raza and brought a turning point in the latter's life. Indeed, with his reviews, art activities and lectures on art delivered at the Bombay Art Society, Leyden was to virtually steer the course of modern art in India in its formative years. Emmanuel Schlesinger, an Austrian Jew who had fled Germany and arrived in India, was also a great patron and collector of art. A pharmacist by profession, he had started the Indo-Pharma company in Bombay. It is said that he had a huge collection of art that he had been forced to leave behind in Germany. Perhaps it was to compensate for that that he would frequently buy works from Raza and other artists and bring along other European buyers with him as well.

Intellectual Ferment and Bevy of Artists

If the '30s and '40s were a period of a great resurgence in Bombay, the presence of many talented artists in the city at the time heightened the atmosphere of cultural awakening. Apart from a basic training, this ambience introduced Raza to many other like-minded artists. Besides Kulkarni, there was Shankar Palsikar, Akbar Padamsee, Tyeb Mehta and V.S. Gaitonde. Palsikar was not only well-informed but also very intelligent and a good teacher. Tyeb Mehta speaking about Gaitonde, who joined the group later, observed, 'He was very close to Palsikar and Mohan Samant – technically, not image-wise. They created their own colour by

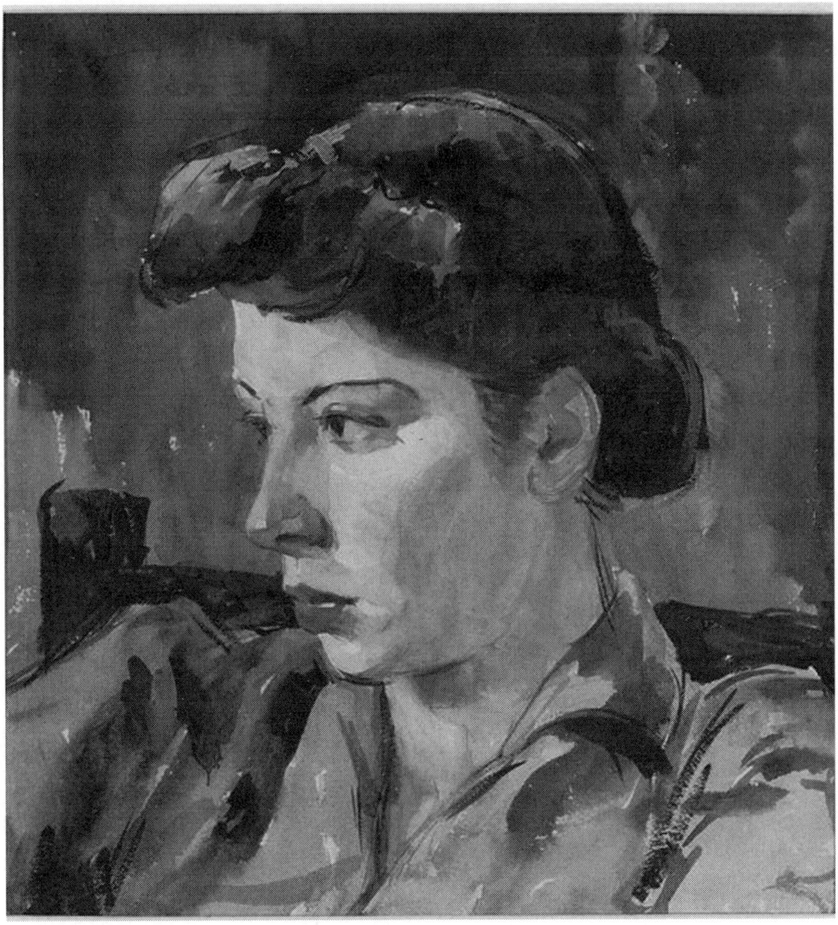

Portrait of Kathe Langhammer by Walter Langhammer.

rubbing cowrie shells on colour which would push one colour into another and create unbelievable texture and colour nuances. This was a technique developed by Palsikar.'[7]

The intellectual and cultural effervescence of the city had many great writers, theatre and cinema directors come together in a rising sense of identity and to address the needs of a nation in the making. And nothing better signified the spirit of the times than the city itself. For it helped each individual, no matter what his class or religion was, to struggle and make ends meet, to rise and to make a name for himself. As F.N. Souza said,

'Bombay with its rattling trams, omnibuses, hacks, railways, its forests of telegraph poles and tangles of telephone wires, its flutter of newspapers, its haggling coolies, its numberless dirty restaurants run by Iranis … its bania horders, its ghati women carrying a million tiffins to the clerks at their office during lunch hour … its machines, rackets, babbitts, pinions, cogs, pile-drivers, dwangs, farads and din.'[8] The city which was sizzling with modern means would be home to young artists who had little source of livelihood and no institutional support.

The Progressive Artists' Group

In Bombay of 1947 was formed the Progressive Artists' Group by the rebellious young Goan artist F.N. Souza. He had been expelled from the JJ School for taking part in demonstrations against the exploitative colonial practices of the British. Raza was invited by him to join the Progressive Artists' Group along with M.F. Husain, K.H. Ara, S.K. Bakre and H.A. Gade. The Group lasted only a few years, but, in their intensity and fervent desire to create an art different from that which existed previously and which addressed the issues of the present, they were to forge a new front. They were to create the first autonomous form of modernism in art which would be inscribed internationally. As Souza stated in the catalogue of the first show held in Bombay in July 1949, 'Today we paint with absolute freedom for content and technique, almost anarchic; save that we are governed by one or two sound elemental and eternal laws, of aesthetic order, plastic coordination and colour composition. We have no pretensions of making vapid revivals of any school or movement in art. We have studied the various schools of painting and sculpture to arrive at a vigorous synthesis.'[9]

Not only did Raza contribute a great deal to the Group but also imbibed a lot from it. As he stated, 'What we had in common besides our youth and lack of means was that we hoped for a better understanding of art. We had a sense of searching and we fought the material world. There was at our meetings and discussions a great fraternal feeling, a certain warmth and a lively exchange of ideas. We criticized each other's work as surely as we eulogized it. This was a time when there was no modern art in our country and a period of artistic confusion.'[10] There were regular meetings, discussions late into the night and the bondedness of a common quest, 'The real common denominator for us was significant form. We were expressing ourselves differently, we had different visions during the early days but what was common was a search for significant form. Each in his own way, according to his own vision. In a painted work, howsoever different it may be, say for example Modigliani and Soutine, who both painted nudes, the approach, the vision is different, the sensibility is different, the way in which paint is applied is different and, of course the temperament of these two artists is different. But the common denominator was significant form.'[11]

The insipid imitations of reality promoted by the art colleges following the British academic system seemed dull and unrelated to their times. At the same time, the revivalist methods of the Bengal School did not appeal to the artists who found it too literary, sentimental and disconnected from the struggle and anguish of their times. Unlike the others, Raza did feel that the Bengal renaissance was important because it drew attention to their culture yet the effete revivalism of tradition did not appeal to him either. They found inspiration in the works of Rabindranath Tagore with his distinct painterly approach, Jamini Roy with his meaningful revival of folk art and Amrita Sher-Gil whose skilful combination of Western and Eastern methods allied with historical reality and the need of the times. The artists were attempting to forge an art which was modern, rooted and connected to the vast changes taking place in the present. They were keen to give a new meaning to art, which would provide a young nation with a sense of self and yet be recognized internationally as a modern means of expression. Inadvertently, in coming together they also symbolized the transcending of the divisions created by religion, region and caste. While their work varied considerably, they were influenced by each other in their styles and themes and were bonded in their aim to bring modernism home.

As the artists evolved their own individual vision, discarding the normal appearance of things and using what the ordinary person considered 'distorted' and 'abnormal' forms, they would often come in for disapproval, even attack. As Tyeb Mehta put it, 'To pick up a brush, to make a stroke on the canvas – I consider these acts of courage in this country.'[12] Modernism with its powerful individual possibilities was for the ordinary viewer an act of betrayal. For instance, in an early exhibition where Souza's own full-length nude was exhibited, it raised much furore. As Krishen Khanna recounts:

> As I walked up the stairs, I passed a rather well-dressed woman muttering to herself. At first I thought she was chanting a mantra. I listened more intently and heard her saying quite audibly, 'Disgusting, absolutely disgusting.' That was a prelude to what I was about to see. It was an exhibition of Francis Newton Souza. Right in the middle of the centre-wall was his self-portrait, in the nude… Of course, females in the nude were an acknowledged and much desired subject matter; but males, inspite of their legacy of Michelangelo, had to keep their underpants on and their flies buttoned up. The police intervened and the 'offending' portion of the anatomy in the self-portrait was suitably covered, thereby attracting still more attention.[13]

Despite their youth and lack of means, the artists travelled long distances to meet at the seafront at Marine Drive, or at the Chetana restaurant or the Bombay Art Society premises and held fervent discussions late into the evening. Their poverty of means only enhanced their determination to forge a common front for modernism. They had not anticipated then that later some of them, like Souza, Raza and Husain would be leading figures in the Indian art world. Much of the Groups' energy was depleted, however, when Souza left for London in 1949, Raza for France in 1950 and Bakre, soon after, for London. Husain, Ara and Gade stayed behind and carried on with the Group's activities – later joined by artists Krishen Khanna, Vasudeo Gaitonde, Mohan Samant, G.M. Hazarnis and the only woman member, Bhanu Rajopadhye (later Athaiya). The meetings were attended by several other like-minded artists such as Tyeb Mehta and Akbar Padamsee. The Group finally dissolved in 1954; but by that time the artists had come into their own.

Dwelling and Despair

During those years of struggle, Raza was staying in Kalyan, which was far from Bombay, but it was all he could afford. A letter dated 9 May 1950 from Sharfuddin Haji Miyan Fakih, member of Kalyan Borough Municipality, Ghas Bazar, states that Raza had been staying at his house on Parsi Lane, Kalyan since January 1949. According to the letter, Raza did not pay any house rent but only the cost of electricity consumed by him.

Not a suburb, Kalyan was a neighbouring town close to Bombay. It would take Raza over an hour to reach the city, yet he travelled frequently to meet the other artists and hold discussions with them. According to Ram Kumar, 'When I stopped in Bombay for a couple of days before leaving for Paris, Raza was living in Kalyan and would come to Bombay twice a week. At that time he would sometimes not even have enough money to buy medicines for his sick wife. I bought a work of his for a hundred rupees in my sister's name and sent it to her… His desire to put an engraved stone marker on his mother's grave could also be fulfilled [only] several years later.'[14] His mother had passed away in 1947 due to a prolonged illness, while staying with Raza in Bombay. It was not much later, in 1948, that Raza's father too died in Mandla.

Towards the latter part of his stay, in 1949, he received a small stipend of Rs 2,500 from the government for developing his art in the context of the rural life in India. In his original application, Raza had selected Kapadvanj, a village in Gujarat, as the field of his work but soon realized that not knowing the Gujarati language was something of a handicap in the region. He then requested that he be allowed to work in Wada, in Thane District where he felt he could work with the people in their rich tradition of folk songs and their languages were Marathi and Hindi, both of which he was well versed in. During the three-month period, he first devoted himself to painting the local people and acquainting himself with their lives. In the second month, he tried to establish more intimate contact with them by giving lessons in drawing and painting their homes to thereby develop in them a 'sense of culture and aesthetics'. During the third month of his stay, he finalized his study of the village and held an educational exhibition and also picked out the local talent and directed them in art.

This experience proved valuable for him as it provided him a first-hand experience of rural aesthetic traditions, apart from getting to know their dismal conditions. While those three months turned out to be very creatively enriching for Raza, he would often be held up for his stipend. 'I haven't received any instalment so far ... This is causing me great inconvenience and anxiety. I had to cancel my Calcutta exhibition ... and even now I feel reluctant to accept any commission which may engage me for some time.'[15] He was impelled to loan an amount of Rs 1,875 which he had spent from the Artists' Aid Fund and requested the authorities to reimburse this sum to his account at the Lloyds Bank in Bombay.

The Artists' Fraternity

Since 1947, Raza had worked in a commercial design studio called L. Rajaram Art Studio, on 44 Bomanji Lane at Fort. He would pay a sum of twenty rupees a month for rent there, a princely sum in those days. It was a small price for him to pay, however, for the liveliness and fraternity offered by his fellow artists of the Progressive Artists' Group whom he met practically every day then. Ram Kumar, who had made Raza's acquaintance during a show of his in Delhi and had instantly become friends with him, came to Bombay for a month during that period and would often meet Raza. 'We met several times each day, sometimes at his Rajaram Studio, sometimes at some Irani tea shop. At times, when it would become very late, some of us friends would spread out mats on the floor of his studio and sleep there. In those days, Raza could not think of anything other than his art. He seemed to be intoxicated by that singular passion all the time.'[16]

The sense of fraternity which existed between the artists can be gauged from the fact that there was frequent communication between them even when they had gone their separate ways. Writing from London to the other artists, Souza maintained his role as the leader, 'What are the future activities of our Group? I think you could work on an idea I have. My mother has a small room on Hornby Road, which I think can be converted into a suitable art salon. Of course if we were six together we could conduct art classes there which could bring us quite a sum of money in fees … but I am not sure of such vague propositions and I have always failed in the activities I have undertaken. But you must keep the group going…'[17] Moreover, there were plans to form an international art group which, however, didn't materialize. 'I have not met any young painters yet and I don't think our hypothesis of forming an international Group will materialize. But I would like suggestions from you. I must have your collective advice. Meet and decide. Are you all coming here?'[18] In one of the letters soon after Souza left for London, he asked Raza if his Kalyan residence could be used after he left for Paris as the headquarters of the PAG. 'I wondered what you were going to do about it when you leave for Europe. I was thinking of it being taken up as Progs Head Quarter on a communal basis. But as we are disintegrated at present I don't think such a scheme is possible even in the near future…'[19] The days away were often isolated and frustrating for the artists and each one thought of writing to one of the other members for they were family. For instance, Souza would write, 'During the past month or so I have been quite melancholic and unhappy, not due to my work but due to the various external occurrences that have deterred me to do so…'[20] And then some big brotherly advice, 'I would strongly advise you to paint now in oils. You are unhappy you say because you have no ideas. Well, I don't think that is true… There are immense possibilities in that medium than you can find in watercolours. And as you work, you will be surprised, you will get brilliant ideas. Don't buy a small piece of canvas. Start big. Do your first oils on large plywood boards, or on large canvases. I am sure in a short while you will be happy with yourself.'[21] This proved to be prescient for Raza as it was indeed not long after that that he left for Paris and started making oil paintings which immediately attracted attention.

After he left for Paris, initially Raza visited India frequently. On one such occasion when he participated in a group exhibition which inaugurated at Gallery 59, run by fellow artist Bal Chhabda, Raza's work was priced at Rs 1,000, a high price in those days, while Husain's work was for only Rs 500. Husain reacted negatively at this and walked out of the gallery. He returned the next day with three paintings that resembled

Raza's work but were priced at Rs 5 each. This immediately thawed the ice and when the group came together in the evening, Husain composed a verse that ran: *Aaj kya ho gaya, paisa khota ho gaya, mamala ulta ho gaya* (Look what has happened today, money has become worthless, everything has turned upside down).[22]

Beholding the Classical

A major exhibition of classical Indian art over the centuries was held in Delhi at the Viceregal Lodge (present-day Rashtrapati Bhavan) in the winter of 1948. Originally held at Burlington House in London between November 1947 and February 1948 and organized by the Royal Academy to mark the transfer of power, it had assembled masterpieces from museums and private collections in India as well as Britain. The exhibition had condensed five thousand years of Indian art, but markedly marginalized the Islamic achievements such as the Mughal miniatures compressing them into one room along with other 'decorative arts' like playing cards and wooden book covers. The exhibition had highlighted the sculptures of the ancient and medieval period presaging the oriental position of the spiritual and symbolic essence of Indian art. This collection was to form the nucleus of the National Museum in a newly independent country. At any rate, in emphasizing this aspect the orientalist in the nationalist discourse came to be inscribed into what constituted modern, national art at the very moment of its birth.

The artists who went to see the exhibition like Husain and Souza maintained a critical distance from its fundamental beliefs but were deeply influenced by its sensual, tactile quality. As Husain stated, 'I came out with a set of five paintings in 1948 after visiting Delhi with Souza where I saw all the Indian works and then I felt I should paint something else. Till then I was influenced by the Expressionists. After visiting the exhibition I combined three periods, the form of the Gupta period, the strong colours of the Basohli period and the innocence of folk art and worked on it and then came out with five paintings which were shown at the Bombay Art Society in 1949. Nobody had seen it – not even Souza. At the opening he caught hold of me and took me to the Irani restaurant opposite and said, "Just tell me, what is this? Have you discovered something new?'"[23] This something 'new' was in fact the creation of an eclectic, hybrid and pluralistic form of expression which revealed the India that existed in the present. For Raza, it would touch an unbroken chord of memories about the richness of tradition he had experienced while growing up in the natural reserves of Madhya Pradesh. This would enable him to evolve his own form of modernism.

The French Encounter

In 1948, Raza, along with filmmaker K.A. Abbas and actor Balraj Sahni, was invited by Sheikh Abdullah to visit Kashmir. He was both exultant about the beauty that met his eye and saddened by the trouble the region faced – this visit led to a series of watercolours that were exhibited in Delhi and inaugurated by Rudolf von Leyden. On the occasion Leyden commented, 'There is a notion that art is a luxury which one cannot afford in the face of an economic crisis. Only a few realize what art can do to raise the moral and general outlook of a nation.'[24] He painted the tranquility of the lake, the autumnal glow of the trees and vegetation, and the wide expanse of the landscape against the white frost of the silent mountains, the bazaars and the pulsating crowds. But he also depicted the charred ruins of Baramulla, stark black against white, totally devoid of people. When the show was held in Bombay, Leyden reviewing it in the *Times of India* wrote:

> Colours have deepened, washes have changed into rich, juicy pigment with an endless play of tones… You will not find many of the hackneyed Kashmir subjects in this exhibition, no poplars, lakes and misty mountains, but plenty of bridges, canals and the bustling thorougfares of Srinagar city. Then like a call-back to the hard realities of life, we face the sombre sketches of unhappy Baramulla with signs of new life stirring among the ruins. As Dr Saiyidain pointed out in his unusually good opening speech, the human touch is always present in Raza's art however much the aesthetic forces of form or colour seem to assert themselves.[25]

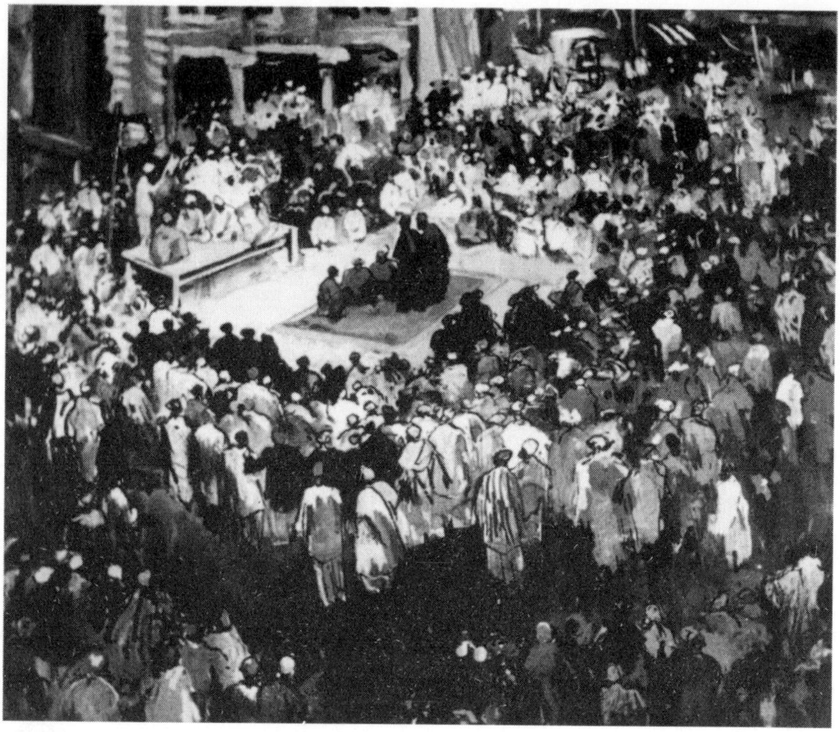

Performance, Srinagar, 1948, watercolour, S.H. Raza.

In Srinagar, Raza met the well-known photographer Henri Cartier-Bresson and the meeting was catalytic for the young artist. On seeing his work, Bresson remarked, 'You are a talented painter. But your work needs one element – that is construction. Try to understand that a painting is built up. Try to see Cezanne. And if you can give structure to your work it will be an entirely different thing.'[26] This encounter was not only the start of a lifelong relationship between Raza and Bresson, but it also initiated Raza's French odyssey, where he would search for meaning in his work.

During Raza's time in Bombay another exhibition made a lasting impact on him. This was an exhibition of large prints of modern French painters presented by the French Consulate in Bombay – exposing him to the works of masters like Picasso, Braque and Matisse. The exhibition left him spellbound and all the more determined to go to France and see the original works. Raza had read *Lust for Life* by Irving Stone on the life of Vincent Van Gogh which had made a great impression on him, '...The anguish, research and ideas of this solitary artist who was a genius but whose work, during his lifetime, was not recognized except by a handful of people...'[27] He decided that in order to excel in his art he needed to go to Paris, the Mecca of the art world, and sharpen his aesthetic tools. Raza applied for a scholarship to the French government for further studies. Intense interaction followed with the French councillor Mr C. Journot, where he was asked why he wanted to go there and he replied, 'The French have mastered painting. I like French painting.' He was asked to name the painters he liked. 'Cezanne, Van Gogh, Gauguin, Picasso, Matisse, Chagall and Braque.' 'What do you think of the works of Picasso?' 'Every Picasso period is significant because Picasso is a genius.'[28] Impressed by his answers, Raza was given a scholarship for two years, instead of just one year. He was advised to learn French intensively and he studied hard for the next two years.

The French Consulate in Calcutta invited him to have a show asking him to be present. Raza's financial situation, however, was not such that he could travel there. He wrote in a letter, 'Regarding my exhibition in Calcutta, I think early July [1950] would be the suitable time. But, I am afraid, I will not be able to come to Calcutta at all – partly due to financial difficulties and partly due to my appointment here... I can have a simple catalogue printed here and send it to you. But I must repeat that at present I am financially very worried and will like to minimize expenses as far as possible.'[29] The Consulate decided therefore to not have an exhibition of his works in Calcutta.

Before leaving for Paris in September 1950, however, Raza had an exhibition at the Institute of Foreign Languages at Outram Road in Bombay. Mr Journot, who had become a good friend of his, wrote apologizing that he was away and could not come for the exhibition. But he had recommended his friends to buy and asked Raza to reserve a painting for him, 'I would like you to reserve for me whatever you choose as best in the exhibition, upto Rs 100.'[30] A list of the exhibition indicates that a painting called *Street* was bought for him for Rs 100. All the works in this exhibition were priced between Rs 40 to Rs 300; and the buyers included Leyden, Langhammer, Schlesinger, Kekoo Gandhy, Raj Thapar (*Flooded Huts*), Wayne Hartwell and others. Dr Homi Bhabha bought the most expensive painting *Bombay* for Rs 300.

In these works could be seen elements of what would become a predominant trend in Raza's paintings in the years to come. The geometrical factor became visible as forms became increasingly simplified. In *Moonlit Night*, for example, the houses are arranged as shapes and create an almost abstract pattern with colours. They occupy no specific location or time. Was this also an expression of his state of mind for the next few years?

The paucity of means at this juncture made all his friends and acquaintances contribute to Raza's departure for Paris. Professor Langhammer gave him his overcoat and his shoes, the Express Block Studio's directors, Jalil and Ashfaq Husain, paid his fare from Bombay to France. Boman Behram, a member of the prominent Parsi family, gave him guarantee in case he was broke abroad. And Raza, equipped and fortified, sailed for Paris in what was to be the longest journey of his life.

After Partition

The largest forced migration in history took place during the partition of the Subcontinent in 1947. The Partition displaced over fourteen million people along religious lines, leaving in its trail large-scale violence and loss of life both during and after it. Moreover, the climate of hostility and suspicion and skirmishes from then continue to shadow the Subcontinent even today. As the author Alok Rai put it: '...There is another sense in which the [experience] of Partition is unfinished business – indeed, it is business that has barely begun to be addressed. Radioactive substances don't cease to be active if they are ignored, or forgotten, or even buried in concrete, as at Chernobyl... Those wounds are festering and the stench is becoming overpowering. The murderers of Partition walk in our midst, our public life is haunted by the ghosts of Partition.'[1]

The trail of destruction and despair that was left in its wake created one of the most apocalyptic moments of human desolation. As many families got divided or entirely wiped out, it did not leave the artists untouched. Many of them personally experienced the fear and disaster of Partition. In one way or the other, art became a barometer of the intense agony that the loss of family, relationships, land and wealth had created. It was a period of virtual erasures of existence in the lives of millions and art denoted those turbulences. Artists in India, like their counterparts in Pakistan, re-created those troubled times in diverse and impassioned ways – reliving that painful period.

Memories and Displacement

In this period of turbulence, the artist B.C. Sanyal was to lose not only his paintings along with his studio, but also the city of Lahore in which he felt rooted. When the Indian National Congress commissioned him to make a bust portrait of Lala Lajpat Rai for its 1929 session in Lahore, little did he know that it would be a turning point in his life. Having received more such commissions, he decided to stay back in Lahore and joined the faculty of the Mayo School of Art in 1929. He, however, came into conflict with the colonial authorities over his ideas and practice which compelled him to leave the institution in 1936. Consequently, Sanyal arranged for his own space in Lahore where he instituted the Lahore School of Fine Arts. But that institute came to an abrupt end with the Partition. Within a few months of arriving in Delhi, he forged an artists' community which became known as the Delhi Shilpi Chakra and reflected the new modern art of an independent nation. The Shilpi Chakra had members like Kanwal Krishna, Dhanraj Bhagat, K.S. Kulkarni, Pran Nath Mago and others, and held its exhibitions in different parts of the city focusing on the struggles of the downtrodden and the marginalized.

Krishen Khanna, also from Lahore, would memorialize in his paintings the intimate conviviality among people of all religions. Speaking of his memories of Partition, he said, 'The evening in Lahore would be penetrated by howling cries as area after area would be set afire and it still haunts me and holds me immobile. I spent several years of my childhood on Maclagan Road which was like a microcosm of what Lahore was. On this modest road lived professors and teachers of considerable distinction as well as my father who taught at the Government College. There was Dr Gurbax Rai, a homeopath who healed even the passerby. He actively participated in the freedom struggle and went to jail several times. During these difficult days his wife would sell fruit preserves. As a refugee in Delhi he continued to live with the same dignity and simplicity. It was fantastic how this small stretch of road had people of every faith and profession and belonging to different strata of society all living in peace and amity.'[2]

Khanna, through many of his works, recalls his childhood memories of Lahore – the city where he grew up. In *Maclagan Road* (1993), the apparently thick impasto surface in red, yellow, brown, black and white can be discerned as a free flowing memory of a vividly remembered area of Lahore, where the halwai sits with his kadhai, the lassi is poured from one glass into another, men sit drinking tea, the garage boys work on a car, among other things.

For Satish Gujral the trauma was vividly depicted like a whirlwind that wiped out everything that was precious to him. Gujral's traumatic experiences of Partition led to many powerful works where with strong, swirling strokes he depicted the untold tragedies of people on both sides of the border. Speaking of his experience, he said, 'The Partition came not just as a political move of the division of the country – but my family was very involved with the freedom struggle. My father was a member of the Constituent Assembly of united India. When it was divided it was decided that his membership should be shifted to Pakistani parliament because his area was on the Pakistan side. When Partition came, my father was in Karachi and I was in Lahore. I had been watching for weeks, firing, killing everywhere but so far it had not knocked at my door. But one day it did and with such force that I and my neighbour had to run to the refugee camp. There I found that more than two lakh people had taken shelter. This was the biggest refugee camp on the Pakistan side.'[3] His father was to get in touch with him soon enough, 'Two days later my father arrived and he said that it had been decided to exchange population and he had been appointed to help people in his own area to evacuate. But no one was willing to drive him there because it was very dangerous. Finally my father agreed that I drive him. We drove from Lahore to Jhelum – a 100 miles which normally take three hours but that day it took us four days because at every step there was looting and killing – murder, rape everything. We had to stop for protection a dozen times. On reaching Jhelum [present day Rawalpindi] we found our house had become a refugee camp.'[4]

The sculptor Amar Nath Sehgal has also left behind an unpublished memoir in his archives, which speaks of his difficult times during Partition. Born in Campbellpur, in what is now the Punjab province in Pakistan, Sehgal (1922-2007) was witness to the holocaust of Partition: 'My nerves were shattered having witnessed the holocaust with millions killed and many more millions uprooted from their ancestral hearths and homes on both sides of the border to seek refuge, solace, security and peace, keeping their bodies and souls together.'[5] Sometime in the 1960s, he wrote *American Education: An Experience*, which dealt extensively with his three-year sojourn in the US beginning in 1949. Shifting to the Kullu Valley in the wake of Partition, Sehgal applied to study sculpture in the US coupled with the motive to 'get out of India'. He wrote in his memoir explaining why the tragedy led to his search for a foreign land: 'I was sad, I had lost my sleep then. I wanted to be away from the environments where there were cries which were unheard.'[6] It followed that Sehgal's sensitivity was quick to respond to victims of natural calamities, wars and poverty. And the remembrance of the tragic events he had witnessed during Partition bears a stamp on his works. His sculptures like *Cries Unheard* (1958) with their simple but highly expressive forms portray human anguish, helplessness, oppression but also a yearning for a better and more humane world.

Separation and Turmoil

In the case of Sayed Haider Raza, his entire family had left for Pakistan and he was the only person to stay behind in India. The difficult times were reflected in the sublimation of many of his paintings which echoed anguish and harked towards unity and harmony. As he stated, 'Partition was an extremely difficult time for us. Our family was absolutely against the division of the country. For us at Damoh, at Mandla, for me in Bombay, the atmosphere was always cordial, we had excellent and affectionate relations with the people around us, and our family was well-respected. Then my brother-in-law had some trouble with the Mayor, people made some remarks that he did not appreciate. Tension mounted. After Partition, there were killings in the region of Damoh, and it became very difficult for my sister and her family. My older brother, Yusuf Raza, who worked as editor of the Hindi journal *Vishwamitra*, was well informed on what was happening. He stayed with my two other brothers. As the tension increased in Delhi, they decided to leave their homes one night. The house was burnt; they found shelter elsewhere and finally arrived in Lahore in Pakistan. My brother had completed his studies in Sanskrit; he was very rooted in the ethos of Hinduism, much better than me, and in Hindi poetry, the Hindi culture. For my sister and her family, life was really degraded at Damoh and they joined the refugee camp, first in Bhopal, then in Bombay and they finally left for Pakistan. Even though the Partition was a tragedy in my eyes, I decided to stay and I never regretted staying back. I am happy to have kept my name, my religion, my passport and to remain an Indian citizen even after fifty-two years in France.'[7]

Raza soon realized that even his wife Fatima wanted to leave for Pakistan as she was deeply attached to her family. He was to be left without any family member as his mother, who had been living with him in Bombay, passed away in 1947 and his father too died in 1948. His mother was buried in Kalyan and Raza would visit her grave every time he came to Bombay, after he moved to Paris. He was not entirely alone, however, even in those early years in Bombay, for the support and friendship of other artists and patrons in the city ensured that his stay was rewarding and creative.

Family Lives

Regular lively correspondence with his family would keep Raza abreast of what was happening in the lives of his siblings and in touch with their triumphs and failures. In turn, he received support and sympathy which, although long distance, partially compensated for the absence of his family. He also provided monetary support to his younger brothers for their art and studies and helped them follow the path that they wanted to. Raza's correspondence with them was intimate and insightful throughout his life, particularly in the early years. The eldest brother, Syed Yusuf Raza, who had started his journalism career in 1939 in Kolkata, had left for Pakistan along with his family in September 1947. After settling down in

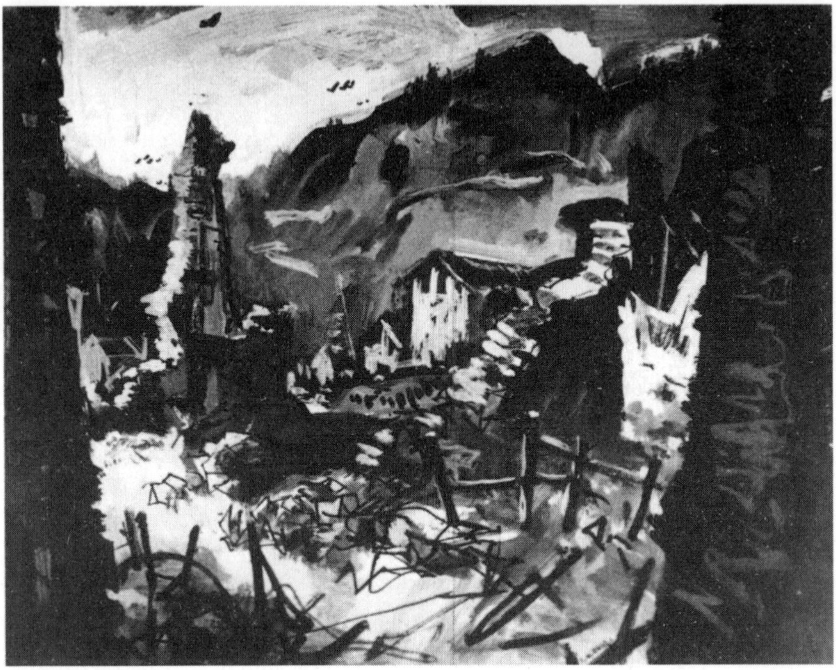

Baramulla in Ruins, 1948, watercolour, S.H. Raza.

the new country, he went on to work for the *Times of Karachi*, for a textile journal, and also produced a monthly art paper *Artistic Pakistan* that ran for two years.

Yusuf's yearning for meeting his brother remained intense, 'How much I wish to meet you. But I have created so many problems that it will still take a few years of hard work to overcome them all. These days I am busy with the preparation for bringing out my own magazine. It would be, I hope, a new type of magazine for Pakistan. Difficulties there are. But with the last seventeen years' experience in all the branches of my line, I am confident about the success of this venture.'[8]

Writing from Paris, Raza would share their common memories after a visit to India, 'There are so many memories – visit to Kalyan, Jabbalpore – where I learnt of the death of Zaki Chacha. Delhi – where I wandered in the streets you lived, met no one I knew, of course, I did not inquire.

I showed in Delhi and in Bombay where the reception of my work was beyond all expectation. AMAZING – HOW MANY ROOTS ARE STILL THERE, in spite of time and distance…'[9]

The brothers continued to exchange news, though it is not clear whether they actually met again or not. When Yusuf passed away in Karachi on 21 April 2001 after a long illness, he had left behind not only his own writings but also his artistic legacy. His daughter, Nahid Raza, is a well-known contemporary artist. The art critic Muna Siddiqui writes of her work:

> No conversation on art history in Pakistan is complete without a mention of Nahid Raza; her career spans at least four decades and her paintings, which are a candid reflection of her life, have been auctioned at Christie's – a renowned international company offering art auctions around the globe… The daughter of a journalist, Nahid had a peripatetic childhood moving from Karachi to Hyderabad and Khairpur and back. Consequently, her schooling was interrupted repeatedly. She recalls that this made her more aware of her surroundings and enriched her in ways that a 'normal' childhood would never have. While growing up, Nahid looked up to her two uncles – Raza, a prominent artist who lived in Paris and Ali Imam, one of the better-known personalities of Pakistani art. When Nahid finished her first year at university, Imam returned from his sojourn abroad and accepted the responsibility of heading the Central Institute of Arts and Crafts at the Arts Council in Karachi. Recognising his young niece's talent, the maestro took her under his wing. At the CIAC, Nahid Raza started her life-long career devoted to art. She recalls how she left Pakistan in the 80s to study art in the US and how this had a profound effect on her work, centralising her artistic focus on her own experience as a woman – as a mother, a daughter and a wife.[10]

In comparison to other artists, Nahid consciously opted for the direction of feminist art. As Siddiqui points out, 'Many female artists do not wish their work to be judged as "feminine", but Nahid is very conscious of her gender and paints with a clear social conscience. Nahid's paintings have hardly been silent on the burden of patriarchy. For those unfamiliar with the painter's work, her first exhibition was titled *Misery*, which followed a messy divorce. For years, she used the necktie as a symbol of masculine hegemony; in her paintings it often signifies the invisible presence of a man.'[11]

Yet Nahid had settled into a more compliant role later, 'But today I see a different Nahid – one who is at peace with her life, surrounded by pictures of her children and grandchildren. And this tranquility is reflected in her paintings. Her new work is, in her own words, wrapped with peace and enveloped in a milky white hue. Ever the spiritual person, the symbolism in Nahid's work draws from her religious beliefs. She has used the *buraq* – the creature is part woman, part horse – that carried the Prophet Mohammed (PBUH) to the heavens in her previous work. For Nahid, this is the culmination of the memory of her recent trip to Mecca, where the cubic Kaaba stands as a central stoic symbol of tranquility and peace.'[12]

Three years later in another exhibition, the critic Veera Rustomji points out that amongst other paintings those of the *Buraq* were significant, 'The two *Buraq* paintings are another reminder of how a woman's role is not solely meant for domestic purposes ... The *Buraq* paintings show a vibrancy of happiness and spiritual belief as compared to the soft demure women in plain white ghagra cholis. The jewels, roses and golden wings adorning the *Buraq* is perhaps a way for Raza to remind her viewers how religion initially valued and placed sacred importance in society for all that a woman has to endure... These three-dimensional incarnations of female figures remind the viewers how resistant women are and that they are really a force of nature to be reckoned with...'[13] Nahid Raza's journey continues to evolve, both as a woman and an artist in Pakistan.

London Days

Ali Imam, Raza's elegant and debonair younger brother who bore a significant resemblance to him, also became an artist of considerable repute in Pakistan. He had followed Raza's footsteps and joined the Nagpur School of Art and later trained at the Sir JJ School of Art. Made to leave

India during Partition, he went on to get involved with the Progressive Writers' Movement and the Communist Party of Pakistan and had to pay a heavy price for it. He had received his Bachelor of Arts degree from Punjab University in Lahore, but was imprisoned thrice for his socialist views in the early '50s.

In Lahore, painters like Moyene Najmi, Anwar Shemza and Ahmed Parvez were beginning to feel the pulse of modern art. Influenced by Shakir Ali, a Lahore Art Circle was formed which Ali Imam joined. In 1955, the group exhibited their work together and it was the first salon of paintings in Pakistan in which the participating artists had exhibited as a group. After three more exhibitions of his work in Pakistan, Ali Imam made his way to London in 1956 and he lived there for over ten years.

He was in frequent touch with Raza while in Pakistan and continued to do so from London as well. When he reached London on 25 September 1956, life was by no means easy. He wrote to his brother, 'I did live without a job for one month but now I am working for a firm as a porter-cum-liftman. It brings me 6 to 15 pounds a week…'[14] Raza wrote to him full of concern and warmth from Paris, 'I believe that exploitation is the sorriest of human activity. But there are many human beings and hence they should exploit each other reciprocally.'[15] He urged Ali to come to Paris in the following month. Ali, however, felt that his art would get affected if he joined his seasoned brother in a raw state, 'I want to be as much away from you as I can. By this I don't mean you in person, but your work. I have only seen three or four of your reproductions – which have resulted in a marked influence of your work in my paintings. Though I am trying to go my own way and am quite near to something very personal, but it will be better if I do not come to Paris for quite some time.'[16] Later, he was to find work as a clerk, 'At last I have found a good job as a clerk in the London County Council. Now, they have found me fit to spill ink on the white and brown paper… I have learnt only one thing in life. For me its equation is a very lengthy one. For every little thing I have to struggle very hard… I have always been very lonely. I could not help it. It appears to be self-imposed at times. This too could not be helped. Life becomes very boring and burdensome at times. I do not know as to when its significant function will be complete. Perhaps never. Why exist then?

Man is basically a coward. Thank goodness that I am a painter otherwise I would have shaken off my cowardice. It is a great relief to work. I used to enjoy painting after 12 hours of work as a porter.'[17]

Ali had brought about thirty paintings with him from home. 'I feel quite confident about my work. I took the risk and wrote a letter to Eric Newton [the artist and critic well-known in the late '40s] to give me some time. He agreed and I was with him for about two hours. He liked my work and wondered as to how I could paint that way in Pakistan. He had some criticism also. He then rang up a Gallery to announce my one man show. But the Art Galleries here are something horrible. They are typically English. They contain mostly horrible stuff. Only a few are modern, but they too are extremely commercial bargains. Secondly it is quite hard for the English to receive an eastern painter with an open mind.'[18] Ali also met Gade and Bakre in London, but it did not seem to have led to anything. 'Gade was here. He saw my work, but was in a patronizing mood. I do not much care about his comments. He hardly impressed me. I went to Bakre's house with him. I saw the fire of a sculptor in him. But my later efforts to meet him did not materialize. He seemed to be too much busy. Hence I did not worry him.'[19]

A little later, however, Ali would see better days. His salary would be enough to see him through and also allow him to purchase art material. 'I am still working in poster colours; but now I will start in oil. In a few weeks' time I will be able to afford it. Two weeks back I bought a heavy overcoat. Things are not as bad as they were before.'[20] Moreover, since his work as a clerk would get over by five in the evening, he had enough time on his hands to paint until late in the night. His work still did not satisfy him but the dissatisfaction of it made him struggle harder. 'I have been working on still lives, figure compositions and have also done some animals and birds – in my own style. But something very essential seems to be missing. I am working desperately to arrest that missing element. My work is getting intense, but is not very satisfying … This period of three months since my return from Paris has been one of great turmoil for me, as far as my work was concerned. I took a great leap and the results – which are most important – are poor.'[21] Raza was quick to reassure him, 'This morning getting your letter, I had quite a shock. I was sure that the visit to Paris will inspire you – that it will agitate and even trouble you. But I am not at all worried. This is just what it should be. Take the risks. They are worth taking. If the growth of work is slow, don't you see that so many of us are devoting all the time to work with no better results… Life is a strange hallucination – painful indeed, but precisely because we can intensely feel it we may do some good work.'[22] Ali had last visited Raza seven years ago and besides enjoying himself, he had also benefited from Raza's artistic views.

Ali's cup of happiness was full when he got to exhibit his works in the main gallery of the Imperial Institute (later renamed as the Commonwealth Institute), London from 7 to 27 January 1958. Raza was delighted with the news and sent him oil colours and some money entreating him to take care of the organizational side of the exhibition, which was necessary. The show itself was a success and not only did some of his works get sold but he received reviews in important publications like the *Manchester Guardian*. A review in *Art News and Review* stated, 'His architectural townscapes are full of interesting forms, and it is instructive to see his reaction to English architecture… '[23]

On Ali's architectural landscapes, Jalal Uddin Ahmed commented, 'In his recent work, he has been concentrating on the theme of "Houses" in which architectural qualities have replaced the earlier emphasis on colour. The sense of "perspective" is conspicuous by its complete absence, and the first impression on seeing an exclusive exhibition of these "empty front elevations", as a critic put it while reviewing his exhibition two years ago, is one of haunting loneliness, perhaps reminding one of Goldsmith's Deserted Village'.[24] Ali's painting of houses in this period were done during different times of the day – night, daylight and in winter when it snowed – yet retain their geometrical forms and a sense of desolation.

After the exhibition, Ali wrote excitedly to Raza, 'Two of my new patrons, Dr Newman the collector and Mr Rice, a young man with lots of money, are taking great interest in me. Their endeavours are to see me a whole-time painter. Mr Rice wants to start a new gallery and intends to have me as one of the painters … I had been to Dr Newman's house again this Saturday. He put my seven paintings in seven different rooms. He has more than a hundred paintings and thousands of sketches and watercolours by the leading painters of the world. It was so flattering to see my paintings hanging side by side with the works of Tropstki, Gurrier, Varnad, Picabia, Lablais and so many other Europeans and British painters.'[25]

In the meantime, Ali had started getting to know Maureen, who had been a colleague of his at LCC. He even visited Raza and Janine with her and eventually married her. But before the wedding, Raza wrote to him in a tone of caution, 'Maureen is a fine girl. She is good looking, uninhibited and straightforward. I prefer her so much to many other girls – who talk philosophy or art. She is human, will love her home and will be devoted to it. Plastic art is however completely out of her domain and this I think is one of the fundamental issue, in which you as a painter will differ with her … I do not know how far you care that a woman should understand your intellectual or artistic aspirations. For some men it's a necessity, for others it is not.'[26]

The relationship did not last long and when the marriage was finally annulled, Ali was distraught. 'As a matter of fact I had been and still am nearly cut off from all my friends for the last four or five months. My work has terribly suffered. I was in such a state of mind that I found myself completely incapable of sublimating my personal problems through my work … Maureen was very unhappy with my moods, my likes and dislikes and particularly with my general attitude that my profession came before everything else. There were constant periods of tension and unhappiness – which kept on repeating themselves… About four months back Maureen decided that she could not lead her life with me and decided to go back to her old boyfriend. I did my best to avoid the inevitable but she was stubborn and persistent that she was not cut out to lead my type of life and that she would be a much happier person with this man of her own mental caliber, likes and dislikes. For the last two months we are living separately…'[27] Although unhappy, Ali was also left with the feeling that it was probably for the best in the long run.

The financial situation continued to plague Ali when Mr Rice stopped paying him the monthly sum for giving him paintings without any explanation. He was forced to take up manual work at the hospital. But finding it difficult, he went back to working for the LCC. 'Last month I applied for the LCC job and was taken back from 21st April. This I did after due consideration of many factors involved. In the first place at the hospital I was putting in 39 hours per week for 6 days to earn only five odd pounds. At LCC I work for 40 hours for five days for nearly double the money and I get two solid days off at week end... In the hospital, it was a manual job and usually I used to get so tired that I could not paint or read. I did very little work during this period. I suffered from severe pain in body which was due to lifting of heavy patients for bathing etc.'[28]

Ali had studied art at Saint Martins School of Art, 1959-60, and later at Hammersmith College of Art, 1962-63. He continued to have shows in solo and group exhibitions in London and received good attention. A highlight was to be selected for the Commonwealth show to celebrate the silver jubilee which was inaugurated by the Queen and where all the major artists were participants. Apart from his own friends, he continued to be in touch with Raza's colleagues like F.N. Souza and Tyeb Mehta in London, Akbar Padamsee who would visit from Paris with his wife Solange Gounelle and M.F. Husain from Bombay. There would be a lively report of their activities sent to Raza to keep him updated. When Tyeb and Sakina had a daughter, Ali wrote to his brother excitedly, 'Sakina gave birth to a daughter a fortnight back. They wanted a daughter and are very pleased about it. Tyeb's work was very well received at Oxford. He sold three paintings out of four. Lately he also sold a painting at Gallery One in a Christmas show. I am mighty pleased about him.'[29] By 1963, he had a steady partner in Lindsay and they not only met Raza and Janine in Paris, but Lindsay also bought a work of Janine's and had written to him, 'I am enclosing 130 F for your painting at the Gallery which I liked and would you please send me the painting when your exhibition is over...'[30]

Despite the even tone of Ali Imam's life and work, the kind of spectacular success that Souza gained in London or the phenomenal rise of Raza's career after the mid '50s evaded him. Perhaps it was time to return home? In fact, his elder brother Yusuf Khan had expressed his wish to Raza that he hoped Ali Imam would return to Pakistan soon, where he could not only do well but also help with raising art consciousness in their own country. 'I wonder what Imam is doing there in London. Would not Paris be a better place for him for studies! Or he may come back to Pakistan. Here the art movement is getting momentum. But there is not a single Art School worth the name in Karachi. The "Art Council" people who are getting lakhs of rupees from the Govt. are all sleeping over this crying need of the day. Imam had a good reputation in Pakistan when he had gone abroad. If he comes back, he may be able to get Governmental patronage for setting up a first class Art School in Karachi. If he takes up this work he will be doing a national service. Besides that – he will be financially well off and will also get enough time to paint. I think by now, he must have developed his individual style!'[31]

Indeed, Ali took the decision to return home, 'I was passing through a very difficult phase of decision. I have now finally decided to return to Pakistan. I will be sailing from Venice on the 16th of December for Karachi. The last many months I have gone through intense struggle about this issue … I am going back only for a few years and have planned things such a way that I will be able to paint whole time, endeavouring to react to the local stimuli and the experiences gained in Europe. I agree with you that full and continuous involvement is absolutely essential in any art form – which I am unable to give under the conditions that have prevailed during the last many years. This factor completely outweighs all other points… The most difficult and sad aspect of my leaving London has been my five years of wonderful association with Lindsay – which unfortunately have to come to an end. She is very sad. She has lately shifted to her cottage and has taken a job locally. We meet at weekends. It is very painful indeed…'[32]

As it happened, Ali's best period came after his return to Pakistan. As he gradually escalated on the artistic scale, he went on to become one of the best-known artists of his time in his homeland. In bringing his Western training along with his own sensibilities to indigenous situations, he would bring about not only a heightened awareness but also an enhancement of artistic space. Ali had made figuration his forte and some of his best works were of a down-to-earth reality of people at work with their implements or animals. In his painting *Farmers*, for instance, we have peasants hoeing the crop in a rhythmic circle which eschews depth or perspective. The cadence of their movement is matched by the juxtapositioning of forms that are individualistic yet bound together in a unity. Unlike Syed Sadequain who returned from Paris in 1966 and incorporated the École de Paris style to his calligraphic forms on the painterly surface, Ali maintained his allegiance to the figure.

In Karachi, Ali founded the Indus Gallery in 1971, which was to play a pivotal role for art and artists in Pakistan. The name referred to the Indus River, which had supported the oldest settlement of Mohenjo-daro of the famed Indus Valley civilization. He ran the gallery from 1971 until he passed away in 2002, and since then it has been managed by his wife Shahnaz. With the gallery and his own work, Ali was at last satisfied. He was an art critic, art promoter and an art educationist to many artists at the Indus Art Gallery. Some of the noted artists that participated in this gallery's exhibits were Sadequain and Ismail Gulgee, among many others. Known for his integrity and authenticity, it is not surprising when he wrote to Raza, 'Since I received Presidents' Medal for Tang-e-Imtiaz last August and Suddre-Azam Award, a shield and a cash award of Rs 3000 both of which I did not receive, there has been a lot of jealousy against me and some journalists have written very nasty and unfair articles against me. I have never worked for rewards or awards. I have only worked hard and sincerely and those social benefits have come my way without my trying for them.'[33]

Ali had settled down in Karachi with his wife Shanaz and two children. As he wrote to Raza, 'Children are growing into fine thinking beings – Shahnaz is the most wonderful wife and mother one could have…'[34]

Ali Imam died of a heart attack on 23 May 2002 in Karachi. Apart from relatives and friends, representatives from many art galleries where he had been active for many years expressed sorrow over his death. Salima Hashmi, a noted educationist of Pakistan and the daughter of Pakistan's renowned poet Faiz Ahmed Faiz spoke about her childhood days when Ali Imam, then a member of the Communist Party of Pakistan, used to visit them while her father was in jail. 'At that time people avoided us lest the wrath of the government might fall on them. But Ali Imam used to come to visit us in Lahore all the way from Rawalpindi.'[35] According to a report, 'Ms Hashmi reminisced that Ali Imam used to exhibit the works of those artists who did not want to limit themselves to the art genres that had enjoyed state patronage. "When I came back from England, where I had gone to study, I realized that through Indus Gallery Ali Imam had taught people to appreciate art, enjoy art and, more importantly, buy art works." "In his last days," she observed, "Ali Imam had enjoyed the role of an 'elder statesman of art'. After all," she added, "he had a great sense of humour."'[36]

Different Routes, Common Aims

Apart from the distress of being uprooted, Raza's siblings had to start their lives from scratch in the newly formed nation and had financial constraints of an extreme measure. When his only sister Mohammadi Begum, whom we hear little of in Raza's collection of letters, was ill and could not be treated for lack of money, Ali had written to Raza, 'I have received sister's letter yesterday. She is ill again and wants some money (Rs 200). I am trying to send her something.'[37]

Raza's younger brother Syed Hasan Imam, along with his wife Taj and four children, made his way to Kuwait to find a means of subsistence. There Hasan initially started a small laundry business, but he had to give it up when it suffered heavy losses. Soon after, he found a job as sales representative for Kuwait Airways and his wife started working as sales representative for Trans Arabia Airline in Kuwait. His constant demands for money at a time when Raza had to also look after his friends visiting Paris eventually made him write to Hasan that he would not be able to spare much as he too had his limitations. Hasan was quick to reply, 'Anyway I think I am wrong in understanding the people who live in west. I think they become so mechanical that feelings and heart has no place in their life. But Bhaijan I am born in east and still live in east. We have a heart, feelings and understanding. We do believe in rules, laws and mechanical system. But we do certain things on sentiment ... But I never knew that I don't have a brother in Paris and a machine who believes in system laws and discipline. Who wants everything done business like. I am sorry it was my mistake. The language of your letter has hurt me a lot.'[38] Exasperated beyond measure, Raza wrote back, 'I did what I could with the means I had. However I want you to know that I will never do it again. Never in my life a favour has been asked from one with such insolence, with such disregard for me and my feelings, for my time. But I will excuse you as you know nothing about me nothing about my values, nothing about my ideas on the east, nothing about my health nor my own problems. You confound sentimentality and human emotion. None of your letters ever contained any real thought [or] motivating material and I am not interesting in banalities of everyday living. So we have to end this correspondence reciprocally futile for both of us.'[39] Despite this, the two were to keep up a correspondence for Raza found it difficult to break with any member of his family.

In fact, to his youngest brother Syed Mohsin, who could barely complete his education and had to ask Raza for frequent help for as little as five pounds, he generously provided as much means as he himself could muster. He wrote, 'For all the time with letters in my hand, my mind recollected all the precious memories and incidents of the past (which are very distinct in my mind) particularly those of the last few months in Kalyan when my ailing mother lived her last. She died in my hands and the last few words she spoke related to you.'[40] Apart from monetary help, Raza would often counsel and encourage him and these spoke for his own beliefs in life, 'But you can take a lesson from me, Mohsin. This letter can help you more than all the financial aid I could give you. That, if you can understand it there is nothing beyond a man's reach. Everything is possible. Only one must be made of a special stuff, must be determined and firm like a rock and must be capable of putting in hard work persistently.'[41]

Eventually, Mohsin landed a job as a lecturer of economics at Lyallpur in September 1957 but hoped to specialize in the subject in London. The conditions described by him of teaching could be true of any university in south Asia, 'Every moment that I pass here is a long journey of time. I do not like many people – they are insincere. Friends and relatives are all selfish. There is favouritism and nepotism everywhere. The abilities and qualifications are not of much importance. Even the hard work does not pay here…'[42]

To Mohsin's relief, at last he got admission in a London university and reached the city by October 1958. In a year or two, he even visited Raza with his girlfriend, later his wife, Rosemarie Geiger. Raza wrote to him after the visit, 'We liked very much indeed Rosemarie. She has most charming manners and a lovable personality…'[43] Soon after the visit to

Paris, the couple found that Rosemarie was pregnant and Mohsin wrote to his brother, 'This has put us in a very difficult position. We love each other and it would be a joy to unite ourselves in matrimonial ties. But it seems rather premature. It will have a direct effect on my course of action and would cause a delay in my obtaining the degrees from here which I must ultimately secure.'[44] Raza, however, felt that Rosemarie would make for a stable and good partner to Mohsin and that the two should marry. The wedding took place on 17 December 1960 in London and soon after the couple left for a holiday in Switzerland. Their first daughter, Christine, was born in April 1961.

After quitting an initial stint at a hospital, Mohsin applied for a teacher's post. In the meantime, he got a wine butler's job at a West End restaurant, 'The work is very interesting and it seems that in wine there is quite a lot to learn. They are giving me good training and I think that it is not a bad idea to know a little about wines.'[45] When Mohsin was appointed as a teacher in a senior boys' school for mathematics and religious instructions, he found the prospect of regular wages and an interesting job to be very exciting, 'I am sure to find it interesting and already I am going through the Bible and the gospel of St. Mark. I had already read Bible some time ago out of curiosity. Most of it is like Quran. In Quran of course, there are some major changes to suit the then prevalent social conditions.'[46] Early in the following year, Mohsin was able to purchase a house in Romford, Essex, near his school by taking a double mortgage. Its repayment of twenty pounds a month was less than the rent they had to pay. Indeed, domesticity settled in with the birth of his second daughter, Yasmine, in October 1963. 'It was certainly an experience for me as I was with Rosemarie all the time and actually saw the birth take place. It is difficult to get a place in the hospital if you have your own house and the conveniences which many others are deprived of.'[47] As for Christine, 'Christine is quite thrilled by the baby whom we call "Yasmine" – quite a nice name – and wants to handle her just like one of her dolls. She hasn't shown any jealousy yet. Yasmine has been quite a good girl during the night and has not kept us awake more than is necessary.'[48]

The continuous correspondence with his brothers was a source of comfort and gratification for Raza as he had been separated from them in a definitive manner. The family suffered many hardships because of being uprooted during Partition, but were able to tide over them and settle down in the newly formed country. As Raza wrote to Mohsin, 'I recollected in this remote place [Paris], lost in my work, that once I had a family life which was abundant with care, love and affection. I was the favoured one to have heavenly parents and affectionate brothers and sisters and we had a pure and divine upbringing. Our joys and sorrows were common and we lived and struggled collectively. Damoh of 1930s! Time passed; circumstances and intentions separated us further and further. Yet we met. I can travel back and have distinct glimpses of short meetings at Nagpur then Kalyan and the happy and sad days together. Then came partition and later I took a boat and reached Marseille on the 2nd Oct. 1950. Two years of detachment. Am I perhaps a gypsy to wander from place to place and to feel perfectly at home in the place my work takes me? Intellectually I understand it, but in states of emotional devastation or depression I feel terribly distressed for most of my actions. There is a conflict in ideals and I feel miserable.'[49]

Paris, Mon Amour

It was an uninterrupted journey by sea, broken by the lapping waters, which Raza undertook in September 1950 and that finally brought him to Marseille. He was accompanied by Akbar Padamsee, who had also decided to live and work in Paris for a while. Raza recalled, 'When the ship left, I looked at the shores of Bombay with tremendous emotion in my heart. Slowly, the country receded and the boat took us over into the space of the ocean.'[1] Akbar Padamsee vividly remembered the journey he undertook after speaking to Raza, 'No. I didn't know anybody and I was in the School of Art, so there was no one – I was 18. Raza was six years older than me.'[2] He elaborated, 'We went by the same boat – *SS Stetenham* – an English boat. It was a wonderful trip with him. You know I was reading a lot of books and Raza didn't know English. His English was poor or nil. And he was trying to study. So the books I read, I talked to him about them. He said, "Wonderful, when did you read them?" I said, my brother Nuruddin has a big library.'[3] According to Akbar, he also learnt how to knot a tie on the ship and would practice it for hours.

They reached Marseille eleven days later on 2 October 1950, where a representative of the French government greeted them and put them up in a hotel. The next day they travelled to Paris by train and were received at Gare de Lyon by Ram Kumar at eight in the morning. Kumar had been a writer, but absorbed by art, he had borrowed a small amount from his father to come to Paris where he studied under André Lhote and Fernand Léger between 1950 and '51. He had arrived just before his colleagues Raza and Padamsee; and together they were to create a segment of the camaraderie they had left behind in India. A room had been fixed for Raza at Rue Delambre in Montparnasse by the French government; this was where all the important painters, French and otherwise, lived and worked. Raza did not take long to freshen up and rush out to see the city he had dreamt about for so long. 'It was an extraordinary experience. I loved these boulevards and buildings and the look of the cafes and houses. I discovered at the crossroad of Boulevard Montparnasse and Raspail an enormous statue of the writer Balzac by the sculptor Rodin… Now, here was a great sculptor portraying a great writer. The city honouring these two artists was fantastic and the solidity and sculpturesque quality of the statue right in a public place was a revelation to me.'[4]

On seeing a poster announcing an exhibition of Matisse at Maison de la Pensée Française, Akbar and Raza went to see it – the very first show that he saw in Paris. 'It was extraordinary in the sense that it worked with two dimensions, nearer to the Indian concepts in which we were getting involved and interested. It was not the realism of the post-Renaissance period. It was solidly constructed, where colour prevailed… Around us there were beautiful men and women, well dressed. Musical concerts being announced, other art events. There was a poster which said in French, "Life begins tomorrow." I said, "No, life begins today."'[5]

Although Raza's dream had come true and he was at last in Paris, the city after the Second World War was a place emptied of its magnetic draw. It had been the metropolis of the twentieth century where artists, writers and thinkers had congregated to realize their art and to lay the paradigms for modernity. As Gertrude Stein wrote, 'The reason why all of us naturally began to live in France is because France has scientific methods, machines and electricity, but does not really believe that these things have anything to do with the real business of living … And so in the beginning of the twentieth century when a new way had to be found naturally they needed France … But really what they do is to respect art and letters, if you are a writer you have privileges, if you are a painter you have privileges and it is pleasant having those privileges ... well that too is intelligent on the part of France and unsentimental, because after all the way everything is remembered is by the writers and painters of the period, nobody really lives who has not been well written about and in realizing that the French show their usual sense of reality...'[6] The grand impresario of art in Paris, Stein lived there for more than thirty years and oversaw with her companion Alice Toklas a salon on the rue de Fleurus that served both as the hearth for the expatriates in the city as well as the artists of the period such as Picasso and Matisse. Her role in patronizing the masters of the new French painting was crucial if somewhat overbearing.

Gertrude Stein's vivid writing of the period recalls the encounters made with ease and intelligence with the masters. As Stein mentions in *The Autobiography of Alice B. Toklas*:

> We went up the couple of steps and through the open door passing on our left the studio in which later Juan Gris was to live out his martyrdom but where then lived a certain Vailliant, a nondescript painter who was to lend his studio as a ladies dressing room at the famous banquet for Rousseau, and then we passed a steep flight of steps leading down where Max Jacob had a studio a little later, and we passed another steep little stairway which led to the studio where not long before a young fellow had committed suicide, Picasso painted one of the most wonderful of his early pictures of the friends gathered round the coffin, we passed all this to a larger door where Gertrude Stein knocked and Picasso opened the door and we went in ... He asked us to sit down but as all the chairs were full we all stood up and stood until we left ... Against the wall was an enormous picture, a strange picture of light and dark colours, that is all I can say, of a group, an enormous group and next to it another in a sort of a red brown, of three women, square and posturing, all of it rather frightening. Picasso and Gertrude Stein stood together talking. I stood back and looked. I cannot say I realized anything but I felt that there was something painful and beautiful there and oppressive but imprisoned.[7]

This was the Paris that Hemingway loved, where it was possible to live well even with little means and to avail of the city's enlightened role in art and literature such as the famed library and bookstore Shakespeare and Company at Rue de l'Odéon. His *A Moveable Feast* published posthumously is an account of the city, '…We loved, and learned, and fought our way back into.'[8] Yet all this was to change after the Second World War. None could give a better account of those difficult years than Sylvia Beach, the young Jewish owner of Shakespeare and Company:

> Then suddenly the Germans swept over France. As they came nearer and nearer to Paris, the population fled or tried to flee … I had resisted all the efforts of my Embassy to persuade me to return to the United States … Instead, I had settled down to share life in Nazi-occupied Paris with my friends. Also, as I went about with François, [her Jewish assistant] I shared with her some of the special restrictions on Jews – though not the large yellow Star of David that she wore on her coat or dress … We could not enter public places such as theatres, movies, cafes, concert halls, or sit down on park benches or even on those in the streets. Once, we tried taking our lunch to a shady square. Sitting on the ground *beside* a bench, we hurriedly ate our hard-boiled eggs and swallowed the tea in our thermos bottles, looking around furtively as we did so. It was not an experience that we cared to repeat.[9]

The War was to leave the great city depleted of its rich human resources. Hemingway wrote in his posthumously published short story 'A Room on the Garden Side' about the importance of Paris. In it, amidst talk of Marcel Proust, Victor Hugo, Alexander Dumas and Charles Baudelaire, a group of soldiers, along with the protagonist, gathered at the Ritz Hotel implicitly wonder if the heritage of Parisian culture can recover from the dark taints of fascism. Hemingway's alter ego Robert then realizes that he must leave the city if he must preserve its meaning in his own memory, 'The town would never look the same again unless you left it when you should.'[10]

Despite the effervescence, the Paris that Raza saw had changed from the early part of the century and suffered from a sense of exhaustion.

The haunts of the artists and writers, like Café de Flore, wore a deserted look and the masters were present by their absence. The École de Paris had run its course, leaving behind the last remnants of abstract art with painters like Pierre Soulage, Nicolas de Staël and Serge Poliakoff. The scene had shifted to New York even as Paris harboured a melancholic nostalgia for the masters of modern art. When one of the last of them, Nicolas de Staël, committed suicide in March 1955 at the age of forty-one by leaping from his eleventh story studio terrace in Antibes, Paris mourned.

Yet Raza was fortunate to have his colleagues in Paris. Ram Kumar recalled:

> When Raza first arrived in Paris in 1950, I was there at the station to welcome him. I still remember how, even as he alighted from the train, he was infused with enthusiasm for Paris, and how within minutes he was talking about the Louvre and Picasso. I attempted to introduce him to other dimensions of the city – the place, the people, the weather, the life – but he was lost in other dreams. He was already planning his schedule of study, when he would work and when he would visit other exhibitions and museums in the city. He valued time immensely and wanted to use it for work and work alone. He felt he might never get such a chance again, and wanted to experience this once in a lifetime opportunity to its fullest – little did he know at that time that he would be spending his life there.[11]

New Horizons

The artist was to visit the museums in a systematic manner to look at the original works which he had wanted to for so long. He could hardly wait to go to Jeu de Paume the next day, where he stood transfixed before a portrait of Vincent Van Gogh and tears came to his eyes. Next to that portrait were the well-synchronized works of Cézanne and Raza studied these with great interest for they consisted of great depth and complexity. He also found Gauguin extraordinary and closer to the oriental aesthetics he was familiar with.

Raza was to join the Alliance Française to improve his French. Soon after he was to get admission to the École des Beaux-Arts and was allotted to the Atelier of Heuze, a well-known portrait painter. In the course of the time that Raza got to know Heuze, the latter said to him, 'Look, Raza, ultimately you have nothing to learn at this school. Of course, you can practice, which is good. Art expression is practical work: paint and study. I would give you every possible instruction ideas that you would like to know. Ask me questions, but work. At home you are already a mature painter. You come from a great civilization and culture. I will give you all the papers that would be necessary but come and see me once a week at least.'[12] Raza found Heuze to be right and that the training did not happen in the school where the students were rather immature but for three or four friends he'd made who had talent. Amongst those students was a young girl who was not just pretty but talented as well, and Raza became very friendly with her. She was Janine Mongillat.

In those early years in Paris, life was very busy for Raza. As he wrote to Mr Journot, his friend and the French Counsellor in Bombay, some years later, 'Please forgive me for the delay in writing to you. Often and again I thought of doing so informing you about me and my work, my happiness and my problem… My first attempt was to acquaint myself with the art treasures of Paris and to have a general knowledge of the history of art in Europe – both ancient and modern… My approach has been, of course, like that of a student of 'aesthetics' rather than that of an archeologist or a historian… The Ecole des Beaux-Arts opened in the middle of October and I joined it as "Etudiant Libre" (that so because I am over-age). I have taken the painting course of the morning and the drawing classes in the evening. As I told you in Bombay, I wanted to do a lot of drawing and painting from life and I am as convinced now as before of the importance of drawing as the fundamental basis of a good painting. I have of course, the afternoons and holidays for my experimental work and for studies in museums and libraries.'[13]

Raza was working harder than ever and appeared to have barely any time on his hands. He was driven because it was a make-or-break situation. But there was a sea change in his work as well. He wrote to his younger brother Mohsin, who had asked for financial help, 'It's not asking too much from a brother (who himself feels morally bound to help you) for assistance. I even like the confident tone of your letter. But dear one, do you know that this one is not the healthy young man of 1940s, proud and confident, who could work 16 hours a day and whose work brought back money surer than the surest trade? All has changed with me now. I have undergone a period of study and evolution for which I had to pay with my blood and the realization has cost me my life. This is no mystic statement – actually I refer to the skeleton I am reduced to now – my physical being which cannot now stand four hours' work – my frail hands which at the age of 30 tremble constantly. Nor do I wish that the above statement should give impression of complaint. I am, on the contrary, happy indeed to have lived and lived fully and my way, according to my own values and to have worked for the sheer joy of working ... Now some facts about my life. My work has completely changed. The pictorial conception I am developing is totally different – which I will not deal with, since it will take me pages to explain. I will only show one difference which is very significant and which at the moment concerns us. This is that I need now at least four to six weeks for a painting – if I work regularly – whereas in Bombay I used to leave home with six papers tucked under my arms – and by the evening I will come back with atleast four paintings – sometimes all the papers were covered. Now this one painting for which I give more than a month [of] hard work is sold for about 300 rupees – which is hardly sufficient for a month's expenses for one person in Paris. The only fortunate thing is I sell almost everything I do and so far I haven't starved.'[14]

Apart from art, Raza read French writers voraciously to understand their culture and thought. He became acquainted with the writings of Jean-Paul Sartre, Andre Gide, Andre Malraux, Paul Valery, and others. The angst-driven writings of existentialism of which Sartre and Camus were the chief votaries cast a spell on the writers of the period. As it was understood at the time, it was a philosophy of solitude where the burden of giving significance and responsibility to one's life was bestowed on the individual and was removed from the comforts of a Universal Being who ruled the world for us. The popularity of existential philosophy in literature as well as plastic and cinematic arts rested on the fact that it did away with the conventional notions of universal order and even the acknowledgement of scientific verities. Yet it was not a philosophy of 'negation' but of 'nothingness' where the universal certainties were now no longer available. The angst of the post-Second World War order as seen through philosophical and popular literature were, as Deepa Nag Haksar pointed out, 'Existential "angst" does not really mean a "neurotic worry". It is the embracing of life with its uncertainties, its polarities and conscious flexibilities. "Joi de vivre" can also be "painful" – "painful" in the sense of "experiential realities" of life itself.'[15]

Raza's own predilection for subliminal forces drew him to Malraux. He felt, 'I was particularly moved by the book of Andre Malraux, *Les Voix du silence* [The Voices of Silence]. Once again it struck a deep chord in my mind and heart, these voices emerging from silence. Precisely this used to happen when I looked at paintings, sculpture or when I heard music. Andre Malraux was not only extraordinarily attracted to the human condition of the arts, he also dwelt on Asia, besides Europe and America. His visits to India and his contacts there were very well known and his book was an important discovery for me.'[16]

Most of all he was spellbound by the poetry of Rainer Maria Rilke, whose diaries were a continuous source of inspiration for Raza. A saying of Rilke's haunted him for the rest of his life, 'God give me the grace to write a few verses which will prove to myself that I am not the least or the lowest of man; that I am not in fear of those I have criticized and disliked.' In Rilke's famed *Duino Elegies*, a state of silence is evoked which was used by Raza almost as a daily prayer when he would enter his studio every morning.[17]

Raza, however, was dissatisfied in some ways with the Beaux-Arts. 'I have not been very happy with the morning classes... My uneasiness has not been so much due to the method of teaching, but due to the atmosphere of the atelier in which I am working. Not only the students are very amateurish in their works and ideas, but, to my mind, they are too full of youth, joy and play. There is a lack of discipline in the atelier and sometimes they get noisy disturbing everyone... Fortunately, during the last two months the atmosphere has improved and the noisy moments are fewer. My professor Mr Heuze has taken to me very kindly and he is happy about my work in general and when I show him my landscapes – he insists on every student seeing them. Unfortunately he is going away now and Mr Dupas is succeeding him. '[18]

Raza kept himself as busy as he could. 'Twice a week, I attend lectures at Ecole du Louvre, 1) Histoire general de l'art and 2) art d'extreme orient. These lectures are useful supplemented with slides, though at times they become rather archaeological. But as a student there I have free access to all the National museums and libraries specially of Musee Guimet with its most remarkable collection of books and photographs. There is a tremendous scope for studies here and I am really living a full life.' He was content for the moment with his life, 'I am very happy, indeed, Mr Journot and I am deeply thankful to you. I have been giving myself to work as if I have only two years of life left and must make the most of my time. The problems of living in Bombay and the stagnation in my work during the last two years, had marred my enthusiasm and delayed most of my projects. But I have regained confidence as much as my health which is considerably improved since my arrival. I feel healthy – mentally and physically and see new possibilities. I am working independently just as I would like to in an atmosphere most congenial for studies…'[19]

To Strive and to Live

Though Raza found it very stimulating to be in Paris, after two years, by 1953-54 his scholarship was over and a difficult period began for him. To make a living, he began giving Hindi lessons to some French people. He also worked with the well-known actress Martine Caol in a film called *Lola Montés* by Max Ophüs. The director of the Club des Beaux-Livre de France asked him to design books for French writers. As he wrote to his close friend Rajesh Rawat, 'This is the eighth book for the Club – an excellent novel *Les Vicking* by Paul Vidlar. I do not always get books of my choice or the book which suit my pictorial vision. But then I have more work than I can really manage. The Editor is proposing a special Edition de Luxe for the end of the year which will mean atleast two months [of] hard work. And then another book by Victor Hugo. I am not yet a rich man but I have enough to live well, pay my rent regularly, eat well, and when necessary visit what is worth visiting. I have bought a Montrilette – do you see me going about in this crowded city? So far I have not injured anyone and I am not killed either, nor do I intend to do so.'[20]

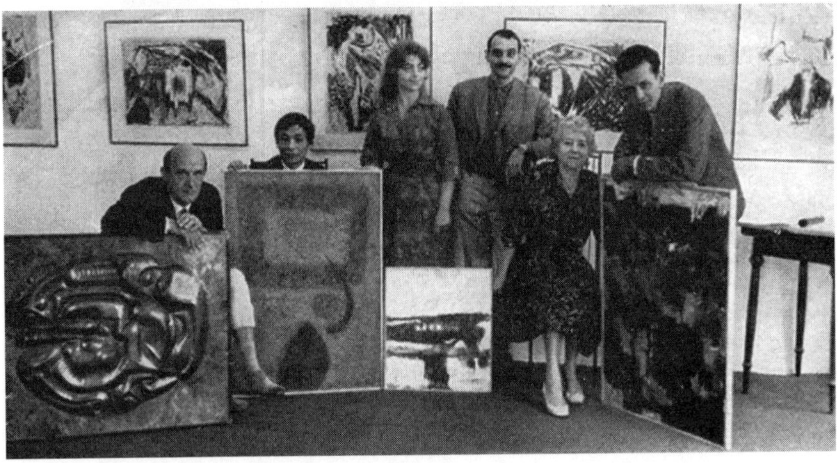

Raza with Lara Vincy (extreme right), Paris.

Raza continued to work hard. His earnings just about enabled him to stay on in Paris and allowed him to paint. A new gallery was opened at Rue de Seine by Lara Vincy – and she visited his studio, liked his work and offered to show his paintings. Raza agreed to it and his works were shown there along with Morvan, Bella Briselle, Besson and others. His paintings attracted enough attention and some of them were even sold. The gallery then proposed to him the idea of a regular consignment of work where they would acquire his paintings in advance. It helped that the gallery at Rue de Seine was very well situated, both art critics and art lovers would regularly visit it and see his work. Raza went on to enter into a contract with Galerie Lara Vincy that said he would show exclusively with them. This agreement lasted from 1955 to 1971, and allowed his work to be viewed by a larger audience. The London collector John Levy, who was well acquainted with India, came to see his work at the Galerie Lara Vincy and acquired a few of his paintings. Since he was very much interested in both Indian classical music and art, Levy would make Raza listen to his records and tapes and acquired more and more of his paintings over time.

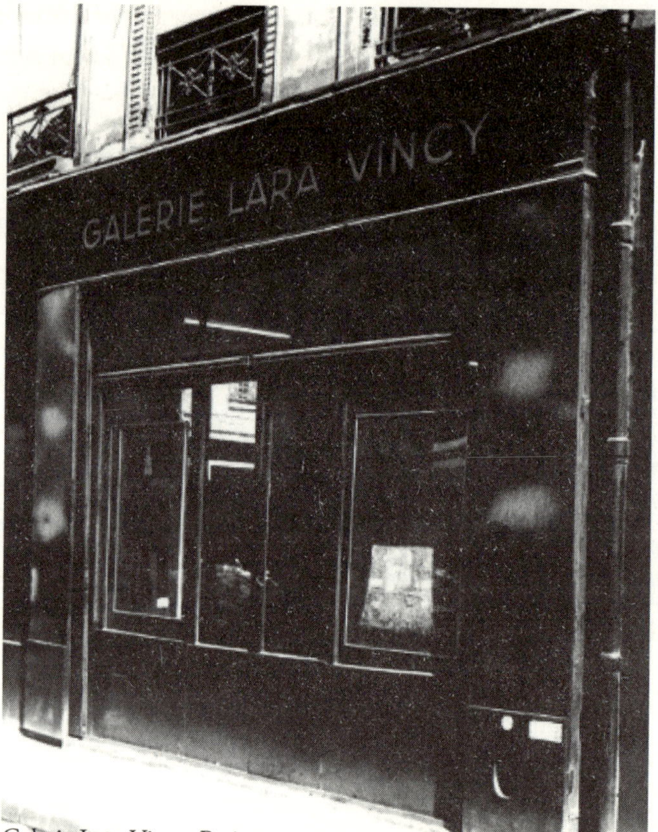

Galerie Lara Vincy, Paris

Raza's connection with the Progressive Artists' Group had continued in one form or another even though he was thousands of miles away. The first to write to him was Professor Langhammer's wife Kathe, '…I think you are very lucky to have such a nice room and for such a cheap price… Prof. once led the discussion at Mulk's place about art in Europe at present. Unfortunately, he was very tired when he came there and the lecture was not very good … Owing to my jaundice I could not attend Mulk's lecture. I was told by Schlesinger and others it was good in principle but a bit confusing which I am afraid is always Mulk's way as a lecturer. Now the progressive group has decided to a have a full course of modern European painting, starting with the Impressionists. The first evening will be on the 26th [October] … I have shown your letter to my husband,

Mr Schlesinger, Blauskopf and I took it to the meeting of the progressive group, but Gade took it there and kept it until we left. Krishen who misses you very much told me he also had a letter of yours. Now, my dear boy, I hope that you are well and are taking care of yourself. Write to me again because both of us are very much interested in your progress. Prof. sends his kindest regards…'[21]

In many ways, the Group was still his family, and he would meet Akbar regularly in Paris.

Recalling those days Raza said, 'Once in 1952, after dinner, Padamsee accompanied me to where I was staying in the campus – and then I accompanied him back to where he was staying and we were constantly discussing.'[22] Ram Kumar went back to India after two years but he visited Paris again and stayed with Raza in 1958, '…I had planned to work in Paris for some months after exhibiting my work in Poland, and had written to Raza about my intentions. He suggested I stay with him for a week, and use that time to search for a suitable rented place. He had two tiny rooms and a studio in an old, two-storied house behind a building. I had been at this place for about four days when he told me of a two-room flat next door that might be available for rent. He had apprehensions about my proximity affecting his work schedule, but seeing my situation he was prepared to risk it. Assured that I would vacate the flat in four months, the landlord rented it to me for a pittance.'[23] The two artists would cook and work together and there was great bondedness and camaraderie. 'I cooked and he washed the utensils and swept the floor. During those four months I came to know him closely. We spent countless summer evenings talking to each other as we walked the streets of Paris. At home drinking tea, sipping red wine after a meal, we had never-ending conversations about art, memories of India, friends and their work. In the mornings, tea mug in hand, he scrutinized and pondered over the canvas he had worked on the previous day. All visitors were welcomed in the evenings with warmth, but during the day even close friends were met and dispatched quickly.'[24]

He was boundlessly generous with friends even though he had limited means. According to Ram Kumar, 'There was a point when I was going through a severe shortage of money, and it became clear that once my small fund came to an end I would have had to return to India. As luck would have it, I met an old American friend who wanted to see my paintings at home. There was also a chance that he might buy one! He had heard of Raza and was excited to know he was my neighbour. Raza was very happy when I told him this; but then he suggested that he would go out when the American friend arrived so that the latter neither met him nor saw his work and, therefore, concentrated exclusively on me and my work. He believed that he would increase my chances of making a sale. And that is exactly what happened.'[25] While Raza knew that it would be good for his work to stay on in Paris, he expressed his homesickness for India by meeting and entertaining his Indian friends and artists, 'Rising through the layers of his mind, memories of India often shook Raza, but it seemed as if changing his decision of living in Paris was beyond his control. He would write a few lines to take the edge off his pain. A hope burned constant that as soon as things eased a bit, he would return to India and perhaps retrieve a fraction of what he had lost in the meanwhile. He welcomed every Indian painter who arrived in Paris with open arms, even extending financial help when the need arose…'[26]

In 1954, on a trip to Paris, Krishen Khanna and his wife Renu tried to visit Raza at Cite University. But they couldn't find him there at the time and so left a note for him. Raza went to meet him the next day and was full of affection. He asked Krishen what he wanted to see in Paris and took him around. 'I said I have to go to the Louvre. So we went to the Louvre and he said, "Do just what I tell you." When we entered the Louvre he said, "Shut your eyes and hold my hand." I literally shut my eyes and put my arms on his shoulders. He led me through a labyrinthine way which I couldn't see. When we went to this one little place he said "Open your eyes." I opened my eyes and there was this *Pieta d'Avignon* wonderful, wonderful painting of Christ by the Master of D'Avignon. Very sensibly it was given its own room and there is nothing else – just one bench. That's the way to see it. I know every inch of that painting. This would be around mid-fifteenth century. It doesn't have the kind of trimmings which are there to ensnare you. It's really like a drawing but also a painting. It's flawless. He has descended from the Cross. The artist is anonymous. It's a single painting. When we were leaving he told me to shut my eyes again and took me out. Just one painting I saw in the Louvre. He was very sensible. People become gluttons and they don't really understand anything. In the evening we sat talking and talking and smoking. He was a very heavy smoker. The whole night passed talking.'[27]

Pieta d'Avignon is indeed a distinctive work situated in the inner recesses of the Louvre. As the art historian Lawrence Gowing observed:

> The agony of the picture is suffered with a rare restraint. No demonstrative expression could match the tragedy of this body, distended as if dreaming. We are in the presence of the simplicity of sorrow. Against the bare skyline, in the gray-gold of the medieval twilight, the scene seems inexpressibly grand.[28]

Pietà of Villeneuve-lès-Avignon, as it is known, is considered an outstanding painting of the late Middle Ages. Its authorship was disputed but later it was accepted as the work of Enguerrand Quarton. It is distinctive from previous depictions of the Pieta by its restraint and beauty. The composition with the Virgin's hands together in prayer, rather than clutching the body of Christ, the curved back form of Christ's body like an arc, and the stark, motionless dignity of the other figures is very different from other works of the Pieta made around this time. The delicacy of the painting is heightened in the specificity of the portraits and the elegant gesture of St. John's hands at Christ's head. It is sometimes thought that the painting which came from Villeneuve-lès-Avignon, just across the Rhône from Avignon, depicted buildings on the left background which are an imaginary representation of Istanbul and the church of Hagia Sophia. This is a likely assertion since the city had fallen to the Ottomans in 1453, a few years before the estimated creation of the painting and the Pieta here could be considered as a lament to the fall of the eastern part of Christendom. At any rate, it holds the viewer standing before it spellbound by its unique qualities.[29]

Apart from the fellow Indians, Raza also made friends amongst the international community of artists. Among them were the French, Jean Porcher and Pierre Henri, and the Lebanese artist Chafiq Abboud. In a letter to Souza, he wrote, 'We discussed a lot and there was a constant dialogue at all levels, like in Bombay, as it was in the times of Modigliani,

Soutine, Max Jacob and Apollinaire in the 20s: a vital and healthy activity almost lost among the artists today. It was a very enriching time.'[30] Interestingly, Abboud and Raza's journey are comparable in that they spent most of their life in Paris but became influential painters in their home country. Abboud also remained attached to his oriental roots, recalling oral storytelling from his grandmother as well as Byzantine icons in churches that would eventually radiate in his works. His encounter with the School of Paris led him to move from a Lebanese tradition of figurative and landscape painting to a colourful personal abstraction.

Friends and Lovers

The other members of the Progressive Artists' Group wrote to him often and among them Souza's letters were the most frequent. There were playful discussions about women and domesticity. 'This one French girl we were so keen to meet and take lessons from happened to be with false eyes and what not. We had idealized her all the two days we spent in contacting her and we had in mind besides learning the language, many other sweet dreams. After the first meeting and consecutive disappointment we worried about getting rid of this beauty queen. It came easy as that evening she was with some friends too busy to bother about us and after half an hour's waiting we left, even without a usual "Au Revoir". We haven't met her again and I hope we don't.'[31]

Souza would even joke about Akbar's flings in the letters. 'I hope Padamsee will start work with renewed vitality and energy. In a way, I was glad to hear from him that his Venus had vanished, before the little cupids came flying about all over Paris, and before complications ensued because he is still a youngster. As for you dear fellow, you are the luckier. As far as I have read some biographies of famous men, most of them seduced other men's wives, and troubles evolved, but ultimately, everyone went on happily. Therefore in a way I envy you. You are however taking it all too seriously. It is nothing at all, old boy. It is part of life, and if you get the chance again, I would advise most wholeheartedly to do it again. You say your experiences with women have ended in tragedies. Not at all,

Raza. Your wife is a magnificent looking woman and I know she made you happy often, you told me so. Women are delightful creatures; they are like frivolous toys, and man plays with them when not at work, as a recreation.'[32]

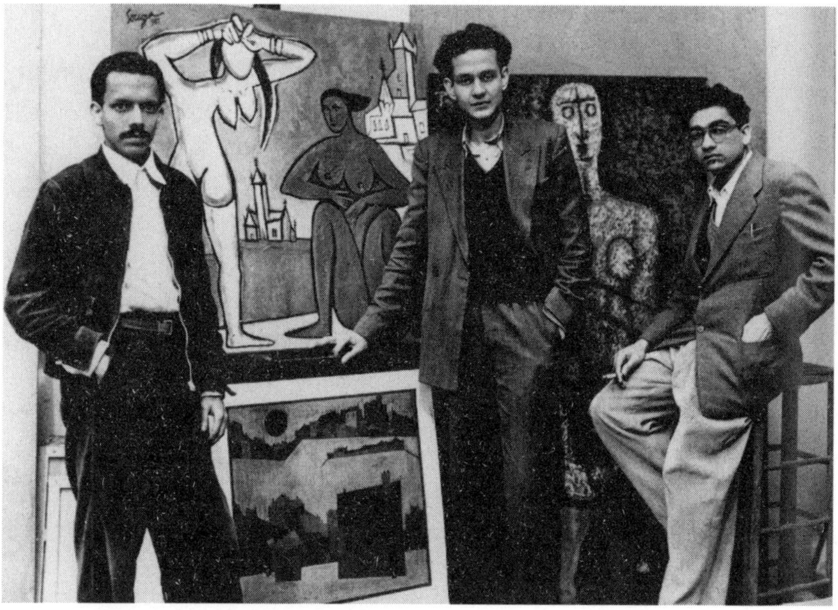

Three artists in Montparnasse, Paris, 1952.
(from left: F.N. Souza, S.H. Raza, Akbar Padamsee)

Despite his seeming indifference to a woman's individuality, Souza was overjoyed when his firstborn, a baby girl, arrived in May 1951 in London. His tenderness and concern for his wife Maria and daughter are shared in a moving letter to Raza. 'I thought she would be asleep, like the rest, who were all in the seventh heaven, dreaming of angels. But my baby was wide awake looking around at the world though she can't see anything just yet. She gave a pretty hard time to Maria. She was to arrive on the 23rd in fact, but the little thing thought she will not budge. "Miserable world, I shall not get out from here where it's nice and warm and comfortable." Poor Maria went through it all quite splendidly…'[33] While thanking him for sending him ten pounds for his own use he also mentions that 'I have sent the 10 pounds to your wife. But you rascal, you never sent me her name and address. Instead you sent me her uncle's or someone's name!'[34]

The exchange of letters between Souza and Raza acquired a frequency when the artists decided to have a joint show along with Akbar Padamsee. In the preparations for the exhibition, letters would fly to and fro. Souza pointed out, 'Your development is miraculous, marvelous, though it had its humorous side. Today you are worried about a drop of water spoiling your delicate fragile landscapes. In the old days you used to paint in the heavy monsoon and keep them landscapes out in the rain (at least it looked like it) to get the beautiful-dirty monsoon effect and the messy yellow hammer look.'[35]

There would be animated discussions about his art and finally about the show for which all three – Akbar, Raza and Souza – were busy preparing. There was a proposition that M.F. Husain also join them for the show. 'I am beginning to turn over in my head the "Idea" of having an exhibition in Paris – a last fling so to speak, along with you. Having Husain in is wonderful – "Quatre Peintres Indiens". We are not really concerned what the other artists will think or say about taking in Husain in our Paris show. Neither is the fact that Husain happens (to my mind not accidentally) a Muslim. We could kick the breath out of any bastard who says ours is a communal partnership. What worried me is what explanation we should give the French public about the addition. Between the two of us, the public understood the presence of Baby Akbar – but now Husain – and between the three of us – complete with beard and all – well; we will have to ask Rostand the biologist to give some explanation for the new arrival.'[36]

Their first exhibition, however, for reasons unknown did not have Husain. Held at Galerie Saint-Placide in 1952, it aroused both interest and curiosity because it could not be placed in any known category and yet had marked painterly qualities. The thirteen-odd paintings on display were sold and went to important collections. Significantly enough, larger galleries began to take notice, and Galerie La France, which had promoted painters like Soulage, Menessier and Zao Wou-Ki, invited Raza to show his work. Following that, the three painters were invited to another group show at Galerie Creuz in 1953. That show too went off well and many of the works displayed were sold.

Raza was in his element and decided to do a tour of Italy to look at the famed Renaissance painters. Tall, slim and handsome, he attracted women almost instantly and it might be said that he was also drawn to them. In a letter to Akbar written from Venice, 'There is so much to see and so much to do that I have been running like a mad man all these days. We went to Ravenna, Fervera, Padova and now for almost a week we are in Venice. This place is remarkable. I have chosen for work the dirtiest of streets and the oldest of houses, where no one, it appears, has painted since they discovered that houses can make a painting ... Lydia's presence has done me a lot of good and it has changed her completely. When she arrived she was pale and almost lifeless and now she is in perfect form, full of laughter and gaiety. Naturally, this is a nuisance, being together with a girl, I am obliged to waste a lot of time, and so I would have worked well only alone. But I do not regret it. On the contrary I am back to health...'[37]

Raza's first exposure to Italy seems to have been fantastic. 'I have begun to love Italy. I was terribly disappointed with whatever I saw in Florence and the parts of the country I saw from the train on our way. Of course I saw a lot in Florence, including the Masaccio, but it was only in Ravenna of the 6th century mosaiques that I was really thrilled. Padova with Giotto was another treat, but I agree with you, without seeing yet Assisi that his later work tells so much. I loved the town, made several sketches here in Venice, I haven't gone to a single museum I am working.'[38] With his money running out, he had to cut his visit short in Rome and fly back directly to Paris.

There is no further mention of Lydia in any of his letters after this point, for Raza was being drawn like a magnet to someone else almost without his knowledge. His warm intimacy with his fellow student Janine Mongillat had begun to change its hues to passionate tones. His feelings brimmed over when he met her, and he could hardly contain himself. In this heightened state, he felt he had at last found the woman who would answer all his prayers. Little did he realize that it would be much more and lifelong. Perhaps the Paris he was looking for was symbolized best by this lovely girl who was a talented artist as well.

Despite a measure of success in his work, however, Raza seems to have been strained for money. He wrote to Akbar, 'I have had plenty of worries during the year, but somehow I have managed my affairs. At the moment I am at a crossroad and really there are things I just cannot manage alone. I must have a place to live in here. There is a chance at hand and two rooms are available from January for a rent of 1,500 francs a month for both of them. They are on Rue Grenita near Rue St. Denis. But there is a reprise to be paid and the sum is 100,000 frs. It's a bargain and I must secure this amount somehow, as an opportunity of this kind will not come again. Here I hope to arrange 50,000 frs. Perhaps some more, as the house is to be furnished atleast with a bed. But the rest I must secure. Give this matter a very serious consideration. You know the house problem in Paris. It is almost impossible to get a room for less than 8,000 frs a month. Here I shall have two rooms. To do serigraphie one must have an atelier. Perhaps I could even give you one of them and may be both if living for one becomes an impossibility in Paris. In fact I am determined to stay on longer and find my way out here and I shall do all I can to make it possible.'[39] He was to resort to offering his works cheaply, 'Would you be able to help me out. Talk to Solange, Nuruddin, Shahbibi. Maybe you could talk to Alkazi and Roshan, Husain and Peerbhoy. I could give six paintings at Rs 100 each. Could they buy and pay in advance?'[40]

If Paris was a city where Raza's meagre means made it difficult for him to live comfortably, it was also the city that provided an opening panorama of possibilities to him. For the moment he felt blessed that he was there and the struggle to survive made him feel more alive than ever. Those early years by the Seine would be embalmed in his memory.

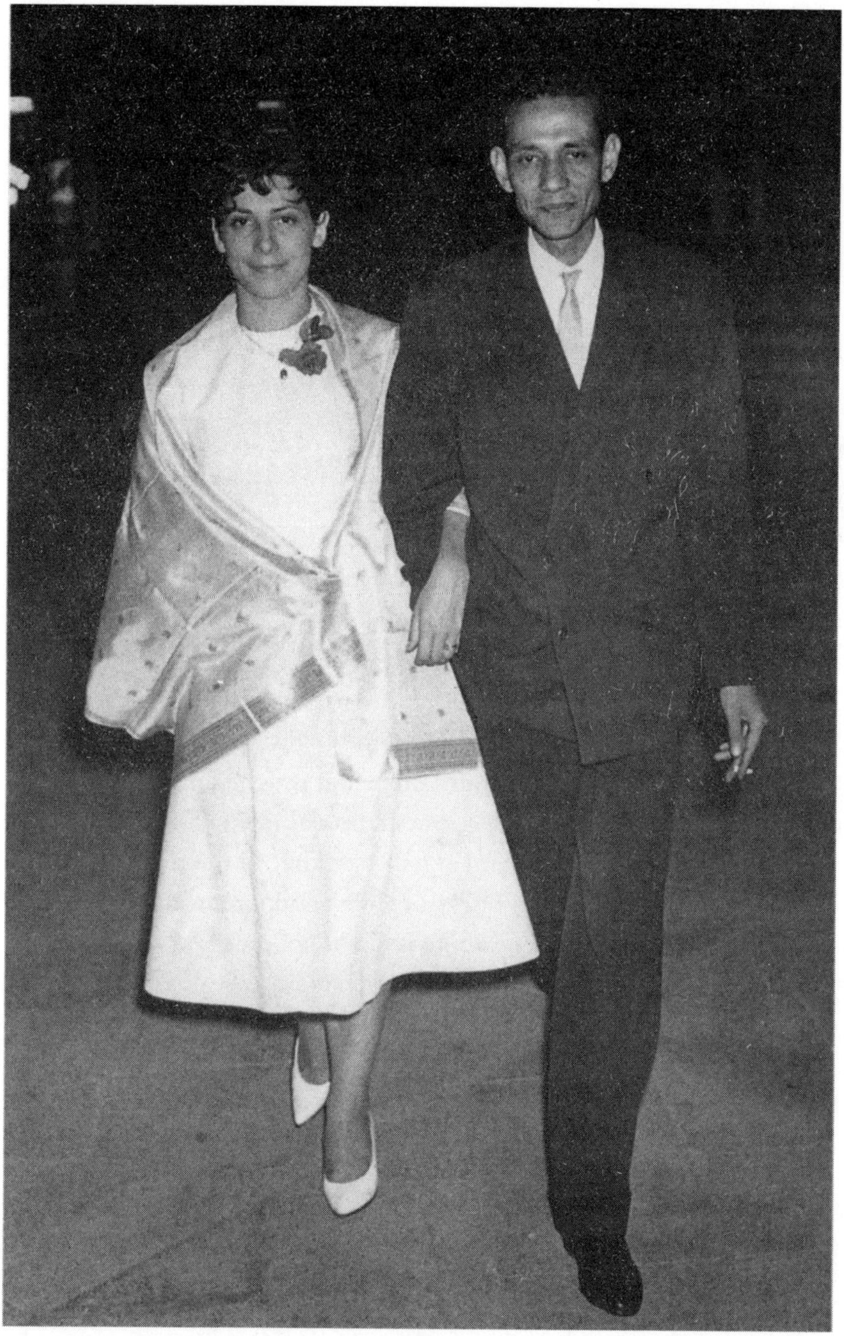

Janine Mongillat and Sayed Haider Raza, Paris.

The Burning Landscape

By the mid-1950s, Raza had made Paris his home. Although he was still hard-pressed financially and lived with a sense of nostalgia for his own country, but being based at the centre of the world of culture had provided Raza with a consciousness of the formal and international connotations of art. As he said, 'France gave me several acquisitions. First of all, *le sens plastique*, by which I mean a certain understanding of the vital elements in painting. Second, a measure of clear thinking and rationality. The third, which follows from this proposition, is a sense of order and proportion in form and structure. Lastly, France has given me a sense of savoir faire: the ability to perceive and to follow a certain discerning quality in life.'[1] For the next fifteen years, he was to work doggedly, persistently, with great strength and determination, inspired primarily by the formal construction of Cézanne and the passionate exploration of colour by Van Gogh.

Initially, Raza had worked according to the aesthetics he had imbibed in Mumbai. There under the influence of artists such as V.S. Gaitonde, Shankar Palsikar and J.M. Ahiwasi, he had painted on paper with gouache and rubbed cowrie shell onto that to instil colours in a manner similar to Rajasthani and Jain miniatures. After two years in Paris, however, he switched to oil painting which would mark his work in the '50s. Thick paint loaded his palette knife or brush, wrapping his canvas with residual memories. He found a new freedom in both the subject and the medium by this change. According to Rudolf von Leyden, 'The gouache technique in tempera was to give way to impasto in oils. The change of medium and manner were not merely technical but signified a fundamental change of attitude. The scholar, who had measured and calculated, burst through the confines of a limited understanding of colour and space-created-by-colour into a sphere of full realization. The transformation created such passion that one could best describe this age of Raza as the age of the Lover. The triumphant handling of paint, this living in paint can only be understood as an act of love.'[2]

According to Raza, 'By the time I left for Paris I was so taken up with the Indian style and the Indian concepts that for two years in Paris I worked in the Indian style: landscapes, housecapes, earthscapes reconstructed … But then I started studying Cézanne seriously. I went to the museum again and again and tried to understand construction according to Cézanne … I read the book of Kandinsky *The Spiritual in Art* and I studied particularly Cubism in which paintings were very carefully constructed. I also went to the extent of finding out what Mondrian and Vasarely had done with pure geometry and what Nicolas de Staël did to it. There were the works of other major artists, some of them still alive, others no more, which were a part of the Parisian scene.'[3]

The first major exhibition of Nicolas de Staël after his death in 1955 was at the Museum of Modern Art, and it left an impression on Raza. He felt that Staël had made a bid for pure painterly values in a masterly manner and at the end of his life had gone back to drawing inspiration from nature, which was against the intellectual trend of the period. 'But I understood in my own way that you can fly very high but have to come back again to nature and life: again and again to those elements which are a source of experience and inspiration for anyone, poet, writer or painter … He had gone very abstract, very sensual, very non-realistic … There was a whole lot of art expression to be surveyed but what was important was that ultimately you came back to yourself…'[4]

Medieval Houses and Churches

The '50s signalled a feverish intensity in Raza's paintings. This was when he traversed the wild terrains of Brittany and the lush valleys of south France to suddenly come upon a row of medieval houses or a stark, white church. These would be placed in a timeless space in his works, devoid of human presence under a burning sun interfacing with a cataclysmic reality. The perspective in these works were both aerial and frontal: the townscapes, which did not reflect any known reality, would glow in their own ambience. The artist painted with a raw immediacy, embalming his canvases with the primaries, the raw red of the earth set off by burning ochre and charred black. Though timeless and ahistorical, these works were at the same time layered with time resonating the arch of his journey from a small village of a few hamlets in Madhya Pradesh to the vast universe of a cosmopolitan city. Inspired by Cézanne in Provence and Van Gogh in Arles, he would set the world aflame, for the space was his for the taking and the colours were conjured from the rich palette of his country.

Art historian Geeti Sen pointed out, 'These paintings could be placed in India or in Sienna or in Catalonia. They are souvenirs of the kind which memory filters through its deposits. They have emerged from the fire, "la forge", chastened and purified. Uninhabited, abstracted, yet concrete. There is nothing anecdotal; only the essential remains.'[5] The vibrant tones would set the landscape on fire and the contours of houses and churches dissected the plane to interface with myriad realities. The artist skilfully melded the careful structuring of compositions inspired by École de Paris with the glowing tonal variations of the Rajasthani and Pahari miniatures drawn from Indian aesthetic traditions. Thus in *Haut de Cagnes* (1951) the black sun hangs from a feverish orange sky over a row of cubicle houses shorn of all life. These houses dot the landscape interspersed by the spread of flaming sienna where the earth and the sky are an extension of each other. The low horizon reminiscent of the miniatures is matched by the two rows of houses that lie in parallel to each other in a structural balance. The painting could be a shimmering reflection of the world made anew.

In *Black Sun* (1953), night and day coexist with each other while the glowing houses under the black sun stream across two sharply divided

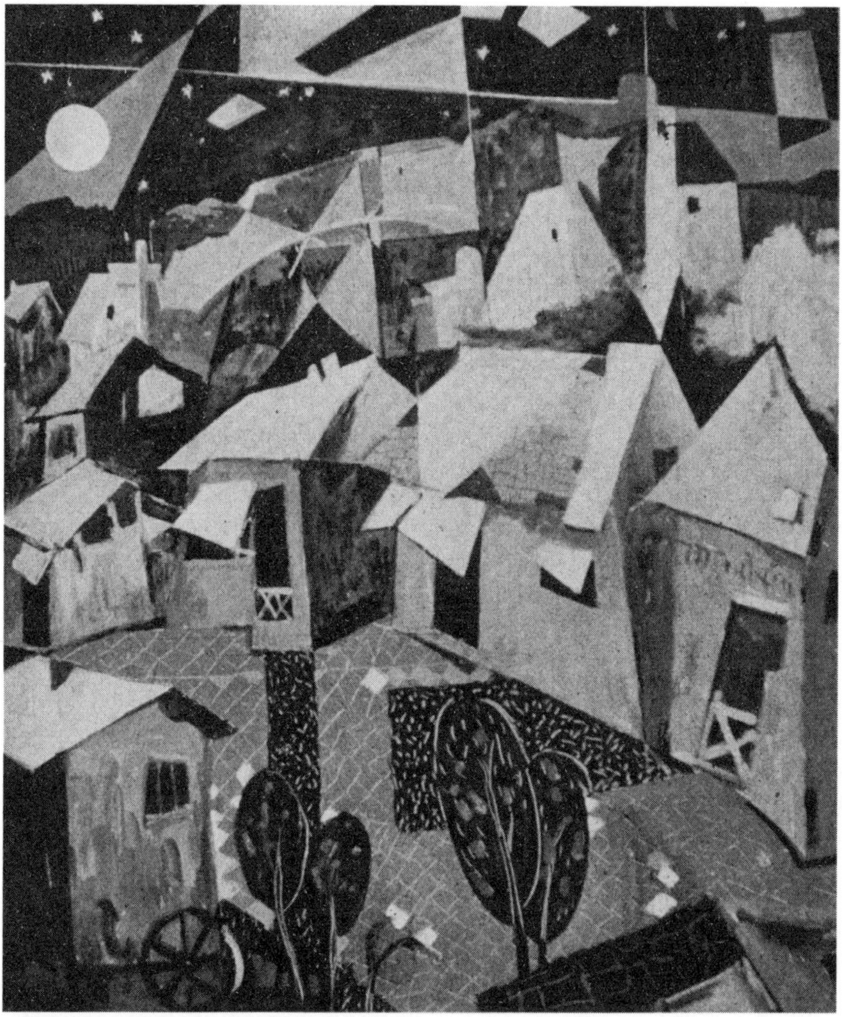

Moonscape, 1950, watercolour, S.H. Raza.

landscapes bridging and uniting them. Did these also reflect his inner binaries of anguish and hope as he glided from night to day? The dark sun was to shadow Raza throughout his life, reflecting his own persona and at the same time being reflected by it.

His *Ville Provençale* (1956), made in thick impasto was created as if in a hallucinatory state. A garland of houses in flickering orange, steaming red, sienna and indigo seem to stem from dark undulating land as if in a dream.

Their uneven shapes and towering spires create the only sign of life, while all else lies still and asleep. The wedges of colours segue into each other and their burnished surfaces create a gem-like effluence illuminating the darkness. These could be the geometrical shapes which haunted his dreams, stemming from his consciousness of a new world of order and structure he was moving into. He had gone to Provence in search of structure and entranced by the medieval houses and churches had laid them in Cézanne-esque spatial tilts where the object would be highlighted, becoming a thing in itself rather than a representation of reality.

Paul Cézanne had painted the Sainte-Victoire mountain from the window of his house at Aix-en-Provence in the south of France over and over again. His stated aim was to organize nature according to the harmony of geometric forms and, thus, he painted Mont Sainte-Victoire in long-views, mid-views and close-ups. With each painting, Cézanne was getting closer not just to the mountain but to the balance and structure of the painting. A fascinated Raza found that to paint the mountain the artist had to become one with it and could not be distracted by extraneous elements. His own work acquired the same obsession which he had found in Cézanne's, with cubicle houses being studied manifold times.

His lush colour palette overlaid those compositions and created epiphanic orchestrations of tones and shapes.

The glistening white houses and churches bewitched the artist when he traversed the lush terrains of south France. 'The French landscape became a dominant theme of my work from 1954 to '65 … I went to Brittany where I painted French churches and villages … I went to the central part of France … and to the southern part called Provence: in the villages dating back to the middle ages the houses were beautiful. The look they gave to furniture and architecture was a subject of study… The wonderful thing is existence, which should be understood, to be enjoyed.'[6] Later, Raza acquired summer residence at Gorbio, a picturesque village with cobbled streets, sandwiched between the Maritime Alps and the Mediterranean Sea.

The nights haunted him, so did the mornings, as the germinating world of forests and rivers, which had driven the restless child away from his studies, comes alive in these paintings. A daub of orange here, a flash of green elsewhere, demarcate the area between the dark of the night and glowing colours of daylight. These could be his experience of a once known space while growing up in the forests of Madhya Pradesh in central India. The stillness of the night with its eerie sounds and shapes would reverberate for the young boy in the darkness. In the daytime, the enthralling spectacle of the village with its diversity and colours would weave a spell on him. As the artist stated himself, 'The most tenacious memory of my childhood is the fear and fascination of Indian forests … Nights in the forests were hallucinating; sometimes the only humanizing influence was the dancing of the Gond tribes. Daybreak brought back a sentiment of security and well-being. On market-day, under the radiant sun, the village was a fairyland of colours. And then, the night again. Even today I find that these two aspects of my life dominate me and are an integral part of my paintings.'[7]

In many of these paintings, we see the emergence of brilliant colours and shapes from the enveloping sombre tones where the two are juxtaposed and interconnected implicating a perpetual coexistence of dualities. This wholly contained unity of diametric opposites serves to create the spellbinding effect of the works. And the bewitching dualities of light and darkness, epiphany and despair, stillness and movement would mark the artist's oeuvre in the ensuing years.

In the work *Eglise* (1953) exhibited at the Venice Biennale that year, the bare outlines of the village church and houses nearby can be seen. Their glowing shapes in the dark are like the fireflies Raza had watched with fascination during nights in his childhood. But the night itself becomes a source of fascination with its nuanced shades of black and its areas of brightness and darkness. If his studies of the blazing light of countryside France with its white medieval houses and churches had been a set of smouldering paintings, the images of the night which were exhibited in Venice showed a strange shadow of unknown depths. On seeing *Eglise*, some verses from Rainer Maria Rilke's poem 'At the Brink of Night', a poet whom Raza read frequently, come to mind.

My room and this distance,
awake upon the darkening land,

are one. I am a string
stretched across deep
surging resonance.

Things are violin bodies
full of murmuring darkness,
where women's weeping dreams,
where the rancor of whole generations
stirs in its sleep...
I should release
my silver vibrations: then
everything below me will live,
and whatever strays into things
will seek the light
that falls without end from my dancing tone
into the old abysses
around which heaven swells
through narrow
imploring
rifts.[8]

The brutal intensity of these dark works glistened in the black night. In a painting like *Church* (1957), the black steeple pierces the sky and the charred roofs burn against the ignited orange sky. As Sen described, 'Do we recall the anguish and despair of Van Gogh? Be it village or town or church, the world according to Raza was aflame. It was being forged anew through the crucible of recollection – baptized through fire.'[9]

Then again, Raza painted Corsica on visiting the small island where Janine's grandparents hailed from. The painting *Corse* (1958) is a homage to the beautiful island with its rugged mountains, green valleys and the quaint stone and brick houses that glitter in diamond white against the deeply textured dense black. His rich landscape paintings from this period have colour as its flesh and organic form and the anatomy of the line can barely be discerned.

International Sphere

The painting *Ville Provençale* was exhibited at the Venice Biennale in 1956, which was more focused on four Indian artists who had garnered a favourable response in Europe: M.F. Husain, Dinkar Kaushik, Akbar Padamsee and S.H. Raza. This as well as the earlier show in 1954 had been initiated and organized by the late diplomat and UNESCO ambassador, the intrepid Madanjeet Singh. Indeed, the year 1954 was a watershed year for the Indian art scene: it saw both the National Gallery of Modern Art and the Lalit Kala Akademi being established; and it was only five years before that that the Progressive Artists' Group had had its first exhibition in Bombay in 1949. Madanjeet Singh travelled to Bombay, Madras and Calcutta, collecting works from both private and public collections for the show in which thirty-two Indian artists, including iconic names such as Amrita Sher-Gil, Jamini Roy, M.F. Husain, S.H. Raza and F.N. Souza, and fifty-nine works in total were displayed. The Indian Pavilion in 1954 was inaugurated by Sir Ronald Adam, in the presence of Luther Evans, then director-general of UNESCO, and as many as forty paintings there were sold at a time when Indian artists were virtually unknown in Europe. The first-ever exhibition of Indian art at the Venice Biennale had created a stir of interest, but Singh himself had considerable difficulty acquiring the works from the National Gallery of Modern Art in Delhi which only agreed to part with them at the intervention of the Prime Minister Jawaharlal Nehru.[10]

The London show of 1958 of seven Indian artists organized by the well-known art critic George Butcher, however, was a climactic moment for art. The show included the works of Husain, Raza, Padamsee, Ram Kumar and Mohan Samant. There was extensive press coverage in the *London Times.* In Bombay, Bal Chhabda's Gallery 59 was established in the year 1959 and Raza's works were exhibited there – this was regarded by Raza as a genuine 'homecoming'. In the same year, the first major book on Raza written by Rudolf von Leyden was published in which the latter wrote, 'Raza is in India on his first visit after almost nine years. He has painted here but no distinctly new element is visible in his work as compared with what he had done lately in Paris. I am sure the new Indian experience will come out and express itself, if not now, then later.'[11]

The Venice Biennale booklet of 1956 introducing modern Indian art of the period mentions, 'In the paintings presented it is easy to see the synthesis between Oriental Art and Western Art. Despite using modern western techniques, in their canvases you can see the vitality of colours and the harmony of the tropics which are representative of India. Surely the painters have rediscovered their own personality in the art production of India, a slightly new direction.'[12]

Indeed, what was being manifested was virtually modernism in the making. Inspired by international modernism and harking back to their own traditions as well, the Indian artists were rigorously reinventing it for themselves and their fellow men. Their form, colour and composition while tuned to plasticity was also informed by the brilliant colours, the two dimensionality and the calligraphic style of their country.

Prestigious Award

The year 1956 was significant in other ways as well for Raza. In July that year, he received the Prix de la critique and was the first foreign artist to receive the prestigious award. As many as sixteen of the most important art critics writing for French, Belgian and other foreign papers in Paris had formed the jury, which had decided in his favour. The entire press covered his work along with reproductions. With that prize, Raza entered the league of artists like Debre, Kito, Buffet and sculptors like Cesar Balduccini or Sugai. The award entitled him to have an individual exhibition three months later. A joyous Husain sent him a poetic message, 'Mubarak-Mubarak. My hearty congratulations on this happy occasion of your first one-man show in Paris and for the critic's award. *Tu shahi hai parvaaz hai kaam tera, tere samane aasma aur bhi hain…*'[13]

And Raza wrote excitedly about it to his friend Rajesh Rawat:

> The story of the six years is something I cannot narrate it now but I cannot help thinking about it. The years of scholarship. The years of

> struggle, suffering and work. People and situations. I hope I can talk about it at length later. Perhaps I do understand about life a bit better but in any case my work has grown.
>
> I wonder if you know about this Prix de la critique and what it represents. I am sending you the invitation of the exhibition which will show the jury and other details. Most of the members are the art critics of various papers here. They chose 16 artists who have shown during the year and in Paris and then there is the final selection the price is given to one artist only. The exhibition of all the artists' work is done every year in July. The winning artist has three pictures and the rest one of each. Later the whole exhibition goes to Japan. Again the winning artist is given a free exhibition for the month of September … I have already some critics who are defending my work with attention which makes me forget the indifference of the previous years.[14]

That year Raza rented a big room at Place Maubert, unknown to anyone, and hid himself there for three months working from morning to night. At the end of this period, an exhibition was held at Galerie Saint-Placide in October 1956. The exhibition was widely appreciated and erased doubts even in the minds of those who still had some. 'Thank God! The material worries were over. It was henceforth a question of working hard, developing my technical command and understanding values in painting.'[15] After this exhibition and winning the award, an exciting phase began for Raza. He was able to rent a three-room space in a loft in the Latin quarters in the Pantheon and isolate himself to concentrate on his work.

His small loft was situated in an old neglected building in the courtyard but was very convenient for work. The proprietor, being an art lover, was very sympathetic to his work and appreciated it. Raza was visited here by innumerable critics who interviewed him and wrote about him. He was also able to engage with Waldemar George, a senior art critic in Paris who had discovered Soutine and Modigliani in the '20s and had been writing in an outstanding manner about the painters he cared for. He was also fortunate in getting to know the critic of *Le Figaro*, Claude Roger Marx. In addition, Raza became acquainted with the well-known critic Jaques

Lassaigne, who went on to become the director of Musée d'Art Moderne de la Ville de Paris and also wrote about Raza's work. He also met the surrealist poet, Philippe Soupault, who looked at his paintings and said, 'One is thrown into a world unknown by these works.'[16]

A year later Raza was to make *Village en Provence* (1957), a six-feet-long panoramic view of south France in blazing colours. Unlike his earlier works where he concentrated on form and structure, here the artist celebrates colour in all its brilliance. As Leyden pointed out, 'His colours take on an entirely new complexion. Brilliant reds and yellows stand out against large looming forces of black and deep Prussian blue. Shapes dissolve in seas of colour which are by no means unorganized and fluid but seem to move and evolve within the space of the paintings.'[17]

Was it from this south of France that Raza painted *Village and Church* (1958), a work of dazzling opposites? The diagonal placement of the structures creates a dynamic interplay between light and dark and between the vivid articulation of form and non-form. The glistening white roofs, chimneys and the conical church spire which are pivotal to this work demarcate the area between the dark of the night and glowing colours of daylight. Made in thick impasto, the deep red, coal black and luminous white interpenetrate and create an intricately woven tapestry of nuanced experiences. The shadows and shapes of houses, trees and mountains are throbbing and alive in the work even as the vibrant palette draws from the rich colours of the miniatures and the germinating world of forests and rivers of his childhood.

Raza was more intent than ever to work hard and succeed. As he wrote to his friend Rajesh, 'I have invitations for several exhibitions – to which in the past I had no access. Remember – the canvas we carried to Café dome in the metro – and well so many others – where constantly my work was refused. During the next few months I will have to be more disciplined, though I must say I have greatly reorganized my time. Rue Chaptal is out of the way for everyone. Hardly any artists around – few anyway that I know. Only my friends care to come and see me. And there are only a few of them. Janine I see almost every day. Padamsee and Bagali come occasionally. At present Bagali is in London and Padamsee has rented a

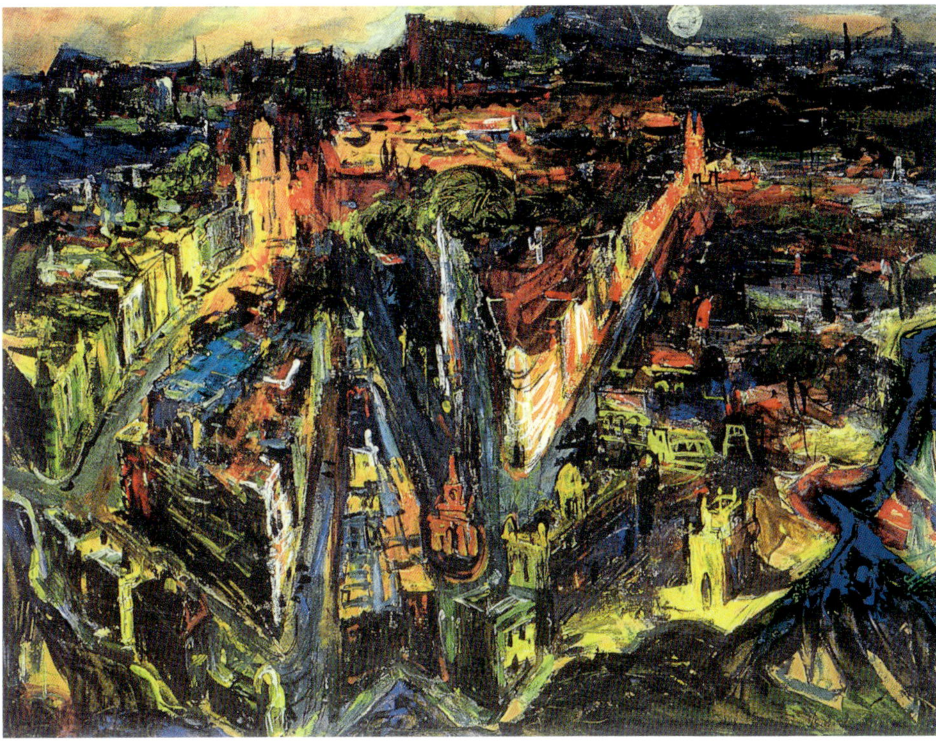

Bombay, 1964
Acrylic on paper
69 x 90 cm
S.H. Raza

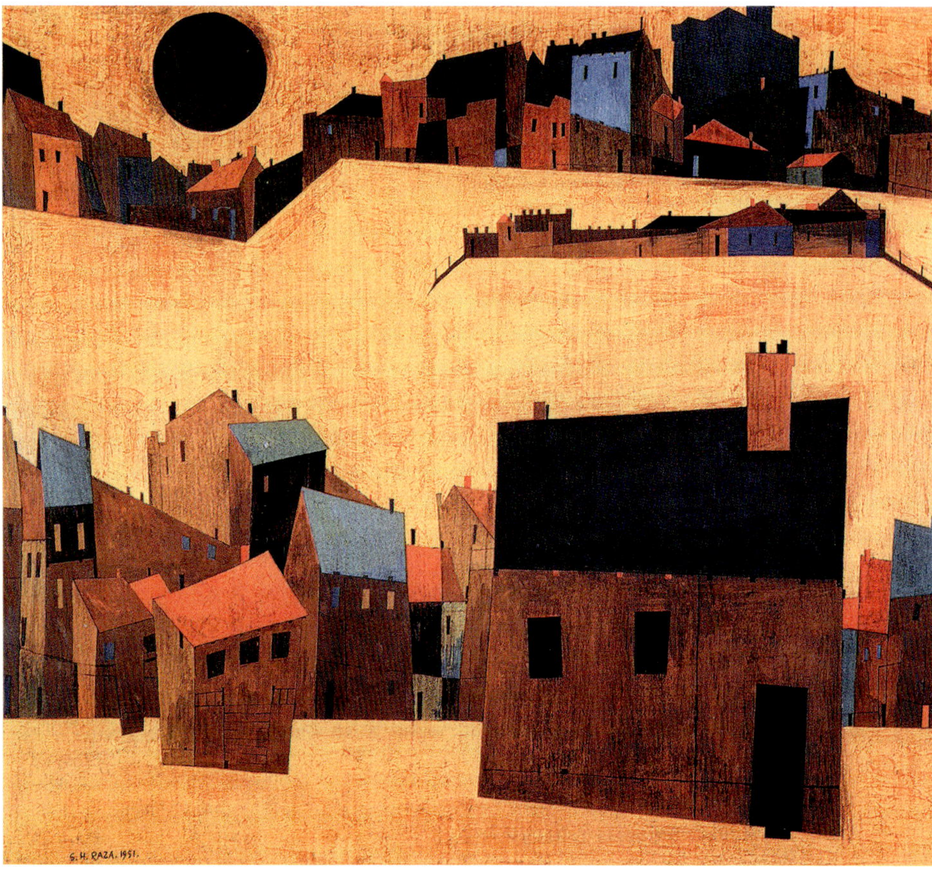

Haut de Cagnes, 1951
Gouache on paper
S.H. Raza

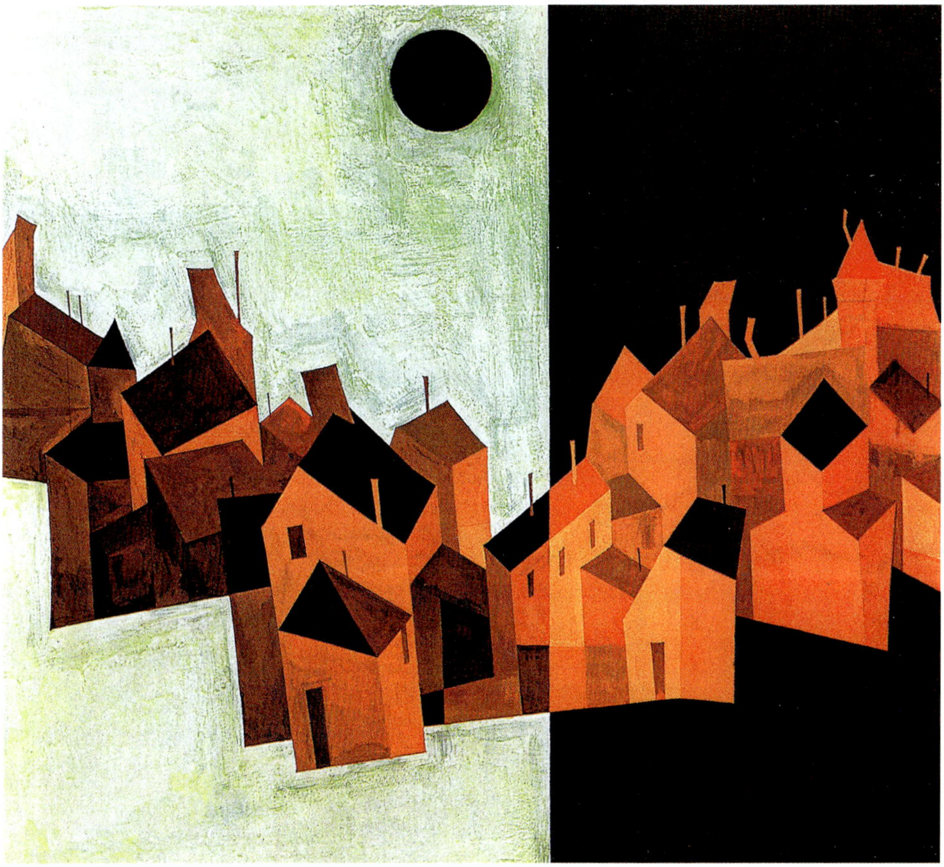

Black Sun, 1953
Gouache on paper
45 x 47 cm
S.H. Raza

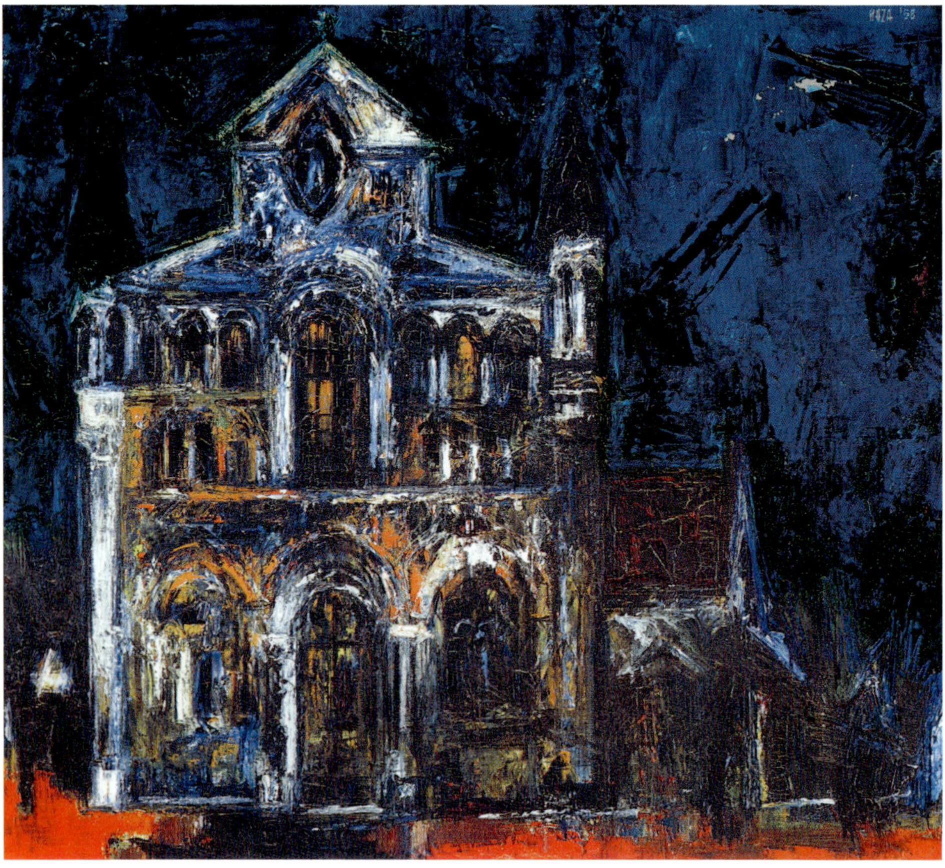

Chapelle Bleue
Oil on canvas
S.H. Raza

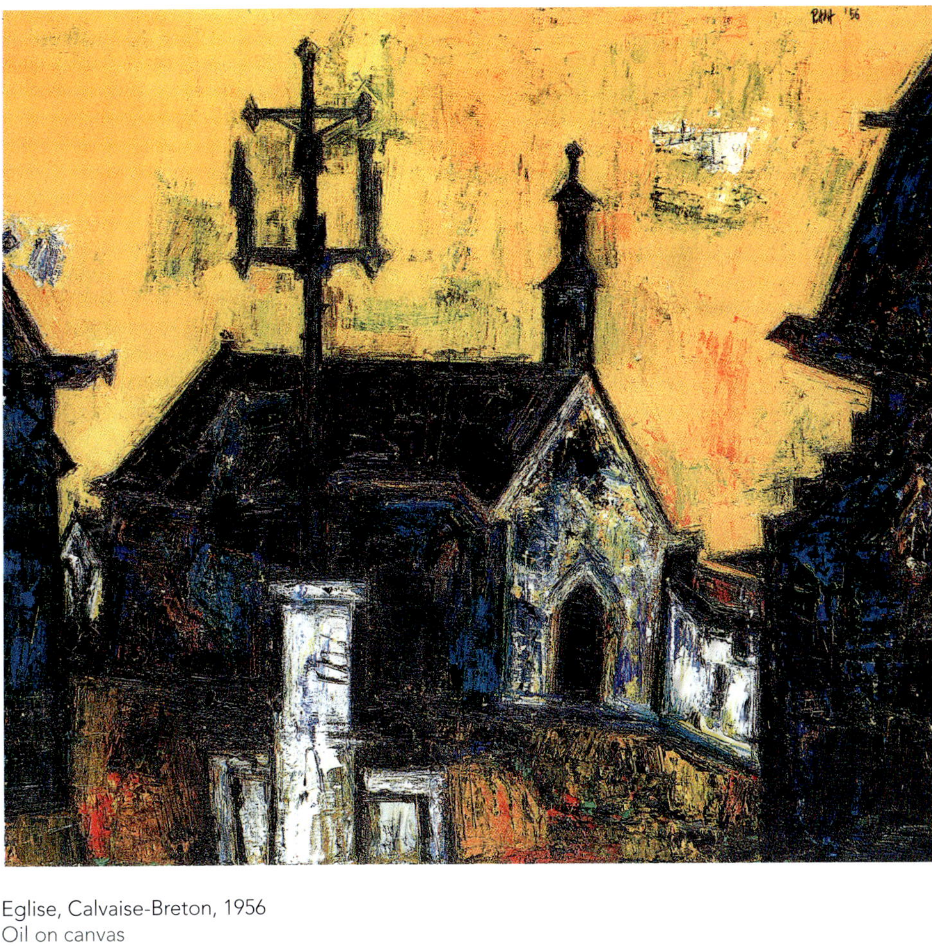

Eglise, Calvaise-Breton, 1956
Oil on canvas
S.H. Raza

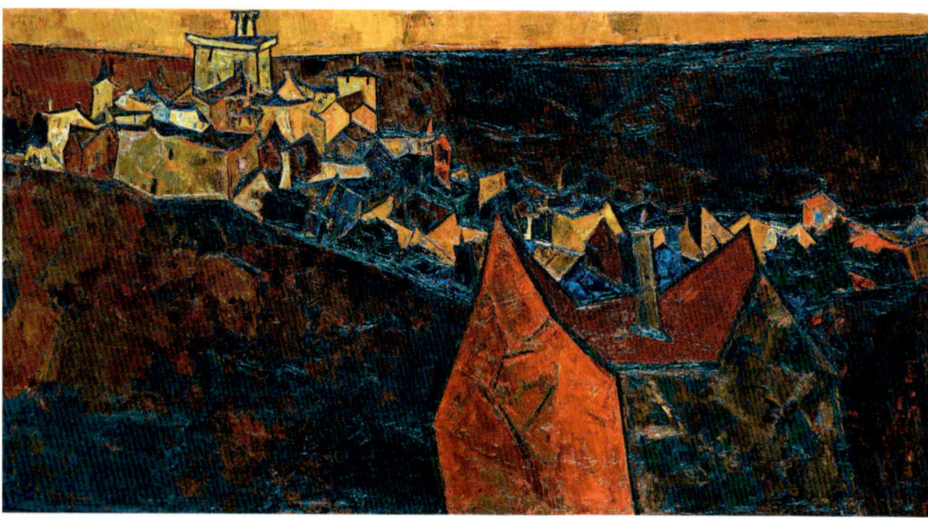

Ville Provencal, 1956
Oil on canvas
S.H. Raza

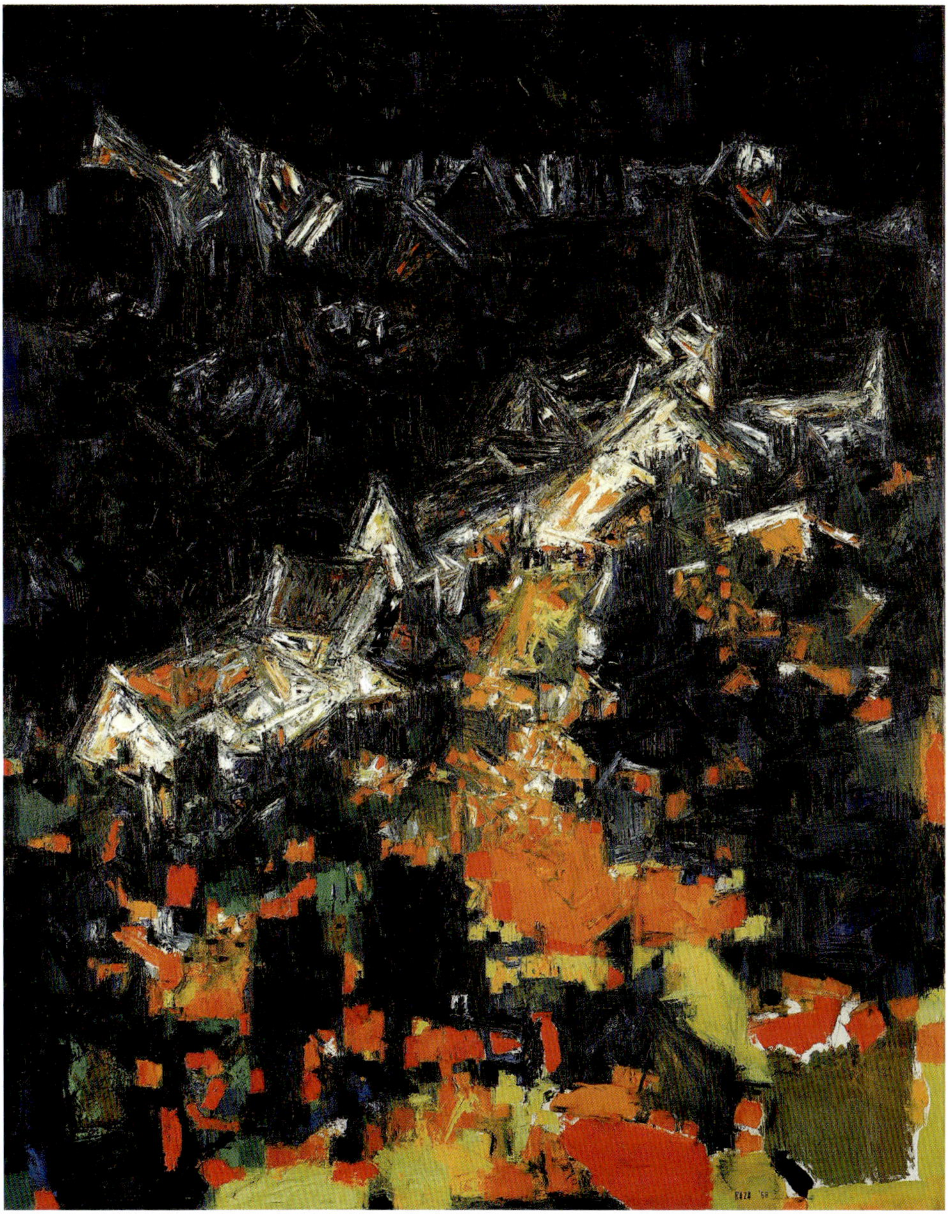

Village with Church, 1958
Oil on canvas
161 x130 cm
S.H. Raza

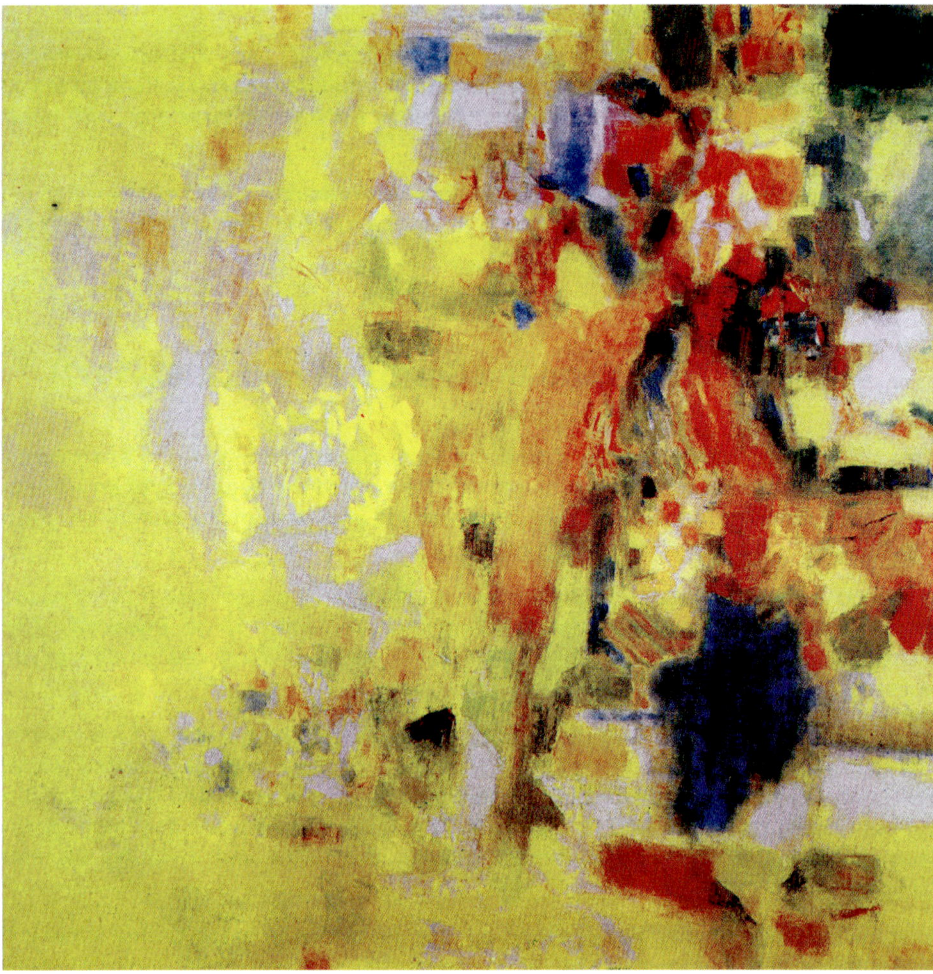

Summer, 1964
Acrylic on canvas
190 x 190 cm
S.H. Raza

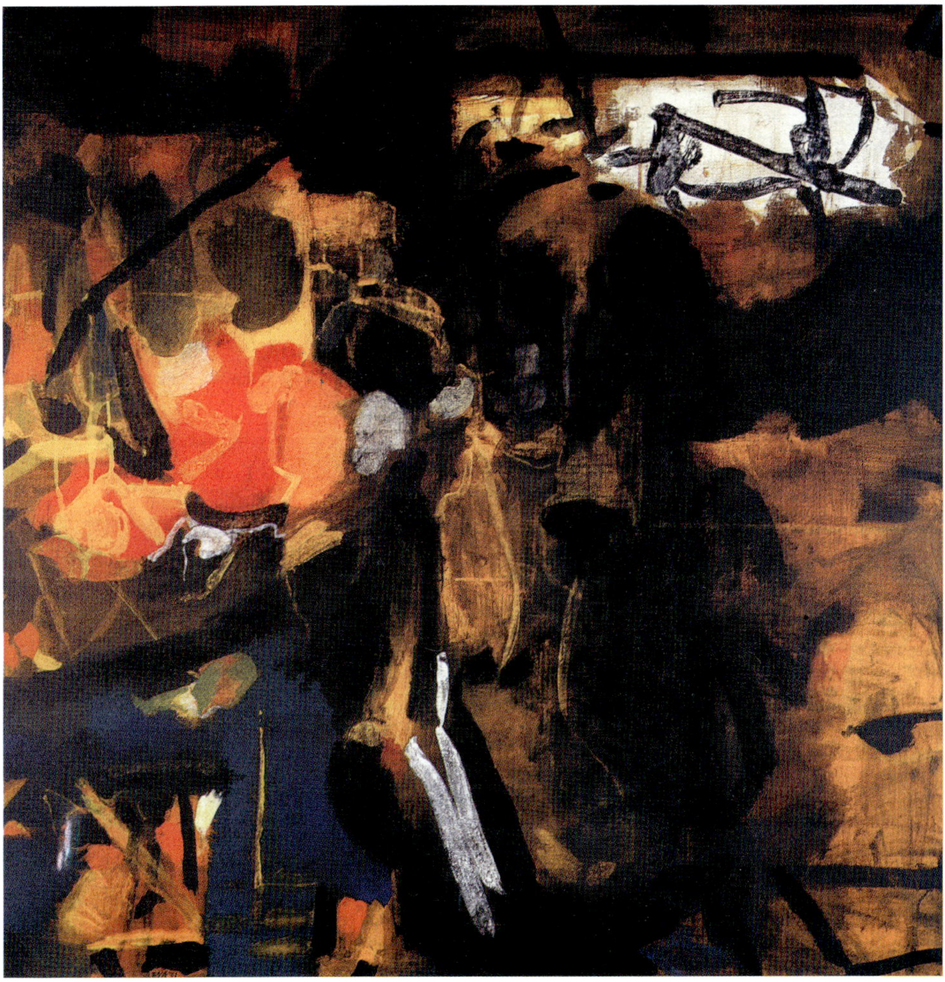

La Forge, 1971
Acrylic on canvas
120 x 120 cm
S.H. Raza

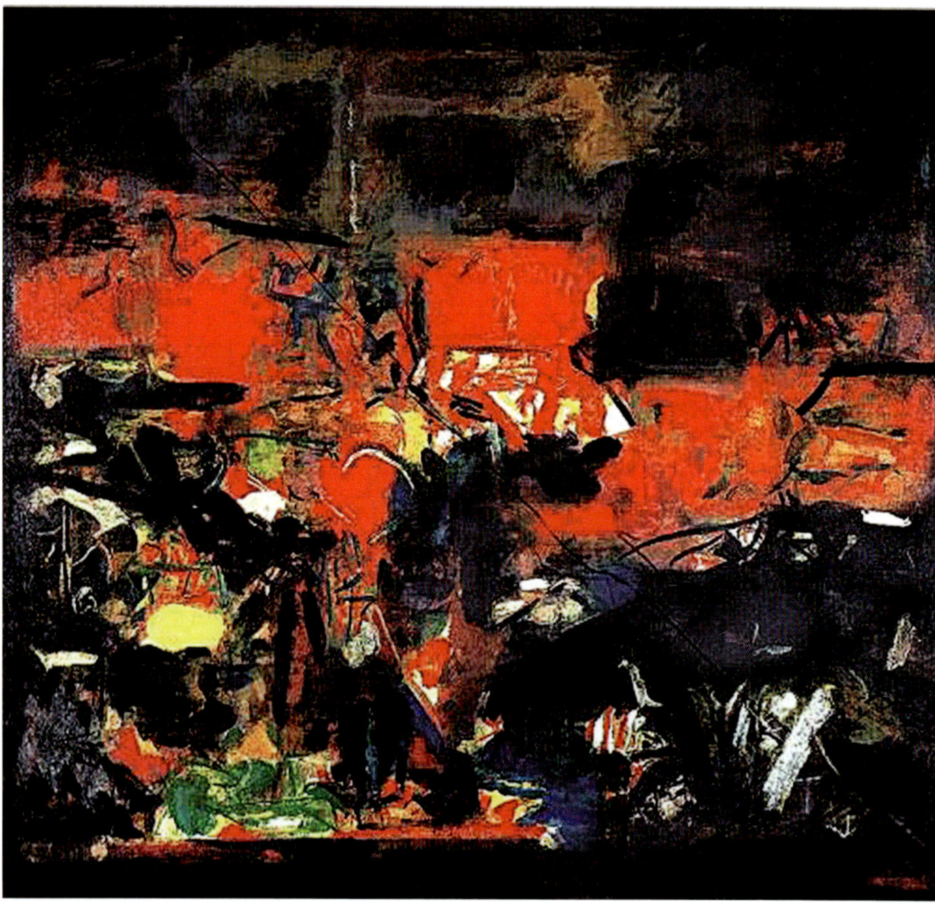

Tapovan, 1972
Acrylic on canvas
159.7 x 188.9 cm
Courtesy: Private Collection
S.H. Raza

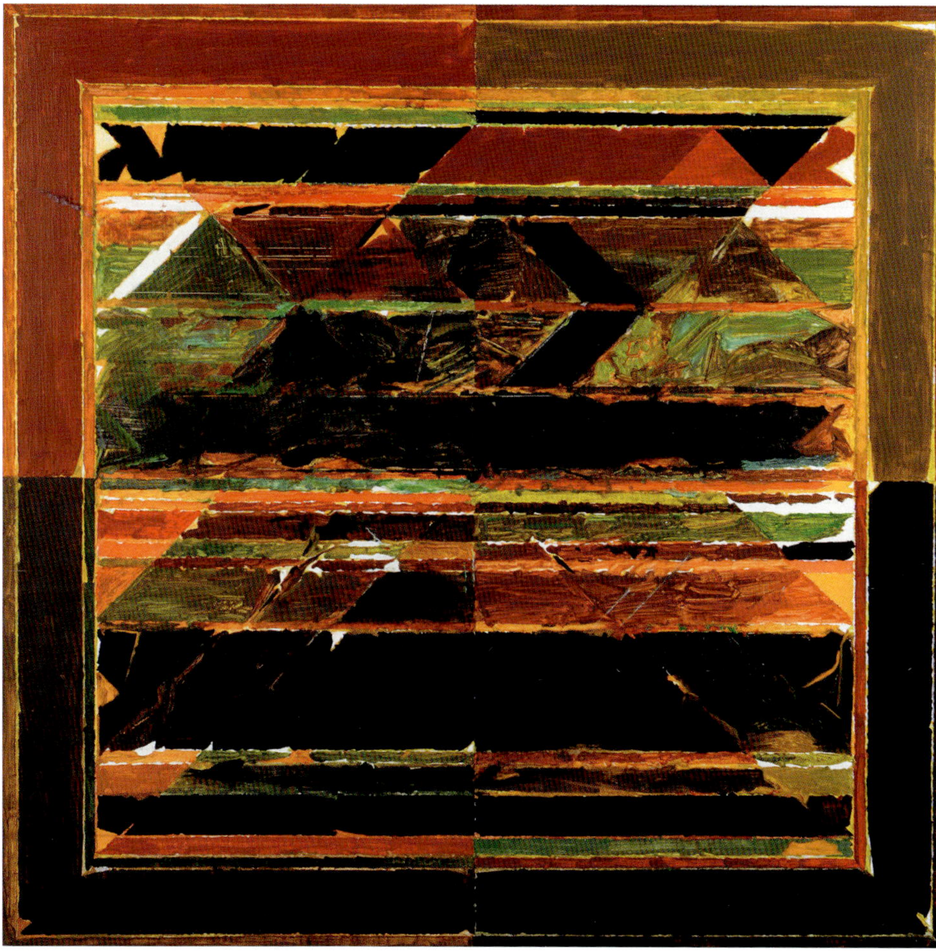

Untitled, 1982
Acrylic on canvas
80 x 80 cm
Courtesy: Private Collection
S.H. Raza

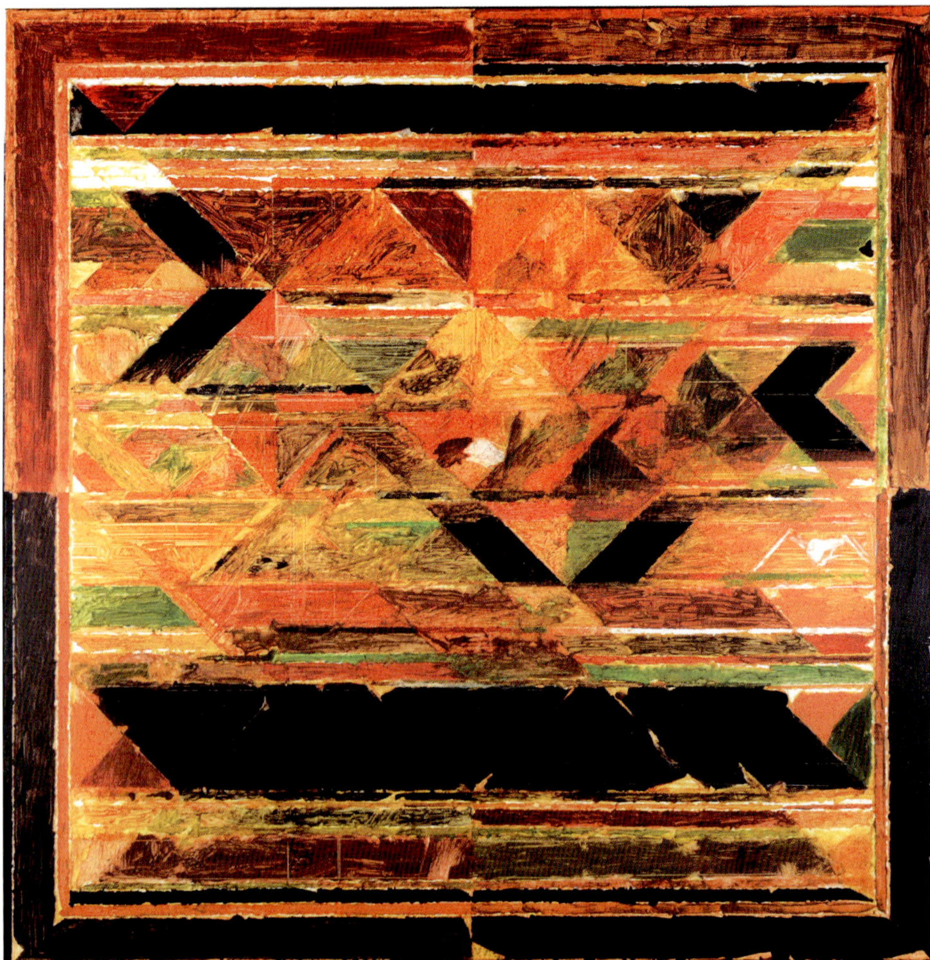

Untitled, 1985
Acrylic on canvas
120 x 120 cm
Courtesy: Private Collection
S.H. Raza

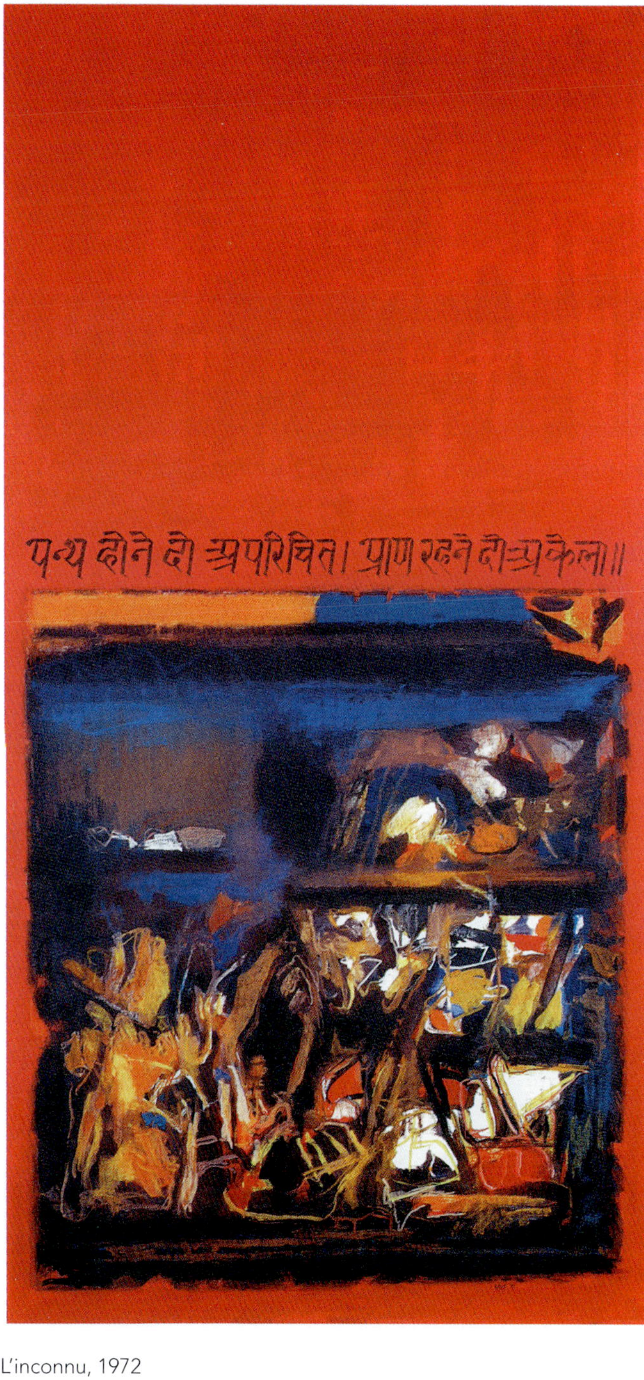

L'inconnu, 1972
Acrylic on canvas
200 x 100 cm
S.H. Raza

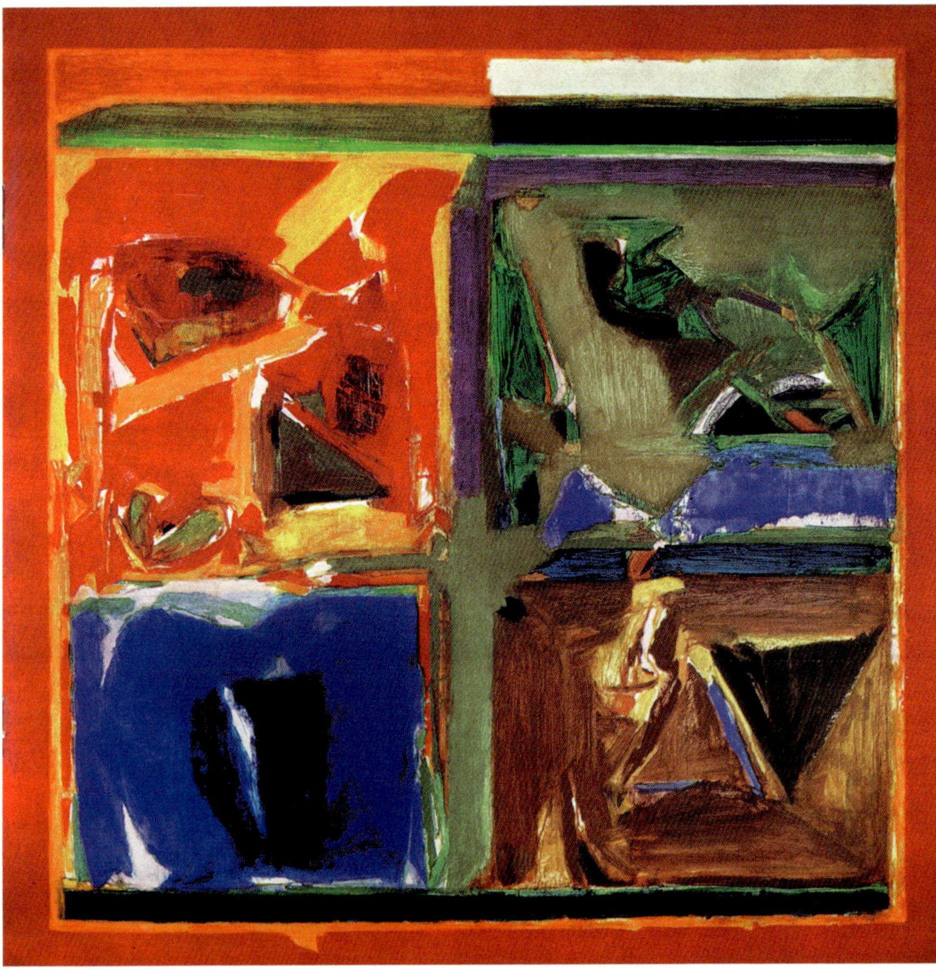

Rajasthan, 1975
Acrylic on canvas
S.H. Raza

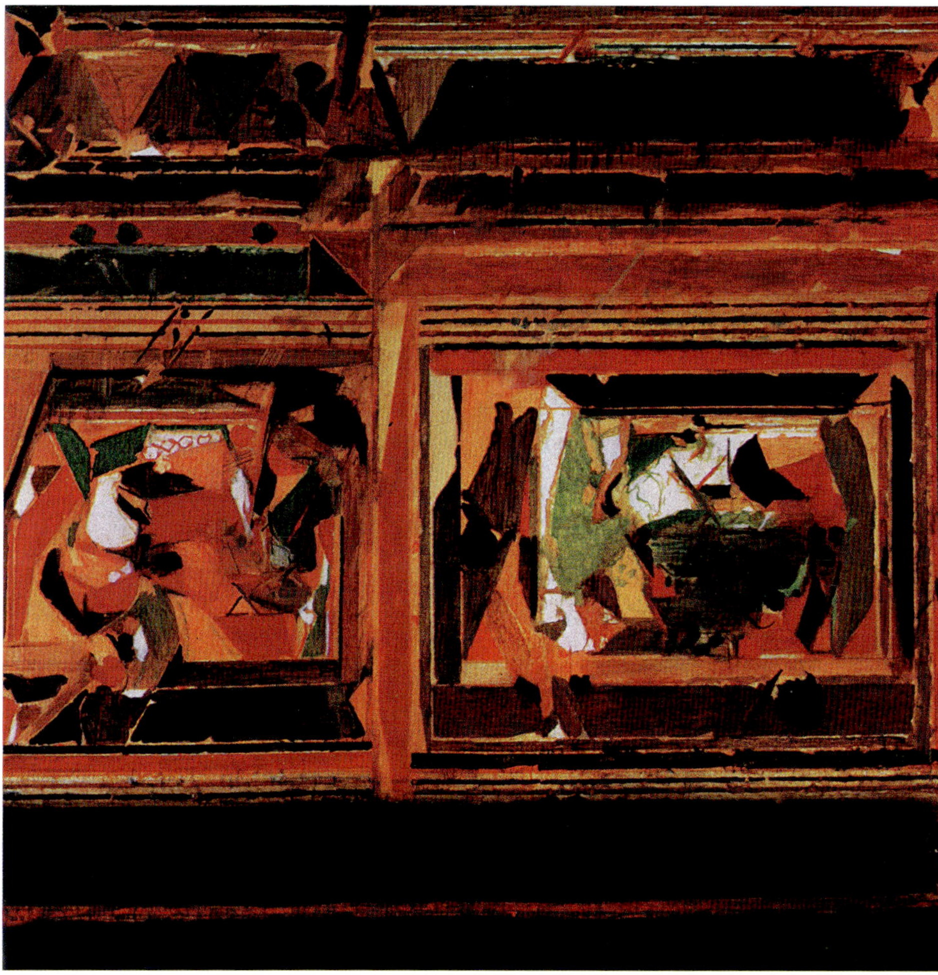

Rajasthan, 1983
Acrylic on canvas
175 x 175 cm
S.H. Raza

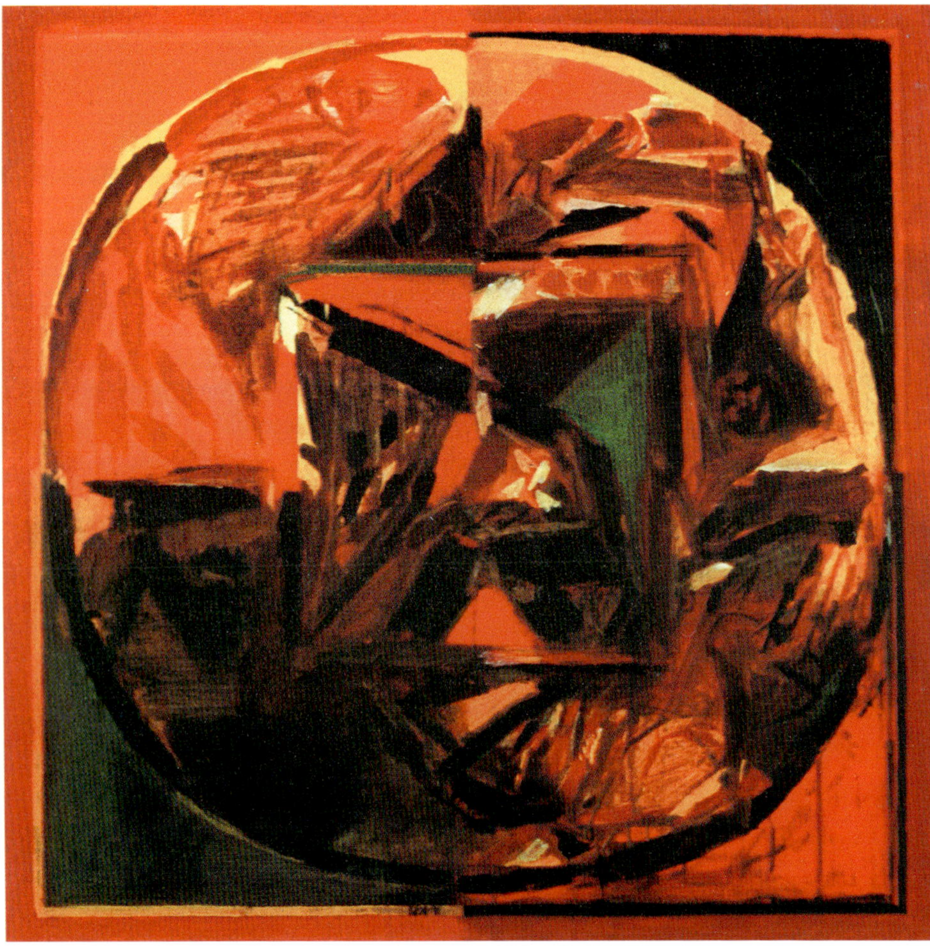

Mandala, 1975
Acrylic on canvas
S.H. Raza

studio almost 65 km from Paris. My room is quiet, the neighbours simple factory workers. Madame Grillet my proprietaire is like my mother. I am working to the maximum.'[18]

Raza was not only invited to the Venice Biennale that year but he also began to show all over the world from the Tokyo Biennale in 1957 to the UK, Brussels, Sao Paulo, New York, and many other places in the following years. Indeed, he had moved to another stage in his work and life. The shapes dissolved, sweeping strokes of brilliant colours lashed the canvas and the dark, still centre became more luminous than ever.

Period of Fulfilment

Raza may have begun to gain international recognition, but the most important aspect of his life was yet to be addressed. His marriage to his wife Fatima was a frustrating affair. For one thing, it was difficult to meet her as she had moved to Pakistan and it was not possible to have a long-distance relationship. But more so, the marriage had soured even when he was with her in India because of incompatibility. Fatima could never understand Raza's intense involvement with art and the long hours he spent devoted to his paintings. Perhaps she would have liked him to take up a regular job and bring home a steady income. In any case, art was not her domain and she was unable to relate to him on that level.

According to Raza, 'I was passionately involved in my work as a painter and it was difficult for her to understand my ambitions. She was deeply attached to her family which went to Pakistan after Partition. And she joined them there. I was deeply rooted in India where I had the care, attention and affection of my teachers, friends and co-workers.'[1]

During this period Raza's brothers would often entreat him to call her to Paris. They would write in their letters to him that she was in a poor state and that he should take pity on her. Even his aunt, Fatima's mother, sent him a warning note: 'Haider mian, salutations. Look, be careful. I am the eldest in your family and it is compulsory to give me respect. You need to seek my good wishes and not my ill will. I feel that the lies you have been writing to us is because you have got taken in by the wrong people … Now I am writing to you that you come and take your wife. You declared your undying love for her and married her and stated that you were willing to give up your life if I as your aunt did not get you married to her … Remember the times when you would go to high school with your books tucked into your sides. You would make up a lot of things about your love for her. You were either crazed for love or showing that you were… I am warning you that be careful or I will come and teach you a lesson which you will remember for the rest of your life. I have been quiet all this time but now I am angry… My daughter has received proposals for marriage from well-off families. They meet her and find her a beautiful and noble person and want her to marry into their family. But your wife does not agree…'[2]

His aunt even suggested that Raza had been mixing with the wrong sort of people, much like his own father, '…Be wary of the devil who has reached Europe and is encouraging you to ruin my daughter's life … Your father also listened to his brothers' wrong advice and created turmoil for my sister [by marrying again].'[3] She ended with the final trump card, 'If you do not reply properly to my letter then I will, as a representative of my daughter, come to France and appeal to the President De Gaulle and get a good lawyer…'[4]

Despite these ominous letters, Raza remained unshaken in his determination to divorce Fatima since the one essential component – like-mindedness – seemed to have been missing entirely in their marriage. With the passage of time and as his relationship with Janine strengthened, it seems to have dawned on Raza that his existing marriage would not make him happy. He wrote to his younger brother Hasan Imam saying, 'I seek to end my marriage and I am determined to see it through. Every letter from Hyderabad [Pakistan] only convinces me that I am in the right including the last letter of Fatima for which I have no heart to reply … What I sought once that my wife shared my life … I had a plan of work – a plan of work worthy of a man. It was her duty to have come and joined me. I arranged a part of her passage money and in spite of my differences with her, I asked her to come – and join my struggle. In reply I got only stupid letters, absurd reasoning, abuses and insults, threats. I took my decision. Now I do not care. I am determined to end this marriage and if necessary I will be prepared to defend my attitude before men and before God... My wife has hindered me in my work constantly. No power on earth will now bring me back to her...'[5]

However, in order to continue his relationship with Janine and to eventually marry her, he had to deal with a divorce which was not easy. As he wrote to his good friend Rajesh Rawat:

> I met Janine's parents. They know now my situation. Their attitude has been unexpectedly very sympathetic. There is no fundamental objection, but I have to hurry up the divorce. They do not know all the aspects of the problem nor do they know that she has been coming home. They have asked me for the eighth time for dinner, several times at their place and they have attended several exhibitions where I recently participated. They seem happy. But I must accelerate things. Fatima and her family know well by now that my views will not change. I have even proposed to pay the Mahr [mandatory payment by the husband to his wife] in two years' time. Well I shall still await some time more. In June it will be seven years that we are separated. They have not replied to my last letter, though Husain's [Fatima's mother] latest ultimatum was for eighth March.[6]

The Wedding

By 1959, Raza was ready to divorce Fatima and marry Janine. He wrote to Rajesh Rawat, 'I am looking desperately for a studio. Janine has been an angel and a comrade. I have also been a good influence on her. She has three Medailles at Beaux Arts, two travelling scholarships, and has passed about 15 concours during the year. To get the diploma of Professera she needs only to pass some three more exams. To Fatima I have written letters, very emphatically to concede to divorce. I have no reply for a month. It is a big problem, yet there is no point in hurrying as I think the matter will have to be paid and I will need some more time to be able to do so.'[7]

With time, Raza and Janine were becoming increasingly close. He wrote to Rajesh, 'Janine is fine. She too has done a lot of good work. I see her family regularly. They have approved [of] me. My effort is to regularize the situation and I hope it won't be long before I could take more concrete steps.'[8] According to Geeti Sen, what Janine found endearing in Raza was that, 'While she might paint on cardboard, he was working on canvas with the finest selection of paints from Winsor & Newton – yet his socks were full of holes! Here was a man who cared more for his work than for his appearance.'[9]

In January 1959, Raza came to Bombay with the intention of staying on until the month of May. He stayed with Rudolf von Leyden at the latter's Nepean Sea Road apartment, and asked his friend Ayaz Peerbhoy, an advertising honcho and an influential person in the city, to help him obtain the divorce. Ayaz agreed to do so, and a request was made to Akbar Padamsee to stand as witness and say that Fatima was not present because of her menstruation. According to Akbar, he agreed to witness but declined to state what he'd been asked to, 'He [Ayaz] said, "You just say she had her periods or something nonsensical like that." I said, "My god, I can never say that." So, he said, "Not even for Raza?" I said, "Not even for Raza." After they left, his [Peerbhoy's] wife said, "There was only one gentleman at that meeting and that was you."'[10] In the end, the divorce took place on 28 February at 6 p.m. with Maulana Syed Abdul Hamid and Maulana Nazir Husain as witnesses. The divorce documents stated that the divorce took place between Sayed Haider Raza and Mukhtar Fatima according to the laws governing Imamia Isna Asri sect. A sum of PKR9000 was sent to her as Mahr and PKR450 for the Iddat (a period that a Muslim woman observes after a divorce before remarrying) from 28 February to 10 June 1959 through a financial agency in New York. With this, Raza was formally divorced from his first wife and not much is known of her trajectory after this.

Raza and Janine were married on 3 September 1959 at a civil ceremony in Paris. The young couple were driven from the wedding by the filmmaker and artist Jean Bhownagary in his newly acquired Mercedes. Although Raza had wanted a Christian wedding in a church, it was not possible as he was not baptized. Well acquainted with Hindu and Islamic philosophy already, he had imbibed Christian thought in Paris and had many Catholic friends who had knowledge of the religion's precepts and beliefs. He was particularly close to Jean Duchesne, the editor of the Catholic journal *Communio*. Raza stated, 'I went into Christian thought and religion which affected me deeply. I read books, went to church, attended mass, tried to study the immensity of the Christian faith and belief where generosity, charity, compassion, forgiveness and many other values are predominant. In studying Hinduism, Islam and Christianity I realized how close to each other these great religions were in fundamental concepts which, unfortunately, people misunderstood, and faith, which should be a binding force, becomes a subject of dispute and quarrel.'[11]

An Indo-French Couple

It is believed that Janine's parents, who belonged to the upper echelons of society, were not too happy with the fact that their only child had chosen to marry not just an artist, but an Indian. But they knew better than to oppose her. According to Jean Duchesne, a close friend of the artist couple, 'I wasn't there at the time. In hindsight I can say that they must have been shocked and sorry and disappointed – while at the same time as French bourgeoisie they were liberal enough to know that this is what French education has taught you – when you read Moliere's plays it is that it is vain and dangerous for parents to object to their children getting married to the wrong person. That is one of the cornerstones of the liberal aspect of the French classical tradition.'[12]

According to Raisa Padamsee, from the French point of view of that time, Raza would have been a very different bridegroom from what French parents would imagine for their daughter, 'I was telling you about the parents – they were very supportive. Because in those days it was very difficult for a French father to admit that his daughter was getting married to a Muslim Indian. And I think Raza waited a long time before courting to meet her father and ask for her hand.'[13]

The father in this case was a high-ranking official in the railways and was in charge of building railway tracks, as he was an engineer. He earned a decent salary and would have liked Janine to marry someone with a regular profession and who was a part of their society. According to Duchesne, 'Her father was certainly a stronger personality, overshadowing her [the mother]. She was certainly more [mild] ... there was a gulf – several oceans wide between Raza and his father in law.'[14] According to Michel Imbert, an art historian and a close friend of the couple, 'Janine's mother had a lot of good taste. All the furniture in Raza's apartment in Paris – the seventeenth-century furniture – all came from Janine's mother.'[15] Michel further said that it was Janine's mother who had paid for many things, 'She was a wealthy lady. She paid for the apartment, the car, everything is from Janine's mother.'[16]

As for the relationship between Janine and Raza, Duchesne pointed out, 'They were a kind of model couple. I think there was no question of each one going his own way. They had to live together. Janine had learnt to cook Indian food for Raza. She would call him Ra for short ... So they had their separate works. She doesn't interfere with his, he doesn't interfere with her. I don't know if you have seen much of Janine's work – she had changed quite a lot. She was able to renew herself because of course everything depended on the materials she used. Janine started from the materials while Raza clearly started from a Hindu world view. So they worked in opposite directions, I would say.'[17]

Yet, according to Duchesne 'There was an unconditional mutual support ... When Janine had an exhibition Raza was there and was very happy it was her and reciprocally when he had one she was there. She came with him to the US – they went together. They really kneaded together in everyday life – they were a very deeply united couple but it was not a couple that merged with each other.'[18] Raza and Janine were different and distinct, and yet harmonious.

Duchesne observed, 'They were two very strong persons. Janine was also a strong person. At one time it seems to me that Janine's work was in part influenced by Raza's work. When we met them especially in the '70s some of Janine's works were influenced by Ra, especially concerning the colour – a lot of black and red and yellow – this is signature Raza.'[19] Duchesne further elaborated, 'She had exhibitions on her own and was an artist in her own right. And this was her parent's desperation – her parents would have liked her to do a clear job and get a regular salary or something.'[20] However, Duchesne recalled Janine's father as expansive and generous, '...He would entertain Raza and Janine and their friends at a restaurant, and I think he once bought a car – to drive them from Paris to Gorbio with all the equipment, brushes and paintings.'[21]

Separate Yet Together

The young artist couple worked together harmoniously but at the same time their works were separate and distinct. In different ways, both delved into their past and the process of working through the accretions of memory came into their art. For Raza, it was his wide encapsulating vision of nature and philosophy that he had grown up with. For Janine, it was her own social atmosphere, particularly her bourgeois and proper upbringing at home which she mostly reacted to.

One reason why Janine was attracted to Raza in the first place was that he was the diametric opposite of the person she was expected to marry. She was to express this in various ways in her art as well. Her art was not symbolic, but earthy and material. As Duchesne pointed out, 'What made Janine attractive to Raza was precisely that she was so different. I suppose it is something I can understand – the woman you love is not just a female copy of himself but somebody fully different. They did have something in common, however, which was the importance of youth. It is said that Janine's work was clearly influenced by all the dos and don'ts that she had experienced as a little girl, and her work was trying to get over all those dos and don'ts. Her upbringing was not especially Catholic but I would say fairly traditional French of her class ... little girls must behave and wear lace and with a proper hairstyle, kind of propriety, kind of middle class propriety. She clearly had an account to settle with this. And what was there in common was this importance of youth. The imprint of youth on their personalities ... but Janine wanted to get rid of it ... somehow, while Raza on the contrary somehow clearly wanted better and ever more fully to assimilate and integrate.'[22]

Raza understood this aspect of her and was patient with it, '...He was extremely nice – perhaps the least natural male you can think of! And at the same time he certainly allowed her to be herself and settle accounts with her youth. So he certainly was a very important aspect of her personal liberation and coming of age. There was always this problem ... in the way she used and reused all those old things and objects and toys and dolls and things like this ... some kind of a spell she was under in her young years that she wanted to get rid of ... the spell that had been cast upon her – and this is consistent with her living with a man who was so different, who did not send her to another prison but set her free.'[23]

Janine's works around this time show an intense desire to exorcise the cast of childhood to set herself free. The barricaded forms done with a skilful eye on composition and colour hypnotize with their drama and power. In one sculpted low-relief work in wood made by her, for instance, the gyrating child in the centre could be demolishing all the accoutrements of a bourgeois lady she is supposed to acquire when she grows up: the fan, the beads, the picture frame, which surround her frame. Was it perhaps because her father was very dominating? But according to Duchesne, 'Her father was not dominating. He just lacked imagination. But it was difficult for him but he accepted it – it was something that was beyond his grasp. But he was not unpleasant and he did help them financially, materially. He was nice with them but he ... Raza was something ... not just ... because he was Hindu [sic] but because he was a painter ... he was somebody who was totally foreign – not just because he came from India. In a way it may even have helped that he came from India, and not just next door. Raza came from so far away, it was normal to be so different, while somebody who'd been born in France – he would have had no excuse.'[24]

Those were idyllic days for the young couple. According to the architect and photographer Jean Paul Roussel and his wife Mijo, '...And then when we met them, I first visited them in Paris, they had some kind of a studio that had been designed and rented out to artists. I don't know if it was by the minister of culture or by the city of Paris. It was in Boulevard Secreten – in the 19th district of Paris in the northeast part of the town. And they had an artist's studio with a storey high room, large window up to the north and smaller rooms for living and they entertained us quite a few times there.'[25] Even as late as in the '60s they lived in a small flat with three rooms and no bathroom where Raza would warmly invite his friends from India to come and stay.

The hospitality and warmth of the young couple made friends wend their way to them in the evenings. To many, they seemed to be an Indian couple who were artists. According to Duchesne, 'The people who didn't know them thought – Janine was quite dark-haired, with a dark complexion as well. Many thought she was Indian too. And when they entertained guests at the Secretan or Rue de Charonne, she dressed up in Indian fashion [in a sari]. People who didn't know them thought he was the Indian painter and she his Indian wife.'[26] She was the very first woman he had really fallen in love with, 'Before Janine – you know he met her when he came to France – he was so young. One doesn't realize but that group of artists – how young they were! Now people are used to travelling. But they were not used to it. So, it was an extreme adventure. And then he goes to École de Beaux Arts, which was extraordinary. And he goes to this atelier and sees that beautiful woman with long black hair – she was beautiful – Janine. A bit manly, may be – but beautiful. And he fell in love with her. So, there was no one before Janine. Of course, he had been married before. So, I guess he had had a sexual relationship with his first wife. But no children…'[27]

Raza's circle of friends consisted of Akbar Padamsee, Ram Kumar and Krishen Khanna. Souza would come visit him too, and along with Padamsee the three initially exhibited together in Paris. The expatriate community in Paris was also a source of friendship and support. There were Indian scholars like Pran Talwar, Rajesh Rawat, Balbir, Jean Bhownagary, Baldoon Dhingra, Jean and Krishna Riboud, Anil de Silva and Philippe Vigier, and also the renowned photographer Cartier Bresson whom he had known since the time he visited Kashmir. On many occasions, they would meet and have heated discussions in Jean and Freny Bhownagary's basement flat having a meal of 'potatoes and ordinary red wine'.[28] And these debates, '…On French art, on Matisse and Cézanne and Fernand Leger were heated, ranging over issues which Bhownagary now describes as "juvenile metaphysics". They were in the process of rediscovering the world, of charting for themselves a new course!'[29]

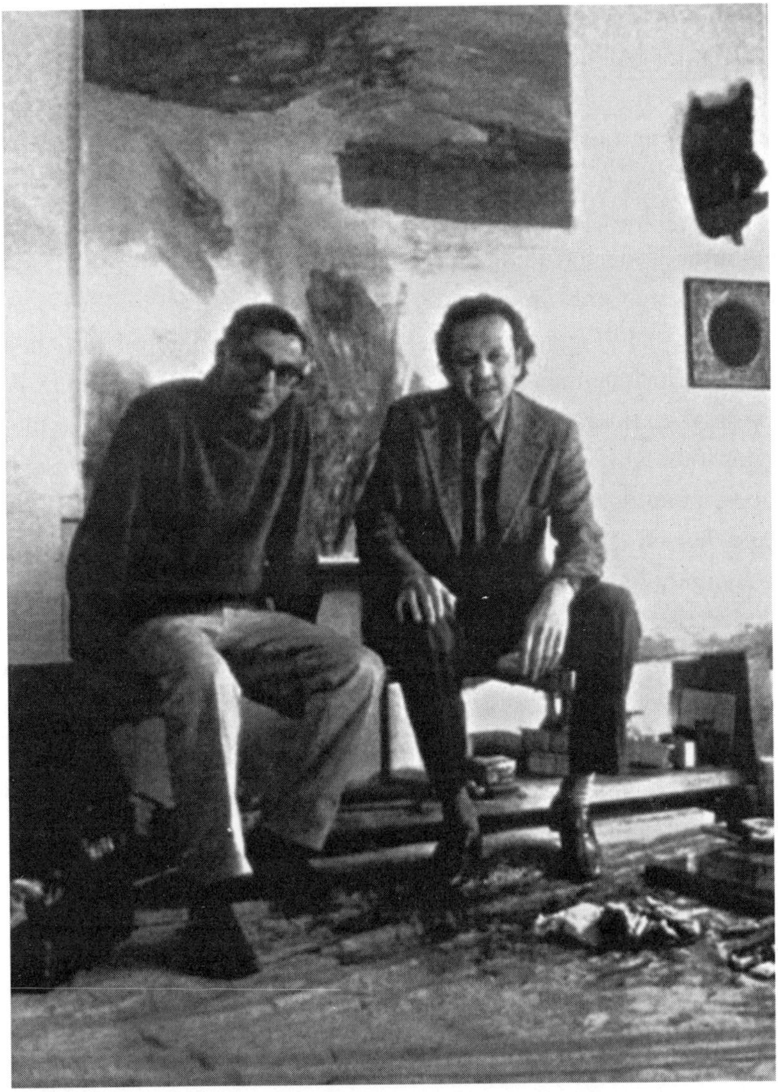

Ram Kumar and Sayed Haider Raza at Secretan, studio-apartment, Paris.

A Time to Remember

Perhaps it was Jean Bhownagary who was not only the closest to Raza at this point but made a significant difference in his life as well. It is not quite certain how the two met; perhaps it was through Souza who mentions in a letter from London, 'Jean Bhownagary will be in Bombay, as he told me, from 10th January. But he said that he will spend most of his sojourn in Poona, at his wife's place. I spoke to him about your coming to Paris. He has been living in Paris for several years and still lives there. He will tell you something fresh from Paris. He flies back from India to Paris after a monthly holiday. Incidentally I will stay with him when I go to France this spring. I have made arrangements to go to Paris by March, he is very keen to meet you and I hope will be of help to you.'[30]

Jean was not only an engaging person but also very multifaceted. He was a potter, a lithographer, a painter and a ceramist, but primarily he was a talented documentary filmmaker. He worked with UNESCO in Paris for more than three decades and the films he directed or produced for the organization won awards at prestigious film festivals. It was during this period that he also worked with the Films Division in Bombay from 1954-57 and then, at the behest of Indira Gandhi, again from 1965-67 when the documentary film in India came into its own. His protégées at the time included the famed documentary filmmakers S. Sukhdev and Pramod Pati. Born to a Parsi father and French mother, he had served in India earlier in Bombay in 1939 at the start of the Second World War when Reuters had hired him as a correspondent. He had also set up the Turkish consulate and briefly joined Tata Sons, wrote scripts for documentaries and cartoon strips and co-authored Gujarati comedies with Adi Marzaban. It was during that time that he developed a passion for magic tricks. As a member of the Toc-H Concert Party he entertained servicemen, hospital wards and POWs; in recognition for his talent, the most influential bodies of prestidigitators admitted him to their fold.

In Paris, Jean and Freny's famed soirées would end with magic tricks. After Jean passed away on 11 April 2004, the journalist Dileep Padgaonkar mentioned in an obituary for him, 'All through my years in Paris, an invitation from the Bhownagarys to visit their home carried the promise of enchantment. Freny could be trusted to rustle up a dhansak while Jean ensured that we washed it down with wines he brought by the barrel directly from the vineyards. But food and drink were just a small part of their hospitality. It is the kind of people who flocked to them and the way Jean entertained them that made our day. The guests were poets, painters, actors, academics, writers and filmmakers. Their banter in English about life and letters continued late into the night... And then as the party moved into top gear, he would perform magic tricks which left the guest speechless with wonder.'[31]

It was in his small basement flat that his daughter, Janine Bharucha, remembers the frequent presence of Raza, Akbar and, sometimes, Souza. In fact, the three would often babysit her together when the parents were out. So much so that she remembers reciting their names together: Padamsee-Raza-Souza in unison for they were inseparable. Janine's vivid memories of her childhood are interlinked with their presence. 'Papa and Mama lived in a tiny little two room – not two-bedroom. It was an underground flat. Papa was broke as well as he was just beginning at UNESCO. And I used to see their feet, their shoes – walking – you know, there was a little window – you could see through from the basement window. And I'd be really happy because they were with us all the time ... I was five from what I remember. And sometimes Papa and Mama would go out so the three or one of them would come and babysit me and I'd see them coming down the stairs and I'd sing ... Padamsee-Raza-Souza ... They were very present, the three of them, in our lives at that time.'[32]

Together they had some good times together. 'They were like the three musketeers – inseparable. Really very sweet. We'd have potatoes with salt, no butter. Everybody was broke! And of course – wine and potatoes. And I made them discover for the first time in their lives, peanut butter. So, I would with a little teaspoon in the peanut butter make a lollipop. Sprinkle a little sugar, make them each eat a peanut butter lollipop. And they had never ever tasted peanut butter! So, I was very proud – that was my contribution to Padamsee-Raza-Souza.'[33]

The presence of Raza was especially important to her and she remembers an unforgettable work of his bought by her father which used to hang in the drawing room of whichever house they lived in. In fact, Jean appears to be Raza's earliest buyer and mentor and had bought the haunting painting *Haut de Cagnes* (1951) from him. Eventually, Raza bought it back from Jean at a low price and sold it for almost treble the cost in the market, Janine noted sadly.[34]

Her apartment is overflowing with drawings, watercolours and pottery made by her father, but also present are works of Souza, Husain and

Padamsee – which were originally a part of Jean's collection. Janine's own artistic instincts, and her sister Asha's, were of course sensitized from the beginning when their house would be frequented by artistes like Ravi Shankar. Raza appears to have first met Ravi Shankar at Jean's house, 'Yes – that happened in our house first. Then Raza started doing the same thing.'[35] And thus, Raza too began inviting Ravi Shankar and others to his home and having soirées.

In some ways, Janine's experience was similar to the one narrated by Jean Duchesne. He and his wife had some of Raza's paintings from the '70s which was one of his best periods, and they had retained all of them except for a large work which Raza asked them to sell at a low price to a collector who had told him that he would set up a museum for him in India. They had refused the collector, but could not do the same with Raza and, so, they sold it to him reluctantly. Later, Jean found on the Internet that it was sold at a high price in an auction in London![36]

The Artistic Duo

An important presence in those days were Jean and Krishna Riboud. Janine remembers, 'They were a really sweet family and I remember going to their place. Satyajit Ray was a good friend of Papa's ... So he had come to a gathering at Krishna and Jean Riboud's house and he had come looking so tired and so sad. Really like the whole world was on his shoulders. And he'd see Papa and his eyes would light up and he'd be alive again. I was so stunned by that.'[37]

Krishna and Jean Riboud were close friends of Raza and Janine and would be frequently spotted at their place. In one letter, Raza wrote to them, 'It is indeed a long time since we haven't met you. We tried to contact you several times hoping to have you in our new home and show you what we have been painting. Janine's second "collage" fairly big size done for the Salle des Fetes in Chouilly-Epernay is leaving the studio next week. We would like you to see it and will be very happy if you could come for dinner on Tuesday 21st October...'[38]

Krishna Riboud (née Roy) was a collector and Jean was a high-flying industrialist who met her at a party in Kolkata and got infatuated. He then courted and married her. Krishna had attended the party for the French photographer Henri Cartier-Bresson given by the editor of *Harper's Bazaar* in the spring of 1947. It was there that she had met Jean Riboud, the chairman of Schlumberger, who would later describe her as 'one of three absolutely adorable, beautiful young Indian girls who were visiting from Wellesley College.' The young couple were not only avid collectors but were also the host of many soirées at their richly endowed art interiors.[39] Krishna was not only a historian and collector of Indian and Chinese antiquities and textiles and a patron of the arts, but she and her husband were also well acquainted with President François Mitterrand, Prime Minister Indira Gandhi as well as General Ne Win of Burma. Their cultural connoisseurship was backed by immense wealth that came from Jean Riboud's heading of Schlumberger, and his transformation of a company with a virtual monopoly in the manufacture of instruments used in oil exploration into a vast global corporation.

Journalist Sunil Sethi mentions, 'Jean Riboud's heroic record of joining the French Resistance and escaping from Buchenwald with the assistance of Communists as a young man matched Krishna's early memories of watching her uncle Soumendranath Tagore, a revolutionary and passionate Communist, being taken away in manacles by the British police at a railway station in Calcutta. Their experiences instinctively put them in sympathy with the Left. Despite their political connections, it was their deep interest in art, however, that made them a formidable partnership. Their fingers were firmly placed on the cultural pulse of three continents – America, Europe and Asia.'[40]

Their vast collection included not only works by artists like Max Ernst, Joan Miró, Henri Cartier-Bresson and Isamu Noguchi, but also the Indian masters like M.F. Husain and J. Swaminathan. Some of their extensive art collection was later donated by Krishna Riboud to Musée Guimet where a separate gallery called 'Jean and Krishna Riboud Collection' is being maintained.[41]

Jean Riboud died in Paris in 1986 and their only son Christophe lost his life in a tragic car accident in Switzerland in 1990. After Jean's death, Krishna continued with her travels for her art and textile collection dividing her time between France and India. According to Sethi, even after the loss, Krishna carried on with her life for 'Personal tragedy did not deter her from her pursuits, nor dim her zest for living. Even after the death of husband and son, she carried on resolutely, travelling to India, China and Japan annually and several times a year to America. For a quarter of a century, hers was a presence to reckon with in the museums and salerooms of the world. When Mme Riboud – the small rotund figure, usually dressed in black and often in her friend Issey Miyake's creations – raised her little finger, scholars paused and auctioneers held their hammer. Only her friends were allowed to tease and cajole and brighten the evening's prospects with the offer of an authentic Persian restaurant in the depths of Westbourne Grove.'[42] Sethi ends on a poignant note, 'Despite the implacable advance of cancer she managed to visit the sites of Pandua and Gaur two years ago. It was only in the weeks before her death that she retreated into her apartment, that tranquil world overlooking the private garden in the shadow of Napoleon's tomb.'[43] Krishna Riboud died at her home in Paris, on 27 June 2000.

A Close Friend

Perhaps the most endearing of Raza's friends was Rajesh Rawat, and there was frequent contact between them to prove that. Raza had probably made friends with him in his student days and the bond only grew stronger over time as they had much to share. Rajesh was a poet to Raza's artistic sensibility, he was interested and involved with India, and he too had married a Frenchwoman, Genevieve, of artistic temperament. They would often go out on evenings as a foursome and those times would be filled with animated conversations. Most of all, Rajesh was Raza's soulmate – someone he shared his innermost thoughts with and with whom he would often lighten the difficulties of his early stressful days. As he once wrote to Rajesh, 'I remember the days at the Cite. Perhaps hardly to be regretted. But the whole mob. Cafeterie Canteen – the same stale conversation. I just could not adjust myself. May be others were perfectly normal, it was only I who took everything so seriously. But then I was convinced that so much of energy was wasted and that's the stuff to be stored and exploited.'[44] Raza would hark back to the early days in more ways than one, 'Those were the days when we read Rilke with so much enthusiasm. I read him less now, but I realize more and more the significance of some of his ideas. I realize them better in the act of living and working.'[45] He had internalized Rilke as he had the French way of life, while remaining consistently Indian.

Raza had many Indo-French friends whom he and Janine would meet frequently as a couple. But most of all, it was his own relationship with Janine which was wholly fulfilling. She was not only a supportive wife but a lively and creative companion as an artist. Her work created a parallel journey to that of Raza's, in its continuous archiving of her own roots and a sense of a larger vision. While he stuck to painting on canvas, Janine experimented with found material in different mediums. In many ways, she was the stubborn counterpoint to his ephemeral heights: earthy, engaging with the contemporary and the material, and wholly alert to practical and daily life. Together they created a meaningful and charmed world of harmony, which took them on a journey that lasted their entire lives. At last, life was fulfilling for Raza. After a turbulent period of hardships, he could finally raise a toast to *La vie est belle*!

Magical Flowers Were Humming

Among a great many letters written by Raza to Janine Mongillat, the ones written in the year 1953-54 were special – for these letters hold in their pages the revelation of the intensity of their relationship as well as his struggle as an artist. By this time, the young artist had begun courting Janine with an earnest dedication as a prelude to their very fulfilling marriage a few years later.

Raza was also poised midway, at this time, between acquiring independence as an artist with his sweeping brush strokes representing the lush natural world of the countryside in France and achieving recognition with the famed Prix de la Critique two years later, which set him on the international route.

The letters he wrote to her are remarkable for their allusion to writers and poets, to philosophical thoughts and, of course, romance. They cruise between disciplines and his personal struggle and are heightened by the alchemy of love. Janine was an artist in her own right and, with her experimental forays, she balanced out the idealism in Raza's outlook. These exchanges are also from one artist to another in what was to be a stimulating and continuous conversation. The letters point to the happiness and turmoil that the young artist had undergone for a few years after reaching Paris. In his poetic expressions, we get a sense of his compatibility with Janine and the vulnerabilities of his life as an artist. Their content, hitherto unknown, follows a sequence and is revealed below in all its disarming candour.

~

9 April 1953

Janine,

I'm thinking of everything that has happened in these two weeks. I'm thinking of the sweet years of my life in Paris too, and of my past in India. The mind requires examination of all thoughts, all acts committed or not, in life…

I think of everything that's happening. It was only in France that I felt free. In India, there were too many things, too many obligations, relations, attachment. It was not possible then, to think clearly, to live as one must…

In a person, there are always the known and the unknown, so continuing dialogue and unexpected exchanges do birth some outcome. We are half certain and half uncertain. We build on this knowledge, on this certainty to arrive at the unknown. Nothing is more beautiful than what doesn't exist…

My ideas have changed over time. The Paris of 1951 is not the same as the one of 1953. Rather it's me who has changed. What pleases me before, doesn't anymore. The Paris that is mine today is so very small, yet, it's the Paris that I love. More than before.

And this old Paris of 1951 has become unbearable. However, I am like everyone else, uncomfortable, but always there, as though nothing can change, as if it couldn't be otherwise…

And everywhere there are galleries with art dealers. Here is a drawing by Matisse, two paintings by Marie Laurencin, and young painters who aren't known yet but who have a lot of talent and will probably be big names in the near future. Every month, there are thirty-six exhibitions in these two little streets alone. Thirty-six painters who show [their work] surviving on hope. As for the art dealer, he knows why he is there, and even if no one comes to browse or buy, he knows how to do business…

It's a market, even worse, a fair, with all the dirty games, false colours, pretensions, affectations, loose prattle, hypocrisy, disgusting prostitution and nothing more. It's heavy. We arrive at the moment when we can't bear it any more, especially because we know that like everyone else, we are part of all this tragedy and that despite inventions, progress, despite culture, religion, knowledge, we have remained on the surface, we have no life, we've understood nothing. And this idea gradually takes on beautiful meaning, that you can only run home to this room, 314, on the 5th floor, lock the door and on your knees read this:

'Dissatisfied with all and dissatisfied with myself, I would like to redeem myself and take pride in the silence and solitude of the night. Souls of those whom I have loved, souls of those whom I have sung, strengthen me, support me, remove me from the lie and corruptive vapors of the world; and you, Lord my God! Grant me the grace to produce some beautiful verses which prove to me that I am not the last of men, that I am not inferior to those whom I despise…'

Completely shaking, I started anew. And yet I wonder why I seem to suffer.

~

10 April 1953

I just read what I wrote. I see that I speak only of myself. I could have addressed this letter as 'Dear Raza', but that is perhaps where its meaning is. I know it's addressed to you. I'm looking deep within, as I present it to you. You don't know me enough – despite your understanding [of me]. If all this were to bore you, you'd tell me. It would be easy to throw these papers in the bin, though be careful, you have to tear this up in the smallest of fragments, as these are only for your eyes, and shouldn't fall into another's hands…

I ran all day today. I'm glad I found Sophocles and some other books that I'd searched for, then got the ticket, permits and checks. It was not fun and I want to tell you this, because for me, with my current concerns, this contact with reality was striking. The reality of this world in which we have the honor of living…

'They have broken my path and to increase my affliction I need no help from anyone.

'Now my soul is melting in me…

'Fears pursue her like a wind, my deliverance from passing a cloud at night pierces my bones and my veins don't rest

'My garment has changed color by the violence of my pain, it sticks to my body and clasps me like the opening of my dress…

'Days of affliction have surprised me, I look like dust and ashes…

'My harp is a lament and the sound of my flute a sob'

But pray, whatever comes out from the bottom of the heart is not enough. I knew that in my childhood and I believe it until today, it takes realization and will to pursue ideas to the end…

Every day brings me to a new discovery. I'm afraid, and this fear is not ordinary. It's not the fear of a child or a big person. It's a creation of this part in me which is all powerful, towards balance and the other [part] which is not.

It's true that one can judge a person only when he justifies himself in the circumstances.

I had misunderstood freedom…

[page missing]

There is greatness in unfulfilled compliments. You have everything you need. There is no reason to see black. Your life is in your hands. You can give it the form you want with your thoughts, with your choice…

I read Paul Valery, here is a part that I like,

'I was twenty, and I believed in the power of thought. I suffered strangely to be, and not to be. Sometimes, I felt infinite strengths.

They fell before these problems; and the weakness of my positive powers would deceive me. I was light-hearted, easy in appearance, strong in the end, extreme in contempt, absolute in admiration, easy to impress, impossible to convince. I had faith in some ideas that had come to me. I take the conformity which they had with my being who had borne them for a certain mark of their universal value; what appeared so clearly in my mind seemed to him so invincible; what the desire generates is always what is most clear.

I kept these shadows of ideas as my state secrets. I was ashamed of their strangeness; I was afraid they were absurd; I knew they were and they were not. They were vain in themselves, powerful by the singular strength that the confidence that had guarded me. The jealousy of this mystery of weakness filled me with a kind of vigour, 'He was too young', you'd say, perhaps.

~

8 June 1953

I wrote to you yesterday, and I did not know if I [am] going to send you this letter. I'd like to retain it, like several others. Being able to grasp thoughts at particular moments already helps [with] my research.

This morning, your letter arrived. I'm going to write to you now, but this paper glows too much before me, and the other one is firmly against the wall.

So, my Sunday thoughts, I send to you.

Klee has always fascinated me. I know him well, and I can't help but see his works as often as possible. This time, I recognize new elements [there, in his work]. Art is based on art. I am convinced. Nature plays a very important role, but it takes a different form, given the shapes already created [by it]. For training, I believe each painter must study and choose his masters. They might become too influenced, but if they bear the consciousness [of the chosen tradition], they must understand it.

I continue on my path, and I continue, even if my masters prevent me from being myself for a while. In Italy, I saw them very closely and they always said to me: 'Go away. Seek your truth'.

Reading Gide here, I found his envoy, a book, in the end, which is true and well written:

'Nathanael now, throw my book [away]. Emancipate what you had! Leave me. Leave me now; you're harassing me; you hold me back, the overstated love I have for you occupies me too much. I'm tired of pretending to educate someone. When did I say that I wanted you the same? It's because you differ from me, in that I love you; I only love you in what differs from me. Educate! – Who then will educate me? Nathanael, shall I tell you? I interminably educated myself. I continue. I never feel at a loss, in what I could do.

'Nathanael, throw my book; don't be satisfied with it. Don't believe that your truth can be found somewhere else; more than anything be ashamed of it. If I looked for your food, you would not be hungry to eat it; if I prepare your bed, you would not sleep [just] to sleep.

'Throw my book [away]; tell yourself that this is only one of a thousand possible postures of life. Look for that which another [person] would have [already] done just as well; [and] don't do it. What another would have said as well as you, don't say it – written as well as you, don't write it. Don't become attached to yourself, except in that you feel that it's nowhere else other than yourself and that you have reacted, impatiently or patiently, ah! [That is] The most irreplaceable of beings.'

My world is annoying. I want to leave it. I am told that there is a lot of movement in St. Germain des Pres. I want to see if there is something interesting.

You know I'm always happy to see you. I will say that it's a need. I don't know if you really get tired with my thoughts. But we're still tired.

Yours,
Raza

~

Paris, 5 July 1953

My dear Janine,

You made me know a feeling that seemed foreign, that belonged to others that I despised, that beautiful feeling of joy, which [now] can be mine too.

In all its fullness, you've brought to me a feeling that I don't know how to articulate, and yet it shows itself in all my letters without talking about it. You've also made me know the exquisite sweetness of moments, which wrongly, I often neglected or ruined. How to write what it has become for me, that consumed days and nights as they came, happy or unhappy, without knowing the existence of this void.

I am immersed in my dreams. Unceasing dreams, sad – if I think, gay – if I surrender to the intensity of pure feelings. I am not searching anymore. Will there be a new way? I don't know. Consequences – I don't think about them anymore.

Janine, I'm waiting for the sweet harvest of smiles, and the end of distressing days.

All yours,
Raza

~

28 March 1954

Janine dear,

I had to write to you all the time to communicate my thoughts, yesterday. I resisted the urge to visit the café at Porte d'Orléans. To see you and not to speak to you would have been more painful.

And now I'm here, it's 11.35. Maybe you're still in the café. Sometimes you look at the door. Perhaps. Me, here alone, I have your eyes in front of me, your eyes from yesterday.

They shine and blind me.

I love them so much that I suffer to see them like this.

Kisses,

R

See you soon

I need to be happy and live. And my happiness, know it well, depends on what you say.

Finding it, I'm deciding to keep it.

~

Paris, 1 July 1954

My dear Janine,

Souza's gallery opening. I went with Rawat and Isabelle, Genevieve had an appointment with the doctor. He is exhibiting around sixteen paintings and twenty drawings. The grand flourish of morose expression – like [all] the things that make you want to kill yourself. Souza was there, standing near the staircase and with a quiet disposition. I said hello and shook hands with him. Not another word. I looked at the paintings and drawings. I was expecting a better and bigger exhibition ... I would have loved for you to be here tonight. I miss you at every step. Fortunately, I can write to you and receive your letters... All of his canvases are of an unspeakable sadness. He truly must have suffered. When considering the quality of his paintings, I found only five or six that I liked. The drawings are excellent ... I left the show after twenty minutes without even saying goodbye.

I want to work like crazy. Janine, write to me as you do every day. I need you to feel close to me – close to me. I am with all your letters now. Before me, I have your pink towel, I just washed it; I am extremely tired of the day. Come, calm me down. Good night.

~

Friday, 12h 10

This morning I was at Mahieus' and an hour and a half of Hindi with Mrs Caillat is never very pleasant, except when I exit her place with 600 francs. When I returned, I almost helped Rawat, who is leaving the city on Saturday. Maybe. This will continue after noon. Yet, I definitely decided to work despite everything.

The only consolation is your letter. My Janine, because of you, I have life.

Your Raza,
[See you tonight]

~

Undated

...He [unclear] told me stories of his school, the dances, his loves, and the life of St. Germain. And then, very kindly, he talked about you, and for the moment his great obsession is to invite you to dance with him. According to him, you are very beautiful. But also very clever. He wonders why I do not learn to dance. 'It helps, you know. It's not too difficult. I'm dancing well now. No, it's not good here, in the city. Ask Janine. You see go see her she will teach you ... etc. etc.'

I gave absolutely no indication [of us]. On the contrary, I asked him some news. The imbecile, he does not know that my tale bathes in the afternoon sun, and that the connection I've established will last for all eternity. He will know it one day, as will everyone else.

It started raining. The little snowflakes fell, which I will never know what to call in French.

I'm happy to think that it's India I spoke of. Or it's only myself [that I speak of in the end].

In one of your envelopes I see the pictures of Nice. Have you met Aga Khan? On this envelope, I'll change the writing and even the envelope, to avoid attracting the attention of evil eyes.

My dear, I'm at the post office. Only five minutes remain left for the last clearance. Two days ago, I received your money order. I don't know how to write about it. I also found a lot of things in the cupboard Janine.

Write to me – know that your letters bring me extraordinary joy, and also the power to work.

To you, Raza
P.S. Do not make too many courtesy calls.

I love you,
Raza

~

Paris, 2 July 1954

My dear Janine,

I am sending you a letter that I want to send to Husain and I want you to send it in Menton. I did not seal it. You can read it. You'll find the form filled up already with my own writing. So close it properly and send it as a registered letter. Additional stamps will need to be added. I've put only a hundred francs.

I will send you the French translation tomorrow. I think the letter is as he deserves it, and it cannot be otherwise, if I want to do what I want to. As [in postscript] I added that I am leaving Paris for the south of France for a few weeks. This is because I want to absolutely not be pestered this month, to be able to work.

I'm in a hurry to put this letter in the post office. I sent you one this morning and I will continue [writing] in the evening.

May I pour into these sheets any tenderness that I feel for you.

Kisses. See you soon.
Raza
It's still the 2nd of July.
Only now it's evening of an eventful day.

And it's a 'me' who's alone and calm.
I boast of a land, rich and voluptuous, all to myself.
I'll go there, to live and to love.
Exclusively.

10.30 p.m. …A drawing is getting worse and worse

Undated

I do not care about literature, *while doing it*, the idea becomes more important than being. And God knows that now it's only being that matters. With my letters, I bind myself to you every moment, I speak, I dance, I laugh, I cry, and without restraint.

Pick them up as my tears and smiles. In this love would be my achievement. I will make it. The bad thing is that I have the terrible habit of thinking too much [maybe one day it will be my strength] I can't help but summarize all the events so far. I think everything is good and right. And that it could not be otherwise. My biggest responsibility is you.

Besides, there is only one thing that can prove me right or wrong: painting. We'll see.

Kisses, good night. See you tomorrow.
Raza

Paris, 6 July 1954, 9.30 a.m.

Have you already risen? Did Marie make you the 'delights' for breakfast? Here I am [again], to say hello and I want it to be done particularly well this morning. Because finally, life is a very beautiful thing. I am happy with your letter and the two postcards. I like this one from Gorbio a lot and I hope to work after that today. Yes, my Janine, I ought to have been in Gorbio at the moment – 7 km from Menton! One day, I'll surely settle in Provence.

My love, this morning is more extraordinary than yesterday. You know that for several days it was bad weather here – I almost took the overcoat [out]. I wondered if the sun is not more generous towards you [where you are]. Fortunately, there is a tremendous brilliance outside, which illuminates the mind/spirit. Your letter arrived at 8.15. On a lonely table, in the cafeteria, I spent a good half hour, reading while thinking. And then, I took a lukewarm and cold shower. I know that the sea of the south is something else, but here in the student house, this is the biggest luxury.

I feel you transform. Janine, my Janine. I love you with infinite tenderness. Your letters show me an ever greater understanding which I wholeheartedly desire. So, I am full of hope, but I think that all that is certain must develop in a natural and substantive way. It will take time.

As for myself, my love is justified because of its exclusivity. This is the only proof when you love. I am obsessed, and I already know perfectly well that nothing can separate me from you now.

I work well. And it's a job where you come to help every moment, and of which you'll be as proud as me. To tell you the truth, I have to travel a lot. The village known as Rouqebrune stimulates the imagination. All elements are within nature. Roman roofs almost resemble an abstract painting. My Janine, such cards will help me greatly/enormously. Fortunately, you know how to choose. Do not hesitate to buy more.

I love you.
Raza

2.15

I worked, ate and after a little siesta I added another word before putting this letter in the mail. The sun is gone. You don't care much for my advice but I ask you not to go very far into the sea. These sports were fun before. Now, you are responsible for your Raza. And I'm also asking you to abstain from being in the water too long if it's too cold. I really want it to be beautiful [weather] and that you get the perfect climate. I cannot wait to see your skin.

I promise you to keep the measure with regard to the wine, I eat well and take care of my health…

~

11 July 1954

Janine,

Preserve my letters.

What is said among the various sensations is little reasoned. Anything impromptu is lost in the air. The acts, the facts, all the stories and the stories [are lost] to a thousand interpretations. Memories belong to an obscure past. These letters are an unchangeable reality that will last. Preserve them.

I'm in. I commit myself by my letters. And I tell you. Because I absolutely need your trust. I need to convince you that there are men on earth who are able to love and who are worthy of love.

I need to make you believe that all true love is exclusive and that my calls are only for one person and that person is you. May God grant me the power to say 'I love you' as it has never been said.

In a few hours I'll be next to you [in Menton]. You will need a provision of the reception. Know that I've never had such ardour [than ever before]. You know the absurdity of my circumstances, and if I come, it is because my whole being is concentrated on you. To reach it prevents me breathing. I need to live.

I come in two days, but from now on, through this letter I propose my life to you and I ask for your hand [in marriage].

I've known you for two years. I wanted you to escape, with all my strength, as much as you did. I had a threatening past. I was lonely, bitter, aware of my circumstances. I did not want to cast a shadow in your path. Months can be spent [like this].

To recount: I saw you turn into a deity. I felt you fill this abyss of my heart. And now I find you scattered in every fibre and every moment.

I am not coming to spend ten days of holidays in Menton. I am coming to establish an affair for all my life, to prove to you my indispensability. Our struggle will be great. You know everything. But with you, I will know how to remove every obstacle. My struggle will have to become yours, my life will hold it, [it will be] ours. It will be necessary that you wish for this same harmony as I do, and the power that we will create together, will know how to overcome everything.

I'm coming to pick you up in my arms. I'm coming over to tell you that 'I love you' as it never has been told. I'm coming to soak my lips in yours. I'm coming to breathe. I already feel the earth shaking, the sky waiting.

Raza

~

Paris, 12 July 1954

My dear Janine,

I rubbed my face with your letter and the sand, and then I kissed it, wherever I signed it.

Tomorrow, at this time, I will have the whole beach to me. I will bathe in the water and the sun. I will let the earth warm me, the wind calm me, the light kiss me and I will kiss your eyes incessantly.

On the station platform obviously, I will be careful. I'll just shake your hand. That would already be a lot.

As far as I'm concerned, I'm afraid of nothing, not men, nor leaders, neither gods. You stand between 'being' and 'nothing', and I chose to be and I will be.

I'll probably bring your earrings. I will put them on you. I assure you, that last night I put them with my things in the bag. Almost everything is ready. I'm bringing 16,000 francs, my return ticket and an inexhaustible tenderness.

Do not worry about this delay. I'm sure of myself. Everything will be alright. Believe that I love you and I'll arrive tomorrow.

It would be wonderful to be able to have lunch together. I will bring a cake and cinzano. You know what I cannot wait to see the most – the colour of your skin.

Dear, I'm sorry you had to search around so much for the room. You could have taken something closer to your house for even a thousand francs, just for a day. And then we would see. I do not like imposing such a task on you. You must warmly thank Marie for me. You know she has always helped me and I am infinitely grateful … By the time you receive this letter, I will already be on the coast. Every moment will come near you. Be as big as the earth to clothe, absorb me.

May the sun shine … Tomorrow at 13:32

~

July 28, 1954

By strange chance, you will spend this birthday of yours on the train. I accord meaning to this trip. My wishes about and will follow you everywhere on you path, in every particle of air.

This is a milestone of a day that brings you into my kingdom. Twenty-five years, a quarter of a century to choose the destiny of a man, to become the Queen.

It is exactly 10h 50. I feel you coming towards me. I am waiting for communion and because of [this] inexplicable joy, I throw flowers everywhere in your path.

Raza

Undated, August 1954

Saturday, 22h 30

Since you've been going to work, I see you in the evening, a little tired, yet happy and smiling, you seem to have changed considerably. First of all, you never looked so beautiful, I swear to you, not even in Menton where there was a real climate of fulfillment. And in addition to this, you are softer, more understanding, bigger, more like I think you are. And so, when you surrender in my arms, I am infinitely happy, as of this existence, even if we only see each other for barely an hour.

Leaving tonight, I thought so and I thought a thousand things about us, so much so that I did not realize enough, that we won't see each other for three long days.

This is ridiculous and it is very sad. My T.S.F. [transistor radio] played sentimental music. Three times I changed it, listened, and stopped. Once they were talking about Corsica [on the radio].

It will be absolutely necessary that we go there, the two of us, where we will have a plot to ourselves and all the time in the world; where no one will come to 'chase us away'.

I have your letter from today, which I read several times, and which I find so full of warmth. Do you know that you write more freely [now] and increasingly better. And do you know that you love me now, and more every day.

I kiss your eyes to say good night.

Ra

Paris, 10 August 1954

My dear Janine,

I read your receipt this morning at 9.15 with great emotion and sorrow.

I think the time came when you could have said that it was me who came to see you. You could have said everything.

I am aware of the consequences, but I think that if you share my life right now, it would be less painful. Because their attitude is really unbearable, and if I exist [in your life] it could not continue for long.

I regret that poor Marie is involved in this affair with which she has nothing to do.

I would love to see you, talk to you now.

On the map of Parisian suburbs, I found 'Champigny-sur-Marne' and I think that I could have come to join you, if there was the slightest indication on your part, or if yesterday you hadn't told me not to come – God knows why.

I would have taken the P.C. to Porte de Charenton and the bus to Joinville and then a taxi from there. I would look for your school everywhere in Champigny and find it because one finds even the good God, if he is truly sought.

I resisted the temptation with all [my] strength because I have to work under all circumstances. If I write, it is to suffer less, to be able to tell you that your pain is mine, and that I will do everything so that these days end as soon as possible.

I still believe that it will be, it would be possible, it should be possible, because of the current pace. I haven't the slightest doubt. You'll see. I know that now everything seems difficult and sometimes, situations are ridiculous. We will come out of this. We will have our freedom, our life, our happiness. You have to calm down. You must think of the sweetness of the future, and that all your hindrances, the difficulties, the sorrows will render us, one to the other more dear, more precious. We will make a life worthy of being lived. All this will happen and you will tell me later: [do] you remember this day and that day, and...

Right now my dear Janine, just think that we love each other and that because of that we will find each other.

Everything to you and forever.

Raza

~

Paris, Wednesday, 22 September

My dear Janine,

It seems that I can't do anything without you. Every moment, I need you and these days where the problem of the room haunts me like a ghost, I wish you were here. Do you see, darling, I absolutely must do something before the end of this month – in October it would be impossible. The number of students at Rue Soufflot is growing by the day and now I have lost hope on this front.

I must go to my friends quickly and ask for the room.

It weighs me terribly, and I'm afraid I'll finally find myself in a hotel after the 15th of October.

Tonight, I made my way home [I spent a tiring day with Schlesinger]; and at home around six pm, I found your letter which gave me great pleasure. My little mouse is with me, I think, and nothing is impossible for me. I sent you a letter only this afternoon and this is my second letter and may be the last in St. Raphael. Trust me, this is only because I don't even know if you find the time to go to the post office to look for it. It's sad to write to Post Restante, when, today I can shout on the canvases that I love it, I love it, I love my little Ratonne. Still, it is convenient that it be so for some time. I really want to write to you, tell you everything I do here, ask you a thousand questions. I hope that this letter will reach you on Saturday or even Friday, and in the meantime you'll write to me to tell me when you come back and if you'll find the time to go to the post office on Monday.

Although, my dear Ratonne, since your departure I worked very little: two portraits. I had to go out with Schlesinger quite often, and I'd like to be excused for yesterday, because I had to work a bit and see people for the room. I also have the receipt of the fair, for little Batailles. Khanna is still here, and I see him often enough. Bengali has been gone for a week and for the best. However, I still had very little time for myself, and I think I could very easily have come to St. Raphael with you. If only the train could have advanced a little more. Yes, on the subject, do not worry about gouaches. I don't need it. I only hope that the drawings and the book do not cause you any trouble.

I can see your father painting. And you, giving him the advice. And your mother, who looks at you both in appreciation. If he takes this art seriously, you could give him the address of a painter, who would be good as a teacher, especially if it is landscape.

Ratonne

My dear, I love you, good night. See you tomorrow.

~

Undated

Dear Janine,

I started the day with your letter. Thank you with all my heart. You know it gives me the strength that I need so much. But with that I have a letter from home too, and from Mr Rawat who has arrived. So, a whole lot of things. Now, it's 5 o'clock in the afternoon. I have your letter in front of me, and the only thing I have thought since this morning, is that yesterday you wouldn't have received my letter, and I am well aware of the mail's disappointment. But dear, I told you that I'll write five days post your departure, I will write very simple, to avoid losing the letters.

Fatima is kneeling on her knees. She is writing things down to explain her point of view, and regrets all the misunderstanding. That, I know, is attitude. They want to see what effect it will have on me. I will write [a mere] two words saying that it is too late, and that nothing in the world can change my decision. In addition, I'll write to Padamsee quickly, to ask for information about Marriage and Divorce. It seems that there is legislation voting in the parliament of the Indians recently which would be in force now.

Abdoulla is kindly bringing me a copy of *World* [magazine] from last Saturday where there are details. I'm going to inquire [further] and I'm sure everything will work out. On, on, on, my Ratonne, concerning the new laws.[3] I do not think there is a variable change in these questions.

Yes, I'm going to ask Solange to give me the appropriate lawyer. I will also know how I can serve a notice here and ask for a divorce, and if the separation for four years is not a valid [enough] reason.

My love, believe that I love you with all of my being, and that I will do everything so that problems are settled in a good way. But know that in case nothing happens, we will go to India to get married.

Spend your days on the sand, under the sun, pay attention to your health, eat well, rest well, and write to me as often as you can. I hope your parents will be nice, but if they tell you mean things, think what you've won is the kindest person in this world, he loves you, and he'll do anything to make you happy. These days will pass. Believe in my will, and truly I am yours. I kiss your eyes.

Raton

I met Abdoulla again. He asked me once more if I wrote to you. I said yes, but I did not write Marie's story. Yes, he said and he wants Marie to speak to you when you arrive. So you have nothing of this business. Do not keep these letters.

Undated
12.30

For three hours my T.S.F. played all the sweet and violent rhythms. Me, I turned in my bed, agitated without being able to sleep. My window overlooks a starry sky where a large and calm moon shines. Between my legs there is a fire.

I think of your trembling lips tonight, which were wet. At this moment, I would have licked them with mine and then I would put my head through them. I would have shaken, clawed, gathered and kissed you. I would have made you sleep and I would sleep too.

I think of your sad face tired by the work of the day. Now I'll put it in the crook of my arms, to make you rest there. I'll have you singing the moon, rocking you, caressing you and I'll make you sleep, and I'll have slept too.

My Janine, I hate everything that separates us. I can't wait to see you.

There are four walls around me and several others. There are floors and stairs and streets. There are districts and a whole underground road, and Pt. of Vincennes the____

Would it be amiable? The sun, tomorrow. Oh, what a weak and painful night.

Raton
8.15

It is raining. I will come despite the sky, despite the deluge. I will chase this 'someone' who is chasing you. At 11.45 am as agreed.

Yours,
Ra
10h

Your tire has come on time. It's raining more. I come.

~

Undated

This Monday afternoon you would have come to see me. Read these lines by Rimbaud again, lines that you already know.

Magical flowers were humming. The turf slopes cradled *him*.

Beasts of a fabulous elegance were circulating.

Storm clouds were piling up on the rising sea made of an eternity of hot tears.

Xx

In the wood there is a bird, his song stops you and makes you blush.

There is a clock that doesn't strike.

There is a pit with a nest of white creatures.

There is a cathedral that sinks and a lake that rises.

There is a little carriage abandoned in the thicket, or that hurtles down the path, trimmed with ribbons.

There is a troop of child actors in costume, seen on the road across the edge of the woods.

There is, when one is hungry and thirsty, finally someone who chases you.[4]

The Watershed Years

In less than a decade since his stay in Paris, Raza had been invited to show in galleries across the world in cities from Tokyo to Toronto and Montreal where the Galerie Dresdnere acquired his paintings and showed his works regularly. It was in one of these exhibitions that Professor Karl A. Kasten from the Department of Art, Berkeley University, saw his works and invited him to teach at the Berkeley Campus in California University. Raza received an invitation asking him, ' ...To serve as guest instructor for the Second Summer session 1962. This will be for the period July 30 to September seven and carries a salary of around $1100. You will be given studio space in campus. It will be necessary to teach from either eight to twelve or one to five for five days per week ... It will be good to see you again. Georgette and I will expect you and your wife to accept the hospitality of our home until you can become situated here.'[1] Raza agreed and also requested for a solo show on the campus during his assignment which was accepted. As he had written to Kasten, 'The visit will, I am sure, throw light on certain aspects of painting problems which greatly preoccupy me, and one on which a good deal of research has been done in the United States...'[2]

Raza had also applied to the Rockefeller Foundation for a six-month stay in New York after his term in California was over and was granted a month by the interception of Thomas B. Keehn. 'I have had a few letters from Mr Thomas B. Keehn. It seems that they will be able to assist me to prolong my stay in New York a month more after my term at Berkeley. But nothing is really decided yet. Mr Keehn is a great friend of artists and I retain excellent souvenir of his stay in India. In his last letter he says he has visited San Francisco, and made it a point to meet you. Mr A.M. Weisblat of the Council of Economic and Cultural affairs (established by Mr John D. Rockefeller 3rd) is also hoping to meet you. These are excellent friends of India and I am sure that you will enjoy meeting them.'[3]

Tom Keehn and his family came to Delhi in 1953 to set up an organization funded by the Rockefellers that would look into village handicrafts. He was also asked to encourage modern Indian art as enough was being done for ancient art. Thus began one of the earliest collections of modern art and his friendships with artists that lasted for many years even after the Keehns left India. M.F. Husain, for instance, would paint in the veranda of the Keehns' huge mansion and would also make some time to interact with him and his family members and bond with them. The Keehns began to make a collection of that period's art with painters like Ram Kumar, Krishen Khanna, V. Gaitonde, Satish Gujral and Husain. The institutional support behind the Indian art scene was partly created by the efforts of people like Tom Keehns. His constant negotiations with American philanthropists like Rockefeller to establish the Indian counterpart to New York's Museum of Modern Art did not quite succeed, but the International Cultural Centre established in New Delhi harnessed the creative talent of the period.

Across the Atlantic

Raza, accompanied by Janine, spent the summer of 1962 in California as a visiting lecturer in the Department of Painting at Berkeley Campus. His studio space was comfortable. He was equipped with an easel, a sink and storage areas and electric lights for night time work. The size of the studio was approximately 20x25 feet.

He was also delighted to know that he could have a show of his paintings on the campus and requested that it be held before the end of the term, in the first week of September. 'It will be the finest contact that I can have with my students and friends. I am fully aware that no amount of talking can really replace work and that in painting only PAINTING matters.'[4] But here stood an obstacle: the Galerie Lara Vincy wanted to hold an exhibition with the Gallery Paolo Alto in San Francisco and they had been given exclusivity on the American Western Coast. Several paintings had already been sent and Mrs Vincy intended to attend the exhibition personally. Hence, the agreement of the San Francisco gallery was also necessary which was eventually given. When the show was held, Kasten and Georgette too went to see it. Lara Vincy who had come down for the show, went to meet Raza and they discussed the new configurations of showing in San Francisco.

According to Krishen Khanna, who was also on a Rockefeller fellowship and travelling in the US at that time, '...We went to see him [Raza] in Berkeley. He was showing then ... he said, "Stay the night with us." He had only one bed so four of us slept on the same bed. When we went on another occasion, a collector was with him and this girl from Raza's gallery in Paris. She was tailing him – who he was meeting, to whom he was selling... At one stage the conversation got so bad they stopped the taxi and I think Janine told her to get out.'[5]

Raza's Berkeley visit proved to be a great success overall. He was to not only make many friends amongst like-minded artists and colleagues but was able to strike a chord with the students who instantly took to him and his work. Karl remembered it fondly later, 'As I write I am transported back to Berkeley and your opening at the Worth Ryder Gallery and the little party at your apartment on Bancroft Way. There was a nice ambience there as I am sure there will be at your opening next week.'[6]

Karl Kasten, an artist himself, and Raza were to become good friends over time. Later, when Kasten was invited to lecture at Lahore University, he had written a note of thanks to Raza, 'At long last an invitation to teach in West Pakistan. You must have received a copy of the letter from Shakir Ali inviting me to join his Faculty for the year beginning this September. I recall your telling me that this is the very thing done all over India – at the last minute.'[7]

Raza had written back to him in delight:

> I was delighted to receive the copy of Shakir Ali's letter to you and later this week your letter. It does not at all surprise me that the invitation from Pak comes so suddenly and so late and I am only sorry that as a consequence, you have difficulties in getting absentee leave from U.C. I hope all the same that the appointment for the spring semester is possible and that you and Georgette can visit Pakistan. We also hope to be in India this winter – December 66 to May 67 and it will be wonderful if you could come there too after your term in Lahore … However, my friendly advice is – that you must fix up the exact conditions for work before leaving. You must know what the salary is – if my memory is good Shakir Ali said it was Rs 3000 – you must know if the passage is paid for both of you and if there are facilities regarding a bungalow etc. … I am aware that this is Fulbright and things must be fairly well organized but even Fulbright – operating in Asia can be effected by local conditions!!![8]

Eventually Karl, accompanied by Georgette, went to Lahore for the spring semester the next year.

New York Enigmas

Raza and Janine stayed in New York after the Berkeley visit. Describing his experience, he said, 'For about three months everything went off well. I had not much experience as a teacher. But I had always liked talking to younger painters and the way it all happened brought me much appreciation from the fifty students who attended the painting section during that summer. The Rockefeller Foundation invited me to New York and in October '62 I spent about a month in and around New York and Washington. I made new friends like Mr and Mrs John D. Rockefeller.'[9]

John D. Rockefeller III collected Japanese as well as Asian art with a passion and was known for his philanthropic and cultural contributions. In 1953, he set up the Council on Economic Affairs, which later came to be known as the Agricultural Development Council, and the Asia Society

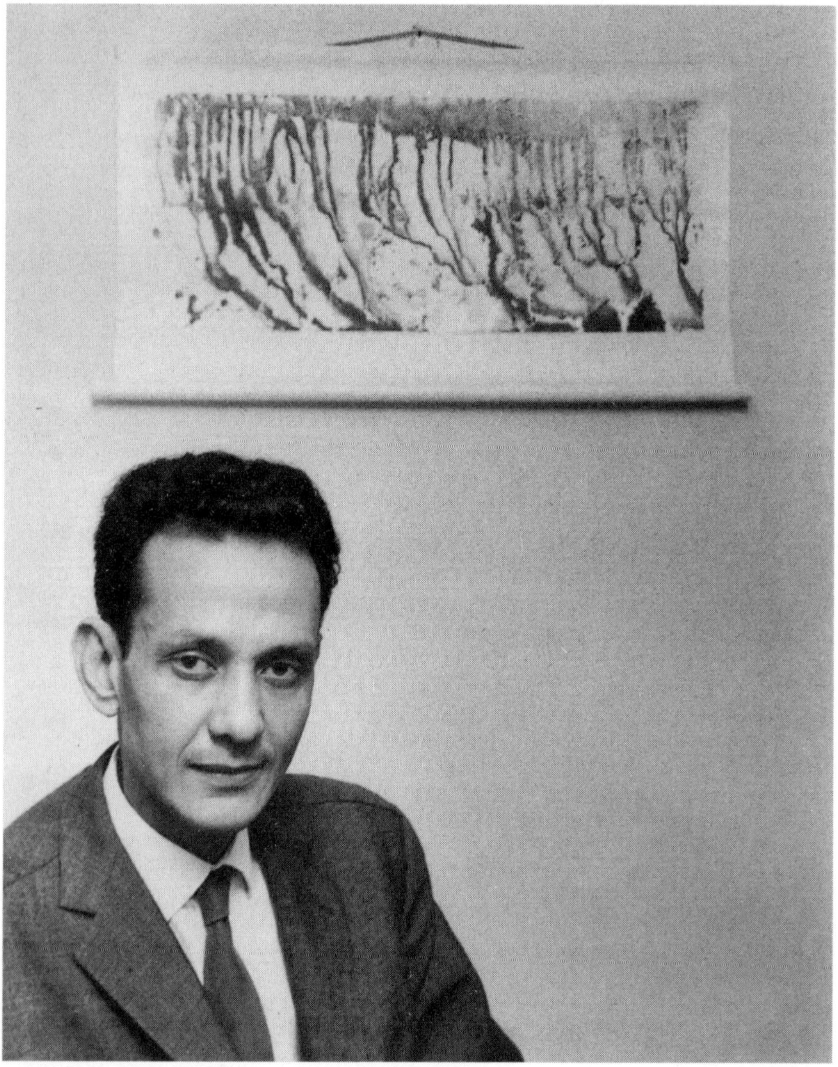

Raza in New York, 1962.

was founded in 1956 to promote a greater knowledge of Asia in the US. It is a little-known fact that the Rockefellers had contributed to the establishment of the India International Centre, the National Museum, the Bal Bhavan and National Children's Museum in Delhi, the American Academy of Benares, the Calico Textile Museum in Ahmedabad and other institutions.

Rockefeller III died tragically in a car accident in 1978, by which time many of his ideas had been given shape and were continued under the aegis of his wife Blanchette Rockefeller. The Rockefellers were indeed friends of the artists and apart from collecting their works, awarded several fellowships and extended hospitality to them during their stay in the US. It was the CECA that had invited Krishen Khanna to the US and followed it up with a stipend for Raza to travel and observe art in America. Natvar Bhavsar was also to benefit from this, as did most of the Progressive Artists and others by the JDR 3rd Fund and the Asian Cultural Council as it was later called.

The Fund, headquartered in New York, had Porter A. McCray, previous director of circulating exhibitions at the MoMA, as its first director and was instituted to bring about greater understanding of the life and culture of people in Asia ranging from Japan to Afghanistan. Rockefeller felt that while a number of organizations existed both in Asia and the United States which were involved with certain aspects of cultural interchange, there was still a need for an organization that would be interested in the field as a whole.[10]

According to art critic and curator Kishore Singh, 'True the JDR 3rd Fund was an important one for Indian artists in the 1960s and 1970s, when India was, to a large extent, cut off from the world, if not politically or geographically, at least through a shortage of funds and foreign exchange that made international travel prohibitive for most… In the country, the art infrastructure was abysmal and where the Fund helped in providing a window to a select few to travel and observe developments in New York and around, the fortunate artists could hardly be thought to be representative of artist movements and practices in that period in India.'[11] Yet Singh concedes that in the formative years of modern art in India, the Fund provided a necessary support, 'It became evident on hindsight that this engagement between Indian artists and the US provided them great space and room for thinking and experiencing alternate realities and knowledge. As we can see, in some cases a change in perspective, or practice, was immediately discernible; in others, it probably just accentuated their thinking, or liberated their sensibility, freeing them to the possibilities of working in ways, or in styles or on subjects they may have previously not considered.'[12]

Inevitably, Cold War politics of the period did not leave the Fund unscathed and despite its undeniable value it came in for criticism from some quarters for being a front organization for the CIA. As Frances Stonor Saunders once wrote:

> The Rockefeller Foundation, no less that the Ford, was an integral component of America's Cold War machinery. Incorporated in 1913, its principal donor was the legendary John D. Rockefeller III. It had assets exceeding $500 million, not including an additional $150 million in the Rockefeller Brothers Fund Inc., a major think tank which was incorporated in New York in 1950 … The convergence between the Rockefeller billions and the U.S. Government exceeded even that of the Ford Foundation…[13]

Yet the fact that it provided an awareness of an international art and culture situation where there was a dire need cannot be overruled. As Singh points out, 'India clearly had a reason to be wary. But while the distrust between the governments continued to rise, artists – and the "culture vulture" McCray alludes to – found there was reason to celebrate their proximity to the Rockefeller Foundation grants which they enjoyed seemingly without any brainwashing – a soft power establishment, while placing, in India and in other Asian countries, former CIA operatives in a new role.'[14]

Rooted and Concerned

A long distance away from India, Raza's concerns were often of the country of which he was still a citizen. He was in many ways a cultural nomad who could travel all over the world and yet remain rooted to one spot. Thus, when the war between India and China seemed imminent, he wrote an intense letter to Krishen.

> Of course, there is the nagging and rather horrible feeling of the trouble with the Chinese which, as you say, prevents one from concentrating. But as, according to Panditji, this whole thing is going to be long drawn

> affair, one may as well get used to the idea and start living with it. As it is with you and Akbar, this has worried me no end and even though there are no immediate hostilities, one cannot take it for granted that there won't be any in the future. I am not at all certain if our government will start hostilities again soon or after a considerable build up when it thinks that it is in a position of relative strength. Whatever it is, one thing is certain – our economic advancement will suffer and we will continue to have to pay for a large defence establishment.[15]

He and Krishen even considered the possibility of organizing an exhibition of artists for collecting war relief funds. 'I agree that we should raise funds as much as we can and as fast as we can. We must be careful not to bungle things in our haste. You may most certainly include the two paintings of mine that you have in the show you are organizing in Paris for the purpose of raising funds.'[16]

Many of Raza's colleagues like M.F. Husain, Tyeb Mehta, Krishen Khanna and Ram Kumar were to record the disastrous human conditions after the Indo-Pak War in 1965. They had been invited by the Indian army to reflect the state of the border areas between India and Pakistan and the detritus of war in these places and show it in their paintings to collect funds for the war widows.[17] Khanna recalled, 'With some ingenuity, the Army flooded an area where Pakistani tanks were, immobilizing them all. Ram Kumar on finding a whole area full of just howling dogs, wrote of them in Hindi. On lifting the lids of the other tanks, we once found a postcard from a friend of the deceased inside, asking, "*Aap kahan hain? Koi khabar nahin.*" Even more poignantly he mentioned, 'A grenade was used to storm a pillbox [a dugout for guards] and we did a picture of the ruins of it. There was a long picture by Tyeb Mehta of the Dograi battle.'[18] According to Khanna, the bodies of the other side had to be buried quickly and, hence, were placed in shallow graves. Animals like wolves would sense these and come at night and pull them out. These were drawn by the artists as well. The purpose of this commission was to speak of the glories of war, but the artists in their work reflected the horror and devastation that followed in its wake.

Raza's own work during his visit to the US and after it was beginning to undergo changes, not the least because he desired a shift in balances.

Krishen recounts, 'In New York, we were together and we were both asked to an interview by a very well-known critic called Hess ... and I had one of my ink paintings there for him to see. He talked to Raza first and he said, "Very French". You know ... which would mean ... And Raza was taken aback and almost in a defensive position. Then he said, "Yes it is, it is."'[19] In fact, Raza had begun to feel that his work had become a pale copy of the French school. His visit to the US was like a fresh transfusion and provided the necessary catalyst for a new stage in his work. As he stated, 'My work held a certain place in the exhibitions in Paris and in France. But I was not really satisfied by being part of the Ecole de Paris. I realized that my eyes were focused outwards, and there was an imperative need to look within myself. Thus began a transformation in my vision, and in my work.'[20]

Raza had been exposed to abstract art in Paris and had considered the works of artists there. Paintings of the American Abstract Expressionist school had also been shown in Parisian galleries from 1951, which included the first one-man show of Jackson Pollock in 1952. In July 1953, twelve American painters, including Pollock, were also shown at the Musée d'Art Moderne. Aside from this, the European CoBrA artists had exhibited as a group between 1948 and 1951 placing emphasis on the expressive immediacy of the gesture. Indeed, the first signs of abstract art had emerged during the First World War when artists like Wassily Kandinsky, Piet Mondrian, Kazimir Malevich, Hans Arp and Kurt Schwitters renounced the 'soulless materialism' of an increasingly capitalistic society and sought a new spiritual force in art. Kandinsky, in his book *Concerning the Spiritual in Art* (1911), emphasized that painting needed to free itself from the transitional and the corporeal and move into realms which are universal, abstract and spiritual. He felt that art had a loftier spiritual vision and that abstract art could communicate this vision.

The early abstractionists, in some form or the other, believed in the spiritual potential of art, which by its universal and absolute values, would rise above the exigencies of individual deviations. In sealing itself from time, however, and declaring that its values were pre-ordained, it was at the same time existing in a void that would deplete its energy. Interestingly, it's a little-known fact that Malevich had been inspired by Madame Blavatsky's theosophical ideas where he saw the vertical as the male principle and the horizontal as the female principle. The cross inscribed within the square had the 'master key' that opened the door to every science, physical as well as spiritual. Mondrian on the other hand had been influenced by J. Krishnamurti and his philosophy of infinite and finite time in a sense bringing the wheel full circle. Although invigorated, Raza had felt that he could not entirely meet the needs of abstract art. 'There is no pure "ABSTRACTION". My work is intimately linked up with life, with nature, with human experience.'[21]

The winds of change from across the Atlantic, however, swept him off his feet when he was there. It was an altogether thrilling experience for him to come into contact with the works of artists like Jackson Pollock, Willem de Kooning, Mark Rothko, Hans Hofmann and others of the New York School during his stint at Berkeley and New York. He found that Abstract Expressionism was a source of renewal as well as of tapping unknown areas within himself. He noted that for Pollock the very act of dripping or pouring paint, the process and the end of painting became its form. To execute an entire painting on the floor, Pollock had begun by the '50s with its large surface covered by interlacing trails of paint and he had to walk around it and see it from all sides and corners. The concept of an all-over, polyphonic paint surface demanded a total physical and psychic absorption in the painting itself. A tremendous unleashing of freedom resulted in not only the autonomy of the picture space itself but also, as Pollock stated in a radio broadcast in 1950, of 'the energy, the motion and other inner forces.'[22]

Primitive Myth

The role of primitive myth had a particular resonance for Pollock, who in 1939 had attended sessions of Jungian therapy in which his own drawings provided material for discussion. From then onwards, there was a consistent allusion to mythic figures and archetypes or to mythic rites in his work and the workings of the unconscious occurred throughout his career. But in his later years Pollock's work became more abstract and references to nature increasingly provided a means of psychic healing.

Willem de Kooning was another artist from the New York school who with the directness and immediacy of paint unveiled his inner workings and replaced a deliberate attempt at construction. He displayed a great deal of energy in the interplay of shapes as areas of colour counteracted against each other. His energetic abstract style, later retaining an element of figuration, made him share, along with Pollock, the unofficial leadership of Abstract Expressionism. In opening the gates for himself and others, Raza was also greatly influenced by Mark Rothko and Hans Hofmann, both of whom were involved with colour-field painting. Hofmann's belief that the two dimensionality of the paint surface creates another reality on canvas and that its spiritual values are awakened by the use of colour, echoed Raza's own beliefs. Hofmann stated, 'In fact, the whole world as we experience it visually, comes to us through the mystic realm of colour. Our entire being is nourished by it. This mystic quality of colour should likewise find expression in a work of art.'[23] The emotive quality of colours in Indian art was not new and this would find a resonance in Raza.

As the chromatic value of the paint itself became the chief concern of these painters, as against the expressive impact of the line, the entire surface became suffused with colour and the scale of the work wrapped around the viewer. 'A dramatic and even physically effective rapport is set up in which the extensive canvas surface and the intense colour suggest something beyond the physicality of the painting itself. Underpinning the extreme abstraction of the work is a constant desire to convey feeling and meaning.'[24] A basic desire to evoke emotions rather than the relationship of colour or form was Rothko's expressed intention.

The colour-field painters, like Pollock and Willem de Kooning in their early works, were also concerned with myth. In a radio broadcast of 1943, Rothko referred to his and Gottlieb's works and said, 'If our titles recall the known mythos of antiquity, we have used them again because they are the eternal symbols upon which we must fall back to express basic psychological ideas.'[25] That the onset of the War and the terror it unleashed was to bring about this interest in the unconscious was obvious, 'In times of violence, personal predilections for niceties of colour and form seem irrelevant. All primitive expression reveals the constant awareness of powerful forces, the immediate presence of terror and fear.'[26] In an attempt to start from scratch, the artists resorted to primitive beliefs and attempted a realization and understanding of their presence in the framework of the present. Following the atrocities suffered by the Jews in the War, for Rothko, the son of Jewish Russian émigrés, the use of the human figure rendered in art became virtually incommunicable. According to art historian Anna Moszynska, 'Colour, light and hieratic disposition of flat, abstract shapes, symmetry and scale became his formal vocabulary, while the living spectator replaced the abandoned pictorial figure.'[27]

In dividing a flat field of colour by a vertical band, the artist Barnett Newman was also attempting an order of the surrounding chaos. Reflecting his Jewish origins in the development of form from disorder and disintegration his work suggested the symbolic birth of a new world following the traumas of the War. Known as 'zip' paintings, when the band first appeared in his works such as *Onement 111* (1948) they suggested a deep theological and ontological basis. As Moszynska points out, 'Yet if the zip divides the surface, it is also an integral part of it; both zip and surrounding field are mutually dependent. The unity of opposite implies "atonement", and this can be extended to the underlying meaning. The zip may be seen as the Divine Light; it may represent order, or even suggest an analogy for the human being in the face of the absolute.'[28]

It was the disasters and disintegrations of the human condition brought by the War in Europe and the migrations to the US which led to the rise of abstract art in that country. But once established, it led to a forceful movement which influenced artists from all over the world. Raza's own progression had made him receptive to these new ideas which he found liberating. For many of his colleagues, the interaction with Abstract Expressionist art and artists also proved to be fruitful. V.S. Gaitonde, who had received the Rockefeller fellowship in 1964, after an initial stint with the figurative, had moved towards abstraction even earlier, influenced by the Bauhaus and Paul Klee's subtle gradation of colour where light and dark values could be weighted. In Gaitonde's later works, the application of paint itself created a highly textured surface with areas of thick and thin paint balancing themselves to reflect light in an entirely different manner. It has to be noted that Gaitonde, along with Krishen Khanna, had visited Mark Rothko's studio and this proved to be a catalyst for his own play of a single, nuanced colour over large expanses. His belief that paint and light itself had its own resonance, its own upheavals and its

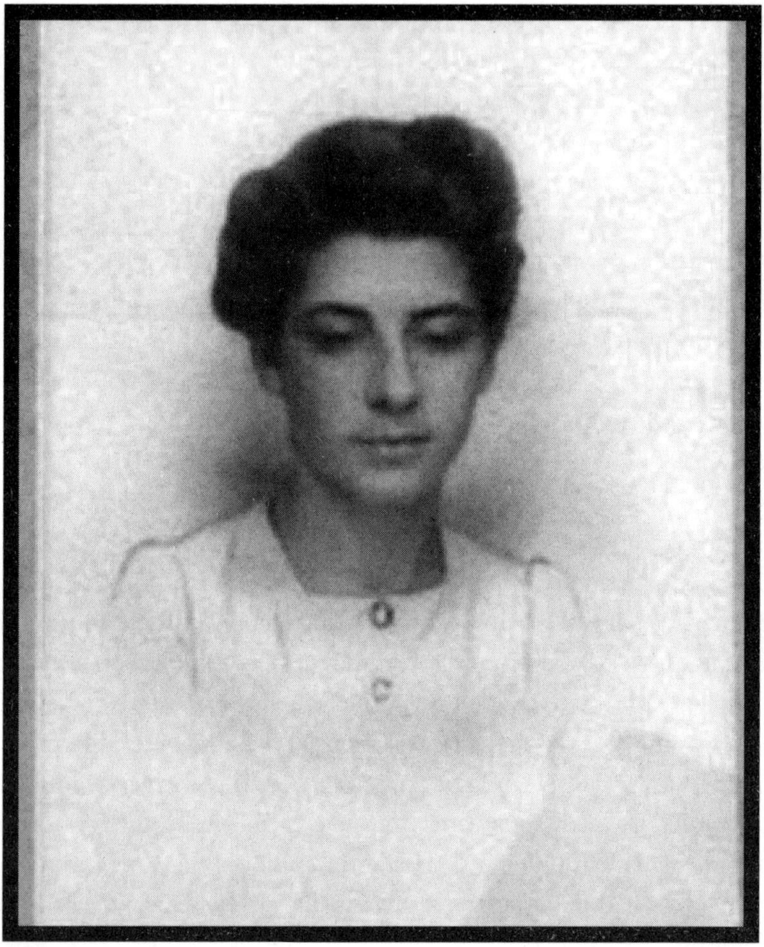

Janine Mongillat

own life preoccupied a large part of his painterly career. For Tyeb Mehta, Barnett Newman's singular division of the surface was to have a definitive influence. If we are to trace the trajectory of the figure, the introduction of the diagonal marks a watershed in Mehta's oeuvre. It took place on his return from the US, where he stayed for a year in 1971 sponsored by the Rockefeller Foundation. Eschewing non-representational art, however, he introduced these matt colours and the diagonal which fragmented and dynamized his figures. As they lunged downwards, the body splintered into pieces came together on the other side. There was a remarkable periscopic effect which electrified the entire picture space achieving a unity of the entire composition.

Raza's trajectory paralleled that of the Chinese-French painter Zao Wuo-Ki, who had not only been his colleague at the Academie des Beaux Arts and subsequently a fellow artist at the Galerie La France but had also travelled in a similar manner from Asia to Europe and then to North America. Zao's work also melded the work of European modernists and the Abstract Expressionists with his indigenous art, creating brilliant canvases with emphasis on light and colour. The journey of these two artists, where the blending of Eastern aesthetics and international art movements had resulted in works of heightened sensibility revealed the scope of post-War global abstraction.

Winds of Change

As he engaged with the new forms of abstract art in the US, Raza found that this mode of disengagement with representation was an entity which could take him to the core of his perceptions. As he stated, 'The pictorial values have always played a major role for me, in Bombay, in Paris, today as well, that is to say, the coordination of colour, lines, forms, their orchestration in space overshadowed the landscape that I painted in India and in France, or even much later when it had more of abstraction. ...In a nutshell, it means that one disregards the visual image but not emotion, feeling or the value of the subject. The most important, are the purely pictorial elements and their coordination. The colours are related to one another, they sing, they fight; they are violent, peaceful, harmonious, according to the intent of the artist ... It is this process, of delving into the core of emotion through visual perception that seems fundamental to me.'[29]

Raza revelled in this new-found freedom in his engagement with fluid brush strokes. Even as his palette changed to expressive use of colours and his medium changed from oil to acrylic, his gestural strokes began to stoke the inner recesses of his imagination unleashing a minefield of memories. 'Thereafter, visual reality, the aim to construct a "tangible" world, receded. In its place there was a preoccupation with evoking the essence, the mood of places and of people. Day and night, summer and winter, joy and anguish – these elementary experiences that are felt rather than seen, became my subjects. They were expressed through emotive colours and forms which became increasingly more gestural.'[30] An atmospheric mood of immersion in light and colour saturates the work *Summer* with its shimmering yellow. In *La Mer*, the aqueous blue textures seem to regurgitate a white brilliance and *La Forge* imbues the canvas with molten red and black embers churning a sensation of burning.

The hot, burning colours and the searing sensations of his land began to flood his canvases as freedom began to be accompanied by memory. Raza's tempestuous gestures, lent fluency by the use of acrylic, were like tongues of flame spiralling in all directions. The lashing reds, yellows and browns of the desert were re-created in *Rajasthan*, his world aflame with incandescent light. Rajasthan, awash with influences of Mewar and Malwa miniatures, is re-created again and again to resonate the recurring climate of experience. There is no recognizable shape, only the fluency of paint and its vibrant movement on the surface. The primary colours – red, yellow and blue – emerge along with white and black to be assembled and re-assembled, simulating the passion and violence of the land. In the later version of this painting such as *Saurashtra*, the frame of the painting, in streaks of red, black and yellow, emphasizes the iconization and the painterly qualities of the work. In the magnificent seven-foot high *Saurashtra* made in the early '80s, the burnished reds, earthy browns, sunset oranges and canary yellows are loosely bounded to create a symphonic composition.

The indigenous traditions of his country, where colours express moods, inform his work from this period onwards. Raza had always claimed an affinity with Rajasthani and Jain miniatures, as against the preciousness of Persian miniatures, and the raw, passionate colours of these schools were used to express contemporary reality. In a series of vibrant etchings made in the early '70s, where he expressed his anguish over the destruction of life in the Bangladesh War, the furious whirling pools of reds and blacks on one side are overtaken by an unending stream of blood red on the other or the blotchy red of the surface separates yellow and red and black on the other side – as the colours speak eloquently of brutal realities and their wider dimensions.

The dark of the forests, the flickering lights of the fireflies and the hidden sounds of night as always accompanied Raza's unfolding of memories. In *Forms of Darkness* (1981) the flashing white spaces emerging from the sombre, nuanced black are like resonances of the night. *Zamine* (1971), a larger painting, has a depth of darkness with its coal black, molten grey and earthy brown spread over the surface in loops, curlicues and wedges. In the in-between spaces, red, orange, yellow, green and white can be glimpsed like flashes in the dark. The expressive quality of black with its liquid intensity is highlighted making the night come alive. A blazing ember red emerges from the surrounding darkness in *Tapovan* (1972) and corralles into slivers of green, yellow and blue to create a dense experience of the night. *Tapovan*, or forest of meditation, is in many ways a triumph of Raza's mastery of nuanced abstractions and his spiritual and symbolic engagement with nature. The painting fuses landscape with abstract, symbolic forms into a powerful invocation of mystic expression. In another evocative painting, *La Terre* (1977), the interlocking reds and yellows with the deep blacks and browns create a dynamic surface that is charged with an imperceptible energy. He painted *La Terre* again and again, obsessed with its magnetism and its many-hued tonal variations. In one brooding example painted in the '80s, flaming colours are enveloped within the impending darkness and flit through its fluid surface creating a restless energy. These works reveal the changing shapes and the underlying rhythms of nature. According to Jacques Lassaigne, the art historian and chief curator of the Museum of Modern Art in Paris, 'For all the tragic intensity of its smouldering fires, and the flare of its greenery, the world of Raza hangs in a torrent of possibilities, amid the contending powers of darkness and light. Notwithstanding the storms of life, the artist, true to himself, has acquired the gift of serenity: he has achieved the inexpressible plenitude which, in the Arabian poem, is born of the reiterated syllable signifying night.'[31]

Colour and the absence of colour are equally fulsome for the artist, just as the brightness of the day is always followed by the haunting colours of night. It has to be noted that of this period with its fluency of strokes, evoking memories and desires, the dark paintings with their resonances of night and its throbbing movement on the surface are compelling compositions. It is as if the night with its vibrancy lends strength and energy to the day and creates the shapes and sounds which reverberate in his consciousness.

The interactions between Raza's earlier works and the new ideas of Abstract Expressionism were to lead to a great expansion in his viewpoint. In their planar dimensions, their evocation of the painterly surface and colour and their universalization, the new forms were eminently contemporary. Indeed, it was the very threshold of modernism that had been touched and the works were to lead to epiphanic compositions of light and colour.

Raza's work had begun to receive the approbation it deserved. He wrote delightedly to Karl, 'Here too we have participated in several shows including one at the Museum of Modern Art where to my great delight I saw my paintings hanging on the same wall as Hans Hofmann and Sam Francis.'[32] At last, he was in the league of the masters of abstract art in the international sphere!

A Moveable Feast

Raza's return to Paris brought in a more fluid and gestural style of his work. For instance, in paintings like *L'inconnu* (1972) two spaces are demarcated denoting a division of sensibility. In the upper part there is a swatch of brilliant red inscribed with a line in Devanagari script that reads: *Panth hone do aparachit. Pran rahane do akela.* (Let the path be unknown. Let the heart be left in solitude.) The lower part has a swirl of blue, brown, ochre, orange, red and a glimmering white and is encased in a flowing red border. It is the binary of light and colour that influences the artist. As he allows himself to wander, there is a conjoined vision which emerges. According to Geeti Sen, 'These pictures can be viewed, especially in retrospect, as works in transition – between two ways of treating the canvas, and of using both abstraction and the figurative.'[1] The outcome of this new direction would be seen at a later stage but for the moment the work showed a simmering unity between two diverging streams.

Initially, the city of Paris had provided a studio-cum-apartment on Avenue Secrétan to Raza. But by 1970, he and Janine moved into their own home which was part of an old sixteenth-century convent for nuns. A protected building, this is erected on the Rue de Charonne close to the Boulevard Voltaire. There is a quality of silence in the brown-grey stone building which stands solid with its thick walls even though it is in the midst of a busy city area. According to Raza, 'It was a convent for nuns and has been notified as a monument by the French Ministry of Culture. Actually we have two apartments. I have a room for myself, which is my studio and Janine, my wife, has the other apartment with a studio of her own. It is very important for me to be completely alone and undisturbed. I need to be alone when I am there at the studio; it is nothing short of a temple in the corner. I come to the studio. A few seconds of prayer. I look at what I have done the previous day. I sit down. I think and slowly start talking to myself. There is no hard and fast rule. I may not pick up the brush for half an hour or more if the ideas do not germinate or perception is not available. Once the inner urge is clear, I pick up the brush and start painting for a few hours. It is like being in a sacred space. Very often I seem to wonder and feel very humble.'[2]

Raza loved the building which was very different from the Boulevard Secrétan: a modern structure of glass and concrete. Even though it was a modest place he wrote delightedly to Krishen Khanna about it, 'I have been working at my studio about twelve hours a day. Not painting but cleaning and arranging it. We took charge on the 15th of April [1964] as was agreed and found that a lot of things were to be done. We cleaned the walls – it's all in stone. We have removed the false ceiling to get the beams apparent. It looks splendid. I am so happy Krishen that at last I have a studio and thank Providence and my dearest friends who helped to realize it.'[3] In this sixteenth-century ambience, with its high ceiling and thick walls, the hushed corridor and wooden panel doors, Raza and Janine were to set up home for the rest of their lives.

The poet Ashok Vajpeyi who visited this home several times wrote the following lines:

> Time is not the stairs in the sixteenth century building at Cite du
> Convent:
> made to fetch supplies from the neighbouring market,
> Time is the silence that lives in the veranda in front of your house,
> time is a thin hair that has broken off your brush,
> time is the expectation of mystery in your eyes

time is the vibration of flesh without any fuss
you go outside of time.
Time is the cloth that has been used many times to wipe
paint-stained hands,
Time is the statue of Nandi lying on the edge of Lake Phutera in
 Damoh
which looks at you unblinking even today
as if you are an ineffaceable point[4]

The Young and the Famous

In course of time, Raza was to make his studio in a part of the apartment and Janine was to buy the adjacent space to create her own space. Together they made it into an atmospheric living area which would be remembered by friends. It was here that they would frequently entertain visitors and hold soirées. Food, wine and conversation flowed; and as close acquaintances like Raissa Padamsee remember, Janine could whip up a good meal at a moment's notice. 'They were a real couple. She was organizing lots of dinners and concerts also … and Janine could organize a dinner in ten minutes. I have seen her once making a Charlotte – very nice to accompany a very sophisticated French dinner, and she put the things just like that – amazing! So, they could host a lot. And I remember my parents and I going to their place. I think she [Janine] was also very maternal to him because when she passed away she told someone, "Look after my Ra."'[5]

The young couple had many people visit them, including the musician Ravi Shankar, the sarangi player Ram Narayan and many others. Jean Duchesne recalls, 'We also had evenings – dinners. At that time, early … I remember evenings there, of talks about independence of East Pakistan – Bangladesh. I also remember an evening with Ravi Shankar – hosted by Raza … private concerts – lots of people invited…'[6] The artist Akkitham Narayanan said, 'In the beginning, Raza was very fond of music, so always there would be some musician – mostly instrumental – Ravi Shankar, Ali Akbar Khan. There was the vocalist, Amir Khan … the audience was mostly French, very few Indians. Mostly his friends … it was a house concert – sitting on the floor mostly … sometimes he would have cinema shows – Cinématheque – that was the place. Sometimes they would have an opening of a festival of cinema.'[7]

The journalist Dileep Padgaonkar would drop in and would entertain Raza and Janine with songs of Vitthal Panduranga. Raza recalled, 'I have been meeting them all through these years and at times at home when they ask me: "You are so attached to India, why don't you come back?" I tell them I am there. I have always been there. I never went elsewhere. I have the same heart and mind. If you don't believe me, ask the Narmada, ask the Vindhyachal and Satupura.'[8] Krishen Khanna too visited him often there and availed of his warmth and hospitality. By this time, Khanna had left his bank job and taken to painting full time. He described the event to Raza in a letter, 'I finally left the bank on 22nd November [1961]. Bal, Gai and Husain came at 3 o'clock to take me out. It was a regular ceremony. We went to Bombelli's and had coffee and Bal presented me with a gold tie pin the shape of a palette! I have been enjoying my freedom since then. I have never felt happier in my life and have been working with tremendous enthusiasm and zest.'[9] To mark the occasion, Raza in turn celebrated by having a dinner in Paris with his friends and toasted Krishen with champagne.

A constant visitor and, in many ways, a mentor was the French photographer Henri Cartier-Bresson. He was, as we know, a strong catalyst for Raza to come to Paris and search for structure in his work. His advice to Raza when he had met the latter in Kashmir in 1948 was of the need for construction in his paintings and Bresson had counseled him to study Cézanne, which had been singularly useful in terms of Raza's work. Bresson would visit Raza frequently and would take his photographs, which became master studies of the artist at work. He would also be present at his soirées enjoying the interaction with other Indian artists and feasting off the food he had grown used to in India.

Raza and Bresson's points of view converged in privileging the day to day, the ordinary events of life, 'When you have poetry which is highly sensitive, and a text, which is highly intellectual, it has its own pleasure, its own joy … But I have always given importance to life, day-to-day life… The starting point is always nature. Henri Cartier-Bresson photographed the moments of play of children, photographed peasants, tanks and rivers, people taking a bath. He was there on the day of Mahatma Gandhi's death. These photographs were taken on the spot, from life, sometimes of great men, sometimes of ordinary people.'[10] According to scholar and critic Michel Imbert, 'Cartier Bresson suggested that Raza visit France to improve his technique … with Cézanne and … he stayed always close to Cartier-Bresson. I remember when I was twelve or thirteen going for dinner in Paris … with Cartier-Bresson – it was amazing in the house in the Paris apartment with Rivoli … amazing people, famous writers and artists and around Janine … they knew a lot of people, they are the big, they were the first collectors of Raza's paintings in Paris and in Gorbio – they arrive from Paris, from Germany, from Norway. Not one person – many. Around Janine there were people of taste – they understood very quickly the importance of Raza's paintings.'[11]

One of the photographs he took of Raza remains unforgettable, 'There is another photograph of Raza from the late fifties, a second study, this time by Henri Cartier-Bresson which gives us another dimension to the artist. Considering that it is a photograph only six years later, the difference is remarkable. The mood is stark, sombre, almost austere. He stands alone in his studio, more mature perhaps (with a crew cut) and looks subdued. The gaze is reflective, inward-looking. Yet for all this, he seems more assured of himself, and responsible for his position. The common factor is a quiet determination which is evident in both the portraits.'[12] Raza wrote a grateful letter to him, 'Do you know the immense joy you did by coming and doing me the portrait I needed so much. I like it very much indeed and let me tell you again that I will respect your conditions: integral reproduction without cut or retouch of the photograph you have marked. I know it is difficult to repay … but if it pleases you, I should like you to choose one of my paintings during this year – if you find something that pleases you and Ratna. The catalogue is under print. I have put a lot of work on it, a lot of effort really and I hope the result will not be bad…'[13]

Bresson was not only a photographer of heightened sensibility but was a friend, philosopher and guide to many artists from this part of the world. If he had been instrumental in Raza's growth as a painter, he was also very close to the Sri Lankan artist George Keyt and had encouraged and prompted him too to exhibit in Paris. He and his Javanese wife, the dancer Ratna Mohini, had been one of the most sought-after couples in the Parisian social circles of those days. Bresson was known to take timeless photographs of life's fleeting moments, such as his iconic photo series on Mahatma Gandhi.

The art critic Waldemar George would visit Raza and discuss his work for hours, interviewing him and writing about his work in appreciative though not uncritical terms. Later, Raza got acquainted with the art historian Jacques Lassaigne who wrote about two of his exhibitions and gave him good advice. 'He was very much for abstract painting and my landscapes were far too figurative. I remember him telling me, "You must go beyond this. I am sure you will."'[14] Lassaigne had served as president of the International Association of Art Critics and as the chief curator of the Museum of Modern Art, Paris from 1971-78. He was known chiefly for his books on art, some of which had been translated into English. Raza was also visited by the young critic and curator Pierre Gaudibert who served as the first curator of the contemporary art section of the Museum of Modern Art, Paris but later left because of his criticism of the President Georges Pompidou. 'He appreciated my works, acquired them for the museums and wrote two or three articles which were published and whose ideas also influenced my work.'[15] The elegant Dominique de Villepin who was ambassador in India from 1989-92, a poet and an aesthete, also visited Raza and engaged with his work both then and later when he was the prime minister of France from 2005-07.

A fellow student Pierre Henri from the École des Beaux-Arts and his wife Josette were regular visitors as well and would also travel with the young couple. According to Raza, 'It was Henri who initiated me into the French mind, French aesthetics and a certain attitude to realistic painting which was also prevalent at that time.'[16]

Flow of Indian Artists

Even if it was past the time of the greats of modern art, Paris continued to attract a host of artists from Asia and other countries who came to sharpen their tools and create their own trope of modernism. Apart

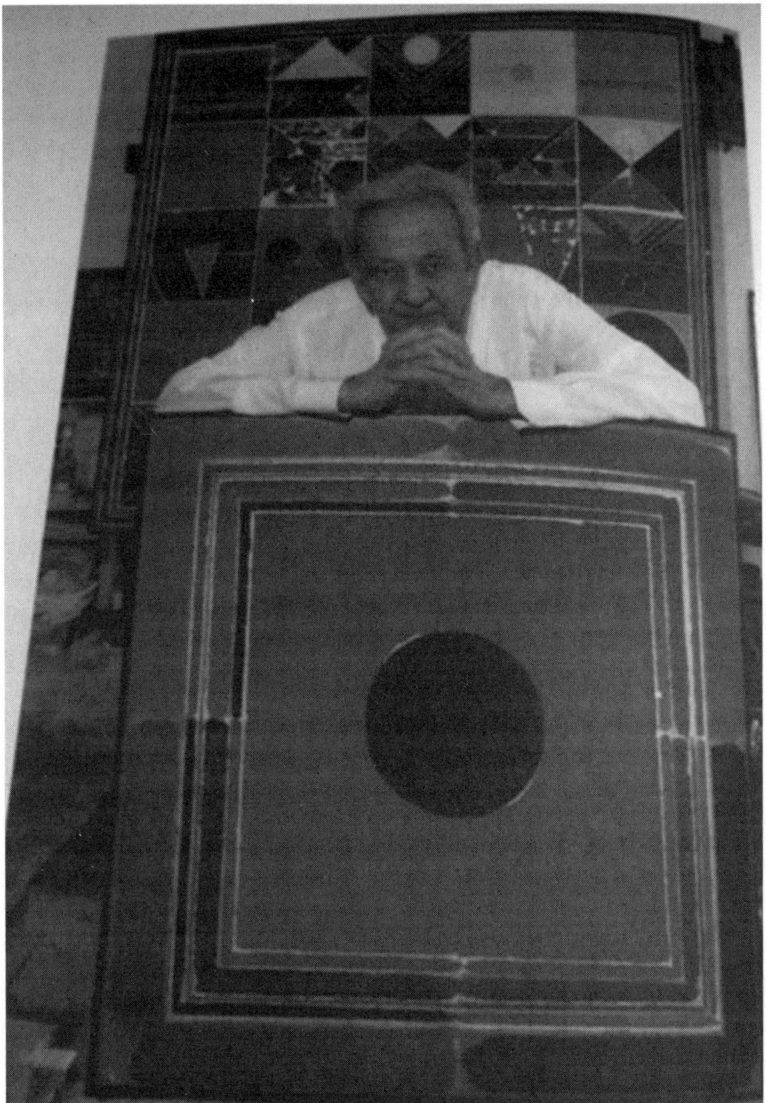

Raza with his Bindu painting.

from Amrita Sher-Gil, a whole generation of artists were to converge in the city from India in the '50s and '60s. This was partly an act of decolonization where they were to free themselves from the colonizing influence in their home country inasmuch to establish their own personal and national identities. Art historian Devika Singh points out, 'But the number of Indian artists living in France significantly increased after the Second World War... Whereas the city may no longer have been the uncontested centre of the art world after the Second World War, many foreign artists seem to have benefited from the freedom of representation Paris afforded... Moreover, one of the characteristics of Paris is that it had nurtured the avant-garde movements shunned by colonial art education and whose legacy Indian artists claimed – knowing that art schools often remained, even after 1947, the inheritors of colonial curricula... In this context, embracing European movements partook of an agenda of cultural deconization.'[17] Ironically, the somewhat asymmetrical relationship with France in India because of its colonial gaze was matched by the freedom of thought and representation that Indian artists acquired in France.

The Santiniketan-trained Krishna Reddy (1925-2018) had also come to Paris in 1950 after being a student of Henry Moore at the Slade School of Fine Art, London. In Paris, he worked under the sculptor Ossip Zadkine, following which he joined Stanley William Hayter's Atelier 17 in 1951. At Hayter's Atelier 17, Reddy initially assisted Joan Miró in attempting a multicoloured print that could be made in one instance, where the tedium of several inkings and registrations could be avoided. While Miro left this process, Reddy along with Kaiko Moti kept at it until they eventually created the first multicoloured viscosity print. The thick textural work, almost hand-moulded, was somewhat akin to sculpture. Reddy's discovery of the principle of colour viscosity has greatly simplified technical processes while at the same time increasing the expressiveness and intensity of the image.[18]

Krishna Reddy felt that it was at Atelier 17 that he encountered a cross-section of artists from all over the world. His disquiet with Paris began with the 1968 student revolt, which he expressed in iconic works like *Demonstrators* (1968) where rows of protesters stand like a barricade in an almost abstract composition of limpid ochre and black. Although he was to leave Atelier 17 and Paris shortly afterwards, he found it a magical place of interaction with people of various colours and practices of which he benefited considerably. Reddy was to leave for New York in 1974 where he would engage with the Abstract Expressionist wave which was to overtake the art world. According to his wife and fellow artist, Judith Reddy, 'Krishna never really left Paris in his heart and mind. He felt rooted there and would visit it every year to reconnect.'[19] Reddy's own affinity with the vast universe of nature led him to make works of studied elegance and lushness of water, forests, vegetation and even tiny insects. He passed away in 2018 but left behind a legacy which needs to be recognized for its richness of details and sensuous preoccupations.

Although both Raza and Krishna arrived in Paris in the same year, they had in fact come from two different regions in India – Bombay and Santiniketan. Their paths crossed in Paris where they would meet occasionally and exchange ideas. While Raza's work began to resonate with Indian philosophy and forms after a period, Reddy chose to use his Indian experiences as a springboard for further aesthetic expansion.

Also in Paris from 1963-67 was the intrepid Zarina Hashmi who had previously worked with woodcuts in Thailand. She had joined Atelier 17 as a student under Krishna Reddy, and went on to become the Associate Director. This was followed by studying woodblock printing in 1974 at Tōshi Yoshida's studio in Tokyo. She was awarded residencies at Art Omi and at the Women's Studio Workshop in Rosendale, both in New York – where she eventually settled. Hashmi's engagement with the politics of space reflects her own extensive travels and the multiple meanings that the word 'home' came to hold for her. As an artist who was dislocated after Partition, her minimalist work challenges familiar locations like 'country' – the ways in which they are bordered, delimited and traversed, and evoke the memory of being rooted and then set adrift. These locations are used to construct new geographies, imbuing them with fresh perspectives in a globalized world. As Kalidas Swaminathan points out, 'In many works over the last decade or more, Zarina keeps returning to the notion of the "self" in transience through time and place. She seems to have so internalized the "act of journeying" that it manifests in her work in multiple ways. So from the "line drawn across her heart" that divides India and Pakistan, to the places she visited with her sister (as in *Travels with Rani*), to cities she had lived in or travelled through or had seen in conflict (as in *Cities, Countries and Borders*) – all make for an opus of works on paper that weave a vulnerable thread of personal history within the harsher grid of geopolitical time-space.'[20]

Also living in Paris since the mid '50s is Sakti Burman who studied at the École Nationale des Beaux Arts in Paris. Perhaps the only figurative painter from India based in Paris, Burman's use of pointillism and a marbling technique achieved by blending oils with acrylics to create fresco-like works on paper and canvas are unique. His paintings evoke multiplicities of time and place peopled with dreamlike narratives.

Among the slew of artists who made it to Paris from India in the '60s and '70s, Rajendra Dhawan and Velu Vishwanadhan retained a remarkable consistency and unique point of view. For Raza, who befriended both artists, especially the former, there was a close bond and yet a sense of being outstripped by their presence which he sometimes overcame with contesting methods. Both artists used colour as their etymology and created diverse and distinctive forms which began to draw attention.

In the case of Rajendra Dhawan's brooding, sombre creations in cerulean blue, coal black and amber, there was a sense of wading into unknown depths. Unlike Raza or Vishwanadhan he did not claim an indigenist abstraction but painted for its own sake where colours melded together, moving seamlessly into each other. According to the painter and writer Alain Umhauer, who was a close friend, 'It was much more difficult for Dhawan to come out with his paintings in Paris, because the Indian painter was Raza – known for Tantric art. And in the '70s this way of painting had a big success all over Europe because that was the time American people, European people were going to Auroville, Goa etc. … Dhawan was a real abstract artist and he had much more struggle with being recognized.'[21] The comparatively difficult economic situation of Dhawan's family had been compounded by the fact that his daughter had learning disabilities and needed special care.

V. Vishwanadhan's abstract shapes in blazing reds, blacks and greens created a hard-edged tension in their juxtapositions even as their format had diaphanous depths which involve submergence. The jagged divisions of space consisted of accretions of paint which retained a casein-encased glowing density. The primary colours themselves harked back to the creation of mandalas on the earth which he witnessed as a child in his village as well as the later divisions of space within the paradigms of modernism. The artist divides his time between Cholamandal and Paris, even as his work creates a fusion between Indian and French aesthetics. His formulation of earth from different countries were part of a larger project of the five basic elements which constitute human sensibility and films made by him like *Panch Bhooth* which is a five-part series, as well as *Ganga* and *Back to Elements*. The return to essentials like the elements, which is universal and humanizing, impelled the basic drive behind his works.

In a shared but yet very different sensibility is the Malayali painter Akkitham Narayanan, also based in Paris. His paintings are abstract configurations with a fusion of Indian Tantric and European geometric art. The artist composes the picture plane with a division of space into triangles and rectangles which convey a lyrical, emotive experience. The strong reds, yellows and greens are amorphous and smudged in some areas and sharp in others. Within these forms, thin lines suggestive of the forms of cloud and elements like fire and water can be discerned. Also visible are archaic lines reminding one of calligraphic forms.

Making It on His Own

Raza's own career was on the rise even as he left Galerie Lara Vincy in 1971 and launched out on his own. During this time, his friends Bernard and Rashna Imhasly once hosted a show of his paintings in their home in Delhi so that people could come see and buy them. As Raza wrote to Krishen Khanna, 'Rashna plans to release my book in Delhi with a reception in her home. I am suggesting the dates 12th or 20th February. I am bringing two large and five or six small canvases rolled up with me.'[22] Bernard and Rashna (Kekoo and Khorshed Gandhy's daughter) were quite close to Raza and availed their hospitality during many of his visits to Delhi. According to Rashna Imhasly, 'It was featured in *Inside Outside* because it was a Charles Correa house where we had the show. In this house we had a Raza show… You know we used to have that Kunika Chemould shop in Cottage Industries and there's no gallery there anymore… She [Khorshed] wanted to have a Raza show in Delhi so since we've moved to that big house she said, "Can we have a show there and in the evening with cocktails?" We said, "Why not?" Again it was a sell-out. I was so scared. We didn't have clientele in Delhi and [I thought] will we sell enough? Usually these Raza shows were the money earners. We sold everything!'[23]

House by the Sea

In the mid '60s Raza and Janine bought a summer home-cum-studio in Gorbio, a village close to Menton in the south of France. They travelled to Menton where Janine's parents had an apartment and searched around for a place with the element that was most important to Raza: nature.

He once stated, 'We had a studio apartment in the city of Paris. Everything was going in such a way that we had a residence in Paris and also in Gorbio, a small medieval village in southern France which became our summer residence. It meant a lot to me to be able to concentrate and do my work. Living in a great city was a strain although there were beautiful places. I thought that it was imperative for me to go out of the city and to be in a place which was closer to nature, trees and mountains, water, flowers and hills. I think this is also due to the fact that I retain a longing for my childhood days, for the forests of Madhya Pradesh. My wife and I had travelled all through France to choose a place that was in the south because of the warmer climate; secondly, because the village was remote from big cities and we could isolate ourselves and work. We bought a plot there, built up a studio in stone in the style of the ancient villages all around southern France. I must say that sitting on the ground, talking to plants and leaves, being with nature under three or four olive trees and numerous hibiscus and bougainvillea and having a view of the Mediterranean sea amongst the mountains is a rare treat. We spend three or four months every year in the village and then come back to Paris and work.'[1]

The couple settled in Gorbio close to the France–Italy border where the picturesque landscape of the Maritime Alps with the mountains and their sheer drop to the Mediterranean sea evoked memories of India for Raza. Immersed in the hauntingly beautiful village, he painted many of his luminous paintings like *Rajasthan* and *Saurashtra*, among others.

Perched on the side of a hill, with steep-sloped valleys covered with trees and olives growing all over the village and a stunning view of the Mediterranean, Gorbio is an idyllic place for an artist. The main square in the village, which is frequented by its small population, has a grand 300-year-old elm tree with an enormous trunk where many people hang around. The main square also has the nineteenth-century Malaussene fountain, once an important source of water for the village. The cobbled streets and the medieval houses built mostly in the fourteenth to sixteenth centuries, winding through Gorbio, make it a place full of memory and desire.

Back to the Twelfth Century

At first they moved into a medieval twelfth-century house which was renovated painstakingly by them and made comfortable. The studio was constructed by them meticulously at a little distance, near the village square. As Raza wrote to Krishen Khanna, 'I am sitting under my beloved olive tree, in front of a small red canvas, and paints and brushes that are calling to me irresistibly … I have undertaken many repairs in the small piece of land where my studio was built and which now is a little paradise. It is extraordinary that we have been able to make it with meager means, in the most traditional French provincial style, "lieu de travail", "un espace vital", which along with our home up in the village is a very convenient and working solution. I am so happy being nearer to nature, with my trees and plants, with my cat, Bona – a village cat who came to us as if from heaven. I also spend a lot of time in the garden, drawing from the earth and admiring the mysteries and energy of the Life Force manifest all over.'[2]

The place was filled with magic and for Raza it was redolent of a childhood spent in the midst of lush nature and the forests. Yet it had taken several years to renovate and restore the old stone house and the stable below into a habitable space. To this day, the ground floor has a leather-bound visitor's book with entries from guests dating back to the twelfth century.

While restoring the house they stayed at Michel Imbert's, the art scholar based in Gorbio, which was situated directly opposite the stone house. They were to stay at Michel's place for a long time for the renovation of their house was for an extended period. They bought the house in 1958 and renovated it for seven years, moving in there around 1965. The young Michel's parents had known Raza and Janine since before he was born. They had met him when Raza had first come to Gorbio in 1956 – they visited the village and met his grandmother in the square, at the bottom of the castle house and immediately struck a friendship with her. 'It was my grandmother who introduced my father and mother to Raza. They were on the square and she invited them when she saw Raza and Janine – she had quickly a good feeling. My mother remembers that when they came for the first time they were not married. And my grandmother asked Raza – "Is this your wife?" And Raza said, "My future wife!" And Janine laughed and said "I wait a long time and hopefully your grandmother ask this question..." Raza said also my grandmother is like his mother, because his mother was no longer alive. And he always stayed close to my grandmother.'[3]

Michel further remembers, 'Raza would arrive each morning – my mother and father would go to Raza's house and discuss and exchange news every day – and at the end of each day when Raza and Janine came back from the studio, they would stop here and have tea or something and have another discussion. I always saw the four around me in discussion – about life, about work... They learn with Raza and Janine – it was a meeting of minds.'[4]

So when he was born in 1962 he would always see Raza and Janine around him.

'Because I open my bedroom and go into the living room across, and it was Raza's studio ... they would stay long periods in Gorbio because the light reminded him of Rajasthan and he made some paintings of that name in Gorbio.'[5]

The young Michel Imbert, who grew up seeing Raza paint in the next room, also learnt a lot about art from him and, later, wrote a book on the artist, *Raza: An Introduction to his Paintings*. According to Michel, Raza looked forward to coming to Gorbio, 'Mainly because in Paris he has exhibition, preparation, galleries. In Gorbio, you must understand it's work time because he was alone in meditation in front of the mountains. If you look at paintings of 1970 – you will see this is mountains – it's very close. When he's in Gorbio he likes to relax, walk in the country, go up, go everywhere for fresh air, relax, have good local food, enjoy life, and … It was the best period for him to create – more than in Paris. His most important paintings he did in Gorbio because it was really a time for work. Sometimes he stayed six months.'[6]

It was only when Janine died that things changed drastically for Michel, as Raza became distant and no longer sought his company. In the end, when Raza left for India he and his mother lost the close contact they had with the family for decades. And yet, when asked what did he take away from his close association with Raza, Michel always says that he got a treasure in terms of knowledge and sensitivity.

As Michel continues to teach art and at the same time works for the Art Museum of Menton and advises on Raza's paintings for art auctions and museums, his rich childhood experiences provide him with a continuous basis for expansion.

Studio of Stones

The climb up the narrow winding streets to their medieval house proved, however, quite difficult for Raza and Janine. So, they sold it to Raza's Norwegian collectors, Mr and Mrs Bergen around 1997, and moved to the studio where they built some more rooms and decided to stay there as well. The construction was done with stones, which they acquired from near the river and the tiled roof completed the feeling of an aged house, which was what Raza liked and felt most at home in. The façade of the dwelling had a ceramic work with blue concentric circles by Raza. The ground floor was the studio and the bedroom, kitchen, dining and drawing room were upstairs. The green sylvan surroundings of Gorbio allowed them to live and work in peace for a few months in the summer each year. Many important works of Raza were painted here. Their friends frequently visited them here to also enjoy the peaceful environment and keep them company. Mijo and Jean Paul Roussel, for instance, were frequent visitors. An architect and photographer, Jean Paul had animated discussions with Raza regarding the studio in Gorbio when it was being expanded with old stones by the river. Their chateau in Normandy houses some masterly works by the artist couple. Paul even has photographs of the artist and his friends as a memento of those halcyon days.

Here at last was the perfect place to work in repose and fulfilment. Descriptions of the studio seem idyllic. The evocative quality of his Gorbio studio is described thus by Geeti Sen: 'Raza's studio is built of rough-hewn stone with dark oak for the doors and window panes. The patio is laid out with four large stone slabs to sit and view the garden: to meditate. You can hear the call of birds and crickets and the rustling bells of sheep as they climb the mountainside.'[7]

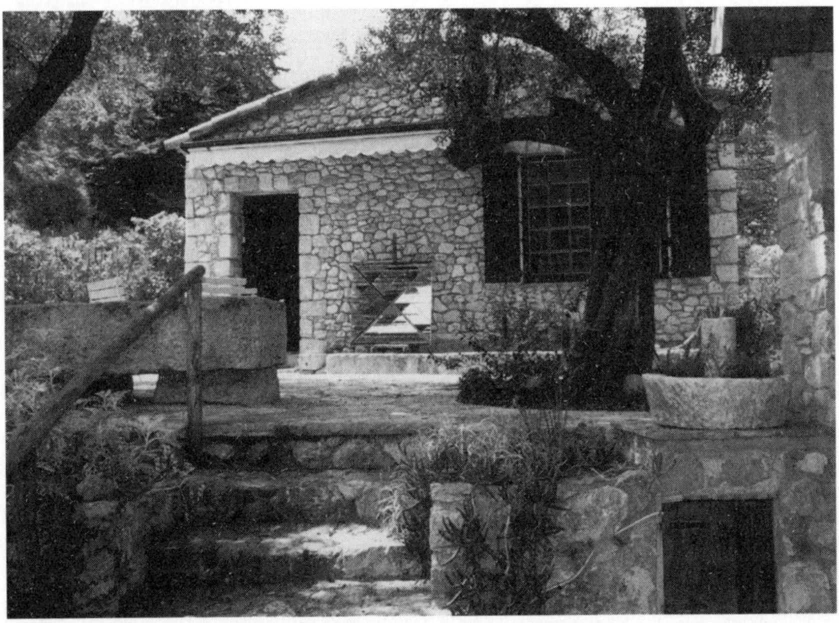

Raza's studio in Gorbio.

It is a rather idyllic garden. 'In this garden of two levels there are variegated greens: the grey-silver of olive, the yellow-green of bamboo, the bottle-green of spiky palm, and the deep intensity of two slender poplars thrusting up into the sky… At night the air is sparked with these perfumes…'[8] The inside was equally magical, 'Within the studio light shimmers from the trees outside and falls upon the window sill that runs one length of wall. Along this sill are arranged various minute objects: a clay lamp and a horned mask from Tunisia, a brass lota from India, a tribal bronze from Raza's home state of Madhya Pradesh, a wooden figure from the eaves of a temple in Gujarat, a few pots with cactus, a pair of Tibetan gongs which when brought together, sound with a deep resonance.'[9]

The couple would wander about painting wherever their fancy took them. 'Outside, Raza sits in the stone patio near the door leading to his studio, in the open air, his paints on the floor, his blank canvas placed on a wooden easel or sometimes on the floor. Janine, his wife and an established artist, is to be found in another part of the garden, working on her collage of assembled tea bags or assembled paper, or occasionally preparing lunch in the kitchen. If Raza's paintings of this time are now pared to their essence, Janine's work takes on the challenge of further complexities: of exploration into new areas and medium of experiment.'[10]

Lured by the romance of Gorbio many friends, artists and collectors would pay frequent visits to Raza and Janine, and continued to remember it for its calm and beauty. An enduring tale is of Ms Erika Blöchlinger, a German philanthropist who ran a home for animals in Bern. She had bought a masterly work of Raza's and cherished it. In her old age, she wanted to sell it for a modest sum and donate it to an animal home while she herself was seeking an exit. A friend of Bernard and Rashna Imhasly, Erika's act could not be more moving: 'Recently, this summer, we visited one of my old people who's in meditation. She had started the Swami Nityananda group in Bern. She had bought a work of Raza. She's very old – now in the last stages of her life. We saw the Raza she had bought and we said, do you know how much it's worth? She said, I bought it for 3,000 francs. I negotiated it and it went for 250,000 francs! She wanted to sell it… She's going to take exit end of this year. She said my body is not working anymore. I want to leave my body. Erika has an NGO for animals and wanted the money to go into that. She's in an old people's home in Switzerland.'[11]

In another account Raza wrote to Krishen about a collector, 'Last week on Wednesday [1987], Henning Larsen [the Danish architect] visited us in Gorbio, with Maneka, a French dancer. We had a great day together, talking about everything on earth. He looked at the painting, we lunched in the village restaurant, and he climbed up the village to see our house, an old peasant farm, dating back to the 14th century. He will go back to Geneva to see the Indian exhibition…'[12]

The exhibition mentioned above in Geneva was the one organized by Helen and Guy Barbier. Guy Barbier had first visited India in 1978 and set up Arthur Andersen & Co. Subsequently, he and his wife Helen and their children made frequent visits and were caught by the myriad manifestations of the country and, in particular, with its modern and contemporary art. They had also visited Raza and Janine in France and bought some of the former's works. The couple is mentioned by Ram in a letter to Raza, 'You might have met a French man called Mr Barbier whose wife is starting a Gallery in Geneva and they want to exhibit Indian artists. I wonder, what response they will get. I have been invited to exhibit about seven pictures in October 1985.'[13]

The Barbiers in fact held a large and successful show *Coups de Coeur* in Geneva in 1987. As Helen wrote about it for an exhibition and auction catalogue of Sothebys in 2019, '*Coups de Coeur* was inspired by a dinner conversation where we lamented that within the narrative of the Festival, there was to be no expression of contemporary art. Guy Barbier objected to this and the result was upon his arrival home, to announce that he had volunteered me to organize a contemporary art exhibit from a collector's point of view – to open in six months, coinciding with the other events under the umbrella of the Festival of India.'[14] The exhibition consisted principally of their collection along with that of Chester and Davida Herwitz, Krishna Riboud, Gurcharan Das and others. It kindled Raza's vision when he visited it, '…I will send you the catalogue of the exhibition *Coups de Coeur* organized by Mrs Helen Barbier. I attended the show on 1st July [1987], and it was indeed very well presented … The figurative dominated, but with sufficiently significant work. You had four large paintings [Krishen Khanna], formally sound and charged with feelings, which went beyond the narrative preoccupations of many others. I truly liked them … I was not so well represented with the three canvases they chose from the Chester collection. I did not complain; I only look at the positive side of things and know that this exhibition, as also the shows in London, Oxford, Paris, New York and Washington, are important manifestations and that contemporary Indian art will soon establish its presence on the world map in a big way.'[15]

It could be said that this was among the few memorable exhibitions that placed Indian modern and contemporary art in the international arena.

An artist who kept in touch with Raza since his early days in Paris as a student was Pierre Henri. Like Raza, Pierre and his wife Josette had bought a studio-cum-living space in Le Ponteil at Saint-Paul-La-Coste and would spend their summer there painting and meeting friends. Their frequent correspondence points to a great deal of conviviality and sharing of ideas. Raza and Janine would often drop in on them on their way to Gorbio and spend a companionable day or two. On one occasion Raza wrote to them, 'I keep thinking of you. Thank you again for your encouragement and help in constructing a roof over our house in Gorbio.'[16] 'We have made Pierre's studio into a small oasis with curtains cutting out the excess brightness and glare and an entirely pink waxed floor – in short, a place where masterpieces are created on their own! …So you see, Le Ponteil is truly getting even better and better every day. We forsee that by next year, a Shakespeare or a Marivaux, depending on the mood and the class of the participants around, to surface somewhere in the Le Ponteil vicinity. Can we count on you being present then?'[17]

Raza-Mongillat Museum

In an adjoining tower in Gorbio known as Tour Lascaris, which is all that remains from the more substantial Chateau des Lascaris that stood there since the twelfth century, there is a small museum dedicated to the Raza-Mongillat collection. The Tour Lascaris had been built to keep vigil over invaders in medieval times. Raza had approached the city mayor, Michel Isnard, also an artist, to house their vast collection of antiquities, artefacts, works of Indian artists and the paintings made by him and his wife. He donated one million euros to the foundation to house and showcase this collection for thirty years after which they could keep it or place it elsewhere but he hoped that it would be the former. According to Mr Isnard, the interest of this yields 40,000 euros which pays for the running of the place. Yet the generous donation did not fail to arouse controversy. According to Mr Isnard, 'He was mostly close to like-minded people… I had organized a meeting of a large group to speak about donations and those who came agreed to make it. But the municipality did not agree.'[18]

The *Independent* reported about this in great detail:

> The village quarrel is an art form in France but a poisonous village quarrel about art is somewhat unconventional.
>
> A generous would-be bequest from an internationally celebrated artist has convulsed the beautiful village of Gorbio, close to the Mediterranean and to the Franco-Italian border. Sayed Haider Raza, a much admired Indian-born artist who has lived in the hill village for 50 years, offered to give Gorbio 20 of his own paintings, worth several million euros.
>
> He also offered €900,000 to create a foundation to help the village to look after them. In return, he asked that the paintings, and some by his late wife, should be shown for a minimum of 50 years in a medieval tower which is Gorbio's pride and joy.[19]

The paper points towards fractious local politics:

> The mayor was delighted. A majority of villagers signed a petition which enthusiastically welcomed the gift. But the village council voted this week by 10 votes to two to refuse Mr Raza's conditions.
>
> The assistant mayor, and political opponent of the mayor, Patrick Truchi, explained: 'Perhaps in half a century, Raza will be considered another Picasso … On the other hand, this stuff may not be worth a rabbit's fart.'
>
> Mr Truchi said that he and his supporters accepted the principle of the gift but could not accept the idea that two of the three floors in

> the Tour Lascaris, a recently restored medieval gem in the centre of the village, should become a shrine to Mr Raza's work.

Others however were of a different view:

> 'We are being offered an exceptional opportunity,' protested the mayor, Michel Isnard, himself an artist. 'How can we let that go begging?'
>
> The future of the artist's collection of his own work, plus several canvases by other painters, including Fernand Léger, will now be one of the key issues in the Gorbio municipal elections next March.[20]

As the newspaper pertinently pointed out:

> On the other hand, how can a village which lives partly on income from tourism refuse an opportunity to be placed on the artistic map of the world?
>
> Mr Raza, 85, is considered to be one of the greatest living Indian artists. One of his canvases was sold recently by Sotheby's for more than a million dollars. His work – both abstract and landscapes – is said to combine the rich colours of Indian art with the 'modernist', geometrical approach of European art of the 20th century.
>
> The artist is travelling abroad and has not made any comment on the controversy back home.
>
> 'They're a bunch of imbeciles,' said a restaurateur in the village. 'What will Raza think when he finds out?'[21]

On visiting it in 2016, we found that of the nineteen Raza paintings in the collection, seventeen of his were on display including the resplendent *La Terre* and a number of Janine's works as well. According to Mr Isnard, *La Terre* had been bought by the village and presented to the municipality. The Raza-Mongillat foundation has many plans to expand but as yet has not fully come into being. According to Michel Isnard, there were plans to turn his studio into an artist's residency but that has not fructified either, as the inheritor is not willing to part with it.

However, in the time Raza spent there which was well over four decades, his name and image has been well established in the village.

He is remembered for visiting the nearby village church, the Church of Saint-Barthélemy, built in the seventeenth century with a baroque-style painted façade and a colourful patterned roof on the clocktower.

He went there everyday for his daily prayers and attended the Sunday mass as well. He would also do his weekly shopping there and stop by at the Imberts for a cup of tea.

Michel remembers that in 1978 Raza's exhibition had been held at the Presbyterian church where clergymen lived, as there was no other space. But now exhibitions were held at the castle which was bought in 2001. The main exhibitions held here had been of Raza, Janine, Marze and Franta, who was a well-known artist from Czechoslovakia. Three exhibitions were held in Gorbio of this group, of which Isnard was the youngest. Though not a collective, there was an attempt by these artists to meet and discuss ideas and show jointly. For Raza, who had great nostalgia for his Progressive Artists' days in Bombay, this was an event he looked forward to but it didn't last for long.

Apart from Raza, Janine and Michel Isnard, there was Emile Marze from Menton whose retrospective was on display at the Chateau. Another artist who was part of this group was Franta and the Castle had three works by him. Perhaps what attracted Raza to François Franta was his tumultuous life which had led him to make works of figures in exile, touched by human suffering. Born in Moravia in Czechoslovakia in 1930, his growing-up years had experienced the political drama of the time. In 1958, he had escaped to the West and after a period of difficulties in refugee camps in West Germany, he had settled in the Nice area, which is where he met Raza and the two quickly became friends. Emile Marze, on the other hand, is known for his painting and sculpture which though have the signifying form, they also point towards a supra-reality. The Hungarian artist Antal Biro, who made abstract, symbolist works was also settled nearby and had exhibited at the Menton Biennale. Among the artists there, it was he who had the greatest affinity with Raza in his approach to colours which he felt had a symbolic meaning. Biro had settled in Menton in 1964 and had even opened a yoga school in Menton to ensure his livelihood after a visit to India where he acquainted himself with yoga and Indian philosophy.

Michel Isnard himself is a painter who turns his eye to the village and to his life there. His figures in their medieval settings but with their contemporary stances seem to bestow a special significance to the village. Many of these are reflective of his own experiences of Gorbio, which he arrived in some forty-odd years ago as a stranger.

Le Corbusier and Cap-Martin

Raza could not have chosen a more artistic area to spend half a year in. The site now known as Cap Moderne consists of the villa of the Irish designer Eileen Gray, and the French architect Le Corbusier's Cabanon and holiday cottages, and the bar-restaurant Étoile de Mer, which are now almost mythical architectural icons in an atmosphere of great natural beauty.

This was, after all, the region where Corbusier (1887-1965) had spent many years. Raza does not mention him but it is unlikely that the two did not meet as he had become a magnetic draw in the area. The year that Raza left for Paris in 1950, Corbusier was appointed Adviser to the government of Punjab for the construction of its new capital city which came to be known as Chandigarh. In the following year during his first visit to India, Le Corbusier went to Chandigarh and Ahmedabad and presented the monument 'The Open Hand' of Chandigarh and started work on projects for the Assembly, the High Court, the Governor's Palace, the Secretariat and the Museum. Not much later in 1952, he built his home Cabanon at Roquebrune-Cap-Martin. This was the only building Le Corbusier had ever built for himself and it was a simple but ingenious beach hut. The Cabanon was completed in 1952, and it became his main holiday home until his death.

The story behind this is equally beguiling. The French architect had first come to Cap-Martin in the 1930s to visit his friend Eileen Gray, the reputed Irish designer who had built a house here and he loved the area and continued to visit it frequently. But trouble brewed when during one of his stays he decided to paint the interior of Gray's villa without her permission. On discovering this, Gray was furious for she felt that Le

Corbusier's paintings had ruined the perspectives of her design. Moreover, she was offended by the subject matter which was that of two women in an embrace, for Gray was a lesbian.

Since he was no longer welcome as a guest, Le Corbusier did come back to Gray's villa in 1949, but as a tenant. It was during that stay that he met Robert Rebutato, owner of L'Étoile de Mer, the café next door where he ate his meals. Friendship blossomed between the two men, and in 1951 they agreed on the construction of a beach house next door to L'Étoile de Mer so that Le Corbusier could have his own space. The Cabanon was designed using the Modulor, a mathematical benchmark based on the height of a man with his arms up. While the Cabanon became infamous for its minimal design and rather hard-edged brutalist setting, the architect proudly claimed that he had a chateau in Cote d'Azur! He worked there every August for eighteen years, sketching and making notes. It was there that he designed his most famous building, the chapel of Notre Dame du Haut in Ronchamp. Corbusier was found dead in the sea off Cap-Martin in 1965.

And it was in this area that the artistic world of Raza and Corbusier would collide, for the stone cottage designed by Raza and Janine was an equally imaginative and nurturing place where the couple spent the summers of the rest of their lives together.

The Indian Eye

In his exploration of colour and its emotive qualities, Raza was to stumble upon his childhood memories and the vast universe of inchoate experience. The floodgates of the past were now opened and there would be no holding back. As he stated, 'I have never really left the deeply rooted, wonderful world of forest and rambling river, hill and sparkling stream. The time spent as nature's child. You see, we lived in the country's core, in Barbaria, Madhya Pradesh, where my father was a forest ranger, and in Mandla afterwards. The lush Kanha thickets were my regular haunts. Highly impressionable at that tender age, I soaked in every single feature of that beautiful landscape. So, I let my mind wander. But that was precisely the problem. It wandered excessively, making me, I'm afraid, the worst, most distracted pupil in my class. So that was when it happened – my introduction to a certain idea which was later to become my leitmotif, an integral part of my art, the very backbone supporting my body of work. This was the concept of the Bindu. How can I ever thank my beloved school teacher Nandlal Jharia? He left an absolutely indelible mark on me. Noticing my restlessness, it was he who made me wait behind suddenly one evening, facing one of the whitewashed walls of the classroom. On this he drew carefully with firm, strong hands, a large, dark circle. Just that, stark against its clear background. *"Is bindu par dhyaan do"* (concentrate on this round spot), he instructed. I tried that. It was difficult not to be distracted at first, but then I got his point. Gradually, blotting out much else, my mind settled down to focus solely at that centre. It was uncanny. Savouring every one of its essential requisited colour, line, tone, texture and space. I found myself riveted.'[1]

When the circle emerged in Raza's work it enclosed vibrant, gestural strokes in passionate colours seeming to enclose radiating energies. An early work titled *Mandala* (1975) signified the notion of a centrifugal force of great dynamism, which by its power could generate the flow of the universe. It was the iridescent centre, which emanated the creation of the cosmos. The emergent image of the circle within the square became the pivotal point of his work. The frame of the canvas itself would have red, black and yellow interlocking and unfolding, at the centre of which, ensconced within a square, would be the throbbing dark circle. The painting *Bindu* (1980) had the black orb as its central axis where the swarming, vibrant red and black courses through the space of the square.

In the masterly work *Maa* (1981), flaming tongues of colours on one side are juxtaposed with the black, still centre on the other, both equipoised as darkness is to light, movement to stillness, action to reflection. The emerging and recessive depths of the painting are the opening gateways of consciousness tautly contained within the flickering framework of red and black suggesting an iconization of the work. Below the painting, in a manner reminiscent of the miniature tradition is the inscription '*Maa lautkar jab aaunga, kya launga?*' (Mother, what will I bring when I return). The yearning for home, with its blazing colours, overflows and is reconstructed in a symphonic movement.

These words from a poem by Ashok Vajpeyi became an oneiric truth for Raza in his sublime creation, *Maa*. It also suggested his own restless longing for the home of his childhood. In the '70s he began to visit India increasingly, travelling all over the country, and in consonance with this, his Indian identity came to the fore. He would seek out writers, poets, artists and philosophers, and found in their writings a spark that would ignite his muse. Raza began to focus on the verses of Kabir, Ghalib, Mahadevi Verma, Agyeya, Gajanan Madhave Muktibodh, Kedar Nath

Singh, Faiz Ahmed Faiz and others; he started using them in his paintings. Very fond of Hindi poetry himself he would often inscribe in his paintings a line or a verse from a Hindi poem and this would give an added visual and metaphorical dimension to his work. Often the Devanagari script instilled in his painting lent it an emphatic meaning. According to Vajpeyi, 'Most times, when he put the word, the word came much later, more or less when the painting was finished ... It was just there and he did not want either the painting to be subsumed by the word or the word to exhaust the painting. He allowed them to coexist in a simple visual relationship.'[2]

Raza was to make a painting which contained a whole poem of the Hindi poet Nirala – an invocation of Goddess Saraswati – inscribed in his exquisite handwriting. Quoting Muktibodh, he stated in another, '*Viswa tama sunya main tahalti hai jagat samiksha*' (This is the idea I've been working on for a long time). The notion of *tama sunya* – the dark bindu. Dark nothingness, but yet charged. Radiating energy in terms of colour that move from black to grey and going in space towards white. That is exactly the theme of my work.'[3] In the belief that from the darkness emanates all light, Raza's dark bindus solidify during this period and their density seems to condense their immense potential. A black concentric circle pulsating with flickering lights, *Bindu* (1987) unfolds where the mother of all colours – black – gives birth to the surrounding red, yellow, white and blue reflected in its rotating orb. It is primarily the plastic qualities which interest him but also it is interlayered with a belief in universal truths, which transcend particularities.

Visiting the Birthplace

Raza had been visiting India since 1959 when the painter Bal Chhabda had had a solo exhibition of his works at Gallery 59 in Mumbai. Janine and Raza had together visited his birth and childhood places in Madhya Pradesh, as well as other areas in India. These visits now began to influence his work as his Indian identity came to the fore. Much of this had to do with the beauty, colour and a sense of joy that he encountered everywhere in the country, despite the extreme poverty and illiteracy that he saw. As Vajpeyi points out, 'Raza felt attracted to the celebrative aspects of

Indian life and art. He could feel that the modernist stance had sidelined the celebrative nature of art overloading it with turmoil, tension and dissonance. For him the moment of rehabilitation of the celebrative in art was not far.'[4]

Raza would visit India every year, especially following his residency in Berkeley. Once when he couldn't come, he wrote to his friend Bal Chhabda that it distressed him a great deal. This was due to a serious vision flaw which he had experienced in 1965. As he wrote, '...We are not coming to India this winter. This breaks my heart every time I think about it. I was so much wanting to come, also Janine. All was set. But we had to decide annulations as I had very serious trouble with my right eye. I have been discreet about this matter, but I will give you precise details. For the last six months, I have fairly high tension in my right eye. They call it Hypertonie Oculaire, an early stage of glaucome. I have excellent vision, and no headaches. Only time and again there is a sort of fog that comes for I do not know what mysterious reason, stays for an hour or two and goes away. I am having the best medical advice that is possible here and three of the most important ophthalmologists have given their opinion. At present it is a treatment with Pilocarpine drops and other tablets. If these have no effect a minor operation will be necessary. We are proceeding slowly and systematically. I am advised to be calm and have as few activities as possible at least for some time. This really is the major problem as a restless person can never rest. All my life I have been either in the frying pan or the fire – and an imposed calm seems rather uncomfortable. But well I have to accept it as an imperative need – at least for a while till the rhythm changes.'[5] It was only in 1993 that he finally underwent an eye operation which restored his vision completely. He made a textured eye in one square and in another wrote 'Drishti' in Devnagari script in the centre and wrote to Vajpeyi, 'For so many years, I had "vision" but finally the eyes are worn out. The tension increased. On 27th May I had the operation at Clinique Franklin. For the first few days I could see nothing but now it's alright. I remember the lines of Surdas... "Do not lose your two eyes, the desire to meet your beloved is there". Do not worry, I believe I will now make my best paintings!'[6] At the bottom, he sketched a close-up of an eye which was almost abstract and in another sketch he wrote *Drishti* (eyesight) with diagonal lines emerging in the four directions. The gift of eyes was a remarkable thing indeed! After the period of disquiet, however, Raza reverted to his artistic routine and things went back to normal.

Recognition in Bhopal

In 1978, he was invited to Bhopal to receive the State honour from the Government of Madhya Pradesh and to have an exhibition of his new works at the Madhya Pradesh Kala Parishad. He also participated in a multi-arts festival featuring classical music, visual arts, dance theatre and poetry. All the paintings from his first show in Bhopal were sold out. Almost a decade later, when Bharat Bhavan, a multi-arts complex, was established in Bhopal, these paintings were transferred to Roopankar, the art museum – one of the largest collections of Raza's work in a public museum. He did not take the money from the sale proceeds in Bhopal, but donated the entire amount to the Parishad for instituting an annual prize for visual arts and Hindi poetry to be awarded on alternate years.

Apart from Bhopal, during his 1978 trip Raza visited Indore, Gwalior and Damoh, where he had first started drawing many years ago. Vajpeyi noted, 'Many were surprised to find that though Raza had lived in Paris for more than twenty-five years, [but] he had not forgotten his mother tongue which he spoke with great felicity and creative force.'[7] It was during this visit that he also visited his village school in Mandala, where he had begun his education and had also established contact with the notion of the Bindu. Vajpeyi pointed out, 'He wished to integrate the essence of his life experiences, his childhood memories, the celebrative aesthetics of India with the plastic skills and sophistication he had so assiduously learnt and imbibed in France. He wanted to return to the age-old tradition through modernity without replacing or abandoning one for the other.'[8]

It was during one of these visits that Raza had another look at the looming statue of Nandi at Phutera Talab in Damoh, where he had whiled away many a carefree hours in his childhood. He found that it had deteriorated considerably, and yet nothing had been done to preserve the ancient statue. Raza managed to convince the authorities to protect it as it was one of the most beautiful things in the town. He spoke about the dire need to restore it to several people during his visit. He was pleasantly surprised when he went there in the '90s to find that they had built a shed for the statue. He had also suggested during his earlier visits that all the statues in Damoh be gathered, many of which had been stored in an unused church outside the town, and that a museum be created for them. 'Seven years later when I went back, there was a newly built museum there and the statues were placed in the museum with lights, duly protected by guards. On this side of the tank, there are temples and on the other side a mosque. It is nice to feel the harmony of the proximity of these presences, if we have the wisdom to take it in this way.'[9]

Raza was particularly touched by the innate sagacity of people in the villages. 'When I went to Barbaria and Bachai, people recognized me and they stopped and began to accompany me. I visited the two villages. There was an old lady sitting next to the tulsi plant on a terrace on the other side of the house and somebody told her that Mr Raza was there. She said, "Yes, I know his father." She said it in the local dialect of Bundelkhandi, the only event that she remembered was the shooting of the leopard by my father. It was so poetic: I was deeply touched. We must learn and preserve our dialect.'[10]

Relics of Remembrance

Raza and Janine also visited other Indian states like Rajasthan and Gujarat. They scooped up the vibrant textures and colours of India by bringing home souvenirs. Their Parisian home was dotted with pieces of embroidered fabric from Kutch, a woven shawl from the Rabaris, the eaves of a wooden temple in Gujarat, a black linga in stone from the Narmada river, a Mary Magdalene from Goa. These were placed on the desk or the window sill, in bookcases or the patio, or the garden at Gorbio. Remnants of his trips to India, these were also memory images that kindled his thoughts and his paintings bringing his India vividly alive.

To Janine these souvenirs suggested images of a diverse and colourful country, which she absorbed with concentration; but for Raza these were symbols that occupied his interior space and solidified his links with India. Janine's collages were built from fragments of her past like

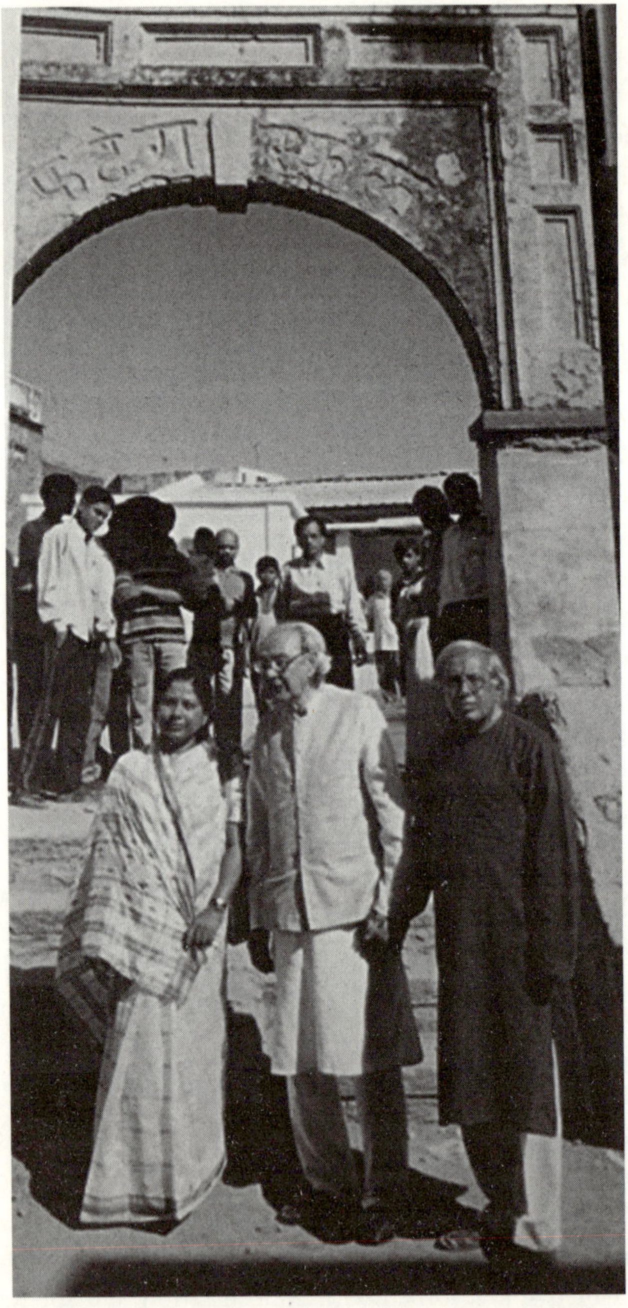

Raza with Ashok Vajpeyi at Phutera School, Damoh 2006.

the gloves, closed boots and laces that straightjacketed her childhood. Her found objects made their way into her frames and even her wedding dress was stitched and spread out as the fabric of her life. As Geeti Sen points out, 'In all works but the papier mâché, which begin from the mid-eighties, she is working through phases of her own life, with the power of memory as recall. There is something in the nature of secrecy about these works – objects closeted are now being excavated and laid bare. It is only in the last, the paper sculptures built out of Indian ribbons and other fragments, which are able to liberate Janine from her own past – so intensely experienced and lived through her work. Here images and colours from India work as a catalyst: she develops a startling and marvellous new sense of colour, of humour, sometimes of the grotesque. This is not nostalgia but joy in discovering new forms and colours which infuse vigour into her work.'[11]

For Raza, the Indian experience was different. It served to, bind him to the sources, shapes and colours he had experienced while in India. According to Sen, 'For him, these forms are not a novelty with which to experiment, but primordial forms which he can only replicate. He brings to his images ancient conceptual thought, as well as the new techniques and formalism acquired in his years in France.'[12] On visiting Kakiya and Damoh in 2006, he had said, 'It is not a question of nostalgia. This is a very deliberate and conscious attempt to go to my own sources, as far as possible to my childhood. In fact, one's life is formed in the first few years of one's existence.'[13]

The well-known artist Satish Gujral, however, objected to, among other things, the use of Indian iconography by artists like Husain and Raza. Gujral even spoke in the media about the denigration of these gods by 'non-Hindus'. This was a deliberate affront to the synergic culture which existed in the Indo-Islamic traditions redolent of the real India. Khorshed Gandhy who along with her husband had instituted the Chemould gallery, which had played an active role in bringing about an awareness of these artists, and who herself was a firm believer in India's secular tradition was to write the below letter to him.[14]

My dear Satish,
This letter should have been written atleast (sic) a month ago – but I have been caught up in a lot of domestic events.

When I read the controversy over your statements regarding Husain and Raza's works, I was both sad and indignant. I had wanted to write a letter immediately to the press stating my point of view.

On second thoughts I felt that Satish is my friend, what I want to say is essentially to him of what my thoughts are on his statements, why do I want to get into the media? Hence I take up my pen to say what I have carried in my heart all these weeks.

1. The first point I wish to raise is that we in India are living through very precarious times where communalist forces are in the ascendency and what we say or do has to be thought through. Otherwise these forces jump in and make capital out of it for their own advantage. I am sure you had a taste of that yourself and must have been surprised as to what LK Advani had to do with your statement.
2. Raza's Bindu is a very meaningful experience for him which has taken him into his early childhood experiences and out of it has evolved a whole new dimension of thinking for this sensitive artist. Without going into the details of a how a Brahmin headmaster taught him this simple exercise in concentration, I hope you will get to read Raza's own clarification some day.
3. As for Husain, I feel he is ingrained in the Indian culture where he thinks and acts in symbols all the time. For him to have wiped out Durga in Bengal was very meaningful I feel as he might very well do with Ganapati in Maharashtra some day! His is a restless spirit which cannot be tied down to norms or conventions and we have to allow him to be what he is.
4. Finally, one humble word: so many of you, our dear artist friends, have found your place in the 'Sun' (the blazing Indian sun at least). We are happy and proud as more of you get your

place in that arc of recognition and honour as you carve out your own unique places. There is enough room for all!!

Yours,
Khorshed

While Husain was castigated by right-wing elements for denigrating Hindu deities, Raza came under attack for his sublimation of Hindu thought. Sadly, the works of neither artist was understood in their modernist stance which attempted to uplift ancient beliefs to the level of contemporaneity and internationalism. Moreover, the tradition itself was an ingrained aspect of their upbringing, and in archiving it they were being criticized for the very thing which they were expected to do: scrutinize its life-giving aspects. Were their intentions being misunderstood because their origins were Islamic? Or were these statements arising out of crass ignorance?

The Essential Indian

On another count, what were the essentials of Raza's own affinities with Indianness? While the colours and concepts seem to have an affiliation with Indian spiritual thought, it is primarily their plasticity which makes an impact. He states, 'The obscure black space is charged with latent force aspiring to fulfilment. Like the universal order of the "earth-seed" relationship, the original form of the Bindu emerges and unfolds itself in black space. All inherent forces unite. A vertical line intersects a horizontal line, engendering energy and light. Space is charged. Contours appear, and colours: white, yellow, red and blue and along with the original black, they compose the colour spectrum of the visible world.'[15]

In *Water* (1986), lavender, blue, coral, ochre, yellow, green and black create a symphonic movement, the flux and flow of the tide constantly changing its shades. A litany of downward pointing triangles can be lightly traced on the surface, formed as it were by the fluctuation of water. As the artist Akhilesh put it:

> For instance take his blue. I am choosing blue very precisely because here is a colour ready to unfold the infinite, ready to unfold its secret depth. A colour in the sky hanging on the head of mankind for thousands of years. A colour spread over three-fourth parts of the earth. A transparent presence in the throat of 'Shiva'. A colour with tranquil memory, with mysterious nature. With pacifying look, hiding the depth of ocean. This blue, exactly this blue is burning in Raza's painting.'[16]

In 1996, Raza made the large painting *The Oceans II* commissioned by the Métropolitaine, Lisbon with deep washes of aqueous blue where panels of circles and triangles alternated to create regurgitating depths.

The Bindu paintings of the '80s are charged with a latent force that is inherent to the medium. His concentric circles of pulsating energy could be related to the dynamism inherent in traditional religious diagrams. But Raza kept an equivalent distance from both, forging his own path. In his own words, 'My present work is the result of two parallel enquiries. Firstly, it aimed at pure plastic order, form-order. Secondly, it concerns the theme of nature. Both have converged into a single point and become inseparable. The point, the bindu, symbolizes the seed-bearing potential of all life, in a sense. It's also a visible form containing all the essential requisites of line, tone, colour, gesture, and space.'[17] As he wrote to Krishen, 'I am still working on the theme of the "point", the circle, and all its inherent composites. The idea is growing. Recent paintings have seen new evolution all by themselves. A strange organic growth: one painting leads to another. One works for two or three months in a state of elevation, and then the superior power leaves: one has to stop and wait. I use that time to see exhibitions, meet friends, write or read books. My favourite authors at present are Mahatma Gandhi and Pandit Jawaharlal Nehru. It is wonderful to read them simultaneously; they were so different in temperament yet worked so closely.'[18]

Neo-Tantric Beliefs

While the broad stream of Indian philosophical thought and, in particular, the Tantric beliefs influenced Raza, he refuted the nomenclature 'Neo-

Tantric' claiming that it was far too complex and that the term did not delve into it deeply enough. In 1983, he declined the offer to participate in an exhibition on the Neo-Tantric movement at the National Gallery of Modern Art and wrote to the gallery, 'My using a circle or a square as key motifs do not make my paintings Tantric, even if I have called them Bindu, Surya or Zamine. I am aware Tantric Darshan is far too complex. I know little about its beliefs or rituals. My involvement in work is essentially with the life of form, and all my efforts are directed towards a coherent pictorial logic.'[19] The Neo-Tantric movement which emerged in the '60s and consisted of artists like Biren De, G.R. Santosh and Prafulla Mohanti, had to do specifically with Tantric beliefs, but could not be linked to Raza's beliefs. In any case, the movement itself had raised some serious reservations. The art critic Rupika Chawla, for instance, who had curated the exhibition *Symbolism and Geometry in Indian Art* at the National Gallery of Modern Art in 1996 pointed out there was an insufficient inquiry into Tantra and an inadequate empathy with the collective psyche. She stated, 'Certainly the function of Neo-Tantra was not that of actual Tantra art or its yantras and mandalas, which were essential as components of ritual and religion.'[20]

Despite this, it has to said that Raza's own preoccupations were akin to much of Tantra's symbolism primarily that of the Bindu. In Tantra, the Bindu represents the indivisible unity of the static female principle and the male kinetic principle, which in their oneness create the entire universe of matter and spirit. It is the smallest unity beyond which energy cannot be condensed and is the creative matrix of the universe – the '*visva-bija*', the world seed, from which all things originate and return. According to Tantric beliefs, the root forms from which yantras or sacred diagrams are constructed are the circle, the triangle and the square. The circle is an expanded Bindu within which lies the notion that time has no beginning or end. The triangle is a primary enclosure since space cannot be bounded by fewer than three lines. Hence, it is the root matrix of nature where, in its inverted form, it is feminine power while the triangle with its apex upwards, denotes the male principle. The square is the substratum, the fundamental base of all yantras, denoting the terrestrial world which has to be transcended. The three in their permutations and combinations constitute the yantras, the sacred diagrams that are used as aids to meditation.

In the significance that Raza attached to the circle and the dynamic realizations of the triangle and the square, he shared an affinity with these symbols. For instance, he was aware of serpent being used as a symbol for traversing the kundalini or the sacred yoni, the female organ and used the device in his paintings. As he stated, 'I am very much interested in the concept of the kundalini – that dormant energy which has to be awakened. Just imagine our sages have said this truth many centuries ago. It is fantastic – when they talk about the serpentine energy. It is fabulous. Our libido is linked to artistic energy and all other awareness. Sex energy is intricately linked up with artistic expression.'[21]

But these linkages for Raza stemmed from a wider belief in Indian philosophical thought, which he associated not only with their immense plastic possibilities but also with their universal connotations. As scholar Olivier Germain-Thomas observed, 'Raza's need for women, money all of this was an artistic need. He was inspired by the Shakti, the spiritual mode which was sexuality enhanced at a spiritual level. For him women were very important and he considered them a source of sexual energy which is the Shakti in Hindu tradition.'[22] Thus, 'Before the call of the white world, Raza was a painter of colours, bright portrayals of genesis, germination, and of the joyous and sensuous feast that Nature offers. He worshipped the feminine, the seed, the tree, the bindu, the sun, the kundalini…'[23]

The stress on his Indian identity stemmed for Raza in the '70s and also arose from a pictorial logic that formed an undercurrent in his work from the beginning. Merely belonging to the École de Paris became insufficient for him, and by the '70s he consciously strove to construct a separate identity for himself. In the '80s, his emphatic claim as an Indian was unquestioned and this became a source of renewal and strength. His position could be compared to that of Souza's based in New York, who had begun to paint Indian icons to retain his identity but which lacked conviction. But Raza's works were not merely exotic. There was a conscious and dogged struggle in him to be Indian in spirit and at the same time to work with the plastic possibilities of the medium stretching them to their limit.

Although they varied in complex ways, painters J. Swaminathan and Raza were not dissimilar in their intentions. Both delved into Indian thought and beliefs, but retained a plastic order in their work which led to works of great aesthetic distinction. Swaminathan's experiences with tribal forms when he was located at Bharat Bhavan in Madhya Pradesh led to works which resonated the symbolic value of geometric forms, notably the triangle, the circle and the square. The inherent values these held for the tribals were used with great intuitive imagination in these works and carried to epiphanic heights. The triangles placed at intersections in their earthy tones of ochre, red and brown radiate a vital sexual energy at the vortex of creation. Chawla points out, 'Evaluated as a unique painter of the indigenous abstract, Swaminathan understood that geometry could be used beyond form and colour, it exists in the very structure of a painting. Miniature painters, for example, have always taken this as an established fact, structurally depending on geometric forms such as the triangle, the spiral, the circle or the parallelogram. Even in his non-geometric "Bird and Mountain" series, Swaminathan's establishment of visual and structural geometry is apparent.'[24]

Drawn from Indian beliefs and practices, the infinite possibilities of symbolic forms, formulated to represent the universe in microcosm and layered with multiple significance was common to both painters. But while Raza's works manifested these forms, hewing from his philosophical beliefs; for Swaminathan the original impetus was provided by the works of the tribals in Madhya Pradesh, which he had experienced directly.

An Inner Call

Raza felt an inner voice in him that had to be answered and at the same time there was a call to carve a niche for himself in the world outside. Could he be considered a professional Indian as some alleged? In other words, was he creating an aura of Indianness around himself in order to create a niche in the highly competitive art world of Paris at the time? Certainly, his brilliant colours, the notion of Indian spiritual thought and the writing in Devanagari script marked him out in a manner in which he was considered modern and yet very rooted. It is worth noting that his artist brother Ali Imam who had come from Karachi to London for training had cautioned him:

> As far as your small painting is concerned, I find it very successful, because of its small size; but I do not know how far you could integrate Indian calligraphy on a large size canvas. When the artists used letters like S and D in their paintings their whole endeavour was to make these letters or words an integral part of the painting and that was accepted by the people who mattered without question. But this task was easy because of the geometric form of these letters to fit in with cubist form. Your problems in the integration of Indian letters are greater…[25]

It has to be said then that Raza's affiliation to this particular brand of Indianness won him many friends and influenced people, even though his work was of the highest merit. If anything, his approach was equidistant from a sheer harking back to Indian spiritual thought and the plasticity of paint. Yet in his creation of an aura around himself, he did make a special bid for an Indianness that marked him out.

At the same time, Raza was deeply in touch with his core, beyond the particularities of any religion and, hence, genuinely believed in divine inspiration. As he stated, '*Divya shaktion key bina chitra nahi banate.*'[26] Then again, 'The small red canvas is staring at me. But the Gods are absent. You won't believe it but I cannot work without the presence of divine forces. They are tangible and real. I have to pray before I start working. They are a link between the unknown and the known, they charge me to a state of "unawareness" and it is only in that "sama", "stimweg" dream-like state, that my best paintings come, without my ever fully knowing how and why. It is a state of grace, inexplicable.'[27] For Raza, the spirituality of his work linked with its plastic possibilities and with an international order, which could be considered essentially modernist. Yet while engaging with debates and discussions worldwide around the formation of modernism, he was an active participant in the creation of an emerging, postcolonial India with its dreams and hopes for the future.

The Circle became a means of encapsulating the wide world. As Olivier Germain-Thomas pointed out, 'If Raza, when he found his path

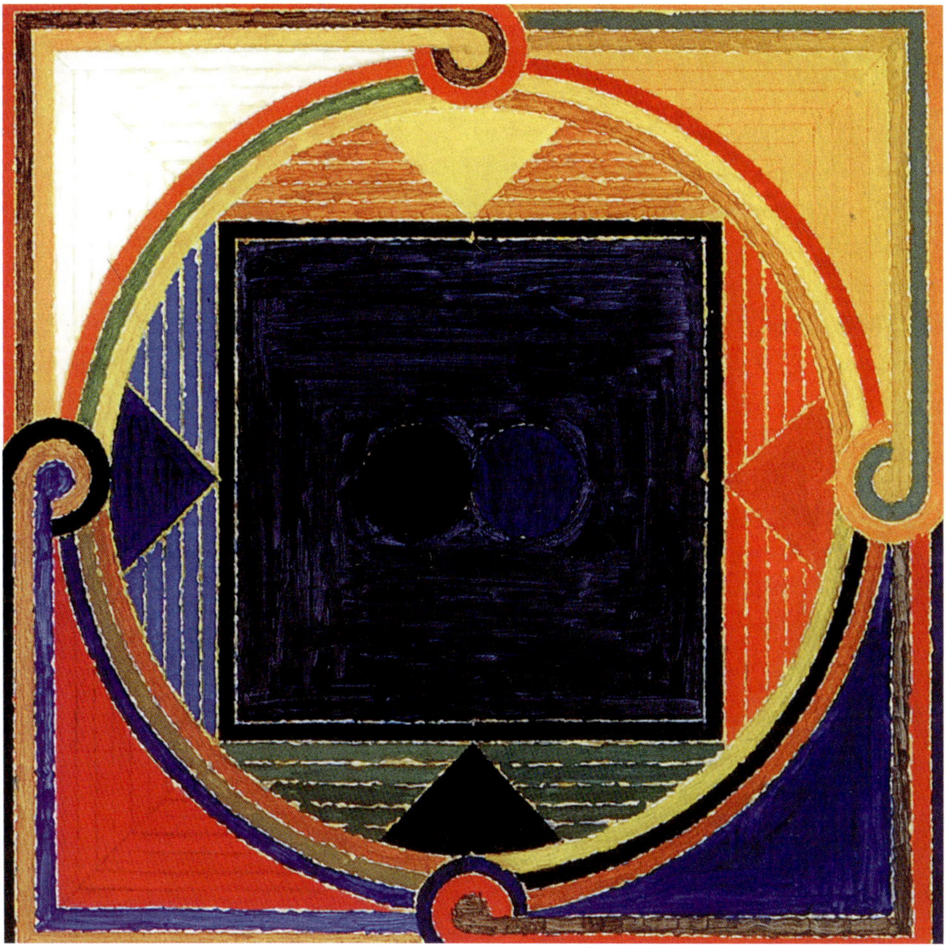

Panchtattvas
Acrylic on canvas
S.H. Raza

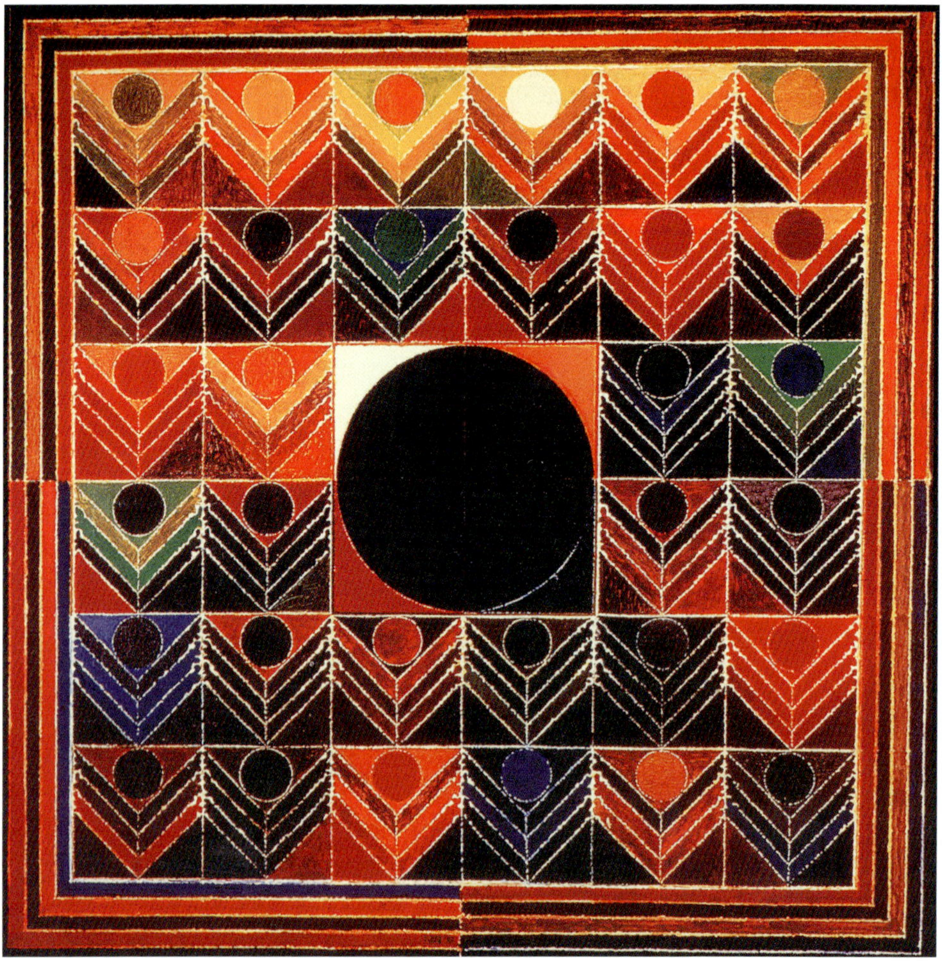

Germination, 1987
Acrylic on canvas
S.H. Raza

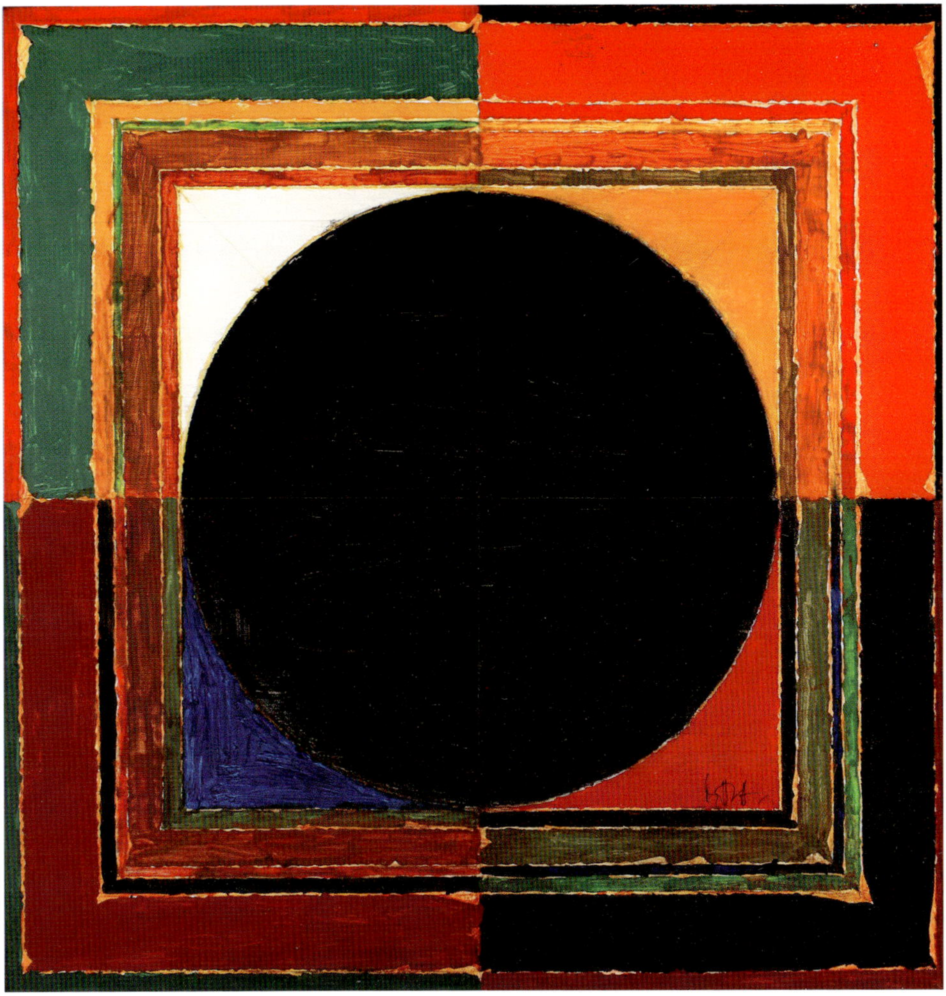

Bindu, 1983
Acrylic on canvas
50 x 50 cm
Courtesy: Private Collection
S.H. Raza

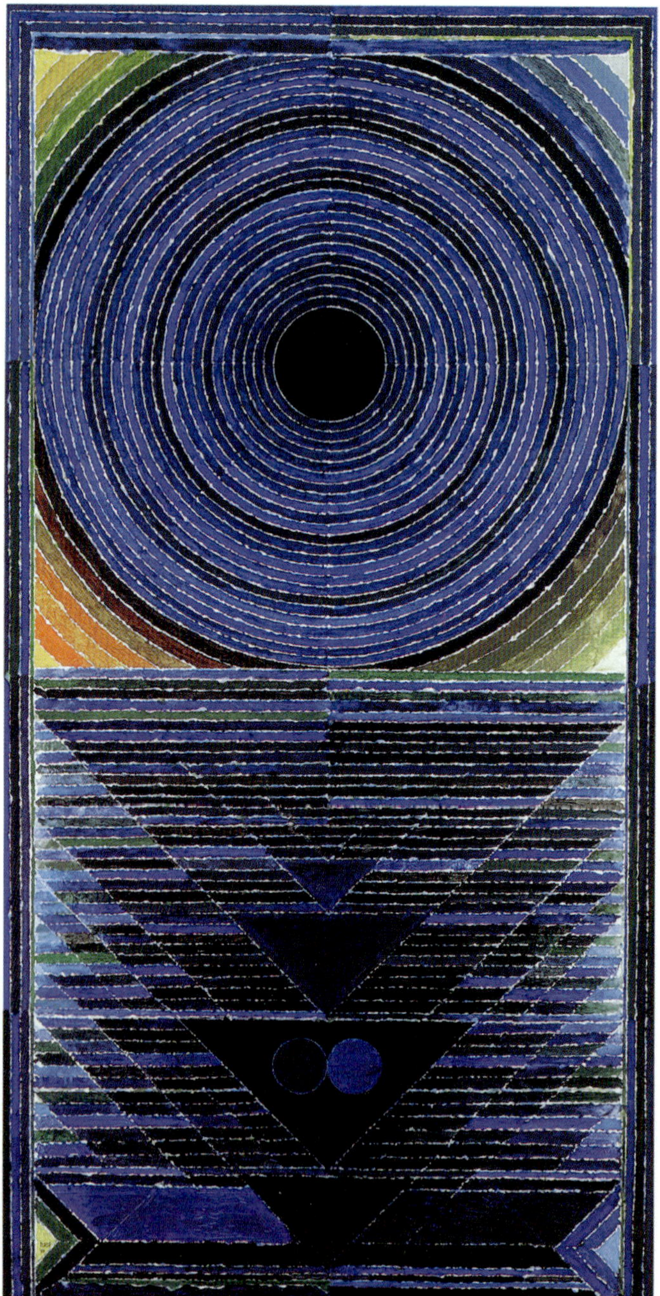

Jala Bindu, 1990
Acrylic on canvas
S.H. Raza

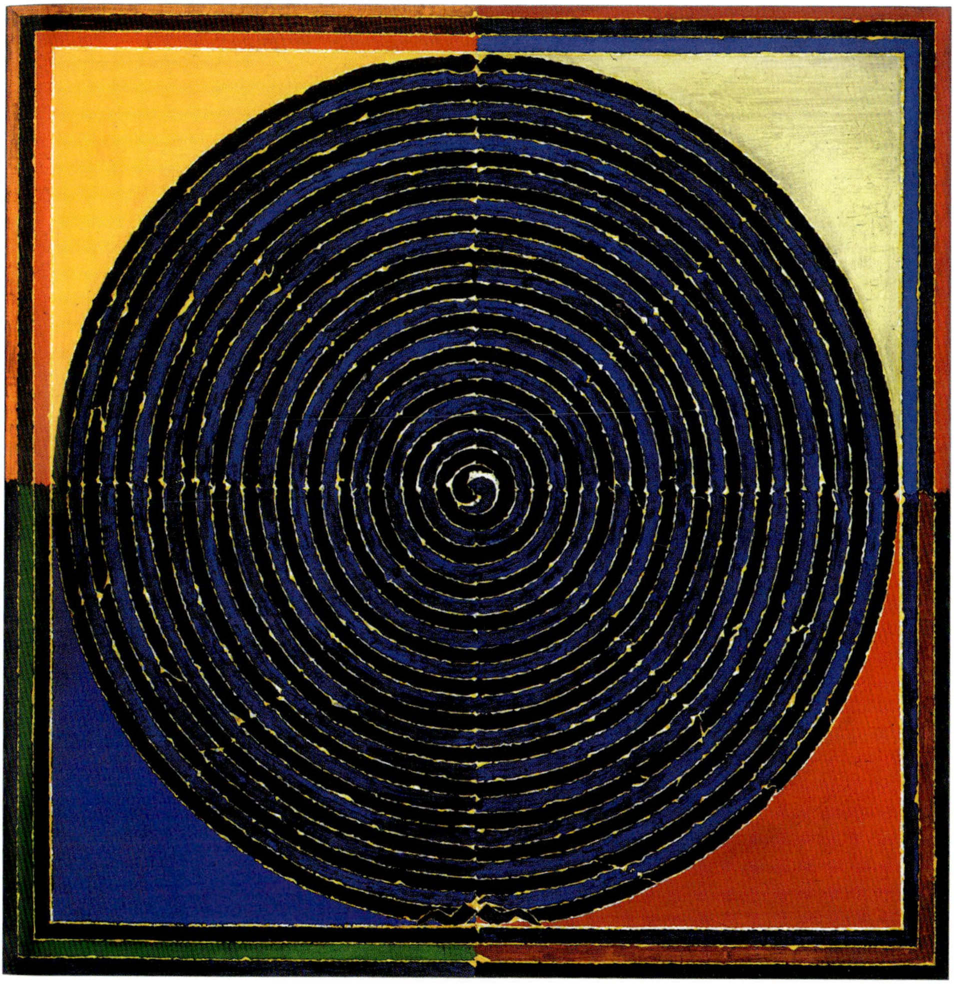

Naga, 1989
Acrylic on canvas
120 x 120 cm
S.H. Raza

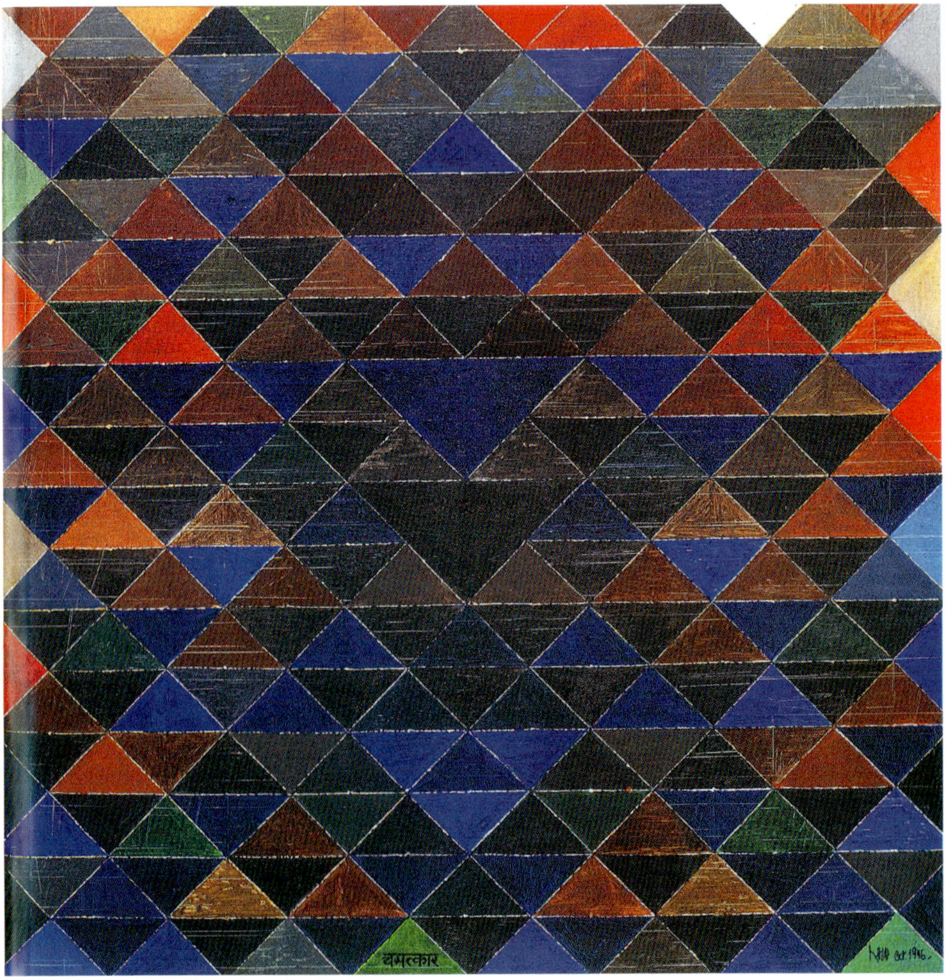

Chamatkar, 1996
Acrylic on canvas
100 x 100 cm
S.H. Raza

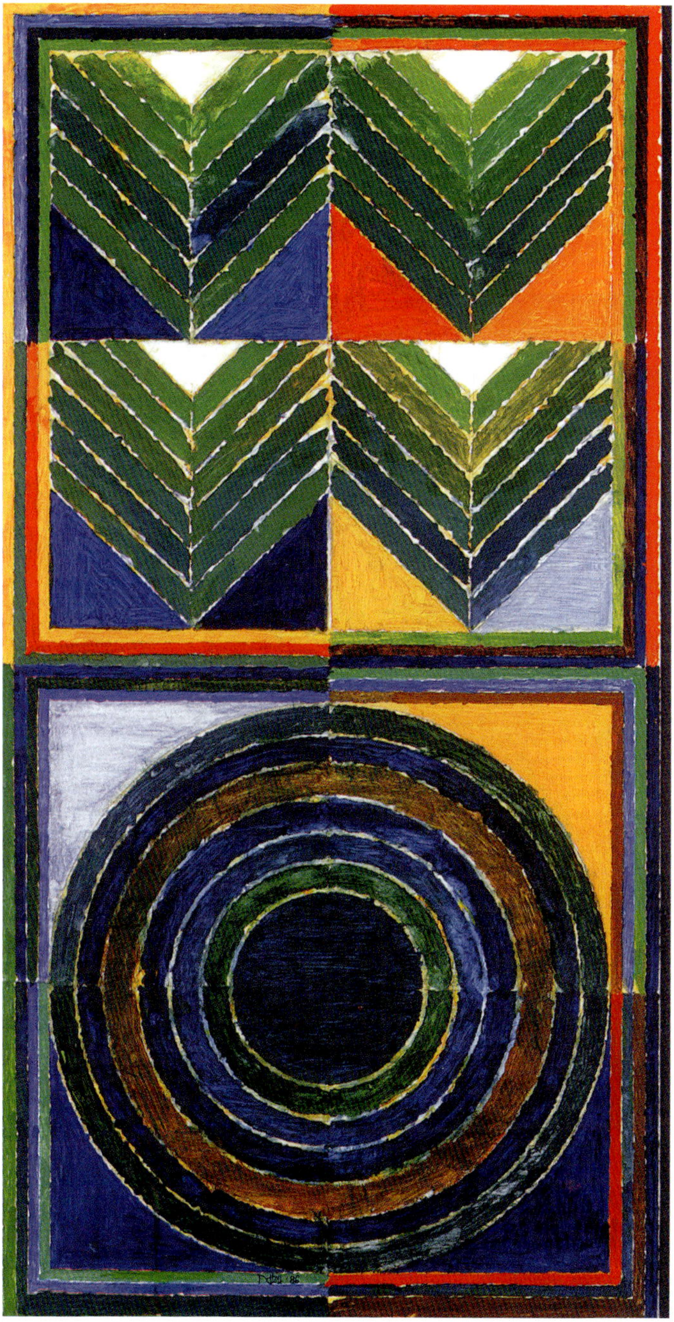

Spandan, 1987
Acrylic on paper
100 x 50 cm
S.H. Raza

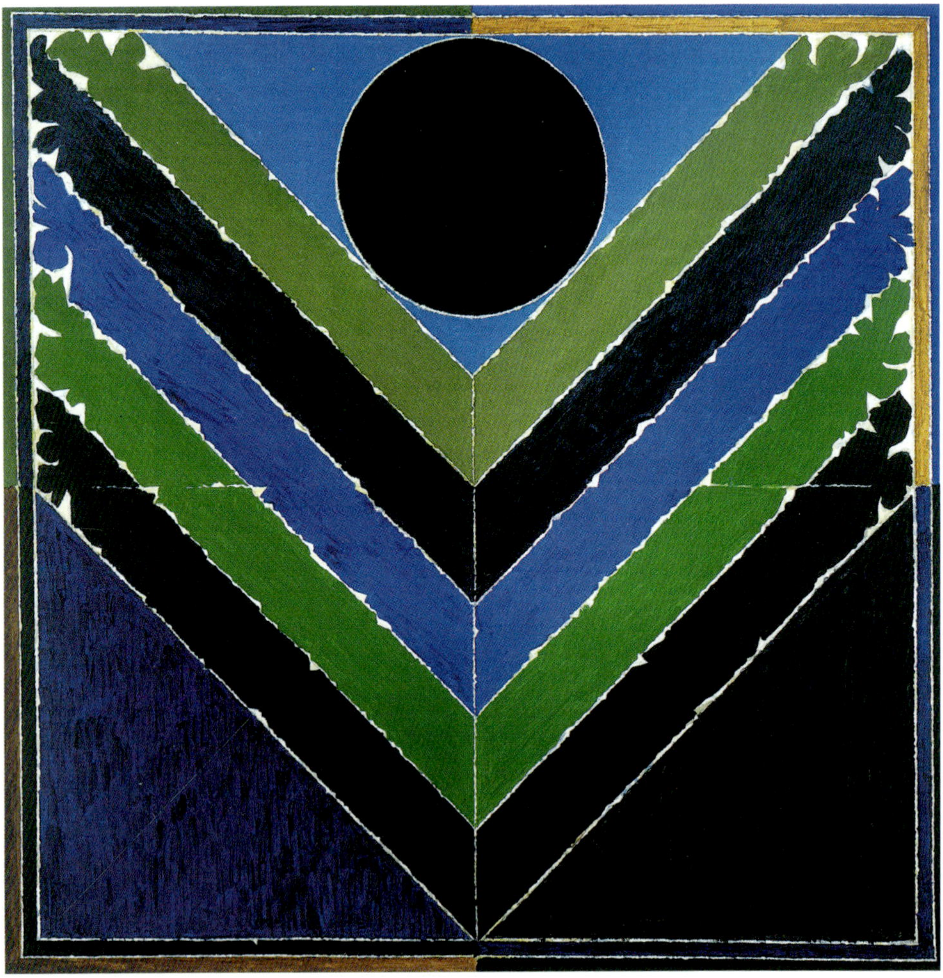

Tree, 1995
Acrylic on canvas
152 x 152 cm
S.H. Raza

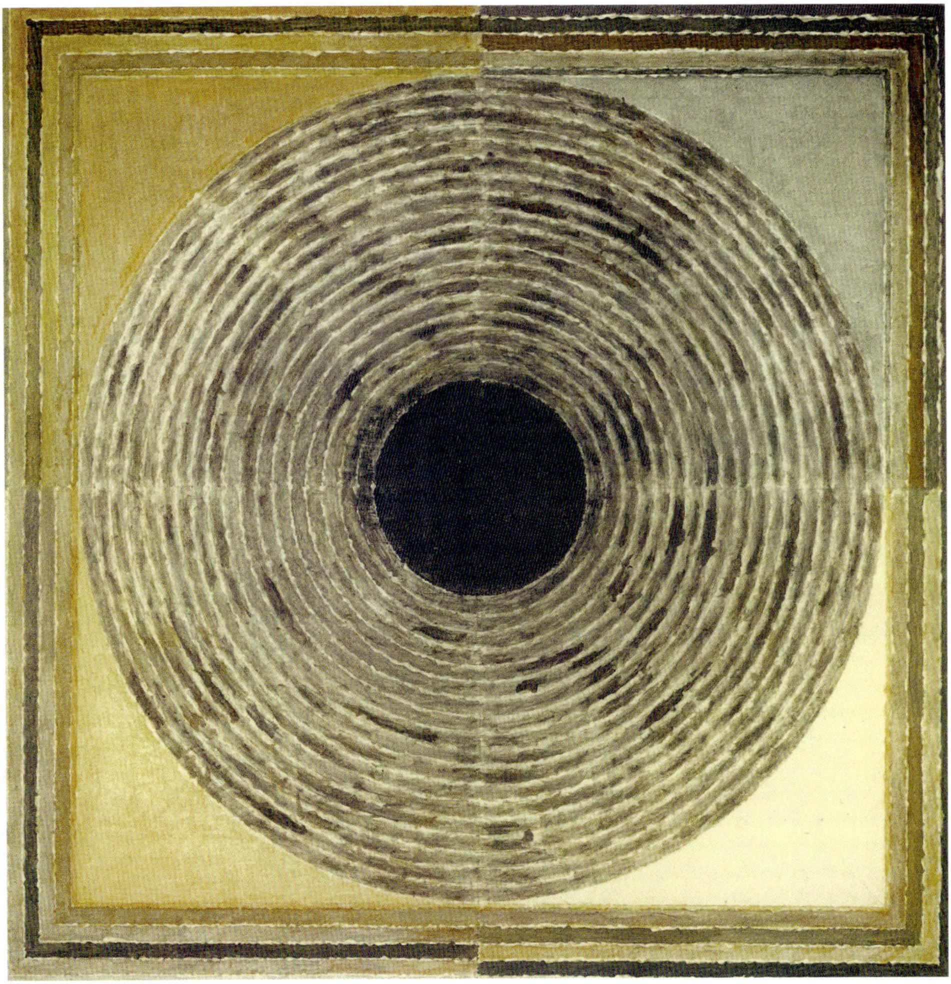

Param Bindu, 1989
Acrylic on canvas
120 x 120 cm
S.H. Raza

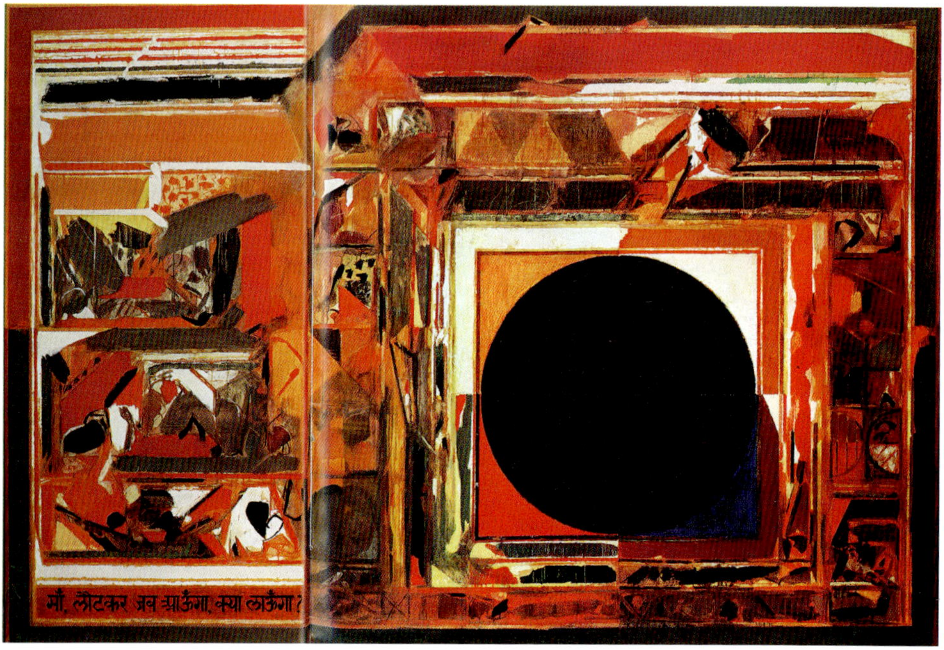

Maa, 1981
Acrylic on canvas
175 x 260 cm
S.H. Raza

The Inaudible Sound
Acrylic on paper
80 x 80 cm
S.H. Raza

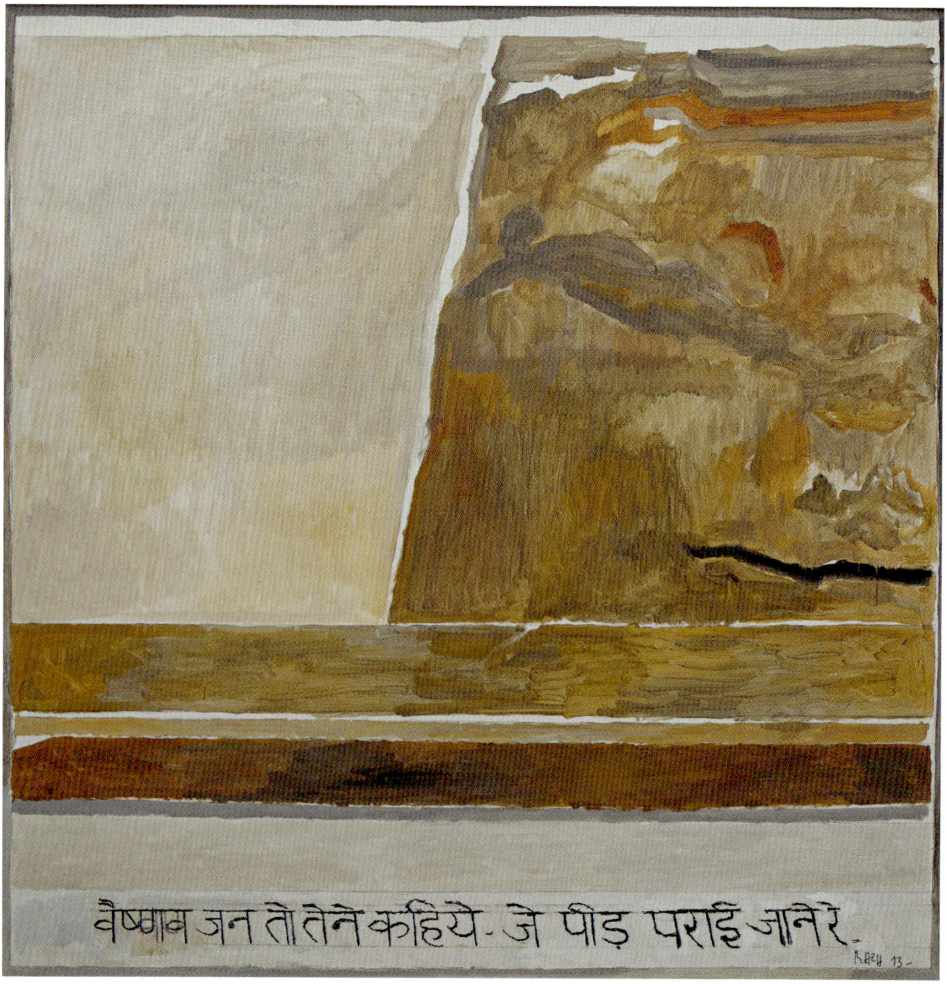

Peed Parai, 2013
Acrylic on canvas
50 x 50 cm
S.H. Raza

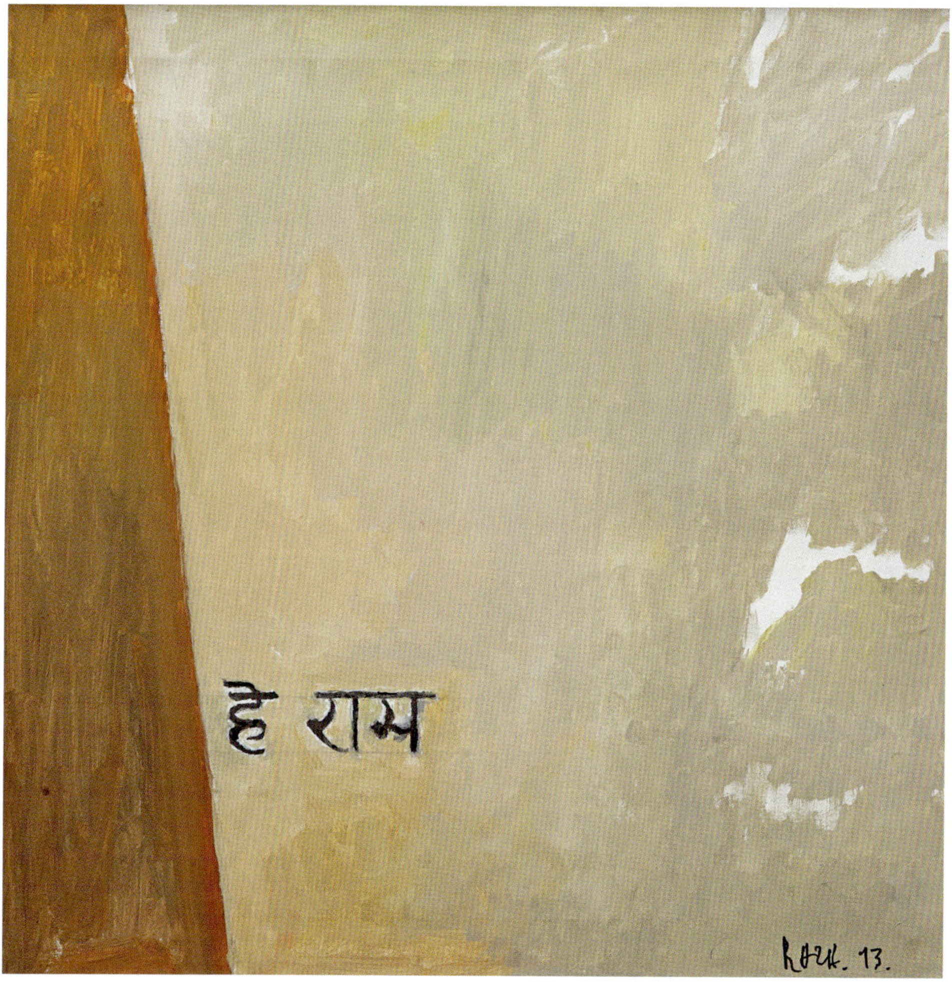

Hey Ram, 2013
Acrylic on canvas
23.5 x 23.5 cm
S.H. Raza

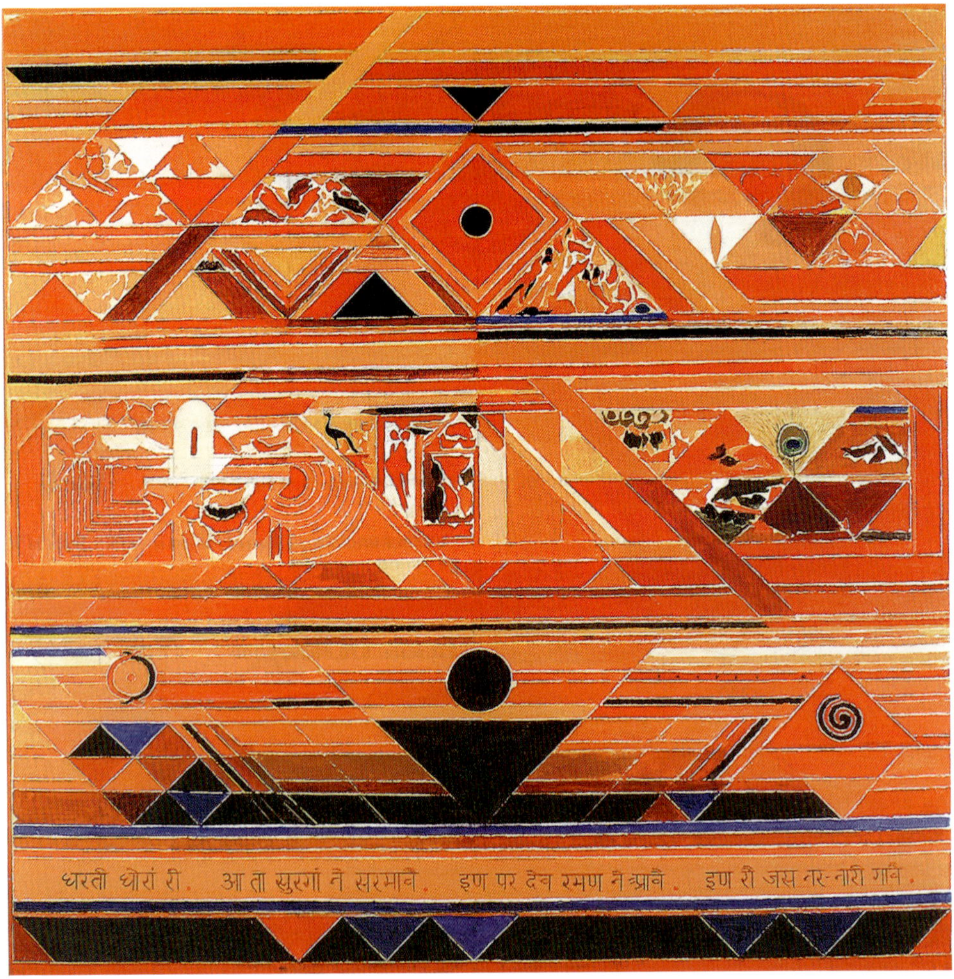

Rajputana, 2003
Acrylic on canvas
59.7/8 x 59 .7/8 Inches
S.H. Raza

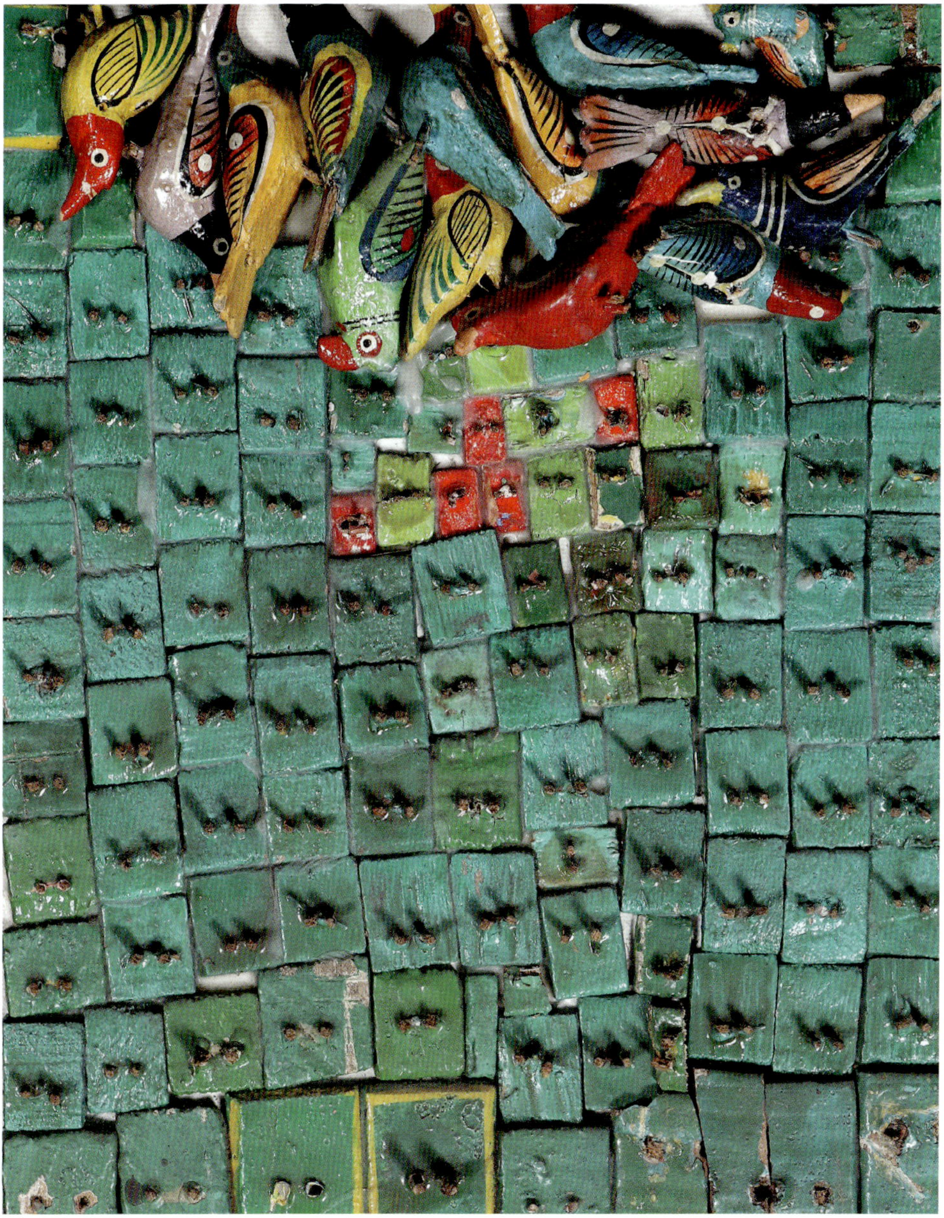

Untitled
Mixed Media
24.5 x 20 cm
Janine Mongillat

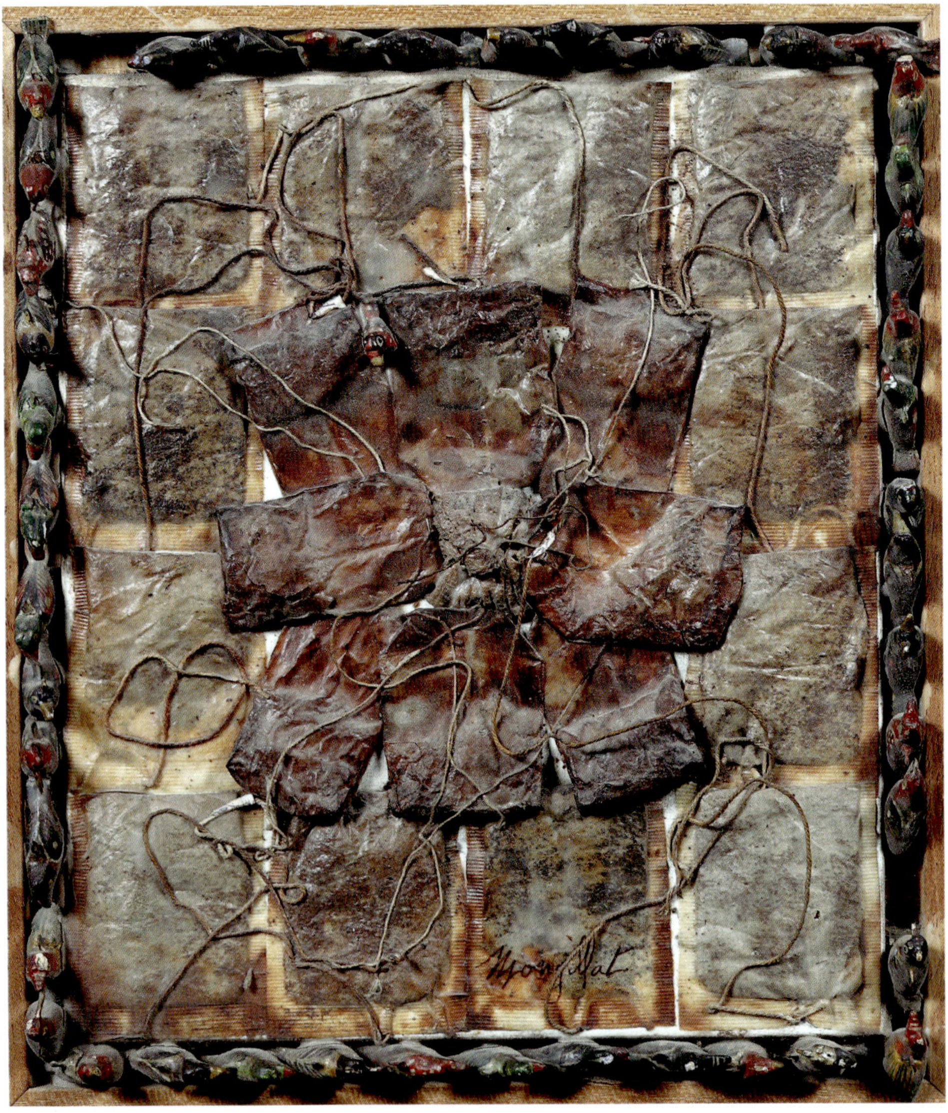

Untitled
Mixed Media
23 x 24 cm
Janine Mongillat

while representing it in his canvases, associated the circle with the bindu, he broadened the scope of its use… Before him, in other cultures which sought the same unit but not openly, the circle said to man that he had the power to raise himself and, thence to give meaning to life even if it were nothing but a parenthesis between two voids.'[28] Inherent in Raza's 'Ankuran' or 'Germination' series which began in the late '80s was the concept that the point carries within it the potential for all of creation just as the seed carries the tree within it. This struck a chord in him when a yoni-shaped stone in the garden of his studio in Gorbio, much like the stones found along the ghats of the river Narmada began to sprout. As he wrote to Krishen:

> My recent preoccupation Germination is the logical 'suite' of the 'Bindu', the seed and my obsessions are real. I do believe that this is the most important part of my life. But without false modesty, I must say that the dynamics of Energy, both in life and in painting, are not easy to explain or express – neither in words nor in paint. This is the objective towards which I would like to concentrate all my energy. The outer aspect is of little interest. Indian painting will not be important if we paint Indian themes only as either lotuses or Indian people. Its significance lies in the concept, the vision and the vitality, and a personal assimilation of things perceived … Can we reach the utmost centre of gravity situated deep within oneself, perceive it in silence and launch the first genuine cry – inaudible like a murmur?[29]

By the late '90s, however, a saturation seems to have been reached. His transition to symmetrical works acquired a humdrum predictability. Despite their immense potential, there is a slippage into the ornamental. Myth and metaphor, with their inherent energy so well amplified in the earlier works, began to be replaced by decorative illustration. In some ways, the Bindu paintings seemed to have reached a plateau and required a form of rejuvenation. As the gallerist Dadiba Pundole pointed out, 'His strongest phase was the late '80s and early '90s when his asymmetrical works and the Bindus reached great heights. The later Bindus were both elegant and at times repetitive.'[30] The cultural theorist Ranjit Hoskote points out, 'Is the mythic archetype enshrined in the symbol capable of speaking to our present experience – is it therefore opening out to history?'[31]

The Stone and the Circle

While in Gorbio, the artist had found a stone which approximated the shape of a key and had an inner circle inscribed on it.[32] It harked back to the many stones resembling yonis found on the ghats of the river Narmada which he had come across in his youth. Raza placed this stone at the entrance of his studio, filled it with earth and planted seeds. The shoots of grass which began to grow from this were inspirational for the artist. He was quick to formulate it, 'The black Bindu is placed in the centre of the earth like a foetus moving in the womb of the mother.'[33]

In *Bija* (1988), the triangles point downward, metamorphosing from umber to sienna, turning into brown and then a deep, earthy darkness. Becoming larger and deeper as they move downward, they place their roots into the earth while in the centre like an orbit is a black circle emerging from a white triangle. An orange tint unites the entire canvas creating multiple movements. In *Ankuran* (1986), primary colours create permutations and combinations of the circle, square and triangle. In *Kaliyan* (1990), in brilliant red, the upper portion has open triangles emerging from each other while the lower portion is inscribed in black with a verse that speaks of the yearning, the meeting and the separation from the loved one. The meeting has as much to do with a spiritual union as human. In a series of paintings titled *Fertility* (1990), the effulgence of colour is emphasized while blank spaces interpose a climactic opposition to the variegated and divided surface. At all times the binaries of light and dark, force and stillness, dynamism and staticity are contained within a uniting whole.

In the Footsteps of Gandhi

Gandhi, as we know, played a profound role in the creation of independent India and fired the imagination of the world as the exemplar of non-violence. With his homespun clothes, austere lifestyle and his simple devices for making the country independent, he was also an aesthete who lived as he believed – that artistic elegance lies in truth. Gandhi's high aesthetic sense lay in the artistic use of ordinary objects by the common man, which he raised to the level of icons. As his grandson Gopalkrishna Gandhi points out, 'He fine-tuned the charkha for instance to make it mobile, light and more serviceable than its archetypes. At the same time, he popularized the hand-held "takli" the "drop spindle," using which is far more complex than might seem, the holding of the spindle at a particular angle, letting the yarn grow out of the sliver at a particular thickness, not less not more and wind itself in a cone that does not go beyond the diameter of the metal disc.'[1] He observes, '"*Sur pakad*" (hold the note) in classical singing and "*sut pakad*" (hold the yarn) are both about staying intact. And that, not just for making a substitute for Lancashire cottons but for what Jawaharlal Nehru came to describe as "the livery of freedom".'[2]

Gandhi meant for the khadi and village industries to be seen as liberating devices, generating self-respect and self-reliance and creating a new trajectory away from commodification and mass production on cultural and aesthetic grounds. More importantly, it was a means of instating a selfhood in the face of the colonial mass production of cotton cloth from indigenous cotton, resold back to the country at high prices.

It was of no wonder that Gandhi struck a chord with artists, both in his lifetime and after. To mark the occasion of Mahatma Gandhi's arrest for protesting against the British tax on salt in 1930, the artist Nandalal Bose created a black and white linocut print of a scantily-clad Gandhi walking with a staff which became the iconic image for non-violence. It was indeed an ingenious image which countered the lofty power of colonialism. In reinstating the might of the ordinary person, Gandhi could not have been depicted with greater simplicity or strength. As the scholar Sunil Khilnani said, 'Gandhi did this with a mixed armoury: He invented, for example, a sartorial ensemble – the dhoti, shawl, cap and staff – that conjured up the village and that he wore in the public territories of the Raj. When Gandhi, dressed in this way, strode past the liveried Rajput guards and into the sparkling Viceroy's House in 1931 (just completed to Lutyens' designs) to meet Lord Irwin, or when he arrived at Buckingham Palace for tea with King George V and Queen Mary wearing a tattered shawl, he punctured the starched sanctity of British imperial pomp. He created his own rituals of power, bringing his artful village cosmology into the heart of the colonial city.'[3]

Nandalal Bose also made around four hundred posters at Mahatma Gandhi's request for the 1938 Haripura Session of the Indian National Congress in Gujarat, which expressively depict ordinary folk like fishermen, farmers, carpenters, ironsmiths, musicians and others. Bose, as before, created a temporary township where all the delegates would stay and the posters were designed to be placed in this area to create a lively consciousness of the people around them. These were produced on handmade paper with pigments made from local stones and were mounted on strawboards with each one being unique and not mass-produced. Bose made images of the local craftsmen and village women engaged in their everyday life melding folk art, the decorative and the calligraphic, signing it off with his personal insignia. He framed these within Indo-Islamic scalloped arches to underline the shared Hindu–Muslim heritage which was inherent to the country.

Mapping the Distance

The magnetism and simplicity of Gandhi has engaged artists through the decades. In post-Independence India he symbolized hope and a diachronic engagement with his beliefs, as artists mapped the distance travelled from his teachings. Gandhi was invoked in a masterly manner by M.F. Husain, for instance, who painted him striding forward (perhaps during the Dandi March) on the strip of road behind and without any facial features. To him, Gandhi was symbolic of the common man due to his ability to survive despite the constant obstacles in day-to-day life. Husain's Gandhi brings to mind the artful manner in which the leader had knitted together his countrymen into a regurgitating mass movement. As Khilnani points out, 'Most importantly, he invented ways in which Indians could occupy and act in the public spaces of the Raj. After Gandhi, nationalist politics was no longer confined to debating chambers, nor did it skulk in the clandestine rooms of terrorism; it poured out on to the streets and maidans in visible defiance of colonial rules, in crowds that literally allowed people to see themselves as a collective body. Before the mass presence of the moving image, Gandhi pioneered a potent theatrical use of processional marches and public meetings.'[4]

Atul Dodiya's fascination for Gandhi, whom he considers an 'artist of non-violence', has steered his work for years. In the iconic watercolour *Bapu at Rene Block Gallery, New York-1974* made in 1998, Dodiya paints an imaginative scene where Gandhi enters the Rene Block Gallery to experience Joseph Beuys' action, 'I like America and America likes me' creating an interaction between Beuys and Gandhi. Dodiya draws connections between the two 'artists' such as their environmental concerns and their belief in the power of the individual to enact change. As Gandhi is known to have said, 'I am not a seer, rishi or a philosopher of non-violence: I am only an artist of non-violence and desire to develop the art of non-violence in the realm of resistance.'[5] Non-violence for him was a dense truth, which was charged with the belief in the unity of all religions and communities and a deep-rooted faith in the power and expanse of the language of humanism. But he was also an artist in a deeper sense and it was no wonder that Gandhi struck a chord with creativity both in his lifetime and after.

When Dodiya visited Porbandar in 1997 to see Gandhi's birthplace, Kirti Mandir, he noticed shallow cabinets there in which Gandhi's personal belongings were kept. These distilled into his inspired work *Wooden Cabinets with Various Objects* in 2002. Dismayed and anguished by the Godhra riots in Gujarat in that year, these nine cabinets were not just a commemoration but are aide-mémoires of sorrow, pain, loss and retrieval. The cabinets showcase replicas of human bones, prosthetic limbs, hand-painted photographs, spades and hammers and other debris of divisive hate which create an anguished despair in the viewer.

In the newly independent country, Gandhi was everywhere – on currency notes, road signs, hoardings, etc. – and yet he was nowhere. His beliefs and ideals had been left behind, even though his name was invoked at every juncture. As the journalist Bernard Imhasly points out, 'Gandhi is alive in civil society, but his virulence is absent precisely where he had positioned himself throughout his life: in the politics of the country, at the intersection between private life and public action. In my journey I did not meet a single politician who reflected on Gandhi's core principle of means and goals, his insistence that both are inextricably linked, like seed and fruit. Even the decent ones among them seem to think that one can build a non-violent society with violent means; that the use of black money, say in election campaigns, can be a shortcut on the way to a transparent public space.'[6]

In navigating the nation-state, none could have played a more profound role than the figure of Gandhi and his engagements with people from all walks of life. Hence, his heightened status merges with the gardener in Sudhanshu Sutar's *The High Performance Intellect* (2010) where he intriguingly walks with a watering can towards the concrete pole with its electric wire heads. The village-city conundrum with its mass migrations and uneven development interface in this many-edged work. The gardener who caught Godse, Gandhi's murderer, came from Sutar's village in Orissa

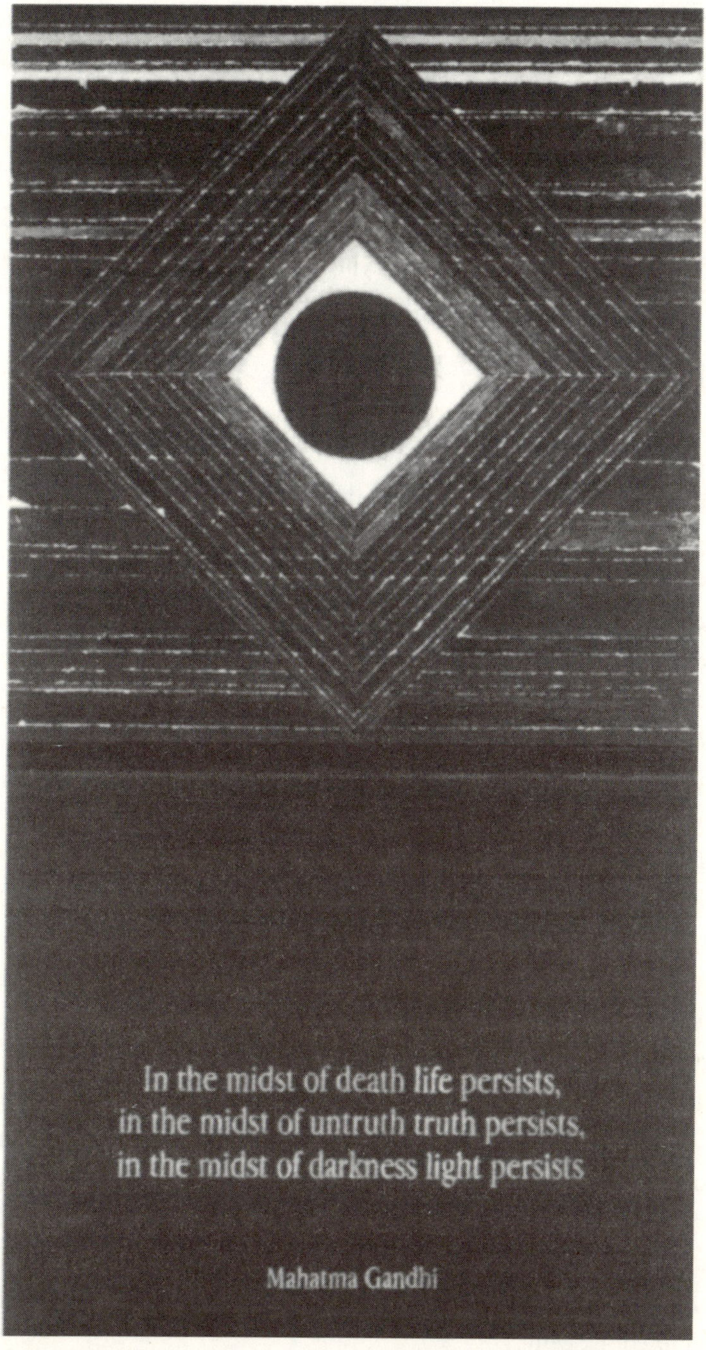

Immanence, 1990, acrylic on canvas, 100x80 cm, S.H. Raza.

and he grew up with tales of his heroism being little known outside the small habitation. When he migrated to the city, the gardener and Gandhi got inextricably intertwined in his imaginative vision. The watering can carried by the iconic figure then is to provide the necessary life impetus to those who are destitute in villages for there can be no progress without this large arc of deprivation being addressed. In Sutar's suite of Gandhi images, we have his engaging persona dealing with the man on the street and the difficult dynamics of his daily life.

He Came to Stay

The magnitude of the role that Gandhi played in Raza's life is something that perhaps even the latter himself did not realize when as an eleven-year-old he went to hear him at a public meeting in Mandla in 1933. Gandhi had come to address the public during the freedom struggle. His father being a forest ranger of the British government, Raza was accompanied by a forest official. On his way to the meeting, he was accosted by the wife of a British official of the Forest Department who rightly assumed that he was on his way to hear the Mahatma. He did, however, reach the meeting but did not remember Gandhi's words later, yet the image of the 'half-naked fakir' with a lathi in his hand made a lasting impact on Raza. He was to say later, '…During my stay in Paris, as my evolution went apace, I realized that Mahatma Gandhi was immense, his acts and ideas truly monumental. Apart from being a politician, he was a great humanist and a philosopher whose thoughts and ideas were intimately linked with day-to-day both at home in India and internationally … He could read a few verses or put it as simply as "Quit India", and the whole nation was electrified and the British had to ultimately leave.'[7]

Later, on having been asked why he did not go to Pakistan when the rest of his family – three brothers, a sister and his former wife had left – he stated that he could not bring himself to leave the land of Gandhi. During his annual visits to India, he would unfailingly visit Gandhi's samadhi and bow before it. When asked what his greatest disappointments were, Raza stated unequivocally:

> My greatest disappointments, akin to unhappiness, were in 1948 when Mahatma Gandhi was assassinated. It was an act of an individual who had convictions of his own. It came at a time when we were full of youth and energy. We wanted to take our destinies in hand and in the period of immense enthusiasm and joy, this tragic event took place. I don't know of any of other distress, more important, in my life. We had a sense of void and despair, a sense of sheer outrage. It was, I remember, the same years when I lost my parents. As children, we were not politically conscious. And for different reasons coming from the authority of my father we were really away from any social work or political action. But the national pride was there, the desire to be independent was there. Mahatma Gandhi had mobilized the country as one magnificent source of power. The British with all their might had to leave India and it was independent. And then the father of the nation was killed. No other incident had this acute pain and distress in my life.[8]

Two years after returning to India, in 2013, Raza was to make a suite of paintings on Gandhi which evoke his presence and his beliefs in a vivid manner. Perhaps he would have agreed with the words of the historian Sudhir Chandra, 'We, who once made Gandhi possible because we believed in him, have made him impossible by not believing in him – and this at a time when we – and the world – need him more than ever before.'[9] Raza fervently aspired to awaken his teachings in private and public spaces by his liturgical visual practice. These works seem immanent in his entire oeuvre and have emerged in one stroke to claim a place for themselves. Their astral, evanescent quality, which could dissolve with light, remains entrenched in the mind.

Invocations and Recitations

In *Shanti*, we have the reverberating Bindu with its incessantly emerging concentric circles in pristine colours of light grey, ochre and white where their exquisite delicacy contrasts with their inherent energy. These radiate in four directions creating a dynamic throbbing invocation of Shanti, which could also translate as the abode of calm. The diaphanous colours, however, are anything but still for they seem to be rotating in a ceaseless movement creating a vibrating mantra. Raza had been making Shanti Bindus influenced by Gandhi for some years but the subtle shades of grey here layer the painting with an extra dimension. In this work, which is specifically related to Gandhi, the Bindu emerges from a dusky ground, like the rising sun which makes its way in the sky. The dual juxtaposition of movement and stillness which is Raza's hallmark creates yet another coded significance. It seems to beckon towards the chakra of light and colour which can be reached by wading through the dark wall of ignorance and impediments.

In *Sanmati*, the deep orb at the centre creates a spiritual geometry formulating Gandhi's favourite prayer which speaks of the oneness of all religions. The lines speak of Allah and Ishwar as names of the same God and that this wisdom seems to have been lost in contemporary India. The glowing circle creates bands of yellow, ochre, blue, red and its nuanced shades which radiate and transform in different directions. A believer himself, Raza, until the end of his life used to visit church, temple and mosque, losing himself in meditation. According to Vajpeyi, 'Raza did not observe any rituals but sought through different religions true and enduring spiritual communion. Here again, I feel that the unique spiritual institution the Mahatma created in the "Prarthana Sabha" with renditions of multi-religious scriptures and meditative silence was the inspiration behind Raza's practice … Raza was not just a Muslim keeping intact his faith in Islam, but also a person inspired by and rooted in metaphysical concepts of Hinduism and, occasionally, Christianity.'[10]

The circle reformulates itself into bands of colour in *Satya*, where the density of grey gradually leads to a translucent light above. The delicate transparency of the upper layers, however, can only be reached by wading through the darker zones below which create a sombre, earthy ground. The struggle has to be gone through rather than evaded and side-tracked into diversionary and destructive routes. Yet, the pure brilliance of truth reaches epiphanic heights when it is attained.

One of Gandhiji's favourite hymns, 'Vaishnav Jana To' by Narsinh Mehta, defines true men of God as those who understood the pain of others. In *Peed Parai*, Raza breaks away completely from the Bindu format and moves towards abstraction. In this dual panel, the frenzy of colours in red, yellow, brown and white give way to an incandescent glow on the other side and the two aspects seem to be consistently intertwined as well as separate. In their startling binaries they speak of the overcoming of base emotions to reach heights that are human and compassionate. The awareness of dualities, which could be surpassed, was in itself a humane act. Yet, the felt reality of others alone would draw out the human being in oneself and make it a life worth living.

In the painting *Swadharma*, Raza drew inspiration from Vinoba Bhave that everyone should heed his inner calling and act accordingly. The inspirational words are written by him in dark letters over a glowing yellow background. The blazing paintings seems to suggest that your radiance emerges from a realization of swadharma. It was clear to him that his own dharma was to paint and that he would abide by this throughout his life.

Hey Ram

The almost abstract work *Hey Ram* that he painted first is also the most poignant. The assassination of Gandhi, which had moved him deeply, is invoked in the last words of the former when he fell to the ground after being shot. In *Hey Ram*, we have a glowing, burnished yellow interspersed by wedges of white in the centre reflecting both purity and ascension as the misty red engulfs the canvas. The layers of diluted pigment are applied in overlapping glazes to create an effect of saturation of colour which are yet ephemeral. In many ways, it harks to the early works of Mark Rothko made around 1947 before his iconic forms crystalized where the raw immediacy of the colours is undiluted and convey an intensity. Rothko stated of these works, 'I think of these pictures as dramas… Neither the actions nor the actors can be anticipated or described in advance … ideas and plans that existed in my mind at the start were simply the doorway through which one left the world in which they occur.'[11]

In a similar manner, Raza made visible that which existed in a latent form in the subject and within himself. The column of brown at the side is akin to the destructive forces which have to be combated to reach the pure incandescence of light. The solidity of the column also suggests a resilience of the spirit which survives even if the physical body is no longer sensate. This is the most abstract and immensely moving of Raza's works on Gandhi.

Raza created a canvas with Gandhi's teachings written in black over a sunset background. His words, Raza believed, were almost like holy scriptures and in inscribing them he was creating an immortal act. The last line reads: 'There is God where there is love.'

One is reminded of the words of the thirteenth-century Sufi poet, Rumi:

O you who've gone on pilgrimage –
where are you, where, oh where?
Here, here is the Beloved!
Oh come now, come, oh come!
Your friend, he is your neighbour,
he is next to your wall –
You, erring in the desert –
what air of love is this?
If you'd see the Beloved's
form without any form –
You are the house, the master,
You are the Kaaba, you![12]

Of the paintings of Gandhi and his statues all over the world which evoke his life and teachings, Raza's paintings can be forefronted because they make an impact on the mind. With their diaphanous lights that create ambulatory patterns, they eke out the essence of Gandhi's existence and project it in subtle yet forceful ways. In Raza's Gandhi, we have the most abstract depiction of the great leader's powerful beliefs.

Memory and Longing

There could not have been a more harmonious couple than Raza and Janine. Their lives were strung together like a melodious tune which played incessantly. And yet they were very different from each other. Raza was the dreamer, the idealist, embedded in philosophy and spirituality and rooted to his traditions, all while being modern. Janine, on the other hand, was down-to-earth, practical; while being sensitive and creative, she also looked into the nitty-gritty of things. Their art varied considerably, with Raza's having blazing colours and sublimated abstractions and Janine's earthy tones and use of day-to-day objects like teabags for creating works with material devices. Yet the two synchronized with each other like a sublime symphony, their parallel lives flowed together and their separate and supportive existence formed the mainstay of their art and their lives. As Michel Imbert put it succinctly, 'They were a good couple because they functioned well together. Raza was a painter – strong, and sometimes difficult. With Janine everything was soft and easy … and she looked after everything – the house, the bank, the car though she didn't drive – Raza drove.'[1] Together they created the yin and yang of life that Raza painted in flaming colours. As Raza's favourite poet Rilke would have said, 'Love consists in this, that two solitudes protect and touch and greet each other.'[2] Although Janine and Raza had separate apartment-studios on the same floor, they were together in all other ways. '[In the morning] I was at my studio and she at hers, we met for lunch, and after lunch I went to my studio again. It was a serious organization … we would go to exhibitions together. Of course, there were the evenings and the nights. I was very fortunate.'[3] And indeed their engagement with each other seemed consistent and strong. 'The two of them really appreciated and admired each other. Every time he would be talking about his art, she was totally attentive. Then he would go into the other room to see her work and he would be completely absorbed…'[4]

In many ways, they had only each other and that brought them even closer. Most of their acquaintances seem to feel that they didn't have children because they wanted to devote their time and energy to their work and each other and felt that it would provide them with greater satisfaction. Janine herself had been an only child and, therefore, had led a protected life with a careful tutoring of the dos and don'ts of an upper-class French family. She had gone to a Catholic school in Paris but she seems to have been tired of its rigours and in later life tended to stay away from it all. Indeed, it was Raza who went to church regularly on Sundays and at other times. Janine had never suffered any material want and even after marriage most of her practical needs were taken care of.

Installing the Past

In her earlier works, Janine attempted to free herself from her gilded cage and she did this with a fiery energy. In a low relief work made in wood, for instance, which hung in Raza's studio, a frenzied child seems to be gyrating wildly surrounded by broken bits of decorative furniture. Around her in disarry are a picture frame, a fan, beads and other accoutrements of upper-class existence. She holds a painted wooden parrot in one hand, perhaps indicating a symbol of regeneration.

Her later work, partly because of her interaction with Raza and the visits to India, became more and more elegant and multi-layered. Beginning with touching the earth, it would soar the skies. Janine's work was in many ways ahead of her times – she often used found objects and installed them on the surface going beyond the space of the canvas. According to Ashok Vajpeyi, 'Janine, besides being the wife, was also a creative and lively companion in art. She was solidly rooted in modern French life and culture and her work followed an interesting and parallel path to that of Raza. Unlike Raza who stuck to painting on canvas, Janine experimented rather boldly with different materials. She used teabags for creating both paintings on canvas and sculpture. She also made use of almirahs, dolls, shoes, frocks, old books, etc. to create new art assemblages recapturing her French childhood memories, her Corsican experiences.'[5]

According to Jean Duchesne, 'There were several stages in Janine's career. In the beginning there was always collage – which is different to Raza. And one characteristic of her work was that she always used raw materials from everyday life. And those raw materials were recognizable in her works... Then there were more and more objects that were reminders of childhood ... dolls' dresses, also old pieces, cards, lace, also pieces of dolls themselves...'[6] There seemed to have been an outrage in her against her own upbringing. Bernard Imhasly points out, '...There's an element of violence in the childhood paintings. A work, for instance, looks like a whip ... I remember she also made some allusions to childhood suffering from what I remember – I mean she was never explicit ... but there's that drawing of that dress ... see that opening ... and there's that childhood sexuality that plays into it.'[7]

Writing on Janine's early works, the critic Christian Pouillon points out, 'With a bit of magic and a bit of daring, what Janine Mongillat presents to us in Reliquaries is a kind of highly governed knitting together of things stored away, a renovation of those secret and gendered spaces that the solitary child she once was carved out of the world. Or are these transformations made by her double, Alice? An Alice who never received training in art and crafts, such that the assemblages have more meaning then her intuition and intimacy could ever give them.'[8] The comparison with Lewis Carroll's Alice brought out the dark fantasies that Janine seems to have worked out in her assemblages. According to Pouillon, '...These works place recognizable objects from the past reconfigured into a world which is poetic as it is bizarre. And this seems to be her particular talent right from the start ... Because this language must make us see the world differently, it slightly shifts what would otherwise seem so familiar, questions what we think we know, and communicates a particular vision and feelings. From this point of view, the assemblages and installations, like the future paper sculptures, are from here on out linked by discernible emotive, philosophical and aesthetic data."[9]

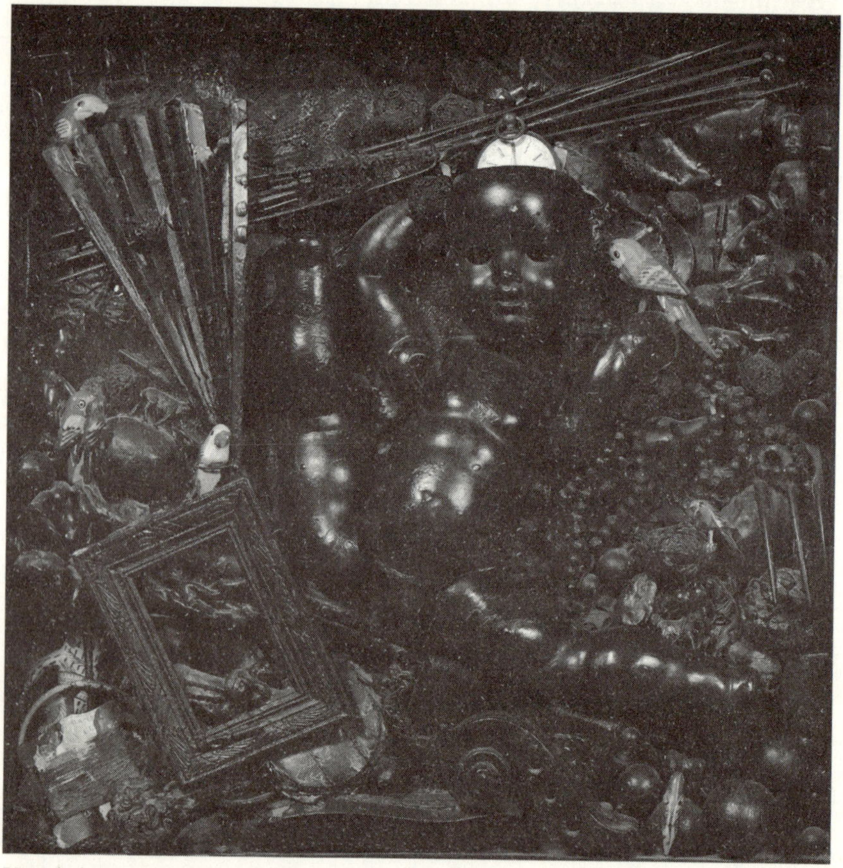

Untitled, mixed media, 42x42 cm, Janine Mongillat.

Janine's objects and views transformed due to her visits to India with Raza and freed her from her own interiority as she entered that of another. Enthralled by the colours and diversity of objects and figures, she infused the profusion of divine and demoniac effigies and recreated them in her own subterranean manner. 'After 1982, she produced polychrome sculptures that freely add moving, grotesque and sometimes troubling demons and syncretic marvels to mythological demons.'[10] What is more, even at this stage, the wooden animals with their hollowed bellies and backs, containing powders and perfumes, are like memorials to the past created by her. By the time it was the '90s, Janine's mastery of modelling material, and particularly art paper, gave way to the flight of *Dancers* which are tiny statues in suspense, in full movement, and yet frozen in place. As Pouillon said, 'This time the work is completely extroverted, joyously and vitally formal, a characteristic belied only by the Dancer's eyes set into the face-masks above oblique postures and baroque drapery. They are perhaps metaphors for the busy fingers of the woman sculptor.'[11]

In one of her imaginative pieces, she creates Hommage à Pina Bausch (1991) – a homage to the famed modern dancer Pina Bausch – where the immensely mutable form seems to be turning like a gust of the wind! Returning to the two-dimensional, Janine's large triptych *The Wedding Dress* is a composition of immense humour and wit. As Pouillon points out, '...The big triptych called *The Wedding Dress*, as caustic and troubling at times as it is funereal, showing the persistent traces of India, and in particular, the many-headed figures in a composition whose resonance is quite evidently mythical.'[12]

Tea Ceremony

Not long after, Janine was to collect teabags and assemble them with great craftsmanship on her canvases creating an immensely textured surface. The small variations in their alignments and their delicate balance would be like the very symphony which she had orchestrated of her own life. Gèrard Barrière elucidates, 'For Janine Mongillat, little talismanic pockets full of secret memories or elusive dreams, the first teabags, appeared in her work as a part and parcel of a singular, untamed project of personal archaeology, a celebration of the intimate rites of memory or, more broadly, of cosmic phantasm.'[13] Dowsed in acrylic, these would generate their imprint on pages which were like the impressions of a wandering soul. 'All that was left of them were fossils, remnants, traces. All that was left were the prints they had left behind, lined up across paper or canvas like a text to be chanted, an obsessive rhythm, a palimpsest open to infinite deciphering … The prints began to appear as so many X-ray photographs through whose transparency one could make out the discreet movement of chrysalides before metamorphosis, or the miracle of Amravati, when the Buddha multiplied his glorious image to infinity or the glyphs of some sacred writing that bears a revelation as essential as it forever inaccessible, or even for one of the works, the ghostly face of the Holy Shroud.'[14]

The teabags interact with cavorting strings balls in a joyous binary of harmony and chaos, *Mandala aux Sachets de thè* (2001) and their inner dynamics are contained within the rectangle symbolic of universal harmony. In her *Birds of Benaras* sculptures, Janine was to imaginatively recreate the wooden birds she had found in Benaras into assemblages of ascension and descent. The rows of birds of different hues placed atop a painted wall would both be harbingers of the final curtain and the ascent to a higher flight. In their hard-edged feathers and bold, brazen eyes the birds ring around the circle of life and death in a perpetual dance. They are scattered around the field where a wooden Ganesh sculpture stands over a stack of wood, which could be a funeral pyre in Ganesh Puja (2001). The birds form the very narrative of her journey and are displayed in the exhibition of her work after her death, which was held in Gorbio from July to September 2002.

There was a playful as well as a poignant quality about the small objects Janine collected and wove into works of art. Bernard Imhasly observed, 'Whenever she came to Bombay, she would disappear for days in the markets. And she was fascinated by these little paper ribbons which you hang up. I remember once, she just had this kind of box and she put these lightly rolled up papers into them … they were all rolled up, squeezed – beautiful.'[15]

Birds of Benaras

Rashna Imhasly pointed out, '…She always asked us to find little birds and animals, when we came from India – we used to buy those little boxes – wooden birds and animals – small ones which she used to put on her figures, or in her boxes... She used to collect paraphernalia like that... Her whole kitchen cabinet she had done as a montage... The entire cabinet in Paris looked gorgeous.'[16]

Unlike Raza, Janine was not a flamboyant artist with brilliant colours, yet she had a sombre depth and an inventiveness with forms, which made her work distinctive. She had had several exhibitions and was part of many collections. But she was also a supportive partner and for her, in many ways, Raza and his work came first. If her works reflected her expansive inner space, she was also known to keep herself in the back when Raza was seen as the famous painter. Yet she was his muse and protector.

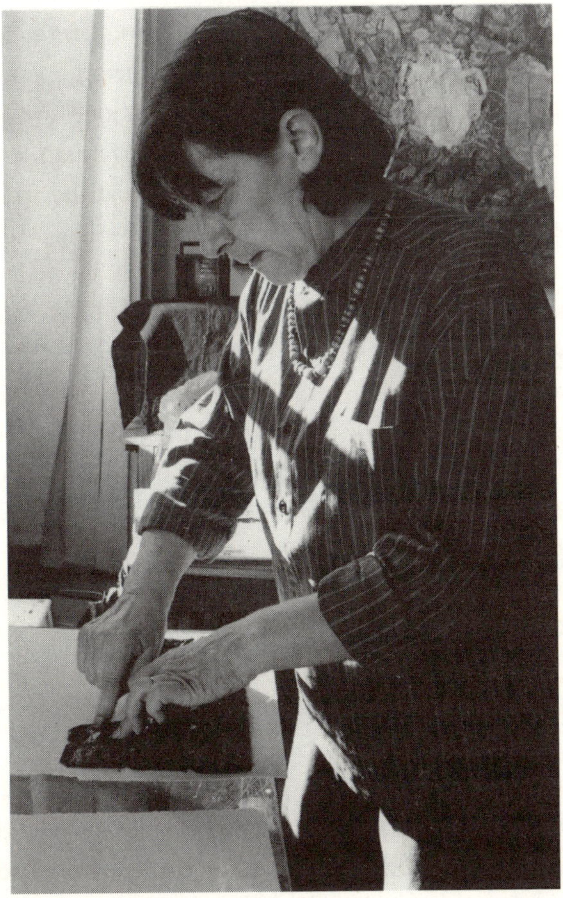

Janine in her studio in Paris.

Friends speak of their collaborative presence in art on visiting them. As the cultural and film writer Latika Padgaonkar points out, 'The first of Raza's paintings to grace our house dates back to 1967. My husband Dileep was a student in Paris then, and had struck up a friendship with Raza. He bought a small Bindu work, paying for it in instalments from his scholarship money. Many years later when we were back in Paris, Raza and Janine's house was a regular draw for us. We would lounge in his workroom, chat spiritedly about this and that, sip wine and gaze at his paintings-in-progress; or stare at Janine's startlingly inventive sculptures, wondering whether we would ever possess any.

'Then, one day, Raza had enough of our stares, our stealthy glances of admiration … My heart beat hard as the eyes went from one gorgeous painting to another … We spent long and anxious moments making up our minds. But we gazed longest at the large "Untitled" work that was to become ours … He then walked us to the adjoining apartment which was Janine's studio. "Choose," he ordered. We looked at the array of Janine's paintings and sculptures, and finally opted for a collage that had been hanging for many years, not in her workplace, but above their dining table.

'The works arrived three days later, and Raza with them, armed with ladder, nails, drill and hammer. He tore open the covers and personally supervised where and at what height the works should be placed in the living room … The effect of the painting and the collage was instantaneous and electric. On one side, the room lit up like a fiery yet ambiguous half-set sun; on the other, nightfall had begun, a mysterious dark sky with patches of light.'[17]

The Darkening Sky

The spell was broken, however, a little before the turn of the new century. Janine was diagnosed with cancer. She had not been well for five years, and the last two of those were especially painful. According to Michel Imbert, 'She fell down on the street and broke her wrist and when she arrived in the hospital they took her blood and understood that she had cancer … It was too late. It had spread … she had a lot of treatment but it was too late. My mother remembers that she didn't want to go to the doctor when she first felt unwell. They spoke together, even though my mother explained that women should have check-ups. But she didn't want to go.'[18] She was at a stage where she could receive only palliative care at the hospital. According to Imbert, 'Raza didn't want to understand. I was there in front and Raza said, "Don't say that! It's not that."'[19] 'Janine asked to have prayers said on her behalf. Luc [a close friend in Gorbio] and Michel met the priest in the chapel at the hospital and explained the situation to him after which prayers were held, which Janine attended. Following this the priest came to her room and also said prayers there. It seems that Janine knew that it was critical at the beginning of the year but didn't tell me or my mother or anybody.'[20] By this time she had isolated herself. According to Jean Duchesne, 'We lost contact with Raza when Janine fell ill. I remember going there and she was ill. He said she didn't want to see anyone so I was not allowed to see her. There was no reason for insisting…'[21]

Just when Janine seemed to be recovering, her illness took a turn for the worse and she passed away in April 2002. Raza was heartbroken.

> I am left alone. Yet, not alone since Janine in her home, in our home, remains a presence. Without her it is so lonesome. But this is the cruel fate: I now have to fill my loneliness by work, by activity, by my paintings. I get exhausted but not bored. I cannot leave art because art is life for me: it is the only evidence that I am, that I'm alive and that I can still touch and see the world through my colours.[22]

In her last phase, Janine turned towards the toy birds of Benares: at first using colourfully painted ones, and later bare, unpainted wooden toy birds almost like bidding farewell to the world, which had India pulsating through it. 'In Janine's entire artistic career this was the first time, in her last phase that she turned to India. The birds of Benares found residence in her world.'[23] According to Rashna Imhasly, '…He said that she's very ill but she's very private. And she doesn't want to share this with other people. It's her thing. And then he showed me … he said this is one of her last paintings. And it's a black egg with hands – of girls – coming out from underneath the black egg. And in the last month she had put birds on it – as if her spirit is ready to go. And I said this is such a powerful picture

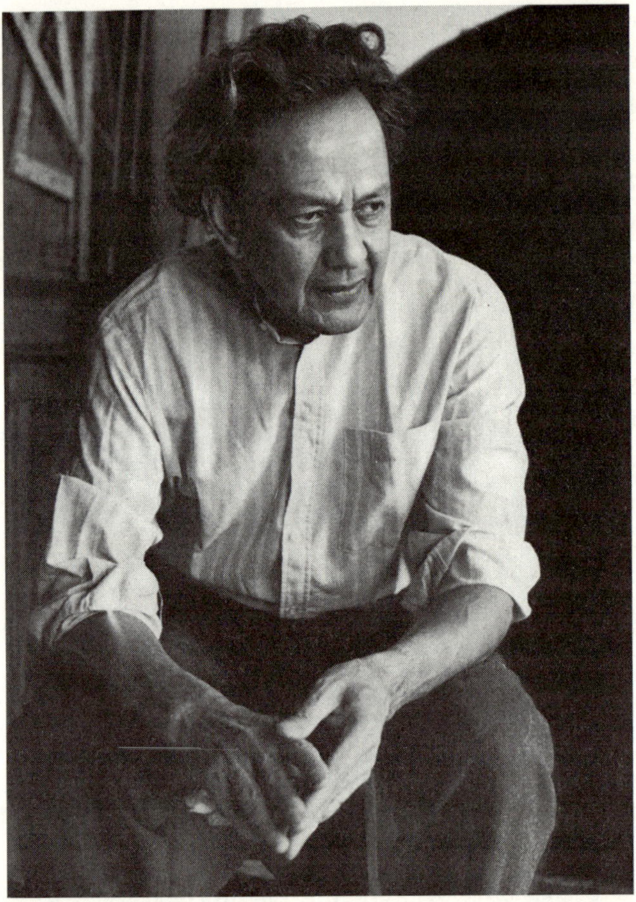

Raza in a thoughtful mood.

and I really want it. So, I bought it. It's a beautiful piece – it's like a little sculpture.'[24] According to Michel Imbert, in her last days she was thinking of India. 'She spoke only about Udaipur and Lake Palace. "Promise me you must go one time to this place – it is wonderful." And she wanted to have in the hospital 2-3 photos about Lake Palace because she had stayed 3-4 weeks with Raza in Udaipur.'[25]

Janine was buried in the graveyard at Gorbio, next to her parents. And Raza professed that upon his death he would like to be buried in the same cemetery close to her, if he died in France. And even as the birds from Benares ascended to another sphere, they would remain forever in his memory. One is reminded of the poet and lyre player Orpheus in Greek mythology who went to the underworld after the death of his wife Eurydice and secured her release from the dead, but lost her because he failed to obey the condition that he must not look back at her until they had reached the world of the living. Raza too would continue to search for her in the void within. In *Sonnets to Orpheus*, Rainer Maria Rilke recalls:

> ...Go,
> and if the earthly fades and has forgot
> you, whisper to the silent earth: I flow.
> To the onrushing water say: I am.[26]

Henceforth, her memory would sweep Raza's canvases like a flood and would continue to lash the shores forever like the frothing waves.

Mother, What Shall I Bring When I Return?

The elegiac works made by Raza in the '90s were an offering to silence and a luminous reflection. The other-worldliness of the Bindu, even as an all-pervasive calm emanates from it, would set the tone for the years approaching Janine's death. In paintings like *Param Bindu* (1989), concentric circles made in colours of yellow, ochre, green revolving around a dark centre create an ethereal zone of ascension. In *Naad Bindu* (1989), the diaphanous sheaths of grey, which turn white at the edges and revolve around a black disc, convey a sense of gradual movement to an upper world of light and sound. The painting, according to Raza, has elements of sound resonating through its vital rotations. The monochromatic canvas, which expands into a translucent space transfers an exquisite delicacy even as its tonal variations create an atmosphere of meditative silence.

In many of Raza's works of this period there is a consonance between music and art, implying that the two heighten and amplify each other. In Indian aesthetics, the Ragamala paintings embody the 'raga' or the melodic note, as personified by the figuration of a man or woman and their meeting or separation and the climate of seasons or time of the day in which this takes place. The Ragamalas of the seventeenth century had musical notes which were metaphorical figures and contained as it were the essence of music. The alignment of music to art can also be related to the sound theories of Kandinsky in which associating colour with form, he aimed at affecting a totality of experience. In *The Spiritual in Art*, Kandinsky emphasized that a painting needed to free itself from the transitional and the corporeal, and move into realms which were universal, abstract and spiritual.

Raza's world too became more ethereal as his spiritual vision became heightened by the approaching separation from his wife. In a work made after her death, *Shanti Bindu* (2004), pale shades of yellow, ochre, grey concentric circles move around a central white space which seems like a void or work of the same nature made two years later has the words 'Om, Shanti, Shanti, Shanti' like a chant addressed to himself. His paintings of this period have bright, flashy colours and often shapes in disarray which speak of an inner chaos.

After Janine passed away, Raza was shell-shocked, lulled into silence and almost unable to contain his grief. Visitors remarked about his experience of her absence in an unaccountable manner. The gallerist Khorshed Pundole stayed at his Raza's house in Paris barely two months after Janine had passed away. She speaks of the time, 'I was put up in Janine's studio and she must have worked there in the past with glass eyes. So, they were all over the place and there was barely any light and all those eyes were gleaming all over the place. It was so spooky especially since she had passed away recently. And the odd part is just before we left his studio, when he went to drop me to Janine's for the night, he showed me pictures of her when sleeping. Or I assumed she was sleeping but they were actually pictures of Janine in her coffin. And I have a phobia of coffins and closed spaces so it spooked me completely. I didn't sleep at all that night.'[1] Was this an embalmment or a pact with death?

Apart from Janine's physical absence, Raza also faced immense problems in coping with the day-to-day life after she was gone. She had handled all his practical affairs and this complete dependence on her made him feel helpless. The artist Sujata Bajaj, whom he had nurtured since she was a young girl, came to Paris and helped with handling some aspects of this even when Janine was there and began to participate more in his life. She had applied for a scholarship from the French government at Raza's behest. When she received it and reached Paris on 22 October 1988, Raza was waiting for her at the main railway station. According to Sujata, 'He knew and respected my Gandhian parents and over time became my ange gardien… When Janine, Raza's wife fell ill, he felt many a time distraught and needed support and company. It was our good fortune that my husband Rune and I were there for him in times both good and bad just as he had been for us in our times of need … I never realized when a reversal of roles emerged and Raza started to think of me as his ange gardien.'[2]

The Path to Nowhere

As his loneliness and vulnerabilities started coming to the fore, Raza was to find outlets which would take him on a path which diverged considerably from his journey thus far. He met Sabrina Guiglionda, an attractive person who came from Monaco and who actively supported Raza in his public project at the Chateau in Gorbio. Along with Raza, she became a member of the Association du Vieux Chateau. Sabrina became intimately associated with Raza, according to Michel Isnard, and she also actively helped in the project of restoring the Chateau and holding exhibitions. It is not clear how long this relationship lasted but she was to marry someone else later and now lives in Iceland.

There was, however, someone else waiting for him in the wings and this was to be his last call. A dealer in Monaco realized that he could actively trade antiquities from India with Raza, which are believed to be fakes, and in exchange obtain Raza's paintings as payment. A considerable number of his paintings went to the dealer in this manner. Finally at his behest, a masseur, Devina Rughoobar, was sent to Raza in Paris. An attractive young Mauritian who could speak both French and Hindi, she had come to Paris at the age of fourteen to study and could speak French fluently. She could speak Hindi because her grandfather hailed from Bihar and had been taken to Mauritius to work in the sugar factories. It seems that Raza not only succumbed to her charms, but also allowed her to take over all his affairs completely. She was in fact a faux companion, a Jekyll-like occupation of his inner self by someone else's spirit.

His dependence on her became more and more acute as he became completely malleable in her hands. According to Ashok Vajpeyi, 'Veena [as Devina was called] met him in Paris as far as I know. She operated for quite a few days as agent of the antique dealer informing him what was happening – if a new painting was being made. Raza didn't bother too much about money – what came, what went. As a result, some money might have exchanged between them So, his generosity became his enemy... And then a point came when he became almost a slave. In daily life, he needed help. There was a Portuguese maid servant who was with them for twenty or twenty-five years and she used to come three-four times a week and do everything – wash clothes and clean the house, buy groceries. She was removed and she disappeared. So, the old set vanished and Janine's flat was occupied by her. Now the occupant was right there on the pretext that she would take care of him.'[3]

This was to continue for the next few years in Paris, as his friends became more and more distanced from him. According to Michel Imbert, 'Raza was like my second father – it was very difficult for us to see that man who changed completely. Before that around Raza and Janine – there were exceptional people, very talented, architects, lawyers ... After that more and more some very strange people – we were very afraid, we were in shock – my mother, myself and old friends ... For example, there is a lady in Paris who was a lawyer, wife of a big collector of Raza. They met in Paris at an exhibition and he says to her "Bonjour madame, hello madame?" She cried because he couldn't remember. He has another mind, he looked the same ... but he changed completely.'[4]

He had changed to such an extent that his regular friends now found it difficult to spend time with him. According to the gallerist Sharan Apparao who was close to the couple, Raza was very different while Janine was alive, 'And I want to give more credit to Janine than to Raza because I think her values were important for him. Because in the later years I found that – of course, when you live with somebody you become like them. And I think because she came from a very solid background it had a big influence on him. And after she died, I found so many things changed. I worked with him till just after her death. And I realized there were too many people with too many agendas and I just stepped back and whatever I heard or saw after that was not to my taste. So, I just took a back seat.'[5]

The gifting of a considerable amount of finance, his possessions and his apartments in Paris and Gorbio to Veena was the final act. Raza had wanted his Gorbio house to be used as a residency for Indian artists and writers, but that never happened. The cesspool of his life deepened even further widening the distance from the heights he had reached. Would there be a way out of this detritus of existence?

The Wheel Comes Full Circle

Eventually the person who came to his rescue was his close friend and colleague, the poet and writer Ashok Vajpeyi. Watching with concern his steady deterioration in mental and physical health, he finally persuaded Raza to return to India. 'He was kept by her in a miserable condition – old pre-cooked food, kebabs kept for days. It became a huge problem.'[6] He also pointed out that by settling in the country of his birth he had a role to play, where a foundation could be set up in his name which would advance cultural and artistic activities and, hence, enhance humanistic growth. And so Raza arrived in Delhi to settle down, bringing the wheel full circle for that was where his ancestors had lived until the 1857 Uprising. For Raza, it was a true homecoming, 'I love my country and want to spend my last years here. I'm very happy to return to India. India is mine and I am all Indian. Despite living in France for sixty years, I remained an Indian citizen, maintained relations with my country and read the Gita Pravachan and Ramayana. I continue to read and write in Hindi.'[7]

Vajpeyi spoke of his great generosity even when he arrived without much means, 'He came here finally in December 2010. He walked in straight to his home and found that this was a nice place. Veena was with him. After two-three days he gave me very unobtrusively an envelope. He said that "I had taken out 30,000 euros from the bank. From this 17,000 got spent on the way – Veena wanted shoes, etc. The balance 13,000 he gave to me." So, I said "What will I do with this? You keep it." He said,

"No, you keep it. I won't be going anywhere." So, after that in his bank account here there were thirty to thirty-five lakh rupees to start with.'[8] He remembers other instances of his generosity, 'Once I told him there is an international mass at Notre Dame next Sunday so why don't you go. So, we went in a taxi and as we were nearing Notre Dame, he took out a ten euro note and kept it and took out another ten. By the time the meter showed six, so I told him ten will be good enough. He said, "No, no, he drove us through Paris so well and so smoothly." It was a Sunday morning and there was hardly any traffic. It came (the final amount) to seven euros and he gave twenty. That was the kind of generosity. I don't know anyone who cared so much for younger people and not just in visual arts but in poetry, music, dance – he would spend huge amounts on them.'[9]

The Meeting of Ways

Ashok Vajpeyi had known Raza for a long time and their journey together was memorable. He had gone to meet him first in 1978 when Raza was visiting Bombay and had invited him to Madhya Pradesh. He persuaded him to come to Bhopal on behalf of the Madhya Pradesh Kala Parishad where he would be honoured and an exhibition of his works would be held. 'So, he quite liked the idea and until then I did not realize that he had a deep yearning for his home state because I had never met him and had no means of knowing. So, we said we would like you to come, show, have a seminar on your work and we will take you to the major art colleges in MP. He finally agreed.'[10] Raza visited Bhopal in 1979 and the visit proved to be very fruitful. He had a solo show, met many young artists and writers and a foundation was set up. The journal *Poorvagrah* edited by Vajpeyi came out with a special issue on Raza and apart from the cover, the entire issue was mostly designed by Raza where he wrote detailed notes on his 'Utsav-79' experience (Issue 35-36, November 1979-February 1980).

In time, Raza became more acquainted with the richness of the Indian culture in which he had grown up. He was enthralled by classical music, dance and art. According to Vajpeyi, 'You see he was brought up in nearby Nagpur. So, there was not much music … and anybody who had heard Ravi Shankar – by the time Raza came to Bhopal – Ravi Shankar was an international celebrity and all that. But vocal music – and this is where it made a lot of difference to him because he was encountering Dhrupad and they were the proper Dhrupad singers. There would be forty-five minutes of total abstraction in the human voice. There is no image, there is no word – it is alaap and it has no word, no image and it is a very geometrically constructed – this is something akin to what Raza himself was seeking and trying to do. So, it matched wonderfully in that sense because he was very struck by Dhrupad. And later in fact in 1980-81, instigated by Mani Kaul, I had started a Dhrupad Kendra in Bhopal to which the other Dagars from Bombay – Zia Moinuddin Dagar – the rudra veena player and the vocalist Zia Fariduddin Dagar came. But that was after Raza had left. Later in 1980 when we happened to be visiting France – by that time Mani Kaul had made *Satah Se Uthata Admi* and it was chosen to be shown in Cannes. I visited Cannes and that was the first time I visited Raza in Paris on my way up and down. And it so happened – Mani Kaul of course was there – there was a concert of Zia Fariduddin Dagar who happened to be there, in the studio of Raza, which Mani Kaul and I had organized. And he invited some of his friends, because he was quite enamoured of that music. And later there was a concert on the river Seine.'[11]

This engagement with Indian culture was enhanced for Raza when at Vajpeyi's behest Bharat Bhavan was set up in Bhopal in 1982 as a comprehensive multi-arts centre. 'The point was that Bharat Bhavan came in 1982 – he was not able to make it at the time of the inauguration. He came soon after and he was very, very impressed for a few reasons. One was that something in his home state of this kind is happening. In a manner of speaking Bharat Bhavan was a counter UTSAV. Instead of having it for a week we had it there all the time. There was a museum, poetry, library, music, exhibitions happening. There was a repertory headed by B.V. Karanth … Bharat Bhavan was very vital – what it became was because of the fact that it was a kind of multi-arts centre. There were centres, but Raza sort of became a part of that because he had seen UTSAV. So had Swami for that matter. We used to have every year in UTSAV an exhibition – a solo show in which we've had Husain, Akbar Padamsee, Ram Kumar, Swaminathan and Raza. Imagine, in the '70s they were all there and then in one show in which Vivan Sundaram, Sudhir Patwardhan, Nalini Malani ... these people were there. The UTSAV continued even when Bharat Bhavan came into being, and then it sort of was eased out because it was no longer necessary to do that for a week only because it was already being done in many different ways, etc. This was a kind of cultural awakening for Raza. He paid the highest tribute personally – he wrote in one of the letters that after Santiniketan, in post-Independence India this is the first major cultural institution. It is the Santiniketan of the New India...'[12]

Raza's exposure was both rich and enhancing. 'He told me that he had never seen in his life so much music, theatre, dance, poetry, etc. because it was all concentrated in a week and he was part of it. So, for him this was very different from the kind of reception he would get in Bombay or other places. There had been many, but this concentration and the fact that he was the most pursued, chased, highlighted artist. Not that he made any special effort to do it – it almost happened automatically. He was such a charmer. And the press was completely amazed that this man knows so much Hindi, living in France [for] so many years. Already when he came, he had been in France for twenty-nine to thirty years. It was quite a thing to find such a person – his elegance, general appearance, very handsome man ... But equally the impression on him must have been made which gave him a sense of belonging to a different world [when he had seen the most senseless manifestations] in this festival, of which he was a part. So, all said and done, although France had seen all kinds of movements, etc., the kind of seamless proximity that one could come across here was quite different from what he must have encountered in Paris – or for that matter in Bombay ... So, he got I think re-routed in a sense, effortlessly, and by sheer force of circumstance ... And the long relationship we developed was entirely due to that.'[13]

Bharat Bhavan had B.V. Karanth directing the theatre department and artists like Swaminathan heading the art department. The latter, though somewhat languid in his bearing, had been solely responsible for the fillip he gave to tribal artists of the surrounding areas like Gond art, for he visited them and encouraged them to make use of their experiences to reinvent their tradition in visual terms. Thus, came about the most vital and rich tribal art section of the Bhavan, and the works of Gond, Bhil and Warli artists – the fruits of which are being reaped to this day. Regardless of Swaminathan's angular relationship with the Progressives, he could link up with Raza. 'Swami came in 1980-81 and when Raza came he was very enthusiastic to show him around and Raza was very generous in his compliments to him. And we met at various parties at my place, etc. There was complete cordiality then. So, to that extent Bharat Bhavan had been able to overcome that distance I think. Partly also, there was a period in Swami's case when it was also geometrical … Swami had by that time also encountered in a big way a lot of tribal art. And a lot of tribal art is geometrical – use of totems and other things. They might not be neatly geometrical but they are geometrical … all said and done…'[14]

The Making of a Masterpiece

Raza was to participate generously in the activities of the Bharat Bhavan's dynamic cultural schedules. He also corresponded and exchanged ideas regularly with its chief initiator, Ashok Vajpeyi. In turn, Vajpeyi used to visit him in Paris each year and would have fruitful exchanges with him there. Although Raza was fluent in Urdu, Hindi, French and English, he felt most at home with Hindi. According to Vajpeyi, 'He used to say Hindi is my mother tongue, not Urdu … This was because his family is very open … His father was not strict about these things … He was deeply interested in Hindi poetry. I didn't know this until he came to Bhopal. Only one book of mine had come out by then – *Shahar Ab Bhi Sambhavna Hai* – a collection of poetry that I gifted him and he took it with him back to Paris and he got very interested and felt that he didn't know what is happening in Hindi poetry today because he had read only his textbook poetry – Mahadevi Verma and others. He didn't know the changes that had taken place. So, he became very interested and insisted that after that whenever I come to Paris to bring with me the collection of Hindi poetry which had been published till then and which would interest him.

'The interesting thing that happened about this was this book of mine – the first book published by Jnanapith which had a poem – "Maa Lautkar

Jab Aaunga" – that was the title. And some time in the '80s – early '80s or late '79 I think, I got a call from him saying that he's doing a large painting. And he wants to use a line from my poem "Maa Laut Kar Jab Aaunga". This poem has an interesting history. It was that I came from a small-town middle-class family. I had landed up here in St Stephen's to do my MA. The intention behind sending me here was that I should qualify for the IAS. And on the way I lost interest in that supposition to get in the IAS. That I got into it was another matter. There was a blank sheet at the end of the paper, it occurred to me that I'm going to go back without having done what my family wanted me to do. So, a line came to me – *Maa laut kar jab aunga kya launga.* So I started writing the poem. The invigilator watched me for a while that I'm not writing anything in the answer book – doing something else – I said, "No sir, I'm writing a poem – it has nothing do with..." [The invigilator then said] "You are writing a poem? You are supposed to be writing the exam." So, that was the original draft which later got converted into a slightly longer poem.

'Raza was struck by this poem and turned it into a painting and then converted it as a letter to the country ... A person who is gone and if he returns, what would he bring? It became a striking painting and was shown in the Triennale and then it was fondly acquired by Husain and Chhabda for Rs 19,000 ... It became priceless later ... I used to tease him [saying], "This is a painting which in some ways belong to me – I have a copyright on it!"'[15]

In another collaboration, Raza's elegant painting, *Naad Bindu*, was placed as the backdrop for a Kathak recital and a poetry reading session by Ashok Vajpeyi at the Avignon Festival in France in 1995. The event marked the synergic conjugation of a trilingual form of art reviving the ancient Indian belief that all art merged seamlessly into each other. This was performed for four consecutive nights at a white chapel in Avignon and some of the paintings of Raza were brought on the stage on wheels enhancing the event. According to Vajpeyi, 'The meticulous geometry, furious colours, ecstatic energy and the drive towards silence and purity of his art were explored sensuously in dance-music-poetry in their own way each illuminating the other, each reaching for the other without ceasing to be oneself.'[16]

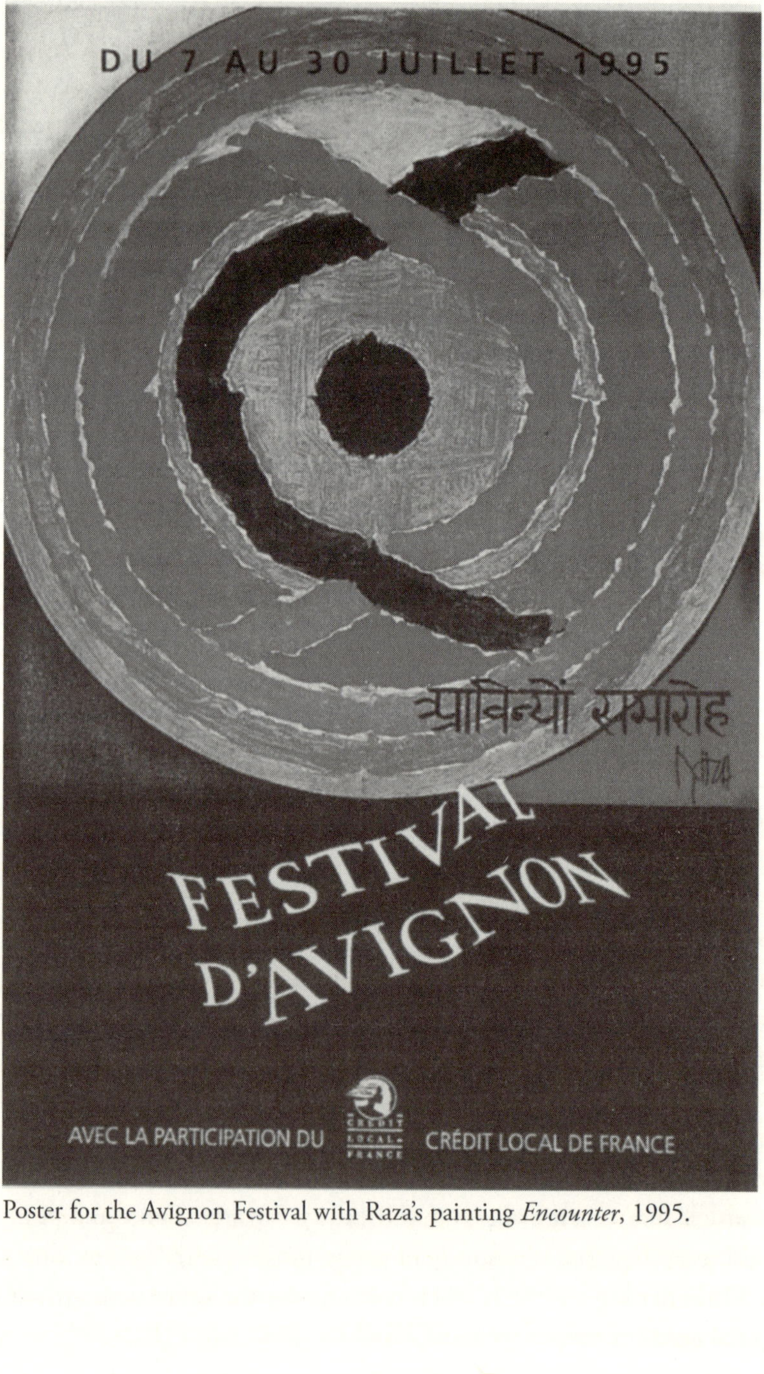

Poster for the Avignon Festival with Raza's painting *Encounter*, 1995.

Return to India

It was this friendship that led to Raza's return to his home country. At Vajpeyi's constant persuasion for over a period, Raza finally came back to India in December 2010. In June that year his seminal work *Saurashtra* (1983) sold at an auction in London for a sum of Rs 16.3 crore – creating a new record for Indian art. Four years later, his *La Terre* (1973) realized around Rs 21 crore at another auction in New York. Yet again the large-scale work *Tapovan* (1972) broke his own record with a sale at Rs 29 crore at a New York auction in 2018. But Raza remained as non-assuming as ever saying that he had never left India and that in spirit he was always there.

A two-storeyed house was found for him in Safdarjung Enclave area of Delhi, which would eventually be his home-cum-studio. Earlier in the year, while still based in Paris, for about three months he had stayed at the artist Manish Pushkale's place which was close by and from there he would travel to other parts of India. Manish, who also hails from Madhya Pradesh and is much younger in years, has in many ways been influenced by Raza's works and yet also stands apart from him. His intense involvement with colour has led to nuanced tonal variation that provide a sensual depth to his work. His subtle brushstrokes create sheaths of diaphanous light in overlapping colours evoking a multi-layered experiential reality. As Vajpeyi noted, 'One way of reading Manish Pushkale's magnificent work is to realize that it leaves us free. Indeed, the reading locates us in a pulsating space to discover its layers and complex layering and to resonate it with our personal memories which then taken together bring into being what could be called rich, intense visual ideas…'[17]

According to Pushkale, Raza not only painted every day but often in the compound of the old pre-Mughal thirteenth-century ruin, Chor Minar, opposite his house in his indubitable manner. The somewhat receding presence today of Chor Minar, or the Tower of Thieves, belies the role for which it was originally constructed. A minaret with 225 holes, the local legend has it that it was built under the rule of Alauddin Khalji, of the Khalji dynasty (1290-1320) and was a 'tower of beheading', where the severed heads of thieves were displayed on spears through its 225 holes, to act as a deterrent to thieves. If this was true, Raza was then the prince of thieves for he painted sitting in the sun, in the cold Delhi winter, as a silent spectator of the infamous legend and made works of loss and recovery.

Raza settled back in India after a gap of sixty years. Initially, he was visited by Veena every year. On one of her visits, he beseeched her that she allow him to make his Gorbio flat into an artist's residency but she refused flatly. Vajpeyi observes, 'Every time she came to Delhi, she wanted money. Once Raza had to be hospitalized because there was such a fierce fight. The only way was to prevent her [from coming] was to write her a letter and to the French Embassy in Delhi as well as the Indian Embassy in Paris. So, he did that and in his last years she stopped coming.'[18] Vajpeyi points out, 'This coming here at least enhanced his life because here he had a much larger support constantly and regularly and he was not supposed to be doing anything but paint, which is what he always wanted to do. After Veena stopped coming, in four years he did something like four hundred paintings – good, bad, indifferent but four hundred paintings is not a joke.'[19] Raza received the Padma Vibhushan in 2013, and in 2015 he was awarded the Commander de la Légion d'honneur – the highest French honour.

Setting Up the Raza Foundation

Sponsored by Raza and initiated by Ashok Vajpeyi, the Raza Foundation was set up in 2001 and became a focal point on his return. In a sense, in its multi-arts approach it was a continuation of the Bharat Bhavan scenario. It supported, during Raza's lifetime and after, visual arts, poetry, classical music, classical dance, cinema, architecture, photography, crafts and similar ideas. It holds several talks, panel discussions, festivals, and supports and funds artists and institutions on cultural matters. The Raza Foundation realized his dream of supporting and promoting all forms of art in the country, which he had always been attached to. It is no idle boast when Vajpeyi states, 'A Foundation set up and financed by a great artist owed it to him and his memory, to his vision and legacy that its resources are used for relocating the arts in our times at the centre of critical and civic attention. In an atmosphere of hatred and bigotry, of violence and disruptions, arts offer a solace, a residence of a new spirituality which restores to the ordinary people the love and lure of reality, of cosmos and of the complex inner world we all have.'[20] In addition to its cultural events, the Foundation has a large publishing programme where it brings out books on art, literature and poetry both in English and Hindi. It is worth noting that during his lifetime Raza did not allow the Foundation to incur any expenditure on him or his art. The Raza Foundation started naming events such as Raza Utsav only after his death.

Many friends of Raza like the gallerist and life trustee of the Foundation, Arun Vadehra, felt that his return to India was a good move and benefited not only Raza himself, but also others. It was the final act according to him, 'I think when he lost Janine, he somehow lost his interest in Paris. He started coming to India very often and I totally encouraged him to shift to India because he would get all the comforts here – people to serve you and we are there for all the support he needed…'[21]

Once Raza had a fall and was in a wheelchair, but he continued to paint every day. As it was noted by the journalist Aarti Dua in the *Telegraph*:

> Every afternoon, Syed Haider Raza manoeuvres his wheelchair into the studio of his new home in Delhi's Safdarjung Development Area. Uttering a prayer, the country's foremost living Modernist painter then clambers onto a chair on a raised platform and sets up his tools in front of his easel. Then, for the next three to four hours – and sometimes longer – the nearly 91-year-old artist shuts out the world and loses himself in his painting. 'I am going to be 91 soon so I have to be very careful about my health. I'm usually tired. But I paint regularly in spite of this and I'm very happy to be able to do that,' says the painter, who's best known for his famous Bindu series of paintings. Raza sits and paints nowadays after he fractured a thigh bone in a fall six months ago. His easel is set on a wooden frame so the canvas can be moved up or down to suit his restricted movements. Yet, neither age nor injury has dampened his passion for his art.[22]

His constant companion and confidante in this period was Sanjiv Kumar Choube, member-secretary of the Foundation. His energetic support and sympathetic ear made Raza's stay in India after a long gap a viable and comfortable proposition. According to Choube, 'He would sit patiently for hours unraveling his life and remembering the smallest person who helped him with gratitude.'[23] In course of time, Choube has become a repository of knowledge about the artist's life and that of his times.

The Last Call

Raza continued to paint from his wheelchair. He also carried on with the practice of uttering some poetic lines before beginning his work. It was usually a verse from Rilke, a poet he was very fond of. As Vajpeyi pointed out, 'Because unlike others, Rilke was very quiet, a poet of silence, a meditative poet which suited him very much. In fact, he used go every day when in Paris to his studio and do a kind of prayer which was inaudible. I once asked him about it and he said, "*No, no mantra – Rilke ki hai ek poem – woh main yaad karta hoon.*" It was something like "Listen to that voice buried in silence" – we have it somewhere. It has something to do with an inner voice and silence which I thought very much to be his kind of thematic.'[24] And it was this inner voice he was listening to while making his last painting. The black Bindu was beginning its circular route on the canvas.

It is the artist's prerogative to subvert linear time and the compartmentalization of history and to recreate a universe of connectivity and seamless humanity. In this way, the artist swirls his brush and wipes away the cobwebs of time to bring alive an insensate, bewitched and luminous world. Raza had completed a half circle like the moon and while his brush continued to swathe the surface with colour, he had to be taken away to a hospital. The days passed there didn't stop him from thinking about it and painting it in his mind. He passed away in the hospital on 23 July 2016 at the age of ninety-four.

According to Arun Vadehra, 'We were there in the hospital during his last evening. We went around 6.30 p.m. or so and he didn't look good to me and Ashok [Vajpeyi] was also there. We all had long faces at the situation which was totally helpless. We couldn't do anything. The only thing was that while he was breathing there was hope. We knew that we had more or less lost him … Raza sa'ab hadn't opened his eyes for the last 15-20 days. He was in a bit of coma. He would shake a little and sometimes make a gesture, but we didn't know what it meant... '[25]

Ashok Vajpeyi regularly visited him in the ICU twice a day for over two months – once in the morning and then in the evening, as Raza's condition continued to deteriorate. After his death, Vajpeyi ruminated, 'I write these lines sitting in Mandla, a district town on the banks of the Narmada where the great painter Sayed Haider Raza was buried on 24 July 2016, as per his wishes, next to his father's grave. Born in a small forest-village of some ten houses, Barbaria, ninety-four-and-a-half years ago, Raza was one of the six children his parents had. He rose from the dust of Mandala and returned to dust here – he breathed his last on 23 July after a prolonged illness. There was nothing in his humble origins to suggest that he would emerge a major artistic figure of twentieth-century India.'[26]

Not only is Raza's grave situated at Mandla but it was to also become the seat of many cultural events in the years following his death initiated by the Raza Foundation and Ashok Vajpeyi, and enabled by the unending and sustained efforts of Sanjiv Kumar Choube. The district administration of Mandla has also created a new multipurpose art gallery from its own funds and named it as Raza Kala Vithika. A major road has been named as Raza Marg in Mandla.

The goblin of death in Terry Pratchett's acclaimed novel *Reaper Man* famously said: 'No one is actually dead until the ripples they cause in the world die away.'[27] The rich legacy left behind by Raza can testify to the numerous ripples which continue to stir and give direction to others. A mute witness to this is the painting he was making before his death, which rests on the easel for posterity. A black circle whirling on its axis would begin its journey, rising from an ocean of white, and dynamize the room. And the studio remains as if he will enter any moment and begin his work. It is a space which has his journey strewn about and anthologizes his life. On one side are pictures of Jesus, Mary and Joseph and of the Last Supper. Ganesh and Shivalinga are placed next to it, along with small vessels and powders for worship. His own smiling photograph along with Daryav Singhji Rathore, the drawing teacher who changed his life, follows. Elsewhere in the studio are Bapurao Athawale and Beni Prasad Sthapale, his mentors. Medium-sized abstract paintings made by Raza are stacked against the wall. A sofa set, bookshelves with books and a brass Nandi complete the picture. On the left are statues from the ancient period, as well as a painting by Jamini Roy. The wall facing Raza's easel has Janine's work in swirling ochre, black and green, indicating a man and his oxen ploughing the field – like a beacon of life. The middle of the room has the last unfinished work with his palette of mixed colours on a low table. In front of the easel is the wooden cane chair that makes it seem as if he is sitting there contemplating his painting. And as the invisible comes to the fore on the canvas, it is a living testimony to an artist who believed that without divine intervention no picture could be made. The artist who felt that his role was only to make the unknown rise from its submerged depths to consciousness. An artist who never stopped chasing his dreams and following his intuitions and in doing so, he lit the path which others were to follow.

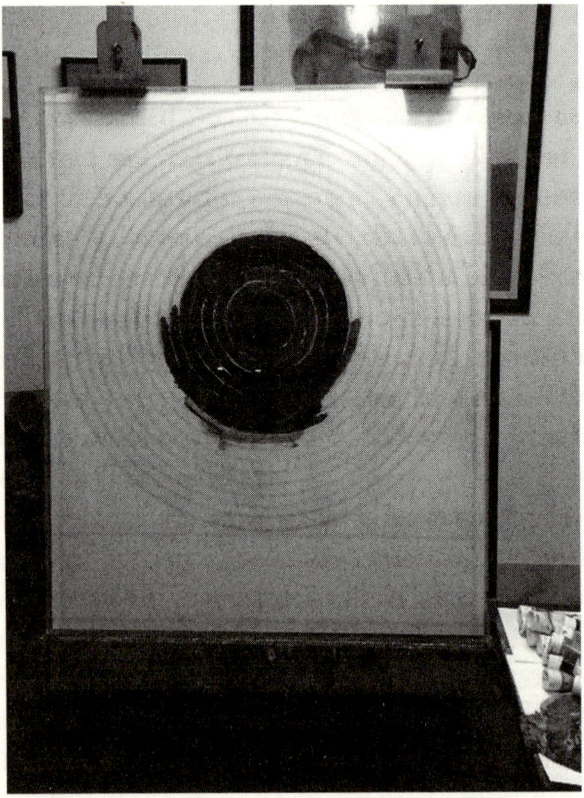

The last unfinished painting, New Delhi, acrylic on canvas, S.H. Raza.

Notes

1: In the Midst of Forests

1. S.H. Raza; Ashok Vajpeyi, *Passion: Life and Art of Raza*, Rajkamal Books, New Delhi, 2005, p15
2. ibid., p14
3. ibid., p14
4. Survival International, 'Tribespeople illegally evicted from "Jungle Book" tiger reserve', 14 January 2015, *survivalinternational.org*
5. *Passion*, op. cit., p13
6. ibid.
7. ibid., p14
8. ibid., p13
9. ibid.
10. Michel Imbert, *Raza: An Introduction to his Painting*, Rainbow Publishers, 2003, p15
11. *Passion*, op. cit., p19
12. ibid.
13. ibid.

14. Pavan K. Varma, *Ghalib: The Man, The Times,* Penguin Books, 1989, p142
15. ibid., p144
16. *Passion*, op. cit., p23
17. Ashok Vajpeyi in an interview with the author, New Delhi, June 2018
18. *Passion*, op. cit., p19
19. ibid., p20
20. ibid.
21. ibid.
22. ibid., p21
23. ibid., p33
24. M.V. Athawale, Principal, Nagpur School of Art, Dhantoli, Nagpur, 8 June 1942
25. K.K. Verma, Headmaster, Municipal High School, Gondia, C.P., 13 December 1943
26. *Passion*, op. cit., p40

2: Bombay: City of Hope

1. S.H. Raza; Ashok Vajpeyi, *Passion*: *Life and Art of Raza*, Rajkamal Books, New Delhi, 2005, p35
2. ibid.
3. Rudolf von Leyden, *Raza*, Sadanga Series, Mulk Raj Anand Publishers, Bombay 1959
4. *Passion,* op. cit., p41
5. ibid., p36
6. Raza in an interview with the author, Bombay, January 1992
7. Tyeb Mehta in an interview with the author, Bombay, January 1993
8. F.N. Souza, *Words & Lines,* Villiers Publications Limited, 1959, p15
9. F.N. Souza, PAG catalogue, Bombay, July 1949
10. S.H. Raza in 'Point of Creation' by Shirin Bahadurji, *Bombay Magazine*, 7-21 March 1984
11. Raza in an interview with the author, Bombay, January 1991. *Significant Form* is a term which has come to emphasize the sensory and formal qualities of a work of art which exist independent of representational qualities. Originally coined by the British critic and art writer Clive Bell

(1881-1964) of the Bloomsbury Group the term became important to denote the 'modern' as against the 'academic' in art.

12. Quoted by Gieve Patel in 'To Pick Up a Brush', Contemporary Indian Art from the Herwitz Family Collection, New York, 1985
13. Krishen Khanna, 'Memories of a Progressive Past', *Art India Magazine*, Bombay, Vol. 2, Issue 1
14. Ram Kumar, *Poorvagraha*, trans. Madhu B. Joshi, Bhopal, 1979
15. Raza to the Education Department, Bombay, 25 March 1949
16. *Poorvagraha*, op. cit.
17. Souza in a letter to Ara, Bakre, Gade, Husain and Raza, London, 17 August 1949
18. ibid.
19. Souza in a letter to Raza, London, 17 February 1950
20. ibid.
21. ibid.
22. Yashodhara Dalmia, *Making of Modern Indian Art: The Progressives*, Oxford University Press, New Delhi, 2001, p75
23. M.F. Husain in an interview with the author, Bombay, January 1992
24. Rudolf von Leyden, *Hindustan Times*, 2 September 1948
25. Rudolf von Leyden, *Times of India*, 1948
26. Raza in an interview with the author, Bombay, January 1992
27. *Passion*, op. cit., p43
28. ibid., p37
29. Raza to Madame Bossennec, Joint Cultural Adviser, Embassy of France, Calcutta, 27 May 1950
30. C. Journot to Raza, Calcutta, 8 September 1950

3: After Partition

1. Alok Rai, 'Forgetting Partition, Remembering Partition', *The Indian Express*, 23 March 2019
2. Krishen Khanna in an interview with the author, New Delhi, November 2009
3. Satish Gujral in an interview with the author, New Delhi, February 2006
4. ibid.

5. Quoted by Siddhi Jain, IANS, 14 August 2018
6. ibid.
7. Raza, *Itinerary*, Carnets Series 1, Vadehra Art Gallery, New Delhi p14
8. Yusuf to Raza, Karachi, 26 January 1962
9. Raza to Yusuf, Paris, 26 February 1962
10. Muna Siddiqui 'A Portrait of the Artist', *The Express Tribune,* 5 February 2012
11. ibid.
12. ibid.
13. Veera Rustomji, 'New Works by Nahid Raza', August 2015, http://artnowpakistan.com
14. Ali to Raza, London, 27 October 1956
15. Raza to Ali, Paris, 28 November 1956
16. Ali to Raza, London, 1 December 1956
17. ibid.
18. ibid.
19. ibid.
20. Ali to Raza, London, 22 February 1957
21. Ali to Raza, London, 23 August 1957
22. Raza to Ali, Paris, 25 September 1957
23. Cottie A. Burland, *Art News and Reviews*
24. Jalal Uddin Ahmed, *Contemporary Painters of Pakistan*, 1958, p52-53, quoted in Grosvenor Gallery catalogue, South Asian Modern Art 2019, London, June 2019
25. Ali to Raza, London, 1958
26. Raza to Ali, Paris, undated
27. Ali to Raza, London, 23 November 1960
28. Ali to Raza, London, 27 May 1960
29. Ali to Raza, London, 29 December 1961
30. Lindsay to Janine, London, 14 July 1963
31. Yusuf to Raza, Karachi, 26 January 1962
32. Ali to Raza, London, 22 November 1966
33. Ali to Raza, Karachi, 2 December 1981
34. ibid.

35. Marjorie Husain, 'Requiem for an art icon – Sayed Ali Imam', *Dawn*, Karachi, 24 May 2002
36. ibid.
37. Ali to Raza, London, 5 December 1958
38. Hasan to Raza, Kuwait, 24 May 1966
39. Raza to Hasan, Paris, 8 June 1966
40. Raza to Mohsin, Paris, 9 September 1952
41. ibid.
42. Mohsin to Raza, London, 5 April 1958
43. Raza to Mohsin, Paris, 14 October 1960
44. Mohsin to Raza, London, 17 October 1960
45. Mohsin to Raza, London, 27 February 1961
46. Mohsin to Raza, London, 31 March 1961
47. Mohsin to Raza, London 9 November 1963
48. ibid.
49. Raza to Mohsin, Paris, 9 September 1952

4: Paris, Mon Amour

1. S.H. Raza; Ashok Vajpeyi, *Passion: Life and Art of Raza*, Rajkamal Books, New Delhi, 2005, p50
2. Akbar Padamsee in an interview with the author, Bombay, February 2017
3. ibid.
4. *Passion*, op. cit., p51
5. ibid.
6. Adam Gopnik, ed., *Americans in Paris: A Literary Anthology*, Library of America, New York, 2004, p81
7. Gertrude Stein, *The Autobiography of Alice B. Toklas*, Harcourt, 1933,
8. *Americans in Paris*, op. cit., p328
9. Sylvia Beach, 'Shakespeare and Company, War and Occupation' in *Americans in Paris*, op. cit., p428
10. Ernest Hemingway, 'A Room on the Garden Side,' *Strand Magazine*, Issue LV, Michigan, USA, 2018
11. Ram Kumar, *Poorvagraha*, trans. Madhu B. Joshi, Bhopal, 1979

12. *Passion*, op. cit., p53
13. Raza to C. Journot, Paris, 20 February 1957
14. Raza to Mohsin, Paris, 9 September 1952
15. Deepa Nag Haksar, 'Reflections on Twentieth Century French Existentialist "Angst"', *Trajectory of French Thought*, Introduced by Dhritabrata Bhattacharjya Tato, French Information Resource Centre, New Delhi, 2004, p119
16. *Passion*, op. cit., p62
17. Ashok Vajpeyi, *Raza: A Life in Art*, Art Alive Master Series, New Delhi, 2007, p61
18. Raza to C. Journot, op. cit.
19. ibid.
20. Raza to Rajesh Rawat and Genevieve, Paris, 10 September 1955
21. Kathe Langhammer to Raza, Bombay, 16 October 1950
22. Raza in an interview with the author, Bombay, January 1992
23. *Poorvagrah*, op. cit.
24. ibid.
25. ibid.
26. ibid.
27. Krishen Khanna in an interview with the author, New Delhi, December 2016
28. Lawrence Gowing, *Paintings in the Louvre*, New York, 1987, p72
29. www.wikipedia.com
30. Raza, *Itinerary*, op. cit., p24
31. Raza to Souza, Paris, 9 November 1950
32. Souza to Raza, London, 3 April 1951
33. Souza to Raza, London, 25 May 1951
34. ibid.
35. Souza to Raza, London, 3 November 1952
36. Souza to Raza, London, undated
37. Raza to Akbar, Venice, 5 May 1953
38. ibid.
39. Raza to Akbar, Paris, 23 December 1954
40. ibid.

5: The Burning Landscape

1. Geeti Sen, *Bindu: Space and Time in Raza's Vision*, Media Transasia India Limited, 1997, p572.
2. Rudolf von Leyden, *Raza*, Sadanga Publications, Bombay, 1959, p19
3. S.H. Raza; Ashok Vajpeyi, *Passion: Life and Art of Raza*, Rajkamal Books, New Delhi, 2005, p56
4. *Passion*, op. cit., p57
5. *Bindu*, op. cit., p66
6. *Passion*, op. cit., p57
7. Jacques Lassaigne, *Raza Catalogue 1980-1990*, Bombay 1991
8. Rainer Maria Rilke, trans. James Burnham, http://www.blackcatpoems.com/r/at_the_brink_of_night.html
9. *Bindu*, op. cit., p66
10. Madanjeet Singh, *The Sasia Story*, UNESCO Publications, Paris 2005
11. *Raza*, op. cit.
12. Information about the Biennale 1956 provided by the Venice Biennale authorities
13. Husain to Raza, 13 September 1956, op. cit., p99
14. Raza to Rajesh and Genevieve, Paris, 1 July 1956
15. *Passion*, op. cit., p56
16. *Bindu*, op. cit., p67
17. *Raza*, op. cit., p19
18. Raza to Rajesh Rawat, Paris, 2 May 1957

6: Period of Fulfilment

1. S.H. Raza; Ashok Vajpeyi, *Passion: Life and Art of Raza*, Rajkamal Books, New Delhi, 2005, p40
2. Fatima's mother to Raza, Hyderabad, undated
3. ibid.
4. ibid.
5. Raza to Hasan Imam, Paris, undated
6. Raza to Rajesh Rawat, Paris, 2 May 1957

7. Raza to Rajesh Rawat and Genevieve, Paris, 1 July 1956
8. Raza to Rajesh Rawat, Paris, 8 April 1958
9. Geeti Sen, *Bindu: Space and Time in Raza's Vision*, Media Transasia India Limited, 1997, p74
10. Akbar Padamsee in an interview with the author, Bombay, February 2017
11. *Passion*, op. cit., p66
12. Jean Duchesne in an interview with the author, Paris, October 2016
13. Raissa Padamsee in an interview with the author, Paris, September 2017
14. Jean Duchesne in an interview with the author, Paris, October 2016
15. Michel Imbert in an interview with the author, Gorbio, September 2016
16. ibid.
17. Duchesne interview, op. cit.
18. ibid.
19. ibid.
20. ibid.
21. ibid.
22. ibid.
23. ibid.
24. ibid.
25. Roussel interview, Paris, October 2016
26. Duchesne interview, op. cit.
27. Raissa Padamsee, op. cit.
28. *Bindu*, op.cit., p61
29. ibid.
30. Souza to Raza, London, 29 December 1949
31. Dileep Padgaonkar, 'Jean's Magic Spell', *Times of India*, 2 May 2004
32. Janine Bharucha in an interview with the author, Paris, September 2017
33. ibid.
34. ibid.
35. ibid.

36. Duchesne interview, op. cit.
37. Bharucha interview, op. cit.
38. Raza to Jean and Krishna, Paris, 13 October 1969
39. www. wikipedia.com
40. Sunil Sethi 'In Memoriam, Krishna Riboud 1927-2000', www.india-seminar.com/2000
41. www.wikipedia.com
42. Sunil Sethi, op. cit.
43. ibid.
44. Raza to Rajesh Rawat, Paris, 2 May 1957
45. ibid.

7: Magical Flowers Were Humming

1. Translator's note: Padamsee soon joined his studio 'Atelier 17'. His first exhibition was held in Paris in 1952. The artists exhibited anonymously, thus he shared the prize awarded by the French magazine *Journal d'Arte* with the painter Jean Carzou.
2. His first wife who is yet to be divorced.
3. Translator's note: This letter concerns Raza's first wife from an arranged marriage who lived in Unified India, and then Pakistan. Raza and Mongillat ran into legal trouble because of this. In this letter they are planning their wedding, while finding a way to annul Raza's existing marriage.
4. Arthur Rimbaud, *Illuminations*, *PN Review 199*, Vol. 37, Number 5, trans. John Ashberry, May–June 2011

8: The Watershed Years

1. Kasten to Raza, Berkeley, 10 October 1961
2. Raza to Kasten, Paris, 3 October 1961
3. Raza to Kasten, Paris, 26 February 1962
4. Raza to Kasten, Paris, 24 March 1962
5. Krishen Khanna in an interview with the author, New Delhi, December 2016

6. Kasten to Raza, Berkeley University, 11 September 1964
7. Kasten to Raza, Berkeley University, 9 June 1966
8. Raza to Kasten, Paris, 23 June 1966
9. S.H. Raza; Ashok Vajpeyi, *Passion: Life and Art of Raza*, Rajkamal Books, New Delhi, 2005, p59
10. Press clipping from *Tarrytown News* mentioned in Kishore Singh, *India's Rockefeller Artists: An Indo-US Cultural Saga*, DAG Modern, New Delhi, 2017
11. *India's Rockefeller Artists*, op.cit., p6
12. ibid., p7
13. Frances Stonor Saunders, *The Cultural Cold War: The CIA and the World of Arts and Letters*, The New Press, New York, 2013
14. *India's Rockefeller Artists*, op. cit., p30
15. Raza to Krishen, New York, 2 December 1962
16. ibid.
17. Seema Chishti, 'When four of India's greatest painters were sent to cover the India-Pakistan War of 1965', *The Indian Express*, 26 August 2019
18. ibid.
19. Krishen Khanna in an interview with the author, New Delhi, December 2016
20. Geeti Sen, *Bindu: Space and Time in Raza's Vision*, Media Transasia India Limited, 1997, p59
21. Raza to Kasten, Saint Fargeau, 23 April 1962
22. Anna Moszynska, *Abstract Art*, Thames & Hudson, London 1990, p152
23. Hans Hofmann, *The Search for the Real and Other Essays*, Harry N. Abrams, New York, 1948, p46
24. *Abstract Art*, op. cit., p163
25. ibid.
26. ibid.
27. ibid., p165
28. ibid., p168
29. S.H. Raza, *Itinerary*, Carnets Series 1, Vadehra Art Gallery, New Delhi Carnet Series, p32

30. *Bindu*, op. cit., p59
31. J. Lassaigne, quoted in Ashok Vajpeyi, *Raza: A Life in Art,* Art Alive Gallery, New Delhi 2007, p73
32. Raza to Kasten, Paris, 23 June 1966

9: A Moveable Feast

1. Geeti Sen, *Bindu: Space and Time in Raza's Vision*, Media Transasia India Limited, 1997, p87
2. S.H. Raza; Ashok Vajpeyi, *Passion*: *Life and Art of Raza*, Rajkamal Books, New Delhi, 2005, p71
3. Raza to Krishen Khanna, Paris, 24 April 1964
4. Excerpt from 'The Moment of Raza', Ashok Vajpeyi's *A Name for Every Leaf: Selected Poems, 1959-2015*, trans. Rahul Soni, HarperCollins, New Delhi, 2019, p50
5. Raissa Padamsee in an interview with the author, Paris, September 2017
6. Jean Duchesne, 2017, op. cit.
7. Akkitham Narayanan in an interview with the author, Paris, August 2019
8. *Passion*, op. cit., p73
9. Krishen to Raza, Chandigarh, 9 February 1962
10. *Passion*, op. cit., p98
11. Michel Imbert in an interview with the author, Gorbio, October 2016
12. *Bindu*, op. cit., p73
13. Raza to Bresson, Paris, 31 March, year not mentioned
14. *Passion*, op. cit., p98
15. ibid.
16. ibid., p97
17. Devika Singh, 'India-France Artistic Exchanges', *Marg Magazine*, Mumbai, September-December 2017, p16
18. Saffron Art, https://www.saffronart.com/artists/krishna-reddy
19. Judith Reddy in an interview with the author, New York, October 2019
20. S. Kalidas, Exhibition Catalogue, 1x1 Gallery, 2010
21. Alain Umhauer in an interview with the author, Paris, September 2017

22. Raza to Krishen, Paris, 24 December 1985
23. Rashna Imhasly in an interview with the author, Alibagh, March 2017

10: House by the Sea

1. S.H. Raza; Ashok Vajpeyi, *Passion: Life and Art of Raza*, Rajkamal Books, New Delhi, 2005, p60
2. Raza to Krishen, Gorbio, 9 August 1987
3. Michel Imbert in an interview with the author, Gorbio, October 2016
4. ibid.
5. ibid.
6. ibid.
7. *Bindu* op. cit., p15
8. ibid.
9. ibid., p16
10. ibid.
11. Rashna Imhasly in an interview with the author, Alibag, March 2017
12. Raza to Krishen, Gorbio, 9 August 1987
13. Ram Kumar to Raza, Delhi, 7 March 1985
14. Helen Ann Barbier with her children Guy-Thomas, Camille and Henri in memory of Guy H. Barbier, Coups de Coeur, Sotheby's catalogue, London, June 2019, p10
15. Raza to Krishen, Gorbio, 9 August 1987
16. Raza to Pierre and Josette, Paris, 19 May 1967
17. Josette to Raza and Janine, Le Ponteil, 24 July 1968
18. Michel Isnard in an interview with the author, Gorbio, October 2016
19. John Litchfield, 'Politics of art: village divided by bequest from painter', the *Independent*, London, 29 September 2007
20. ibid.
21. ibid.

11: The Indian Eye

1. S.H. Raza, 'My Art', *Illustrated Weekly of India*, 19 March 1989
2. Ashok Vajpeyi in an interview with the author, New Delhi, 2018
3. Santwana Bhattacharya, 'The Artist Comes Home', *The Indian Express*, 28 January 1996
4. Ashok Vajpeyi, *Raza: A Life in Art*, Art Alive Master Series, 2007, p98
5. Raza to Bal Chhabda, Paris, 11 December 1965
6. Raza to Ashok, Paris, 12 June 1993,
7. *Raza: A Life in Art*, op. cit., p108
8. ibid., p111
9. S.H. Raza; Ashok Vajpeyi, *Passion: Life and Art of Raza,* Rajkamal Books, New Delhi, 2005, p23
10. ibid., p24
11. Geeti Sen, *Bindu Space and Time in Raza's Vision*, Media Transasia India Limited, New Delhi, p94
12. ibid.
13. *Raza: A Life in Art*, op.cit, p18
14. Letter from Khorshed to Satish Gujral, Bombay, undated, courtesy Chemould gallery
15. *Bindu*, op. cit., p107
16. Akhilesh, 'The Blue which Burns' in *Raza: A Life in Art,* op.cit., p338
17. S.H. Raza, *Artists Today: East West Visual Encounter*, Marg Publications, Bombay, 1987
18. Raza to Krishen, Paris, 10 February 1987
19. Quoted in Yashodhara Dalmia, *Making of Modern Indian Art: The Progressives,* Oxford University Press, New Delhi, 2001, p315
20. Rupika Chawla, catalogue for 'Symbolism and Geometry in Indian Art', an exhibition curated by her for the National Gallery of Modern Art, New Delhi, 14-22 March 1998
21. Raza in an interview with the author, Bombay, January 1991

22. Olivier Germain-Thomas in a conversation with the author, Paris, October 2016
23. Olivier Germain-Thomas, *S.H. Raza: Mandalas*, Art Alive Gallery, 2009, p109
24. Catalogue for 'Symbolism and Geometry in Indian Art', op. cit.
25. Ali to Raza, London, 17 November 1963
26. Raza in an interview with the author, Bombay, January 1992
27. Raza to Krishen Khanna, Gorbio, 9 August 1987
28. *S.H. Raza: Mandalas*, op. cit., p117
29. Raza to Krishen, Gorbio, 9 August 1987
30. Dadiba Pundole in an interview with the author, Bombay, November 2018
31. Ranjit Hoskote, 'Symbolism or Decorative Motif?', *The Times of India*, 3 February 1990
32. Mentioned by Geeti Sen, *Raza Anthology*, Gallery Chemould, Bombay, 1991
33. ibid.

12: In the Footsteps of Gandhi

1. Gopalkrishna Gandhi, *Gandhi in Raza*, Akar Prakar, Mapin Publishing, Raza Foundation, New Delhi, 2017, p54
2. ibid.
3. Sunil Khilnani, *The Idea of India*, Penguin Books, 1999, p126
4. ibid.
5. Quoted in the brochure 'Our Time for a Future Caring' India Pavilion, 58th Venice Biennale, Venice, 2019
6. Bernard Imhasly, *Goodbye to Gandhi?: Travels in the New India*, Penguin Books, New Delhi, 2007, p194
7. S.H. Raza; Ashok Vajpeyi, *Passion: Life and Art of Raza*, Rajkamal Books, New Delhi, 2005, p39
8. S.H. Raza in an interview with Ashok Vajpeyi, 'Gandhi in Raza', New Delhi, 2017, p30
9. Sudhir Chandra, *Gandhi: An Impossible Possibility*, Routledge, New Delhi, 2016, p150

10. *Gandhi in Raza*, op. cit., p32
11. Mark Rothko quoted at a show at the Museum of Modern Art, San Francisco, October 2018
12. Jalal ad-Din Muhammad Rumi, 'I Am Wind/You are Fire', trans. Annemarie Schimmel, www.rumi.org.uk

13: Memory and Longing

1. Michel Imbert in an interview with the author, Gorbio, October, 2016
2. Rainer Maria Rilke, www.rainermariarilke.com
3. Anindita Ghose, S.H. Raza, 'The Last Great Moderns', *Livemint*, 13 January 2012
4. Rashna Imhasly in an interview with the author, Alibag, March 2017
5. *Raza: A Life in Art*, op. cit., p65
6. Jean Duchesne, op. cit., Paris, 2017
7. Bernard Imhasly in an interview with the author, Alibag, March 2017
8. Christian Pouillon, catalogue, Mongillat Retrospective, Centre d'Art Presence Van Gogh, Saint Remy-de-Provence, 4 April to 26 July 1998 and Musee des Beaux-Arts, Palais Carnoles, Menton, 12 September-14 December 1998
9. C. Pouillon, op. cit.
10. ibid.
11. ibid.
12. ibid.
13. Gerard Barriere in an interview with the author, Paris, 26 September 1997
14. ibid.
15. Bernard Imhasly in an interview with the author, Alibag, March 2017
16. Rashna Imhasly in an interview with the author, Alibag, March 2017
17. Latika Padgaonkar, 'Remembering Raza Saab', *The Asian Age*, 26 July 2016
18. Michel Imbert in an interview with the author, Gorbio, October, 2016
19. ibid.
20. ibid.
21. Jean Duchesne, op. cit.

22. *Passion*, op. cit., p96
23. ibid.
24. Rachna Imhasly in an interview with the author, Alibag, March 2017
25. Michel Imbert, in an interview with the author, Gorbio, October, 2016
26. Rainer Maria Rilke, 'Sonnets to Orpheus', *www.rainermariarilke*.com

14: Mother, What Shall I Bring Home When I Return?

1. Khorshed Pundole in an interview with the author, Mumbai, March 2019
2. Sujata Bajaj, 'Raza Saheb' in Ashok Vajpeyi's *Raza: A Life in Art*, Art Alive Master series, New Delhi, 2007, p342
3. Ashok Vajpeyi in an interview with the author, New Delhi, May 2017
4. Michel Imbert in an interview with the author, Gorbio, October 2016
5. Sharan Apparao in an interview with the author, New Delhi, December 2016
6. Ashok Vajpeyi in an interview with the author, Delhi, May 2017
7. Meenakshi Sinha, *The Times of India*, 4 January 2011
8. Ashok Vajpeyi in an interview with the author, New Delhi, May 2017
9. Ashok Vajpeyi an extract from his memorial speech, Paris, October 2016
10. Ashok Vajpeyi in an interview with the author, New Delhi, April 2018
11. ibid.
12. ibid.
13. ibid.
14. ibid.
15. ibid.
16. *Raza: A Life in Art,* op. cit., p130
17. Ashok Vajpeyi, 'The Art of Discovery' for the catalogue *Manish Pushkale: The Painter of Light*, Musee de Guethary, France, 10 September-29 October 2016
18. Ashok Vajpeyi in an interview with the author, New Delhi, May 2017
19. ibid.
20. Ashok Vajpeyi, *Swasti*, Raza Foundation publication, No. 01, 2017
21. Arun Vadehra in an interview with the author, New Delhi, May 2017
22. Aarti Dua, 'The Modernist Master', *The Telegraph*, 3 February 2013

23. Sanjiv Kumar Choube in an interview to the author, New Delhi, May 2017
24. Ashok Vajpeyi in an interview with the author, New Delhi, April 2018
25. Arun Vadehra in an interview with the author, New Delhi, May 2017
26. Ashok Vajpeyi, 'S.H. Raza: A Tribute', *The Mint,* 27 July 2016
27. www.terrypratchett.com

Index

Acknowledgements

My long acquaintance with Sayed Haider Raza and his work is the primary inspiration for this book. I would like to thank him first of all for this engagement and exposure, which has allowed me to map his remarkable journey, and learn in the process. I am grateful to his close associate, the poet and writer Ashok Vajpeyi, for his encouragement and the many insights provided by him which made this book happen. My thanks to the Raza Foundation for commissioning me to work on this biography and also for the use of their extensive material, so meticulously preserved by the artist himself, which has provided a gateway to his life and work. I would also like to thank Sanjiv Choube, member-secretary of the Raza Foundation, for his helpful and ready support for this project. Medha Singh is to be thanked for her excellent English translation of Raza's letters to Janine in French. I am indebted to the Raza Foundation Archives for providing me with the black-and-white as well as most of the colour photographs for the book. All images used in the book are from the Archives unless otherwise noted.

Of the many artists associated with Raza, I am very grateful to Krishen Khanna for the long hours spent reminiscing and recapitulating those heady days in Mumbai and Paris with him. The late Akbar Padamsee, despite the frailty of his condition, also provided insights about the artist. Of the younger group, Velu Viswanadhan and Nadine Tarbouriech in Paris, Akkitham Narayanan also in Paris, Judith Blum Reddy in New York, Gieve Patel in Mumbai and Manish Pushkale in Delhi were very helpful. My heartfelt thanks to all of them.

I am indebted to Rahul Soni, Executive Editor, HarperCollins India, for his incisive editing of the book and his helpful suggestions. Thanks also to Tanima Saha for copy-editing the book. I am grateful to the HarperCollins team for their able handling of the project.

Raza's association with many friends and colleagues in Paris enabled a comprehension of the long years he spent there. In particular, I would like to thank Raissa Padamsee and her husband Laurent Bregeat for spending long hours in their ambient home discussing their association with the artist and his times. Among the acquaintances, the following were very helpful and my thanks to them: Jean Duchesne, Jean Paul Roussel and Mijo Roussel, Alain Umhauer, Olivier Germain-Thomas and Janine Bharucha. I would also like to thank Catherine David, Deputy Director, National Museum of Modern Art, Centre Georges Pompidou, for her many insights into Raza's work. In Gorbio, I am especially grateful to Michel Imbert for extending his hospitality and his incisive knowledge of Raza and his work. The mayor Michel Isnard also needs to be thanked.

In India, I would like to thank Bernard and Rachna Imhasly, Dadiba and Khorshed Pundole, Shirin Gandhy, Arun Vadehra, Sonia Bellany, Kishore Singh, Sharan Appa Rao, Ashvin Rajagopalan, Geetha Mehra and Shruthi Isaac. I am grateful to Nitin Bhayana for his help in the writing of this book. My thanks to Bertrand de Hartingh, Counsellor and Head of Education and Culture Department, French Institute in India, for his encouragement and support for the book. I am grateful to Razia Grover for her transcription of interviews which would otherwise have been a long drawn-out affair, Pratibha Pritam for her research, Shaista Anwar for her translation from Urdu and Jehanara Wasi for her assistance in the French translations.

My heartfelt thanks to all the writers on Raza who are too numerous to mention here, but have all contributed to the making of this book. Last but not least, my gratitude to Maseeh Rahman for his immense patience and support for this work.

About the Author

Yashodhara Dalmia is an art historian and an independent curator based in New Delhi, India. She has written several essays, articles and reviews on contemporary Indian art. She is the author of *Amrita Sher-Gil: A Life*, *The Making of Modern Indian Art: The Progressives* and *Buddha to Krishna: Life and Times of George Keyt*. She has also co-authored *Memory, Metaphor, Mutations: Contemporary Art of India and Pakistan*. Dalmia has curated several art shows such as *The Moderns* which inaugurated the National Gallery of Modern Art in Mumbai and the centenary show *Amrita Sher-Gil: The Passionate Quest* at the National Gallery of Modern Art in New Delhi, Mumbai and Bengaluru in 2014.

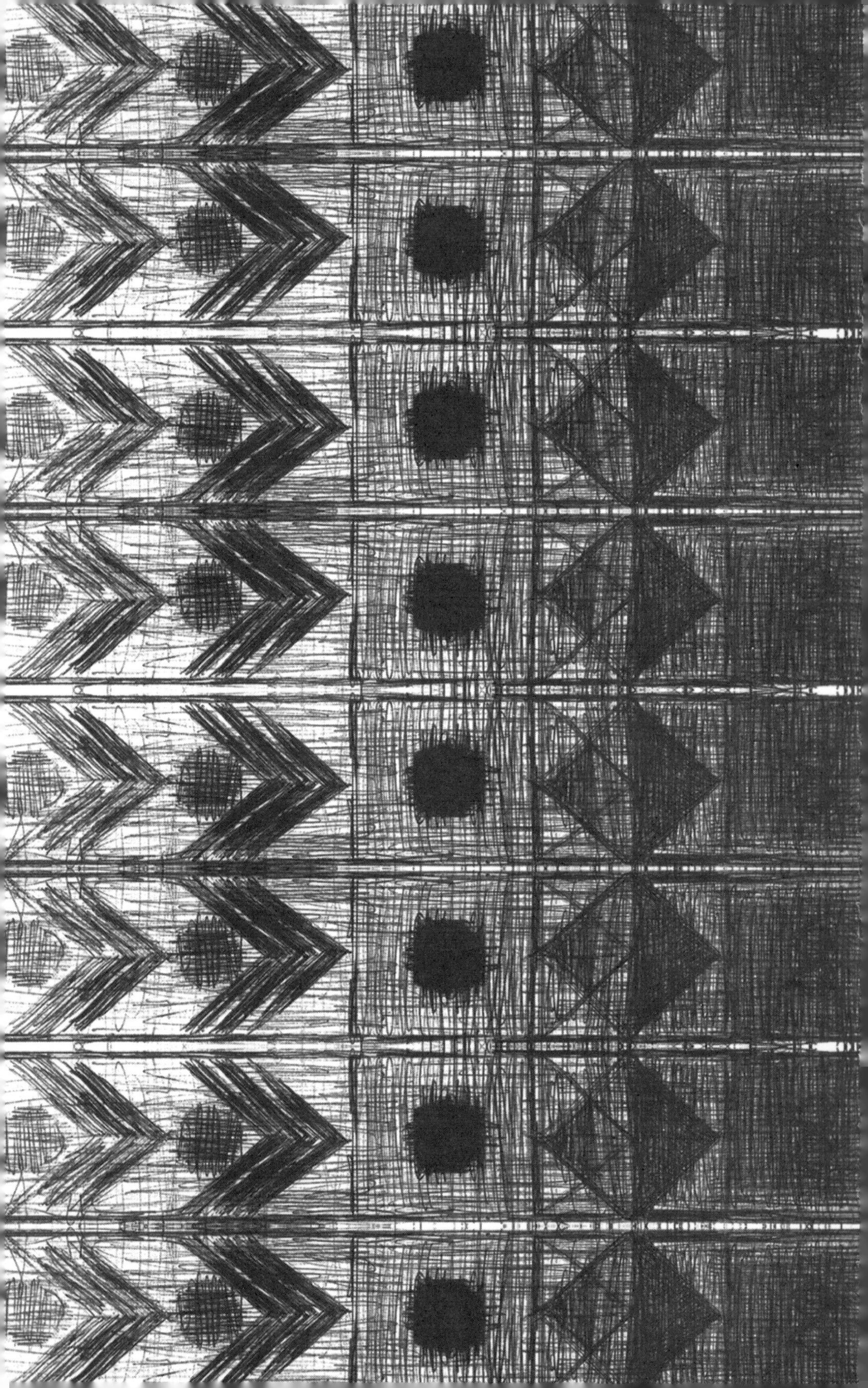